SO YOU
HAD TO
BUILD
A TIME
MACHINE

Books by Jason Offutt

Fiction
So You Had to Build a Time Machine
Bad Day for the Apocalypse
Bad Day for a Road Trip
A Funeral Story
Road Closed

Nonfiction
How to Kill Monsters Using Common Household Items
Chasing American Monsters
What Lurks Beyond
Haunted Missouri
Darkness Walks
Paranormal Missouri

SO YOU HAD TO BUILD A TIME MACHINE

JASON OFFUTT

CamCat
Books

CamCat Publishing, LLC
Brentwood, Tennessee 37027
camcatpublishing.com

Hardcover ISBN 9780744300147
Paperback ISBN 9780744300161
Large-Print Paperback ISBN 9780744300352
eBook ISBN 9780744300178
Audiobook ISBN 9780744300208

Library of Congress Control Number 2020935371

Cover design by Devin Watson

5 3 1 2 4

For my wife,
who has supported me through everything.

"Today's leading scientists grew up on Doctor Who and Star Trek. Every one of us has dreamed of stepping inside the TARDIS or transporting into a parallel dimension. We're close to making that happen."

—KARL MILLER, THEORETICAL PHYSICIST

"The days are strange. I'm not sure why, but something's not right. Has anyone else noticed an odd feeling?"

—BIG CHUCK, KANSAS CITY RADIO HOST

"Issa blass foo gibbidy hoom."

—GORDON GILSTRAP, GNARLY DUDE

CHAPTER ONE

1

IT WAS A WARM, pleasant Kansas City evening, the sun dropping below the skyline as Skid walked home from work. A drink in a friendly quiet place to unwind, she thought, would be nice. Slap Happy's Dance Club was not that place. It was crowded, loud, and for whatever reason Skid liked it. Sitting at the bar, she ordered a vodka tonic, smiling at the people on the dance floor. People she had no interest in talking to. That was a headache she could do without, not that anyone would bother her tonight. She hadn't washed her hair in two days, and she was sporting a sweat-stained T-shirt.

Then some moron sat next to her.

"Hey," he said, startling Skid. That barstool had been empty a second ago. The guy was about forty and dressed in Dockers. A whiff of ozone hung in the air around him. *I hope that's not his cologne.*

Skid nodded. "Hey."

He looked nice enough, but lots of people looked nice. Her father Randall wouldn't approve of him, but Randall didn't approve of anyone.

"I'm Dave," Dockers guy said. "Let me buy you a drink."

Skid froze. *Let me buy you a drink* wouldn't fly tonight. No, sir. Her plans were: Drink. Relax. Go home. Do not repeat. *I shouldn't have come in here.*

"I'm Skid and thanks, but no th—" The bartender set a Bud Light in front of her. "—anks."

"You're welcome," Dave said through the neck of his bottle, and Skid knew this conversation wasn't going to end well.

A frown pulled on the corners of her mouth as she turned away from Dave and looked across the dance floor. A big hairy guy in red flannel stood next to the bathrooms. He could have stepped off the side of a Brawny Paper Towel package. Yikes.

"Is Skid your Christian name?" Dave asked, laughing, "The Book of Marks, right?"

Don't do it. Don't talk to him. Her last relationship ended two months ago when a thirty-two-year-old fool who acted like a teenager thought dating a nineteen-year-old behind Skid's back was a good idea. Spoiler alert, it wasn't. She'd successfully avoided men in her life since that one (*Guy? Jerk? Loser?*) and planned to keep it that way. She wanted a quiet life of watering plants, reading, and sitting in coffee shops ignoring everyone, especially those pretentious types who thought they were poets. She also wanted to find a couple of women who liked to binge watch online baking shows and didn't make her want to jump out a window. Of course, that would mean getting close to someone.

Now there was this guy.

She turned to him. Dave who drank Bud Light grinned at her like he'd just won twenty bucks on a scratchers ticket. Skid never bought scratchers tickets.

"I had a wreck when I was a kid," she said, pausing for a drink. "Russian dancing bear, clown car, motorcycle, and tire skids. The usual. Now, if you—"

"Your last name's Roe, isn't it?" Bud Light Dave said.

"Maybe." Skid cut him a side look then elaborately looked around the bar for someone, anyone else, to talk to besides Bud Light Dave. There were no good prospects, so she decided to finish her drink, leave, and pick up Thai food on the way home. Stopping at Slap Happy's Dance Club was looking like a bad idea. Her eyes briefly met those of Brawny Man, who quickly turned away. The giant stood scanning the room with his back to the wall.

She sucked the last bit of vodka tonic from her highball glass, slurping around the ice. The bartender set down his lemon-cutting knife (absolutely the wrong knife for the job, Skid noted) and motioned to her empty glass. She shook her head.

"I'm a doctor," Bud Light Dave suddenly said, which seemed as likely as him being Mr. Spock from *Star Trek*.

She squinted at him. "Sorry. I don't have any pain. Unless I count you."

Bud Light Dave took a long suck off his bottle. "I'm not that kind of doctor. I'm a theoretical physicist. I spend most of my day postulating space-time."

Maybe, she considered, he actually thought he *was* Spock. She'd dated worse.

"Where?" Skid asked.

Bud Light Dave gazed at a beer poster, the guy holding a can of cheap brew and way too old for the bikini model next to him. "A little place south of town. Probably never heard of it."

"Try me."

"Lemaître Labs," he said, turning to face her. "But I probably shouldn't have mentioned that," his voice suddenly a whisper lost in the music.

She had heard of the place, a government weapons lab. Skid lifted her empty glass and swirled, ice clanking the sides. *Leave. Leave, Skid. Go home.*

But Skid couldn't resist two things: one, knee-jerk self-defense, and, two, proving someone wrong.

"Okay, science boy," she said, setting down the glass. "What's the underlying problem with the Schrödinger's cat scenario nobody talks about?"

A smile broke across Bud Light Dave's face. He smiled a lot. "I knew there was a reason I sat by you." He leaned back on his bar stool. "It's not so much of a problem as it is an ethical dilemma. We don't know if the cat inside the box is alive or dead, but we do know looking inside will kill it if it still is alive. At this point, the cat isn't alive, and it isn't dead. It's alive *and* dead. The would-be observer has to ask himself a question: should I, or should I not open the box, therefore preventing, or perhaps causing, the zombie catpocalypse?"

For a moment, just a moment, Skid considered she may have misjudged this guy. "Yes, but I was going more for chastising Erwin Schrödinger for being a bad pet owner."

This brought out a laugh, and Skid realized Bud Light Dave's smile was kind of nice, and, maybe the way his eyes looked in the dim bar light was kind of nice, too. She shook her head. *No. Go home, now.*

"What about you?" he said. "What was all that about the Russian dancing bear and the clown car? You don't look like the type."

"Excuse me?" Her eyes flashed. She'd dealt with this kind of bullshit all her life and hated it. "What do you mean by 'type'?"

He took a drink and shrugged. "If I may perpetuate a probably unrealistic stereotype: four teeth, gang tattoos, rap sheet, the usual. You seem too well-educated to be a carney."

Standing, she jammed her glass onto the bar coaster. "My father had a master's degree in chemical engineering and worked at Los Alamos National Laboratory before he ran the family business."

Bud Light Dave nodded. "Los Alamos? Daddy was not a lightweight. What's the family business?"

Skid stretched over the bar and plucked the knife from its citrus-stained cutting board. "Hey," the bartender barked. She ignored him.

"A circus," she said. "I grew up in a fucking circus." Skid took a deep breath and drew the knife behind her ear, holding it by the tip of the blade.

Bud Light Dave was motionless. Someone behind Skid shouted, and Brawny Man took a step toward her but stopped. Skid lined up the too-attractive fake-boob model in the Dos Equis poster at the end of the bar.

"Skid," someone said. Bud Light Dave probably, but she couldn't be distracted. *Why are you doing this, idiot? Just walk away.*

But it was too late, she'd put herself in The Zone. Skid's arm shot forward and the knife flew from her fingertips. A blink later the knife was buried an inch into the wood paneling behind the poster, the blade pinned between Fake-Boob's baby blues.

Skid uncurled her hands toward Bud Light Dave and wiggled her fingers. "Ta-da."

A couple nearby clapped, but she didn't notice. She was proving some kind of point.

"So, you were raised in a circus, huh?" Bud Light Dave said, still grinning. "What's your rap sheet look like?"

Good people worked in the circus. Nice people. Sometimes even honest people. Family worked in the circus. Randall's mantra ran through her head—*If something needs done, do it*—and before Skid knew what was happening, she'd pulled her right hand back in a fist and let it fly at Bud Light Dave's stupid face.

The connection was solid. He fell backward in slow motion, the best way to fall, like Dumbledore from the Astronomy Tower, or Martin Riggs from the freeway. Blood splattered from Bud Light Dave's nose as if he'd caught a red cold. A smell, like a doctor's office, flooded Skid's nostrils as he dropped. She twisted her shoulders for a follow-through with her left if she needed it, just like Carlito the strongman had taught her, but she didn't need it. Bud Light Dave was there, on his way down, falling through air that suddenly felt thick and heavy.

He was right there. But he never hit the floor; he simply vanished.

2

The girl was hot. Problem was, her boyfriend was hot, too. He worked out, a lot, or was just naturally ripped like those TV vampires. Maybe the guy was a vampire. Damn it, vampires are so hot. Cord hated good-looking couples. He was in this business for the money, sure, but he flirted with the cute women as a bonus. A pretty boyfriend complicated matters.

"Why's it so hot in here?" asked a man built like the Muppets' Telly Monster.

Cord didn't stop at the question. He held up his left hand, his eyes focused on the EMF meter in his right.

EMF meters were useless. These devices measure AC electromagnetic fields, which are everywhere, even in nature, but especially in the kind of wiring in houses and definitely the Sanderson Murder House Cord bought because it was haunted. Supposedly. He'd installed a few extra devices in the walls to make the EMF meters ghost hunters brought with them light up like they'd discovered something. "Ghosts create electromagnetic fields," he told the skeptical ones who sometimes come through. If someone doubted him, it always made Cord smile. "You forget the Law of Conservation of Energy. Energy can neither be created nor destroyed; it can only be transformed. So, if ghosts exist, they're made of invisible energy, such as, oh, I don't know, a magnetic field. You can prove me wrong, if you'd like."

This would garner some "oohs" from the crowd, and the skeptic usually shut up.

"It's easier to tell when you walk into a cold spot if the central air's not on," Court said over his shoulder. "A cold spot is a sure sign of paranormal activity."

Or not. He didn't know and didn't care. Cord only cared that the people who paid him to walk into a cold spot cared.

Someone in the group of twenty grumbled behind him. The rest of them gathered in tightly to look at the meter Cord held like he was studying it. He wasn't. His eyes were mostly on the meter, but enough on the hot girl in front of him to see her leaning over to get a better look at the readout.

"You see this number here," he told the hot girl, his voice soft, confident, in control. *Cord, you got it goin' tonight.* "Higher than ten milli-Gauss or lower than two milli-Gauss is a background electro-magnetic reading in any normal house," he said, then paused for effect and whispered, "but this isn't a normal house."

Cord smiled as he looked up into her eyes, hazel but leaning toward blue. His eyes quickly dropped back to the meter. The show must go on, and Vampire boy could seriously kick his ass.

"The meter fluctuates," he said loud enough for the entire group to hear, "depending on what appliances are on in the house. The central air, the oven, even a hair dryer can send the number higher." He paused again, holding up the meter so everyone could get a peek. "But a ghost. Oh, a ghost will not only hit a number higher or lower than that—" His right index finger pointed to a yellow light that was not on—yet. "This warning light will start flashing." His finger moved expertly to a red indicator. "But when something really nasty shows up, this baby starts blinking."

A hand raised in the back. "Yes," Cord said, knowing what was coming. "It has blinked red in the house once."

A slight "oooh" came from the group, except hot vampire boyfriend, who stood with his tattooed arms across his chest.

Cord smiled as he inspected the paranormal enthusiasts who'd given him $20 a pop to attend the 9 p.m. Sanderson Murder House Ghost Tour. Six of them had also opted for the $428 group overnight tour (with a non-refundable $200 deposit) where they got to sleep in the beds of the Sanderson family. Replica, of course, but they didn't know that. The Sanderson daughter off at college during Daddy's killing spree had had anything drenched with blood carted off to the landfill after the cops were through with it.

"That one occasion was on the second floor where Delbert Sanderson butchered his wife with a samurai sword in 1984."

A collective gasp filled the room.

"Has there ever been anything right here?" asked a teenage blond kid there with his mother.

"Yes," Cord said, not hesitating, nodding his head from the parlor area toward a darkened archway. "Just down this hall." He didn't like to take groups into that hallway until they'd toured the kitchen where Mrs. Sanderson once made county fair award-winning pies, and the sink where Mr. Sanderson washed the blood from his arms and face as best he could. But Cord played each group how they felt, and this group felt like it wanted action.

He slid his left hand into his front pants pocket and triggered the remote control to an enormous stereo system in a locked closet, its volume turned to 0. *You want EMF, you got EMF.* When Cord pulled his hand out it bore a tube of ChapStick. He popped the cap, applied the lip balm, capped the tube and slid it back into his pocket all with one hand. Misdirection was the shyster's best friend.

"Please tell everyone what happened in the hallway." A tall man of about seventy stood in the back of the group, well dressed and smart looking, but eyeglasses made everyone look smart. "I lived next door when the murders happened."

The tour "oohed" again. *Oh, shit. Shut up, dude.* Cord wore a grim smile when his eyes worked the people who'd paid good money to hear the grizzly details of the Sanderson crime. "This is where Delbert Sanderson chased down his thirty-two-year-old son screaming, 'This is why I never got your teeth fixed,' before he hacked him to death."

The man shook his head.

Goddamnit.

"No, son, that's not quite right," the old guy said. Cord began looking for a reason to kick the man the hell out of his haunted house. He assessed his paying customers, who were all looking at the tall old guy with his air of dignified authority and 'I lived next door' attitude. No one looked at Cord. His stomach tightened.

"I heard the whole thing," the man said. "In fact, I'm the one who called the police that night." The "oohs" turned to "whoas," and Cord's hands turned to fists. "It was hot that Thursday, but not so hot Cecilia—that was his wife—Cecilia had the air conditioning on. She was a bit of a penny pincher." He paused for a second, whether for tension's sake or if the guy just forgot where he was going with this, Cord couldn't tell.

"Well, what did he say?" a woman in nurse's scrubs asked.

The old guy chewed his lip before his eyes widened. "Straightened. Yes, Delbert screamed, 'This is why I never got your teeth straightened.' Then he hacked poor Tommy to bits in the hallway."

Cord relaxed, a muffled sigh slowing escaped his lips. *Time to take back control. Your show's over.* "Thank you, Mr.?"

"Wanker," the man said.

Damn straight.

"So, after Delbert Sanderson screamed, 'This is why I never got your teeth *straightened*,' he chased Thomas Sanderson into this very hallway," Cord said, then took a step forward into the hall, pretending to concentrate on the meter again, even though without his ace-in-the-hole EMF-blasting stereo playing Iron Maiden in complete silence, all he would get was a normal background reading. He waved at his tour group to follow him anyway; it was all part of the show.

The sixty-watt bulb in the ceiling fixture didn't shed a lot of light, but it showed all Cord wanted it to. Although the house had been cleaned and spit polished more times than he cared to count (the house had seemed to be always on the market before Cord realized what gold mine potential it had), there were stains in the hallway's hardwood floor. There weren't any stains when Cord bought the place two years ago, he just thought the suggestion of decades-old samurai sword murder blood helped with the ambiance.

Cord stepped over the carefully applied splatter of cherry wood finish stain ($8.49 per quart and damn well worth it) and stopped. "This is where it happened."

Silence. A heavy oppression sank into the hallway, like everyone had just seen a made-for-TLC movie. And the smell. *What was that? Is somebody using Febreze?* He looked from face to face. Everyone's eyes were wide, their mouths agape.

"Didn't you say the red light flashing was bad?" the hot girl asked, her voice shaky, her shoulder pressed into vampire-boy's chest.

Red light? Cord looked at the EMF meter, the red indicator flashed like a bulb had gone bad on a cheap string of Christmas lights. The numbers on the readout changed so quickly they became a blur.

"Oh, shit," he whispered. This hadn't happened. This *never* happened. The meter only changed when Cord wanted it to change. He didn't think the house was haunted, not really. A scream split the hallway. Cord would have been satisfied to know it came from the hot girl's boyfriend, but everything happened too fast.

A man—who hadn't even paid admission—popped into existence about two feet off the floor, a look of shock on his bloody-nosed face. He fell like he'd been shoved and hit the floor with an "oof."

"What the hell?" came from someone, but Cord didn't look to see who. His eyes were on the man in the white shirt and gray Dockers who smelled like cheap beer and ozone. For a second, only a second, Cord thought he heard dance music. The guy tried to suck air into his lungs and failed the first couple of tries but was soon breathing again.

Something between a gut punch and the first drop on a roller coaster grabbed Cord's insides in a fist. This was a ghost. A real ghost. No chains, no floating and no Scooby-Doo "whooooos," but still, a ghost had appeared in Cord's haunted house. Cord stared at it because his eyes refused to do anything else.

But the ghost didn't look like a ghost. The white oxford shirt was wrong, and so was the blood coming from his nose. If Delbert Sanderson had sliced up his boy Tommy with a samurai sword, why did the splatter on the man come from a bloody nose?

Cord reached out his right index finger and poked the Amazing Appearing Man in the leg just to make sure. The leg was solid.

The man glared at him, confused. "Where's Skid?" he asked before, pop, he vanished again, Cord's meter flashing and spinning like he'd just hit a jackpot at a casino. Maybe he had.

Skid? nearly squeaked out, but Cord clamped down on that momentum-spoiler fast.

"Was that Tommy Sanderson?" the nurse asked. Not to Cord, to the old man.

The old guy adjusted his glasses and frowned.

Oh, please. Oh, please. Oh, please don't ruin this for me you Wanker.

"Well, I wish I'd gotten a longer look at him," the former neighbor said. Cord didn't realize it, but he was holding his breath. "But, Tommy Sanderson? It looked like him. Yeah, it looked just like him."

The breath whooshed from Cord and he sucked in another one, a big one, through a smile. "If anyone in the group is still skeptical about the paranormal," he said. "Please get your disbelief out now." Cord raised his hand to his ear in a bit of stage play overacting and waited one beat, two, three. *This is the best night of my life.* "All righty then. Would anyone like to upgrade their tour tickets to overnight tickets?"

Hands shot up faster than dandelions. *Oh, yeah, the best.*

Cord had no idea what had happened, and he didn't care. As he pocketed the extra $1,500 on top of the $828 he'd already made off this group, he silently thanked the Amazing Appearing Man. Cord didn't realize until morning he hadn't even gotten the hot girl's name.

To hell with it. He had a haunted house to run.

3

Brick leaned against the back wall of Slap Happy's Dance Club next to a sign that that read "Hookers and Johns" and tried not to stand out. But Brick always stood out. Growing up, it was his job on field trips to stand in the parking lot so his classmates would know where to gather. And he wasn't just tall, he was big, professional-wrestler big. This made him seem intimidating even when he told people in a soft voice that he baked muffins for a living.

He checked his phone. Beverly had been in the bathroom twenty minutes. At least a dozen women had come and gone through that door in twenty minutes. *Did she come out and I missed her?* But he knew that was more wish than reality. He scanned the club. It was full of people dancing to loud music hoping to hook up. He didn't want that; he'd just met Beverly, sure, but he kind of liked her.

Beverly seemed like a nice girl when she walked up to him at their mutually-decided first date meeting spot—in the bar area at Il Palazzo Bianco. "Oh, you just have to be Chauncey," she said in a voice that didn't sound like it could ever get on his nerves.

"Yep," he said. "Chauncey Hall." He almost followed that with, "My friends call me Brick," but stopped before the words came out. Being a Chauncey was enough of a burden. He didn't want to explain Brick.

Beverly smiled and looked like her profile picture; she even talked about the things she'd listed:

BEVERLY GIBSON
Likes: Journalism, "Lord of the Rings" (books and movies!), old-fashioned gentlemen and muffins. I love muffins.

Dislikes: Bad grammar, the color Alabaster (It's called white, people!) and shoes.

Quote: "I'm happy with who I am."

Looking for: A nice guy.

Brick decided she was the one he liked out of the four girls whose profiles matched his best. He was happy Beverly liked *Lord of the Rings*, which were his favorite books. *Maybe she likes Dungeons and Dragons,* he thought, then stopped as the words of his mother poured through his head. *Don't tell girls you still play Dungeons and Dragons, Chaunce. It's like telling them you have leprosy.*

During their date, Beverly smiled at him over her wine glass and didn't once talk about eating her sister's placenta like last week's H. P. Lovecraft date Jayna. After dinner, Beverly wanted to stop in across the street at Slap Happy's, then she disappeared into the bathroom.

He pushed open the door to the hallway a crack. A red, glowing EXIT sign hovered over a metal-reinforced door at the far end just past the entrances to "Hookers" and "Johns." She'd had an escape plan. A rock sank in his stomach.

"Not again," he mumbled.

Then the door to "Johns" slammed open and a man spilled into the hallway, slapping into the far wall.

"Hey," Brick said, stepping forward, the spring-operated door to the dance floor snapped shut behind him.

The man leaned against the wall, his white button-down shirt stained yellowish-brown, his face streaked with filth. From the smell, Brick guessed it was hydraulic fluid, but there was another smell mingled in. He sniffed. Ozone? Yeah, ozone, like someone had turned on a room freshener. A crust of dried blood stained the skin under the man's nose.

"That was some dump, huh?" Brick said.

The man craned his neck to stare up at Brick and a light of recognition popped on. He pushed himself from the wall and lurched forward, the smell of hydraulic fluid grew stronger.

"Brick?" the man wheezed. "Are you Brick?"

Brick stepped away from him, studying the oily face.

This oily man took another step, planting his weight on his left foot and nearly dropping to the chipped tile floor.

"Oh, no," he whispered. Blood stained the left leg of the Oilyman's gray Dockers he'd apparently tried to bandage with a rag. "What happened to you?"

The man forced himself upward and grabbed Brick by his shirt, hydraulic fluid soaking into the material.

"Watch her, Brick," the man wheezed. "Watch out for Skid. She's not what she seems."

Skid? Brick looked down at the man, trying to place that face. Was he from high school? The gym? A customer?

"I don't know you, but you need a doctor." He started to reach into his pocket for his cell phone, but Oilyman pulled hard on his shirt.

"Skid's going to kill us all," he said, his voice as close to a shout as he could muster.

"Who's Sk—"

The door to the hallway opened and three drunk girls bounced against the far wall and laughed before righting themselves and stumbling into the bathroom marked "Hookers." The dance music, loud only for a moment, was muted again by the closed door. When Brick turned back, the man was gone.

"Hey."

Bloody, oily prints from flat-soled shoes were all that remained in a trail from the bathroom that ended at Brick. He swung around, but he was alone.

"Hey, buddy," Brick said into the empty hall. Nobody responded. *He has to be somewhere.* But the man hadn't gone out into the bar or out the back. That left only one place. He pushed open the door to "Johns."

Oilyman's bloody footprints started in the middle of the floor, facing the hallway like he'd simply appeared there. A smell filled the bathroom, hospital sanitizer. Brick let the door swing shut and walked back into the bar.

"People don't just disappear," Brick muttered, standing just off the dance floor. The Oilyman had gone, of that much Brick was certain. But he couldn't have gotten far on that leg. He leaned against the wall, his eyes roaming the room.

"No way."

A pretty brunette in a T-shirt looked toward him, then turned away. The man next to her said something the woman probably heard but saw no reason to answer. Her eyes met Brick's, and she frowned. His gut clenched. He turned his head. *No, it can't be.* Brick counted to five, then glanced back. He didn't care about the woman; his attention went to man. It was the man from the bathroom, but it wasn't. This man's hair was combed, his white shirt clean. And his leg? No wound. But it was the same guy.

The brunette's face grew grim, and she pulled the bartender's knife from the cutting board.

"Hey," Brick saw the bartender mouth as she lifted behind her ear.

"Oh, no," Brick whispered and stepped away from the wall, the door crashing open behind him, but he didn't turn to see what happened. Probably the drunk girls. He started to launch himself through the crowded dance floor, but he was too late. The woman threw the knife like she knew what she was doing. It impaled the model in a beer poster.

Two seconds later the man at the bar said something, and the woman punched him in the nose. He fell under a sea of dancers who didn't have a clue what had just happened.

4

Skid stood with fists clenched staring at the spot where Bud Light Dave disappeared two feet above the floor. A few people clapped. One man patted her on the back and pushed something into her grip. Not a smart thing to do until Skid realized it was $20. "It was worth it," he shouted over the music, escorting a woman toward the dance floor. "You've got talent."

I'm sorry. I'm sorry. I'm sorry. Bud Light Dave had vanished. Not in a blizzard of fuzzy 1960s special effects, and not like D. B. Cooper. Vanished, vanished. Like Harry Potter.

"I'm so sorry," she whispered.

She had to run. Skid pivoted, pointing herself toward the door when the bartender stopped her, "Hey!"

She spun again. "Yes?"

"Your boyfriend didn't pay for that last round."

"What? Here," she fumbled the $20 across the bar, nodded and walked straight into a red flannel wall. Brawny Man. Hipster Dan Haggerty. He was huge.

"Back off, Grizzly Adams," she said.

The man shoved his hands in his pockets awkwardly like he didn't know what else to do with them. "What happened to him?" he asked, his voice surprisingly soft and kind for someone who looked like he could cut down trees by flexing at them.

"What?" Skid said, the word squeaking like air out of a balloon.

"The guy at the bar," the big man said. "He had on a white shirt and gray slacks. Where did he go? I have to talk to him."

Skid stopped and looked up at him; his eyes were clear, but his expression was confused. The man looked, well, he looked nice.

"I don't know where he is," Skid said, the shock starting to wear off. "He disappeared."

The man frowned under his neatly trimmed beard. "What do you mean disappeared?"

"The guy went all Frodo Baggins on me." Then she flared her fingers for effect. "Poof. Disappeared."

"Damn it," he hissed, one meat hook absentmindedly pulling at his chin. "He did the same thing to me. We gotta find him."

Hipster Dan Haggerty turned to scan the dance floor. When he turned back, Skid had gone for Beverly's Plan B.

"Well, crap," he whispered.

CHAPTER TWO

SEPTEMBER 2

1

SWEAT TRICKLED down Skid's back, soaking her T-shirt. It was nearly 8 a.m.; she'd left her apartment for a run at 6, hours before the nice Thai family that operated The Dumpling King below her began prepping for lunch by screaming at each other. Not that she ever got up that early, but seeing a man vanish into nothingness will do that to a person. Last night was pinned to her mind, no matter how much she tried to ignore it.

She turned left onto Gerry Avenue, a residential area, mostly because the traffic light on Baltimore and Gerry had turned red and she hated it when runners stopped at the light and jogged in place until it turned green. Showoffs. The houses here were big, nicely kept for the most part, and apparently not good enough for joggers who stopped at red lights, because Skid was the only one out.

Bud Light Dave. Damn it. He'd gotten into her head, and she didn't like it. Not one bit. A man, any man, had no place in her life. At least not right now. But that lab Bud Light Dave said he worked for, she had heard of it. She just couldn't remember the name.

Skid slowed as she approached an intersection without a light. A black Ford Escape with a magnetic sticker that read NEWS on the door turned onto Gerry. *For what?* A crime, probably. That was the only time the wonks came out of their newsrooms. Unless maybe it was for a feature story, but it was about 7:45 a.m. on a Saturday.

Skid jogged across the street. She didn't run this route often, just when the light on Baltimore was red, but the number of cars compared to the houses was wrong. Some cars had Kansas license plates and one was from Nebraska. It was like someone had a party last night and no one went home.

The news car stopped a block ahead of her. A woman in a blue skirt and yellow blouse stepped from the passenger side. She held what looked like an iPhone and a reporter's notebook. Another woman slid from the driver's side and walked to the back of the vehicle, popping the hatch. By the time the driver had pulled out a camera bag and started taking photographs of the exterior of a two-story house probably built in the early 1900s, Skid realized why they were there, at least superficially. The news people were at the Sanderson Murder House.

Skid hadn't been born when the Sanderson man slaughtered his family in that house and wouldn't have heard about the killings if she had. Her father had left the science life and taken over the family business in the early 1980s. The Roe Bros. circus made the circuit from Washington state across the northern US to Pennsylvania from May to September, moving down the East Coast and swinging from Georgia through the Southern states to winter in Prescott, Arizona. Roe Bros. never touched the interior parts of the country and never would have heard the news. That's why Skid had picked Kansas City, Missouri, to settle in; she didn't have to worry about running into family. She knew of the murder house by the tacky blood-splattered sign in the front yard.

A man rushed from the Sanderson house to greet the journalists as Skid jogged by, shooting her a glance and a grin even as he extended a hand toward the first reporter.

Take a picture, jerk.

Blank faces stared into the yard from the windows like the place really was haunted. She'd read somewhere the house rented out for overnight ghost tours, and this must have been a doozy. A few people, including a nurse in scrubs, spilled out onto the lawn, the photographer snapping away. Skid turned her head and picked up the pace, not that she had anywhere to go. Work didn't start until 4 p.m. and it was halfway across town. Security at a Doobie Brothers concert wasn't tough, just a matter of making sure all the stoned Baby Boomers didn't start a riot during "Keep This Train A-Rollin'." Somebody might lose their dentures.

She needed a shower and probably a nap because some asshole had blinked out of existence right in front of her last night, and she hadn't had any coffee. She reached a thumb up to pull a sweat-soaked bra strap back into place.

"Coffee first."

2

The reporter from *The Kansas City Star* stood in the yard next to a sign that read Sanderson Murder House, in blood-dripping letters. Cord's stomach wrestled itself into a knot. Last night had been perfect for business and he had twenty witnesses. Who cared if the ghost wasn't really a ghost? If it appeared like a ghost, vanished like a ghost, and made him money like a ghost, it was a ghost. The people at *The Star* certainly jumped on it. *Thank God for slow news days.*

He'd excused himself from the tour at about 10 p.m. to put fresh batteries in his stereo remote, which came in handy around 3 a.m. when the tour went back into the downstairs hallway to see if Thomas Sanderson fell on the floor again during the Witching Hour.

He didn't, at least visually, but Cord triggered the hidden stereo and the EMF meters he handed out went crazy at the right time. His customers needed to get their money's worth.

But 11 p.m. had been Cord's favorite time of the night. After he bought the Sanderson house, he'd heavily insulated the closet of the master bedroom on the second floor and lined it with refrigeration coils, the motor that circulated the coolant hidden deep in the walls surrounded by sound dampening panels so no one could hear it running. The result was a cold spot in the closet, unexplainable except as a sign of spiritual activity. It didn't hurt that poor Cecilia Sanderson had attempted to escape her crazed husband by barricading herself in that closet and failed miserably. The psychological impact of the death spot coupled with a mystery chill was as powerful as a punch to the face.

Cord steered the hot girl and Vampire Boy into that closet at 11 p.m., and Vampire Boy couldn't take it anymore. He'd been jittery most of the night, and he'd finally started to crack. All he'd needed was a little push. As soon as his girlfriend shivered and said, "Don't you feel that? It's a cold spot," he rushed back out into the master bedroom, leaning himself on the bed the Muppet man had paid $50 extra to sleep on. Yep, it was that cold in the closet; not cold enough to store leftovers, but cold enough to make an impression.

"Fuck this," Vampire Boy said, pushing himself away from the bed and moving his feet like he'd forgotten how to stand. He pointed at Cord. "And fuck you. I'm going home."

"Come on, Roman," the hot girl said, her voice pleading.

Roman? I thought Romans only existed in soap operas.

"No," Roman shouted. Footsteps began to clomp from down the hall. People had paid for a show and this shouting was part of it. Roman moved to face Cord and jabbed a finger toward him. "I want my money back, man. I want it back now."

Cord shook his head. Normally an angry, buff, stupid guy would be the cause of some alarm, but not tonight. This jerk was in his house.

"Sorry," he told him in the same voice he used in his former life as a car salesman to inform buyers their trade-in wasn't worth quite what Kelley Blue Book said even if it was. "No refunds. It's worded that way in the waiver you signed before the overnight."

The waiver everyone signed said no such thing, but Roman wouldn't bother to look and Cord would have that fixed by the time the next tours showed up tomorrow. But tonight? Roman glared at Cord and flexed before he looked to his girlfriend, his face melting from anger to a pout before he left her standing in the unnaturally cold closet.

Oh, yeah. Eleven p.m. had been a magical time.

Cord rushed out the front door to greet the reporter and photographer as they stepped out of their car, barely taking notice of the cute girl in the black T-shirt running on the sidewalk. This was it, his ticket. One good story in the local metro paper and he'd have more tour requests than he could schedule. Cord would tell the reporter about Roman chickening out as they worked their way upstairs. He had to.

3

The sun on his face wasn't the first thing Dave Collison, Ph.D., noticed. Neither was the sensation of something pulling on his leg, although it stopped for a moment before beginning on the other. It was the smell. Something smelled awful.

"Whazizip," he mumbled, although he was unsure of what he was trying to say. His brain was busy matching up enough synapses to figure out what pulled on his feet, and why it had stopped.

"Hey," he managed before summoning enough strength to force open his eyelids. He wished he hadn't. Dave lay in an alley atop a pile of black, festering garbage bags that smelled like rotting fish sand-wiches from All-National Burger, and a homeless man had appar-ently just stolen his shoes. "Hey."

The man, about fifty and short on teeth, grinned at him through a dirty, rust-and-white beard and held up a leg showing Dave his left Aston Grey Leu leather oxford on the man's sockless foot, then did the same to his other leg to show Dave his right.

Dave didn't know what to do so he said, "Hey," again.

The man, in a dirty T-shirt, shrugged his thin shoulders, stuck his hands in the pockets of his dusty, oversized jeans, and hummed as he walked from the alley out onto the sidewalk and disappeared around a corner.

"Goddamnit." Dave lay back on the trash bags. He didn't know where he was, he didn't know why he was there, and he didn't know what happened after he'd met the girl in the bar last night. *Skirt? Skip? Skid.* Her name was Skid. Thoughts of last night began to crawl from whatever hole they'd burrowed into. *Nickname. She crashed a motorcycle.*

His eyes grew wide as a few mental wheels clicked into place. "A full matter transfer," he whispered. "I was in a full matter transfer—twice." *But why?* He examined the alley and determined, as far as alleys went, this was pretty shitty. "Where am I?"

Dave started to sit up, but realized his face felt like something had slept on it wrong. Then the night began pouring out. The beer, the knife-throwing trick, the fist coming at him.

"She punched me," he whispered, and moved a hand to feel his face. His nose was tender but didn't seem broken. "What happened to me?"

Dave pushed himself to his feet, the bad smell sticking to him. His hands went to his pockets. Wallet, keys, phone, all there, but he'd woken in an unknown alley with a dirty shirt, no shoes, and no idea how he got there. "Now I know how Bruce Banner feels."

It wasn't until he pulled his cell phone from his pocket that he saw he was going to be late for work.

4

Skid stopped running at the corner of Tim Binnall Boulevard and stretched. Bud Light Dave. *That son of a bitch. How the hell did he disappear?* That moment at Slap Happy's replayed in her head and made her want to punch him again. She exhaled slowly and raised her arms above her head, leaning to touch her left foot. As she tried to clear her mind, her eyes locked on the street sign. She froze. Her plan was to turn right on Tim Binnall Boulevard, stop at a coffee and muffin place down the street, take another right onto Baltimore, walk home, shower, and collapse onto her bed. But the green sign with white letters didn't read "Tim Binnall Boulevard." It read "Tim Binnall Avenue."

An uneasy feeling crept over her. She'd gone by the "Tim Binnall Boulevard" intersection every day since she left Roe Bros. and moved to a city that was so Midwest, people still smiled at strangers. It was "Boulevard," of that she was certain. Had the city council changed it on a whim? Was this Binnall not worthy of the status of boulevard? A simple vote would be all it took.

Then why had rust grown around the bolts?

"I've seen weirder," she said and started running again.

5

Cord turned off the custom refrigerator in the master bedroom and had no intention of using the stereo remote control for the news crew. Nope. That would be too much of a good thing, bordering on unbelievable. People come into a supposedly haunted house not expecting to encounter cold spots or books flying across the room, so about half the time nothing is exactly what they got. To the ghost hunters and weekend spooktacular enthusiasts, this didn't mean the joint wasn't haunted. It was just another house that behaved like they thought it would. A lot of them came back the next night, or maybe a week later because something would eventually happen.

Cord always made sure it did. Anything to keep them coming back.

"So, this is where it appeared?" asked the reporter. Cord stood in the hallway with her, the photographer and most of the overnight guests.

"The full-bodied apparition," the photographer Carly emphasized. "This is where you saw the full-bodied apparition."

The reporter, who had introduced herself as Beverly Gibson, nodded. "Yes, uh, the full-bodied apparition," she said, her attention not quite there. "Could you... Could you tell me what happened?"

Cord's mouth slid open, then shut almost as fast. The reporter lady seemed like she might be a bit off. Distracted? Sad, maybe? But that didn't matter; this was as big a show as last night and he had to sell it.

"It surprised us all," he said. "Maybe you could leave the question open for everybody. We were all here. Tamara?" The hot girl blushed.

Oh, Cord. You slick smooth loveable bastard.

"Well, we were here. Right here," she said, pointing the palms of her hand toward the spot on the hall floor like she was attempting to hold it down. "And Cord's meter went all crazy."

"Meter?" Beverly asked, looking at Cord.

Expert testimony in three, two, one— "An EMF meter. That means electromagnetic frequency." Cord looked around him at all the rapt faces. He felt like a TV preacher. "Spirits, at least in theory, are composed of energy because—" *The Law of Conservation of Energy? Sure.* "—if the Law of Conservation of Energy applies to the paranormal, the energy of a spirit, a soul if you will, cannot be destroyed. It can, however, be transformed into what we saw last night."

The crowd, his people, was quiet, no one daring to interrupt Cord's show. Except Beverly.

"A ghost?"

Carly pulled the camera away from her face for a second. "Full-bodied apparition."

Beverly faintly smiled. "Of course. Could somebody describe it?"

The tall old nosy neighbor and total Wanker raised his hand. "It was the ghost of Tommy Sanderson."

The hall fell quiet. "What did he look like?" Beverly asked.

Cord took over before he lost any more column inches in tomorrow's newspaper. "A man in his thirties with brown hair, white shirt, gray pants, and a really surprised look on his face."

Beverly scribbled illegible shorthand into her reporter's notebook while Carly snapped the tense expressions around the ghost-hunting group that wouldn't have been any better if Cord had paid them.

Cord almost jumped when Tamara's warm hand rested on his forearm. "He said something to you."

Yeah, he did. 'Help me,' would have been nice. 'I can't find the light,' would have been better. 'My dad still stalks this house,' would be the absolute friggin' best. But twenty witnesses heard what the man had said.

"Where's Skid?" Cord said. "The ghost of Tommy Sanderson said, 'Where's Skid?'" He bit his lip and held it for one, two, three seconds before he looked into Beverly's eyes. "We have no idea what he meant."

Carly clicked a close-up of Cord, who smiled like a stoned Matthew McConaughey in *Dazed and Confused*. Alright, alright, alright.

Beverly pulled the conversation back a step. "But the meters."

She looked at her notes. "The E-M-F meters. What did they do?" She looked at her notes again. "Tamara said they, 'went all crazy'."

Cord slipped his hand into his pocket and fingered the remote control. Maybe a little show wouldn't hurt.

6

The coffee place sat where Skid thought it did, on the corner of Binnall and Baltimore, which was as confounding as was the brick storefront with "Muffin Monday All Week Long!" painted in the windows in bright pink and yellow. A black awning hung over the door reading "Manic Muffins" with cartoon lines around the words to show how manic it was. Two wrought-iron tables with three chairs each sat on either side of the door with fresh flowers in tall coffee mugs in the center of each. Cute. This was cute, and normal. The sun cut through the clear morning sky, the coffee shop looked like a coffee shop, and no one disappeared in front of her. Normal.

Skid slowed as she approached the shop, ignoring the store for a moment and concentrating on the street sign at the intersection. "Tim Binnall Avenue." This sign was faded and slightly bent. It had been there for a while.

That can't be right.

Even though the world seemed almost sane and cheery, she didn't like the feeling in her gut. The kind of feeling she sometimes had when something bad was about to happen, or when she ate at that dodgy Indian restaurant on Washington Street. Moe, Larry and Curry was the worst.

7

Brick squatted behind the counter and stared at the tray of muffins he'd slid into the display case earlier; big, beautiful chocolate chip muffins in sparkly cups topped with pink frosting and Homer Simpson sprinkles. The frown he wore deepened. Brick got to the shop around 4:30 a.m., baked his first batch of muffins by 5:15, had them iced by 5:45 and in the display case by 6. By then, more muffins were ready, some to be iced, others not. But this batch of muffins was different than any he'd ever iced before because he'd used chocolate frosting as brown as mud—and now they were bright pink.

"I'll take a pink one," Katie said, pointing at the rack of muffins that should be brown. Katie was a semi-regular. She was at least 60, maybe older, but came in every morning from a jog. "And a cup of coffee, black."

Brick forced a smile. He'd never had to force a smile with the older woman before. She'd come in on his grand opening and stopped by a few times a month. "You bet," he said, and put a pink muffin in a recycled paper sack, "Manic Muffins" stamped on the front.

"You know," she said as he poured her coffee into a to-go cup. "I had an idea."

"What's that, Katie?" he said, snapping a lid on the cup.

"Well, since your name's Brick, I thought it would be cute if you offered a muffin named Brick."

"Okay. I'm listening." He set her coffee on the counter and picked up the cash. She knew exactly how much, to the penny, and she always left a five-dollar bill in the tip jar.

"Maybe you could make red velvet cake muffins but bake them in little loaf pans so they'd be rectangular on the bottom. You know, like a brick."

That was a good idea.

"And fill it with cream, because you know you're softer on the inside."

The forced smile melted into a real one. "That's perfect. I'll get to work on that."

Katie took her sack and coffee and started walking toward the door.

"I'll have to come up with a muffin called the Katie," he said after her.

She stopped and turned, her face smiling, but her eyes were flat. "I don't think you've got anything that sour, Brick." Then she left, the bell over the door chiming as she walked outside.

"That was weird," he said, turning his attention back to the pink muffins, the conversation pushed into the back of his mind. *How is this even possible?* he wondered, then thought, just briefly, that he might be losing his mind. *Last night's whatever it was, then this. I must have used pink frosting. But—*

The bell over the front door jingled again. Katie, he thought, maybe with another idea, although he had to admit the Brick muffin was a good one.

A cough from the other side of the display case cut off his thoughts. He stood and saw it wasn't Katie, and his day wasn't getting any easier.

"Hipster Dan Haggerty," said the woman from Slap Happy's, the one with the knife. "You?"

The morning had started normally. His phone had blared the annoying default bell chime he'd never gotten around to changing, and he had eaten breakfast while reviewing possibilities of why his computer date dumped him. But the woman who punched the Oilyman in the face? He hadn't seen this coming. *Don't say anything stupid. Don't say anything stupid.*

"I think the universe is trying to throw us together," Brick said, resisting an urge to groan.

The woman exhaled loudly enough Brick knew that, yeah, it was stupid.

Brick shrugged. "Sorry."

"I don't want to talk about last night. Whatever happened didn't happen. I just want a muffin." She pressed her finger against the glass display case Brick would have to clean later. He hated smudges. Parents with little kids were the worst.

"A guy talked to me in the bathroom last night," Brick said.

"I thought there were rules against men talking in bathrooms," the woman said, then nodded to herself. "I'll have one of those pink ones, please."

Brick didn't move. "I turned my head for a second and he wasn't there anymore. It was like he just disappeared." Brick pulled himself up to his full height and crossed his massive arms. It didn't seem to impress her. "Then I see you talking to the same guy at the bar. He was cleaner than the man I saw, and his hair was different, I think. But it was the same guy."

"It was like he just disappeared," the woman whispered.

Brick relaxed. "What did you say?"

The woman seemed to gather her wits back from whatever directions they'd traveled and looked up at him, her eyes made of iron.

"People don't just disappear," she said, then pointed behind him. "I'd also like a coffee, please. Black. What do you call your large?"

"Large," Brick said.

She nodded. "Yeah, that sounds great."

He used tongs to pluck a pink-topped muffin from the case and slide it into a sack, then poured house blend into a large cup made from recycled trees, or recycled cardboard, or recycled toilet paper. He didn't know what his cups were recycled from, he just knew the hipsters who came in spread the word when they realized Manic Muffins was a friend of the environment.

"How long have you been here?" the woman asked.

Brick snapped on a plastic lid the hipsters never questioned him about and turned toward her. "I thought you didn't want to talk."

She pulled a sweat-soaked twenty from the band of her running pants and put it on the counter. "I don't. So, how long have you been here?"

He took the twenty and left it behind the counter to dry, then began to hit buttons on the cash register. "Since 4:30. Why?"

Her face tensed. The woman seemed nice, like the kind of person who'd bring snacks to work, but at that moment she held herself like a fighter, and although Brick had at a good foot and a half on the woman and at least 150 pounds, he suddenly felt if she wanted to hurt him, she could. He counted out the change without thinking and set it on the counter. He didn't want to get too close to her.

"Here." She shook her head. "No, not here. Not today. I mean in this building. How long has your store been in this building?"

How long? "Four years, I guess. Maybe five. You with the Chamber of Commerce?"

A tight grin pulled across her lips. "Four or five years on Binnall Avenue?"

"No," he said. "Boulevard. Binnall Boulevard."

The woman plucked her coffee and the bag with the pink-topped muffin off the counter and barked a laughed. "Ha. I thought so," she said, grabbing her change; at least the bills. She dropped the coinage into the tip jar.

Then she walked out the door. For the second time in less than twelve hours, the same woman he didn't know walked away, leaving him to wonder what had just happened.

"Avenue," he said aloud. Brick stepped from behind the counter and walked to the front window, looking between the hot pink and yellow lettering his niece Amy had written for him. The sweaty woman in black running clothes rounded the corner, going east on Baltimore.

He glanced up at the street sign next to the red traffic light. It read "avenue."

"Well," he said. "I'll be damned."

8

The journalists were nice, Cord determined as he stood in the yard and waved. Carly the photographer waved back before she pulled the Ford Escape into the street. The overnights took that as a cue and said their goodbyes, some promising to book another tour online and bring friends. *Damn straight.*

This was it; he knew. Oh, sure, he'd been interviewed on some of the paranormal radio shows, and a few authors had written about the Sanderson Murder House in books like *Ghostly Kansas City*, *Missouri's Spookiest* and *Show Me Your Ghosts!*, but his house wasn't like the Waverly Hills Sanatorium or the Crescent Hotel & Spa in the national world of ghost attractions.

Until now. A full-bodied apparition witnessed by twenty people would do it, and those nice newspaper ladies would take him there.

"Thank you for a thrilling evening, son," Mr. 'I Lived Next Door When the Murders Happened' Wanker said, patting Cord on the shoulder. "I never liked that boy, Tommy. He borrowed my hoe one fall and never gave it back. Kept barking, 'Hoe, hoe, hoe' at me then laughed all through December. Not saying he deserved to be hacked to death with a Japanese sword, but I am saying I can see why his father got tired of his shit."

Mr. Wanker nodded and walked off to his car.

Tamara waited until all the other ghost hunters had gone before she came out of the house and approached Cord. He sighed, a smile growing across his lips. *Why do birds suddenly appear every time you are near.* It was a song, but it wasn't a question. She stopped in front of him. No arm touching, not even an accidental brush against his shoulder. Tamara had to go back to her life, and that brought her back to reality.

"Hey," Cord said, taking a half step closer. Not invasively close. More like 'I had a great time at summer camp am I ever going to see you again?' close. "You want to go get some breakfast, or something. There's a muffin and coffee place just a couple blocks away. It's—"

She shook her head, her glorious black mane swishing in the same way that made actresses in disaster movies always look like they'd just styled their hair.

"I can't," she said. "I have a boyfriend."

Cord smiled his best car salesman sealing-the-deal smile and gently took her hands in his. She jerked them away.

"He pulled up about five minutes ago," she said, pointing toward the street where Roman stood in a tight tank top outside the door of a Mitsubishi sports car.

"Yeah. Roman. That guy." Cord gave a clench-toothed grimace and waved at Roman before raising his voice. "Hey, I hope you enjoyed your adventure at the Sanderson Murder House. You guys come back sometime, okay? I'll give you a discount." He would in no way give anyone a discount. Not even his mother.

Cord could almost see the thoughts bouncing around Tamara's head as she finally decided to smile.

"Yeah. I'd like that." She stopped for a second as something occurred to her. She laughed. "I might have to come by myself, though, right?"

Cord nodded. *I can only pray.*

"Sure," he said. "You do that."

9

Dave decided not to pace in the alley because of all the broken glass. Sure, Police Detective John McClane would work his way through it and blow up all the terrorists in Nakatomi Plaza, but Dave had sensitive feet. He stood as still as possible and frowned at his mobile phone.

"Yes, Gillian, my GPS shows I'm only two-point-four miles from the lab but—" He looked at his feet and noticed a hole in his left sock. "Like I told you, I was mugged in an alley." A greasy sack from All-National Burger lay crumpled on the alley floor. "I think I'm near an

All-National Burger. The guy took my shoes. I don't want to walk two-point-four miles on a rural highway without shoes."

Silence came from the other end.

"Hello?"

Gillian tapped her pen on the desk loudly enough Dave could hear it over the phone.

"What were you doing in an alley at that time of the morning?" she asked.

Dave took his cell phone from his ear and bit it before saying what he had to say next. "I told you, I thought I saw a quarter." That was the joke around the office. Dave was so cheap he'd get mugged in an alley trying to pick up loose change. Ha, ha, ha. He thought he might as well make it work for him.

She stifled a laugh before the clicks of her keyboard tapped through the phone. "It looks like Dr. Miller is the only one still not in the office yet. If you can catch him—"

Karl Miller. It had to be Karl Miller.

"Yeah, Gillian. Thanks." Dave ended the call and thumbed through his contacts until he came to Karl's name with a Summer's Eve douche as an avatar. He didn't want to call Karl. Karl hired him at Lemaître Labs because Dave's foster father had given Karl a job to work on secret projects for the United States government. Now Karl was the boss, looking for the particle beyond the God Particle, the thing past the Higgs boson, the building block of the Standard Model of particle physics. This was everything Dave had worked for, the quest his foster father had cemented in his mind, and Karl opened the door to let him in. Dave supposed he should be thankful, but Karl felt he owed his foster father and the bastard never let Dave forget it. And something told him Karl Miller, Ph.Douche was responsible for his full matter transfer. Karl also smelled like Cheetos.

But it was only two-point-four miles.

Dave moved his thumb to the call button when something pushed him, like the moment the undercooked chicken vindaloo from

Moe, Larry and Curry, that dodgy Indian place on Washington Street, tells you it's ready to fight its way out. But this was all around him, more like the barometric pressure dropping right before a storm. He looked up.

The glass from his smartphone cracked as it hit the pavement.

10

The volume downstairs in The Dumpling King hadn't quite gotten to "the doors open in an hour" loud by the time Skid climbed the stairs to her apartment, but it was close. She slid the key into the lock of the door from the street, knowing a single girl in the city was supposed to look behind her, but she didn't. A lifetime of learning self-defense from a circus strongman gave her the kind of confidence that usually scared people away before anything sweaty and bruisy happened. The day she moved in, the Thai father Mee Noi (half owner of The Dumpling King with his wife Sirikit) stopped her at the door to the street to tell her it was his duty to protect the women in the building. Circus training kicked in, and since then, Skid had never had to pay for dumplings, no matter how many times she apologized.

The muffin bag skipped across the surface of the small table in her kitchen in front of a quiet Japanese waving cat and stopped before it dropped onto the floor.

"You're failing me, Hayata," she said. "You should've had that."

Skid reached a hand toward the cat and flicked its arm. The back-and-forth bobbing threw a thin, harsh shadow across a wall calendar of adorable kittens. The rest of the tiny apartment was decorated with items any young, sophisticated metropolitan woman should have—a tightly made bed, a framed picture of Audrey Hepburn in "Breakfast at Tiffany's," a Barbie toothbrush, a punching bag and a full-sized spinning trick knife-throwing target with wrist and ankle straps. She often wondered if she brought anyone into her apartment how long it would take them to ask if they were going to shoot porn.

Skid sat her coffee on the table and walked into the living room. Even after a run and not enough sleep, she had way too much pent-up energy, enough to go out for another run, or to down a bottle of wine while watching a cooking show; the one with all the cakes.

Her mood began with Bud Light Dave disappearing in front of her, right in front of her. Now she had to deal with an entire street changing its name. Not completely, just slightly; such a little change most people would never notice. Except people who lived and worked on that street. Hipster Dan Haggarty worked on that street. He'd called it boulevard. He was right.

"What the hell, Hipster Dan Haggarty? What do you know?"

A black leather knife belt with twelve blades hung from a nail she'd hammered into the living room Drywall with a boot. She slipped a four-inch Browning Black Label stainless steel blade from its sheath and flipped it in her hand. The knife was deadly, the kind of deadly people picture ninjas using against helpless nobles in hand-to-hand combat. Double-blade, hollow handle, holes down the length to give it that 'Mama's going to spank you with a slotted spoon' look. She tossed it in the air, grabbed it between her index finger and thumb without looking, then threw it. The knife slammed into the target's left leg.

Skid hadn't aimed at the left leg. She never aimed at the legs. Knife scars decorated the white paint outside the red silhouette of a man clutching his groin, but the body itself? Clean of knife marks, except for this one.

She stood, hands hanging to her sides. Her father, in a tuxedo and top hat, had strapped hundreds of men—mostly cocky, stupid men—to the target and spun them like he was playing the Showcase Showdown on *The Price is Right*. In Portland, Oconomowoc, Hershey and other towns people never meant to go to but ended up in anyway, she'd always planted the knifepoints next to ears, in the crooks between arms and bodies, and so close to thighs that maybe, just maybe, the knife would cut a thread or two on a pair of blue jeans. But it never went in the groin.

Ever.

I need sleep.

Skid walked back into the kitchen and opened the bag from Manic Muffins. A couple of bites, or maybe just the top of the pink frosted muffin, and she'd get some sleep before leaving to work the concert this afternoon. She pulled the muffin from the sack and almost dropped it. The icing was chocolate.

CHAPTER THREE

1

THE SUNDAY *KANSAS CITY STAR*, rolled and stuffed into a plastic bag to keep out rain that was never in the forecast, lay on the sidewalk on Baltimore Street between Clem's Country Diner and a payday loan place that changed names every couple of weeks. Skid looked at her vintage thrift store Swatch as she walked through a cooldown. It was 8:45 a.m. Clem's had been open for more than two hours, and the loan place opened at 8. She had told herself earlier if the paper was still there by the time she walked by with her coffee and doughnut (no muffin this morning, maybe not ever), it was officially hers.

She passed Clem's. The smell of bacon wafted through the screen door. Inside, the counter was dotted with old men in plaid pastel shirts and blue jeans held on with suspenders and a belt. Never can be too careful. Couples in a few of the booths sipped coffee and read the newspaper.

Ha. Monday's paper. If someone had wanted to read Sunday's paper, they would have read it on Sunday. Skid bent and snatched the newspaper off the pavement and stuck it under her arm like she hadn't stolen it. Randall R. Roe didn't tolerate getting anything for free. "Hard work," Skid's father had stated the day he caught her taking a sucker from a basket in the grocery store. She was seven and that was why the candies were there, but it didn't matter to Randall. They walked to their car, a bag of groceries in one of Randall's hands, Skid's small fingers in the other. "Hard work is what makes a person. Study is work. Practice is work. Work is work."

"But it was free," Skid told him.

He stopped, never letting go of her hand. Randall squatted and looked his daughter in the eyes. "Are the clothes you're wearing free? Are these groceries free?"

She shook her head, wanting to pull her eyes away from his deep brown ones, but she couldn't.

He smiled. "If you get things for free, they have no meaning. It's the work that makes them important." He paused, staring deeply at his daughter. "Do you understand, honey?"

"Yes, Daddy," she'd said. Skid hadn't known what he was talking about then. She just wanted to get home and watch TV. She did now. Life, she'd found, is what a person wanted it to be, and sometimes a person had to take a handout when it came.

2

The MacBook Air chirped. Cord sat at his desk in what had once been the sunroom of the Sanderson family, and scrolled through the booking website he'd subscribed to when he bought the house. His page, usually quiet on a Monday morning because most of the bookings were done by weekend ghost-hunting groups or drunk college students who didn't do anything productive until three a.m. But not today, and not yesterday. The computer chirped again. Another booking, this one in December. All his slots for September, October and November were already filled.

Chirp.

Thank you, Beverly Gibson.

Cord knew as he slid the laptop shut and went for his pre-tour ritual (batteries charged, closet refrigeration on, loosen that basement step that had stopped squeaking), that Beverly was only part of it. Cord's real financial hero was Tommy Sanderson, or whomever had dropped out of the air and onto the floor of his hallway. If ghosts existed, and Cord wasn't convinced they did, the person from Friday night wasn't a ghost. He was real. He came from somewhere wearing gray Dockers, and he went somewhere wearing gray Dockers.

The question on both counts wasn't so much the who, or the how, but the where. Where did he come from and where did he go?

Cord went into the kitchen, well stocked with water and soda at $1.50 a bottle. The Keurig, for when the sleepies came to visit, took coins, bills and credit cards. He pulled a hammer from the junk drawer. He'd wanted to keep the feel of the Sanderson Murder House as close to a home as he could, and every Midwestern home he knew of had a kitchen junk drawer.

The problem with a man appearing then disappearing on the spot Delbert Sanderson butchered his son Tommy wasn't the fact that he did it in front of twenty witnesses. Oh, no. That was a present from God, or Jesus, or the jolly fat man himself. Cord needed all those people to see the Amazing Appearing Man then tell everyone they knew about it. From the bookings, it was working as fast as a new government hire whose soul hadn't been beaten into submission. The problem was the same problem all those visiting ghost hunters had. Repeatability. Nothing's real unless it's repeated. That's why Babe Ruth didn't hit just one home run in 1927, he hit 60. If you can't do something more than once, nobody believes it.

"Who are you?" Cord wondered aloud, walking down the basement steps, putting all his weight on the loose step and bouncing. Yep, the atmosphere-building squeak had gone. "And what were you doing in my house?"

Cord knew he had to find the Amazing Appearing Man and he had to find him fast. When he did, he'd have to pay the man to do the disappearing trick again, and the way visitors were clamoring to get inside the Sanderson Murder House, he could afford it.

3

The day-old Sunday edition of *The Kansas City Star* had a problem. Not on Page A1 where idiots from Washington, D. C., Germany, and Russia couldn't get their shit figured out, and not on Page B1 where idiots from various local city governments couldn't get their shit figured out either. It was in the Around The City section, under the picture of a band Skid had not seen Saturday night as she worked concert security. A headline read, "Steely Dan Rocks KC."

First off, Steely Dan never rocked anything. She read the first two paragraphs, just enough of the story to know Steely Dan apparently played from 8–10 p.m. at the Sprint Center, the exact time and place she'd worked. Skid glanced at the folio—September 3. It was the right paper. *Second, I saw the Doobie Brothers. They told me Jesus was just all right.*

But there was that one guy.

The crowd at the gate was quiet because it was the type of crowd that paid to see a fifty-year-old band. Skid stood beside a ticket taker in case of trouble, although the only trouble she noticed was that management had instructed security to wear their crimson T-shirts while she wore pink nail polish. Skid hated her colors to clash.

"But," the guy told the ticket taker. He was about 65 and red in the face. It could have been because of anger, or because it was hot enough for all the concert goers to sweat Geritol. "I bought a ticket to see Steely Dan."

"I'm sorry, sir, but the Doobie Brothers are playing tonight."

Doobie Brothers/Steely Dan. Tim Binnall Boulevard/Tim

Binnall Avenue. Pink-frosted muffins/chocolate-frosted muffins. *What the hell is going on here?*

"May I see the ticket, sir?" Skid said, stepping forward and holding out her hand. He gave it to her without protest.

Steely Dan
brought to you by
Boulevard Brewing Company
Crossroads District
Kansas City, Missouri
7 p.m., September 2
No refund.

Something was wrong, and not just with the ticket. Skid felt it. She'd felt it the moment her fist connected with Bud Light Dave's nose and that feeling hadn't gone away. Things were off, like she'd taken an afternoon nap and woken up groggy. Big Chuck, the afternoon DJ on KYYS, said this on her drive to work, "The days are strange," his voice rasped from the speakers in Skid's car. "I'm not sure why, but something's not right. Has anyone else noticed an odd feeling?"

She handed the ticket back.

"If you don't mind seeing the Doobie Brothers, I think we'll let you in, sir," she said, then turned to the confused ticket taker. "The ticket's legit and it's for today. It just says the wrong band. Must be a misprint."

The ticket taker waved her electronic wand over the bar code on the ticket and handed it back to Steely Dan Guy, who looked even more confused than she did.

Yeah, what the hell?

Skid let the newspaper drop to the table and picked up her coffee from Dan's Daylight Donuts. She hated it when people spelled doughnuts like that. It was just lazy.

"I'm losing my mind," she said over the lid before taking a drink. The coffee was just bad enough to pull her mind back to someplace she knew. She had to admit Hipster Dan Haggarty's coffee was better.

I worked the Doobie Brothers concert. I know I did. She sat the cup down when she realized her hands were shaking. For the first time since Skid had left home (if a trailer in a traveling circus can be called home), she didn't feel in control.

"I'm losing it," she whispered. "There's no other explana—

She stopped. Her eyes looked in disbelief at the picture in the newspaper of Donald Fagen singing something, probably "Rikki Don't Lose That Number," or some other song that gave Skid a headache. Then her gaze dropped to the bottom of the page as she reached for her coffee again, this time with both hands. A headline froze her attention, "G-G-G-Ghost! Spectral spirit spotted at Sanderson Murder House."

The picture with the story, tagged "Star Photo by Carly," was of someone she recognized.

That guy?

She'd jogged past the Sanderson Murder House Saturday morning just as two newsies stepped out of their car, but that seemed like a long time ago. The doofus in the picture (Cordrey Bellamy, the cutline read) had rushed out to meet them but gave her a look and a smile all the same. Skid drank more bad coffee and read the article. When she finished, she leaned back as far as she could in the wooden kitchen chair and stared at the ceiling. She had to go see the Muffin Man.

4

The sky opened and a body dropped from a swirling, purple hole. If anyone had been around (which they weren't), they may have heard screaming, but since the screaming began at roughly 13,200 feet above sea level outside Kansas City and it traveled at about 150 miles per hour, it's not surprising David's screams did nothing but empty his lungs.

He tried to think about why he was falling to his death and how he could mathematically predict his impact velocity if he could just ignore all the damn wind in his ears. The pain in his leg was distracting, but his mind was mostly consumed with Skid.

A purple wave burst from the ground, shooting toward him like a missile. But the wave didn't actually hit David, it enveloped him, caressed him, slowed him.

A second later he reappeared five feet above a metal stock tank.

5

As the young mom opened the door out of Manic Muffins, the bell on a wire overhead jingled. "Bye, Brick," her seven-year-old son Tanner said, waving the hand holding a muffin almost as big as his face, his other hand pinched in his mother's. Tanner and his mom, Serenity, were regulars. They first came in on a slow day while Brick put the finishing touches on a Goliath Barbarian character, and Tanner caught sight of the fire giant on the cover of the Dungeons and Dragons *Player's Handbook*.

"Cool. What is this stuff?" the boy asked, plucking a d20 from the counter.

Brick told him, his eyes lighting up as he described the fun of gutting an orc. Tanner just grinned. About a week later, Serenity came in wearing a frown he thought better of telling her would give her crow's feet if she kept it up.

"I bought him that monster book thing—" she'd said.

"*The Monster Manual.*"

"Sure, fine, whatever. Anyway, that awful creature on the front—"

"A beholder."

"I don't care what you call it, it was horrible. He had to sleep in my bed for a week."

Brick gave her a free muffin for Tanner, but Serenity didn't talk to him when they came in anymore. As for Tanner, well, Brick thought he might be Tanner's new hero, but being someone's hero didn't stop Tanner from smearing whatever covers little boy's hands all over Brick's display case.

As soon as the door shut behind them, Brick stepped out from behind the cash register with a rag and spray bottle. He knelt and squirted some of the blue stuff on the mysterious child streaks. He often wondered if children secreted slime. It would explain a lot.

The bell over the door chimed and light footsteps padded across the polished hardwood floor of the old building.

"Be with you in a second," Brick said, scrubbing the glass with the rag.

The soft, sure footsteps came closer. "Come on up, Hipster Dan Haggarty," the voice said. "We have a problem."

He knew that voice. Brick pulled himself up to his full height and turned around. It was the girl from the bar, the one who threw the knife, the one who punched the Oilyman who wasn't the Oilyman, the one who sweated herself into his business Saturday morning and bought a pink-frosted muffin that probably hadn't stayed pink for long, since the rest of them hadn't. She held a newspaper and coffee from a competitor's business. *Great.*

"My name's Brick," he said. "Before you ask, I used to be a bricklayer."

She took what looked like the last drink of her coffee and set the cup on a table made from a cable spool, then spread the newspaper out next to it. The woman, dressed in jeans and a dark T-shirt, wasn't as sweaty today as she'd been Saturday. Her hair was once again tied in a ponytail.

"Brick? Sure, okay," she said, her tone all business. "I was witness to something weird at Slap Happy's Dance Club Friday night." She pointed toward Brick's vast expanse of chest. "You were witness to something weird at Slap Happy's Dance Club Friday night."

He nodded slightly. "I tried to talk with you about that Saturday."

The woman waved off the words. "I know. I just wasn't ready to talk about it." She paused, her face serious. "I am now. You might think Friday night was as messed up as they come, but it wasn't. Things have gotten worse." The woman dropped a finger on the front page of the Around The City section of *The Kansas City Star*. "Read this, then we'll talk."

6

G-G-G-Ghost!

Spectral spirit spotted at Sanderson Murder House

By Beverly Gibson

KANSAS CITY, Mo. – The backdrop is that of a Hollywood blockbuster. Quiet family, quiet neighborhood, quiet city. Then a little corner of reality snaps and all of this is gone in one wicked night of bloodshed.

Kansas City witnessed such a night on Sept. 19, 1984, when, at 8:50 p.m., Delbert Sanderson crept through his home at 427 Gerry Avenue holding a samurai sword dripping with the blood of his own family. Today, the house belongs to Cordrey Bellamy, 35, a Kansas City, Missouri, native who's not old enough to remember the slayings, but values their place in the infamous part of the city's past.

"The Sanderson murders are legendary, but that legend had started to fade with time," he said. "I bought the house because I didn't want a piece of Kansas City history forgotten."

The slaying of almost an entire family—mother, son and their dog— brings people to the Sanderson house out of an intense curiosity in the macabre and the possibility of experiencing something otherworldly. Bellamy hosts ghost tours at the house most nights of the week and

Friday, 20 guests got exactly what they paid for—the ghost of Thomas Sanderson.

Thomas "Tommy" Sanderson was 32 years old the night in September when Delbert Sanderson chased him down on the ground floor hallway and ended his life. It was in that hallway Bellamy's guests got a glimpse of the past.

Bellamy held an electromagnetic frequency meter (EMF), a device paranormal enthusiasts claim can detect the presence of ghosts. When the group moved into the hallway, the meter went off.

Tamara Hooper, 25, of Lee's Summit, Missouri, was there when it happened.

"We were all here. Right here," she said, standing in the hallway Saturday morning. "And Cord's meter went all crazy."

Seconds later, witnesses claim a full-bodied apparition appeared floating two feet in the air before it crashed onto the hardwood floor still stained with Tommy Sanderson's blood.

Olan Wanker, who lived next door to the Sandersons the night of the murder, stood in the hallway with the other spectators Friday.

"It was the ghost of Tommy Sanderson," he said.

All 20 guests described the same entity.

"A man in his thirties with brown hair, white shirt, gray pants and a really surprised look on his face," Bellamy said.

The experience, however, wasn't over just yet. Tommy Sanderson spoke to Bellamy.

"'Where's Skid?'" Bellamy said. "The ghost of Tommy Sanderson said, 'Where's Skid?' We have no idea what or who Skid is."

Connie Franklin, R.N., of Overland Park, Kansas, who came to the ghost tour right after work at Saint Luke's Hospital, said the event was eerie.

"It was the most exciting—and creepy—thing I've ever seen," she said. "I'm definitely coming back."

Tommy Sanderson may have even made himself known during the

interview. Lights flashed and dials jumped on the EMF meter when Bellamy demonstrated it in the downstairs hallway.

Susan (Sanderson) Meek, the only surviving member of the Sanderson family, was away at college at Northwest Missouri State University in Maryville the night of Sept. 19, 1984. Meek doesn't believe the story of the haunting.

"It upset me when that man turned our house into a tourist attraction," Meek said. "Dad was sick. This sort of thing just glorifies him."

She also doubts the claims of the people who saw her brother.

"Tommy?" Meek said, surprise in her voice. "If there's such things as ghosts and one did show up in my old house, it wasn't Tommy. He was always much too lazy for that."

Ghost tours of the Sanderson Murder House are held Tuesday through Saturday at 7 and 9 p.m. for $20 per person. Groups of six or more can rent the house overnight for $428, $75 for each additional guest.

Contact Bellamy at his website, www.sandersonmurderhouse.info.

7

The step didn't take long. Cord crawled from underneath the wooden structure and stood, surveying the basement, a work bench island surrounded by a sea of electronic devices he not only didn't want to activate, he didn't want to touch. Especially the five-foot-tall circle rimmed with twisted copper wires like the inside of an electric motor. Mr. Sanderson had been a government scientist before he cracked; he apparently took his work home. None of the other owners or renters had been brave enough to touch the equipment either, so it had sat there since 1984 gathering dust and cobwebs; cobwebs Cord refused to clean. Cobwebs were ambience to a haunted house.

The basement was a missed opportunity, he knew; something spooky in the basement could be icing on the paranormal cake. Sure, no one had been killed here on Delbert Sanderson's mad rampage, but this machine, whatever it was, had never been mentioned in the newspapers, so he could call it anything he wanted. Too bad it gave him the creeps.

"I could hook the washer and dryer up to timers," he said to himself into the big, mostly empty room. "Or maybe one to make the light over the workbench pop on and off." But those tricks would be carnival games compared to Delbert Sanderson's stargate, or timegate, or bug zapper. This was why Cord hadn't tackled the basement. He let people down there, sure, but offered no tricks. Ghost hunters knew finding anything supernatural was rare, so he was afraid of ratcheting up the action too much. Someone might become suspicious and as soon as his cover was blown, customers would stop coming, no matter how many people fell into his hallway.

"Maybe—" he started, but an old picture frame stopped his thought. The frame that had come with the house, the one he left because it gave a feeling of authenticity, hung crookedly off a concrete screw over the work bench, the back bent, the glass dusty, but that didn't matter. The size of the thing mattered, and it was about the size of the newspaper section that sat upstairs on the kitchen table. "Hey."

Cord set his hammer on the work bench. Lifting the frame off the screw, careful not to drop the glass onto the concrete floor, he took it upstairs. The step, third from the bottom, groaned as he walked over it. *Success.* If the newspaper fit, he'd hang it by the front door just like restaurants do when they get a good review. *The Star* story made his haunted house legitimate, but this would make it legitimate for visitors from out of town, telling them they were in an honest-to-God haunted house.

He stepped into the kitchen and pushed the basement door closed with his foot. It swung shut quietly. *Gotta work on that, too. If it creaks, they freak.* The frame wasn't exactly the same size as the newspaper, but close enough. A grin wiped across Cord's face.

"I'm just going to clean you," he said, laying the frame on the table and lifting the paper. "And you'll fit just like this."

He flipped the newspaper section and set it face-first on the glass. Eyes stared at him from the back page.

"Holy shit."

8

"Hmm." Brick nodded slightly and turned to page D2, his eyes jumping to D3 before flipping the pages again.

"Hmm?" the woman said. "You read the article, right?"

Brick turned back to the front page before flipping to D4. "You mean the piece on Steely Dan? No. I didn't go."

"No." She rested her hands flat on the table and took in a deep breath. "I did, but it wasn't Steely Dan, it was the Doobie Brothers."

He flipped back to page D1. "Says Steely Dan, here."

"Look, I know what it says," she grumbled, then cleared her throat. "Sorry. I'm just a bit on edge." She took a deep breath and began again. "I worked the concert. I heard them play 'China Grove.' Steely Dan doesn't play 'China Grove.' The Doobie Brothers play 'China Grove'. I might not like it, but that's reality." Although she didn't know what reality was anymore.

Brick lowered the paper enough to look at her, his eyes dark under those bushy eyebrows. "Then why does it say here it was Steely Dan?" He pulled the paper back up and flipped to page D6.

She lowered her voice. "Why does a full-grown human simply vanish?" she asked, then pulled the newspaper down. "What are you looking for?"

"I'm thinking about going to the movies tonight. I'm just seeing what's playing."

She stood and looked at him over the top of the page, a frown on her lips, pleading in her eyes. But Brick didn't see that, he didn't look up. "The ghost story. Did you read the ghost story?"

"Yeah," he said.

"And?"

He shut the section to the back page. "Yes, I read the ghost story. It sounds like this ghost house guy saw the guy from the bar, the one who disappeared. The Oilyman."

"Oilyman?"

Brick shrugged. "Yeah, that's what I called him. You know, in my head. He came out of the bathroom covered in some kind of oil. It smelled like hydraulic fluid."

She sat back down. "Was he wearing a white shirt?"

"White enough under the stains. And gray pants. Except—" Brick stopped. His face may have been pinched tight under all that beard, but it was hard to tell.

Skid leaned closer. "Except what?"

"He had some kind of wound on his leg wrapped in a dirty T-shirt. It was dripping with blood." Brick studied the woman for a second, his head cocked slightly, giving her the impression he was a big, confused, friendly dog. Bud Light Dave didn't have a leg wound, at least not at the time, although he'd been asking for it.

"I—" she started, but Brick cut her off.

"Is your name Skid?" he asked, his voice deep, flat.

She sat back like Brick had pushed her. "Maybe. How do you know that name?"

"Because," Brick said, "Oilyman told me two things before he vanished in a puff of ozone. He called me Brick and he mentioned you." He paused, trying to gauge the look on her face. Confusion? Contemplation? Constipation? A debate on whether she was going to flip the table like it was a Scrabble board? She was hard to read. "He said, 'Skid's going to kill us all.'"

To Brick, it seemed like someone had let out some of the woman's air. "He did? He used my name?"

"Yup," Brick said, laying page D8 face-up on the table. His big index finger landed on the news story, 'Government Scientist Vanishes.' "It was this guy."

A smiling black-and-white two-dimensional Bud Light Dave stared up at Skid.

9

Government Scientist Vanishes

By Beau Branna

KANSAS CITY, Mo. – A physicist for a United States military research facility south of Kansas City, Missouri, is missing, an Army spokesperson said Saturday.

David Collison, Ph.D., a theoretical physicist at Lemaître Labs near Peculiar, Missouri, failed to report to work although he called into the lab under what the spokesperson reported as, "duress."

Collison had apparently been assaulted and robbed of his shoes in an alley behind All-National Burger, 1264 S. Manchester St., Belton, Missouri, Saturday morning, his call for help to the facility logged in at 9:04 a.m. The shattered remains of his mobile telephone were discovered at the scene. Belton Police located his shoes in the possession of Grenada Operation Urgent Fury veteran Gordon Gilstrap.

"Yeah, dis been dang shoe thing he-ah," Gilstrap said. "Issa blass foo gibbidy hoom."

Belton Police Chief Chris Donallen said he doesn't believe Gilstrap was involved in Collison's disappearance, but at this point anyone is a suspect.

"It looks like Dr. Collison slept on a pile of garbage bags in the alley and Mr. Gilstrap appropriated his loafers," Donallen said. "On the asphalt surface of the alley, there are three greasy sock prints covered in what appears to be rotted fish fillets from All-National Burger. Then, the footprints disappear. It's like something just swooped right in and scooped the good doctor up into thin air."

Lemaître Labs coordinator Dr. Karl Miller said it is vital the scientist be located.

"Dr. Collison is an important member of our team," Miller said. "Of course, given his security level, I can't comment anymore. He's classified."

Lemaître Labs, at least publicly, designs weapons for the military.

Collison was raised in foster care in Kansas City, Missouri. He attended college in Illinois and Ohio before earning his doctorate at Stanford.

He has no known relatives. His surviving foster sister Susan Meek could not be reached for comment.

Anyone with information on Collison's whereabouts may call 1-800-555-TIPS.

10

The newspaper fell to the table and Cord sat back, leaning the chair onto its back legs like his mother had always told him not to. The ghost had a face, he had a name and, better yet, he had blinded Cord with science. This was it. This was beautiful. Science was reliable, ghosts were not. His face grew hot as the facts of the story crept in.

David Collison, Ph.D., worked at Lemaître Labs, some government place outside town. Cord thought he'd read something about some super-secret lab building a supercollider, or roller coaster. For all he knew they were the same thing, one just had more buttons. But the government wasn't working on a machine that dropped people into his hallway, were they? Why would they want to do that? It must have been a mistake. How hard was it to dial in a far-away AM station on an old radio? Finding a place for a government transporter to beam a confused scientist must be at least twice that hard. But if

Doc Brown Jr. was involved in building a transporter, maybe, just maybe, Cord could buy one from him, or better yet, rent it.

Or rent-to-own. Like places do for poor young couples who can't afford a refrigerator or living room set.

He could rent-to-own. All he'd have to do is work out an affordable payment plan with the scientist, because a machine that could science fiction–show zap a person from one place to another would be expensive. Like the House of Creed Bespoke Fragrance Journey he'd seen in the Christmas Neiman Marcus catalog. People would be stupid to pay $475,000 to go to Paris to sniff perfume, but for a teleportation machine? Almost a half-million dollars would be a bargain.

Cord didn't have half a million dollars, but he would, eventually. He knew it. The newspaper article had landed him overnight guests for the next three months so, unless jerks decided to cancel, he was looking to make at least $100 grand. Cord rested his chin in his hand and stared at the picture of David Collison, Ph.D.

"Where are you, you beautiful, beautiful nerd-boy?"

11

The empty Styrofoam coffee cup that read "Dan's Daylight Donuts" fit right over Bud Light Dave's newspaper face. Skid didn't want to look at him anymore.

"He said that?" she asked.

Brick reached out to grab the cup. A competitor's product wasn't good for business, but Skid snatched it first. "Yes. He said two sentences," he lied. "He said, 'Watch her, Brick.' Then he told me, 'Skid's going to kill us all.'"

Skid. Skid. He knew my name, she thought. *Of course, he did.* She froze. *This isn't funny.*

Brick studied her face. Oilyman hadn't said two sentences. He'd said three, 'Watch out for Skid. She's not what she seems.' That part

Brick thought was right. If royally bombing on internet blind dates taught him anything, it's that women are a mystery.

Skid pinched her jaw, her face serious as a Hallmark made-for-TV movie. She stood and walked away from the table before turning back toward Brick.

"Things are wrong," she said, punching one hand into the other for an effect she didn't need. "And not just Bud Light Dave disappearing and appearing again. The street name is wrong, too. It's like really's wrong. You know, parallel dimensions. The Mandela Effect. That episode of South Park where Cartman had a goatee."

Brick started to say something, but she cut him off.

"I know it is Tim Binnall Boulevard. I just know it. I know I worked the Doobie Brothers concert even though the newspaper says Steely Dan." She snatched the newspaper and held it up to Brick. "And I know this asshole tried to hit on me Friday night then disappeared. Maybe something paranormal is happening. The Mothman guy, John Keel, called them Window Areas. He—"

Her eyes grew large, like in a Keane painting. Brick didn't like where this was going. "What is it?" he asked.

She turned the newspaper page around. "What's the name of the paper?"

Watch out for Skid. "*The Kansas City Star*, why?"

Skid slapped it back onto the spool table, her finger on the folio. Brick read *The Kansas City Times*.

"Whoa."

"Yeah," she said, turning and beckoning him with both hands. "Put out your 'Closed' sign. We have to go talk to this murder house guy. Now. Like right now."

Brick didn't move.

"Please?"

12

David's head was underwater only a few seconds. He hit the surface of the tank 138 miles per hour slower than when he'd appeared high enough in the troposphere he could have seen his house. His foot hit the bottom of the metal tank in slow motion, then he shoved upward, breaking the surface and scaring the hell out of fifteen head of cattle.

"Moo," they lowed in unison and scattered, although cattle don't really scatter. One starts to run, and the others follow.

"Oh, shit," he wheezed as he grabbed the sides of the tank with both hands, trying to steady himself. His heart pounded. "What is this?"

The cattle, mostly polled Hereford and a few roans, forgot what startled them and began to slowly walk back toward the tank.

David pushed himself to standing, trying to gather what breath his body would allow. He winced when he put weight on his injured left leg, then quickly shifted the weight to his right.

"Hey, you cows," he growled. "Why don't you go away."

The lead bovine stopped and looked at David with dark, brown eyes. "Moo?"

A farm. David had landed on a farm. *Of course. Cows, idiot.* A dusty red pickup was parked near the stock tank on the opposite side of a barbed-wire fence, a John Deere tractor pulling a cultivator moved in the distance behind it. David dragged air into his lungs and pushed it out slowly. *This is not cool.* Things began to fall into his head, the things that had happened since the waves began swooping in and dropping him all over the universe. The pig people with swords, the mushroom people, what he did to Karl, the explosion, Skid. He grimaced. This was all Skid's fault. No, he realized. It was all Karl's fault, everything but the pain—that was all Skid.

There was no one there to see him, no one to ask him questions. David gritted his teeth in a painful grin. Something had interrupted his fall. *Finally, some kind of misguided, misplaced, stupid luck.*

He grabbed one side of the tank with both hands, his breath still coming in hard. He lifted his right leg out of the water and swung it over the tank's side, securing his foot on the dusty, cattle-stomped ground before swinging out his left leg and dropping it like dead meat. He groaned when his foot hit the dirt. Sticking from his thigh was the black four-inch handle of a throwing knife.

It was at that point he decided if he ever saw Skid again, he was going to kill her.

CHAPTER FOUR

SEPTEMBER IV: A NEW HOPE

1

THE CORRUGATED TIN wall didn't so much open as become pudding when Dave passed through and fell onto his face. A cough shot from him when he hit the concrete floor that tasted of dust and motor oil. A spot of blood flew from his mouth and sat for a moment, just a moment, its surface tension holding the shape of a quarter-sized reddish pool before it soaked into the dirt. Dave pushed himself onto his rear and leaned backward, resting his shoulders on the firm tin that had seemed to be the contents of a dessert cup just moments before.

"I don't like this," he whispered.

This dirty tin shop, the hallway with all those people looking down at him, the bar with the pretty dark-haired girl who punched him in the face. These were connected, somehow.

"Hello," he said into the great empty space. His voice echoed slightly. A bird, startled by Dave's voice, fluttered near the high A-frame ceiling, a sparrow or barn swallow most likely. Light came from the crack between the large rolling doors on three sides of the cavernous room; other light leaked in through nail holes that had long ago lost their nails. So, it was daytime, he supposed. He also supposed that, apart from the bird, he was alone.

Come on. Take a breath. Relax, relax. He closed his eyes and breathed slowly, purposefully, trying to clear his thoughts like the corporate meditation guy brought in by Karl had showed them to do. *How much money did Karl spend on that guy? He looked like Jesus.* He shook his head, dislodging the thought.

Breathe. Deep, breathe. In, out. In, out.

Friday. Something had happened Friday. The experiment had been on track. Dave worked late every night for the past two months to make sure the collider would be online September 2, Saturday. He dotted 'i's, crossed 't's and caught a major flaw in Karl's math that may have shut down the whole project for another six months. And Karl was—*What?* Furious. Karl was furious.

"I don't need some kid telling me my math's wrong," Karl shouted at Dave during the launch meeting late Friday afternoon. "Especially one I hired just because I owed his *daddy* a favor." Dave flushed at the jab. It wasn't fair. Karl's mistake—and it *was* a mistake—would send the experiment in a direction no one on the team wanted to go. Karl pounded his fist and talked about the God Particle being nothing compared to what he would discover. Then he—

"Holy shit," hissed from Dave like he had a leak.

After the meeting, Karl had sent everybody home. Dave remembered grabbing his car keys and leaving without saying goodbye to Gillian, without making plans to get drunk with Oscar. He stopped at the first bar he saw on his way back to his apartment, the Happy Crappy, or Happy Slappy, or Slap Happy's. Something like that. Then everything went wrong.

"That idiot," he said. The words came out slowly. "That Cheetos-smelling bastard launched the experiment without me."

A hum kicked on somewhere in the shop, and Dave's eyes popped open. He lifted himself onto stiff legs and walked toward the hum. It came from a hideous, blocky avocado green 1960s model refrigerator. He turned, taking in the entire structure for the first time. Air compressor, drill press, work bench, arc welder, table saw, and the fridge—a beer fridge.

"Hey," he said, his voice echoing through the old machine shed. "I know this place."

2

Light streamed into Manic Muffins through its plate glass windows. A shadow of the window art "Muffin Monday All Week Long!" showed on the polished original hardwood floors. The real estate agent had told Brick the building had been a general store, then a haberdashery in its early days before more modern shops like a hair-dresser and "Tammy's Tanning Oasis" moved in and covered those glorious floors with black and white tiles. He had stripped the tiles and carefully brought back the luster of the wood floors during the remodel. Brick also took down the suspended ceiling to discover pressed copper. However, when he looked up, the beautiful pressed copper from another era was now tin.

"Come on," Skid said, stepping away from the table, waving him toward her like he was a puppy. Brick didn't move. "What did you say your name was? Rick?"

"Brick," he said, his voice soft. His eyes fell from the tin ceiling and onto Skid. "Unless you'd rather call me Chauncey."

"Uh, no." Her face pinched, like she'd bitten into something sour. "That's not going to happen."

"Then it's Brick." He stood and walked behind the counter, poured himself a cup of black coffee. Skid picked up her Dan's Daylight Donuts cup and waved it at him. Brick leaned over the display case and considered this woman, about 5'6", who carried herself like 12th level fighter/mage. "What do you hope to find at the murder house?" he asked.

"I don't know," she said as she walked up to the display case and set the cup in front of him. "But Bud Light Dave was there. He fell out of the air in front of twenty-one witnesses after he'd vanished from Slap Happy's." A look of realization swept across her face. "Right after I punched him. Do you think—"

Brick shook his head. "Seriously?" He blew across the top of his recycled cup before snapping a plastic lid over it. "I think whatever this guy was working on at this government lab, it's pretty important. A missing person case doesn't hit the press for days unless it involves a kid, but his did the next day. Although, if I were you, I'd put some thought into why he warned me not to trust you. I sure am."

She pried the lid off the cup and pushed it toward him. Brick stared at her.

"I am thinking about that," she said, taking the cup behind the counter. She turned sideways to slip behind the mass that was Brick and poured her own coffee. "I'm also thinking about why you saw the same guy, but not the same guy. Why he vanished from the bar, why he appeared back in the bar—"

"Before he even disappeared the first time."

"Yeah..."

Brick nodded. "That's what threw me off. After he disappeared from the bathroom I walked back into the bar and saw you talking to him. Then you punched him."

"He said something offensive." Skid took a slow sip of coffee. "This keeps getting weirder. Why do you think he showed up in the murder house?"

Brick shook his head. "I don't know. Maybe things are just random, or maybe he has some connection there."

"Uh-huh. Yeah. Maybe." She took another sip. "Your coffee's better than Dan's Daylight Donuts."

He turned his head to look at her, expecting something to be different. Her hair, the color of her shirt, maybe she would have turned into an elf, or something. Nothing. She looked the same. "I know," he said. "Dave uses store brand." He noticed Skid's eyes were bloodshot. "Not sleeping well?" he asked.

She nodded.

"Me neither. The last time I looked, my ceiling was copper," Brick said. "Had been for probably 150 years. Now it's tin. I don't like this. Whatever is happening, for whatever reason, it's not fun."

"Ceiling's copper again, Brick."

Brick looked up. She was right.

3

Cord hung the newspaper in the entrance hall right next to the front door. Unlike the time he tried to build a birdhouse for his mom in eighth grade shop class, this looked just like he'd pictured it in his head. He stood, admiring the headline. Well, not the headline. The word in 48-point font read, "G-G-G-Ghost!" The editor who wrote that watched too much Scooby-Doo, although Cord knew too much Scooby-Doo wasn't possible. He liked the subhead, "Spectral spirit spotted at Sanderson Murder House."

"Thank you, reporter Beverly Gibson," He said, but the stupid grin slid from his face. He'd been too much in the moment Saturday morning. He hadn't even asked for her telephone number.

It didn't matter. With the amount of wannabe ghostbusters who'd already paid for an overnight stay months in advance, he had plenty of time to meet nice girls.

A bit of movement through the front window broke his thoughts. People walked by his house often. It was in a residential neighborhood, after all. The crazy few even jogged by, like that girl in black who'd bebopped past Sunday when Beverly Gibson and the one-name photographer showed up. But it was 10 a.m. on a workday.

He leaned closer to the window. Two people walked up Gerry Avenue in the direction of his house, which shouldn't have been odd. Cord's door got knocks from the occasional salesman, sometimes from even a kid hocking band candy, and a mail-man/woman/person still delivered door-to-door here, but these two were none of those. A man, the largest man he'd seen in person, bearded and wearing a red flannel shirt like he was Paul Bunyan, opened the gate to Cord's walkway and a woman stepped in. She could have been a normal-sized human, or even tall, but in the man's shadow this woman with dark hair tied in a ponytail looked like a middle schooler.

What are you doing? Cord wondered and checked the door to see if it was locked, not because of the man, although he couldn't see a lot of his face behind all that hair, but because of the expression on the woman's face. He'd seen that look before on a woman. A chill ran through him.

"No. Go away," he whispered, pressing himself against the wall. Seconds later, a shadow fell over the window on the front door and knuckles rapped. *I'm not here.*

Cord didn't know why he felt jittery. Nothing usually frightened him, not even moronic gym rats named Roman, and Roman had every right to frighten him. Cord even owned a haunted house, for Christ's sake. *Then why—*

"We know you're here," the woman said. "Brick can see you through the window."

Brick?

He stopped. This was wrong. He had no rational reason for his guts to tie themselves into a garden-hose-at-the-end-of-summer mess. He owned a business. These people had approached his business. They must want to discuss a way to pay him money to use his business. They were not here to hurt him. He inhaled sharply because for some stupid reason he hadn't been breathing.

Cord stood straight, stepped away from the wall and opened the door.

"Good morning," he said to the strange couple. "I'm sorry, but tours don't begin until 7. Have you reserved your spot?"

"We're not here for the ghost tour," the woman said. "We're here to discuss David Collison, Ph.D."

Oh, no. "Are you from the government?" squeaked out.

"No," she said.

Cord grabbed the front door. He had to slam it, slam it now, or his life would change. He knew his life would change, and he didn't want it to change. He liked his life just the way it was, thank you very much.

The door came to a jarring stop, and the woman stepped into the house under Brick's outstretched arm.

"You should consider yourself lucky we're not with the government," she said and took a few steps forward to allow Brick enough room to enter the house behind her.

As the door closed, the knot in Cord's stomach tightened. He'd seen home invasions in movies, but they usually involved drugs or kidnapping a senator's daughter or something much more exciting than his life. "What do you want?"

The woman smiled. "Just to talk," she said. "You really need to learn to relax."

4

Dave walked slowly toward the avocado beer fridge, his hand shaking as he grabbed the chrome handle and pulled open the door. What was left of a case of Miller Lite sat on the middle shelf, two Ziploc bags of sliced summer sausage and a partial brick of sharp cheddar cheese on the top. He reached inside and pulled out the sausage.

"This isn't right," he said, his voice loud in the quiet machine shop. Dave opened the clear plastic bag and sniffed. The aroma dragged a flood of long-hidden memories through his brain. Grandpa Sam's farm. He plucked out one of the slices roughly cut by a pocketknife and bit down. The soft, processed meat stung his tongue pleasantly with coarse salt and cracked pepper.

"My God," he moaned. He hadn't eaten summer sausage since Grandpa Sam died. *When was that? Grandpa Sam took me to see E.T., so nineteen eighty-two?* He swallowed the processed meat and put the bag back into the fridge, drawing out a beer before shutting the door. *But this is his shop. This is his beer fridge. His beer brand. His sausage.* When Dave gripped the beer tightly and pulled, the tab came off so unexpectedly he almost dropped the can.

"What the—?"

A pop tab ring hung on his index finger. He hadn't seen one of those for decades. *That's because they stopped making them when I was a kid.* Dave took the tab from his finger, bent it like he'd watched Grandpa Sam do hundreds of time, careful not to cut his fingers, and dropped it into the opening.

"This is wrong," he said, the bird in the rafters fluttering again at the sound of his voice. He held up the Miller Lite. "This is all wrong." Dave pushed his arms into the air and spun like Julie Andrews on that Austrian mountain, trying to take in the machine shed all at once. "Grandpa Sam's dead. This isn't his shed. This isn't his farm. I haven't been dropping out of thin air. Some bum didn't steal my goddamned shoes that cost me over a hundred dollars. I've lost my mind and gone to Crazytown."

He put the can to his lips and took a long draw of cold, foamy liquid, careful to rest his tongue on the opening so he didn't suck the tab into his throat. He drained the can and threw it across the shop. It landed and bounced, clanking into a shadowy corner.

"Hey," he shouted into the machine shop. "It really is less filling and it tastes great. Who knew?"

A noise stilled his hand before he could pull open the fridge again. The sound of tires crunching on gravel hit him like Skid's fist. Someone owned this machine shed. Someone who might like the same snacks as Grandpa Sam and the same beer as Grandpa Sam. Someone who didn't know Dave once had a right to be here and might call the cops on a trespasser.

He padded to the nearest door on sock feet, leaned in to peer through the crack. What he saw almost dropped him back onto the dirty concrete floor.

A man in oil-stained Key overalls stepped down from a dusty brown 1980 Ford Ranger and spat tobacco juice.

"Levi-Garrett," came from Dave's mouth, although he didn't realize he'd said it.

The passenger door popped open and a sandy-haired boy about eight years old slid onto the gravel drive, his white *E.T.* T-shirt clean except for a dark Dog n Suds root beer stain over Elliott's face. Dave knew that shirt, he knew that stain—they were both his. He also remembered the last time he wore that shirt. The day Grandpa Sam died.

"Dear god," he whispered. "Nineteen eighty-two."

5

"Hey, you people can't do this," Cord protested as the big guy clamped a hand on his shoulder and walked him into the kitchen. The jitters that had grabbed Cord at the door left him. Now he was just mad. "I'm a legitimate businessman in a legitimate neighborhood."

"So am I," Brick said, dropping Cord gently onto a wooden kitchen chair.

Cord looked up at him, his eyes narrowed. "Hey. You're the Manic Muffins guy."

The statement caught Brick slightly off guard. "Uh, yeah."

"You have really good coffee." Cord turned toward Skid. "And you—"

"Always the coffee," Brick mumbled over Cord's head. "Why doesn't anybody ever say that about my muffins?"

"—you jogged past my house Saturday morning."

Skid shrugged, her toned, T-2 Sarah Connor arms not lost on him. "I'm sure lots of people do."

He put on the car salesman smile that won him Employee of the Month six times in a row at the dealership. "I never forget a face, at least not one as striking as yours."

Brick shook his head. "Don't."

Cord's smile turned into a grin. "Oh, wow. So, are you two, you know?"

"Nope," Brick said. "I don't really know her, just well enough that using the words 'striking' and 'face' in the same sentence isn't the best idea." While he said this, Brick contemplated the flowery 1970s linoleum and Skid's pink Hello Kitty shoes. Nope. He didn't know this woman at all.

Skid turned a kitchen chair backward and plopped down. "Now, Cordrey," she said through a smile. "Why—"

"How do you know my name?" he interrupted.

She draped her arms over the back of the chair and rested her chin on them. "I read Sunday's paper."

Cord's grin faded slightly. "It's Cord."

A hand the size of a Stephen King hardback slapped against the table. Cord jerked backward and almost fell.

"This isn't about you. This is about the scientist," Brick said, not shouting, but at the same time shouting. "We all saw him on the same night, and he teleported somewhere each time. *Teleported* right in front of us." Brick stood and folded his arms, which, whether he intended it to or not, made him look even bigger.

Cord pulled his cell phone from his pocket and activated the screen. "I've just dialed 9-1," he said. "My finger is about a quarter-inch away from hitting another 1. You two have about thirty seconds to convince me not to call the cops. So far—"

Skid's hand shot out faster than Cord could react and snatched the phone from him.

"Please stop," she said, her voice calm. She slowly pushed herself from the table and stood, slipping the phone in her back pocket. "Something weird started happening to us the night we all met Dave." Her eyes bore into Cord's. "Little things. Street names changed. The name of the newspaper changed. The band I remember seeing Saturday night wasn't the band that played by Sunday morning. Muffin frosting changed."

Brick dropped his hands into his jeans pockets. "How'd it taste?"

She waved him off. "Delicious. Very chocolatey."

"What we want to know," she continued, "is what is Dave Collison Ph.D.'s connection to this house, and do you expect him back?"

"Back?" Cord barked a laugh. "Back? I don't know that guy. I have no idea how he got here. I was conducting a ghost tour and he just dropped out of the air. I have no idea if he's coming back, but—"

"Do you guys smell that?" Brick sniffed and nudged his hairy head at Cord. "Do you have an air purifier?"

6

Grandpa Sam. Dave tried to force himself to relax, but his chest had pulled too tight for that. Grandpa Sam died on the day Dave spilled root beer on his E.T. shirt. The memory filled Dave's head in a flash. After he spilled his soda, Grandpa Sam had laughed, pushed a wad of Levi-Garrett chewing tobacco into his cheek and got out of the truck, only to take a few steps, clutch his chest like Jonathan Kent and fall dead onto the dusty gravel drive. Dave's screams echoed in his head. He had rushed back to the truck and grabbed the CB radio mic, trying to reach anybody to come and help.

Dave peeled his face away from the crack between the door and the wall, tears running down his face.

"Nope," he said, turning and walking into the middle of the shop, the dusty concrete dotted with his sock footprints. "I'm not going through that again." He stopped and looked to the ceiling, the rafters in shadows. "Why the hell am I here?"

The bird chirped.

"I wasn't asking you."

There'd been no scream from outside. *Not yet.* "Maybe I remember wrong." But he knew his brain was trying to lessen the impact of his grandfather dying in front of him for a second time. The day he died was the day Dave felt the world drop away. It was the reason he would follow his foster father's path into physics and try to solve time, to figure out a way to go back and warn Grandpa Sam he was going to die. Theoretically, the supercollider he worked with could create mini-black holes that would supply the extreme gravity needed to disrupt time. If only—

The feel inside the shed changed, like static electricity had suddenly flooded the air.

"No," fell out of his mouth and he rushed toward the beer fridge, stuffing the bags of summer sausage and cheese into his pants pocket and looping a finger into the plastic yoke on a six-pack of Miller Lite. The wave must be on its way and he didn't know when he'd eat again. He'd barely shut the door when the air freshener smell grew heavy and enveloped him.

The little Dave outside screamed, big Dave no longer there to hear it.

7

Silence. Skid and Brick stared into the hall that went from the kitchen to the front room. Cord sat at the table, his hand cupped as if he still held the cell phone Skid had confiscated.

"Uh-hem," Cord said. Skid held a finger to her lips, then turned to Brick.

"You feel that?" she asked. He nodded.

"Feel what?" Cord wanted to stand with them, but he felt like he was in the principal's office.

"Change in air pressure," Brick said, taking a step toward the hall-way. "Like a storm's coming."

Storm? Cord finally stood. "What do you mean, 'storm'?"

"It's just like what it felt like when Bud Light Dave vanished in Slap Happy's," Skid said, ignoring Cord. "The air's heavy. Same smell, too. It's coming from the hall."

This was getting even weirder. "That's where the guy appeared."

"Or it could be anything," Brick said. "If this Collison guy is slip-ping in and out of somewhere, he's also coming and going somewhere. He might not be the only one doing it."

Skid's eyes popped wide. "If it's him again, we can't let him get away."

"What if it's a Siberian tiger?" Brick asked, a hand on her shoul-der. "Or a mountain troll."

She frowned. "How could it be a mountain troll?"

"Of course, it couldn't be a mountain troll," Cord said, his voice a little higher than he would have liked. He coughed. "There's no such thing, but what about the tiger?"

"It's him," she said, "and his ass isn't getting away this time." Skid took off in a dead sprint and dropped into a baseball slide in the hall-way, skimming over the false blood stain and turning to stop on her stomach.

Brick moved into the hall after her more quickly than a big man should.

"Hey," Cord started, but a thump interrupted him, like someone had dropped a duffel bag of meat in his house. He stood, frozen, and watched a full can of beer roll into the kitchen.

8

Another floor. Dave mouthed *ouch* and slid his eyes open as he landed on his chest. He looked up; a pair of brown ones peered into his.

"Yaaaa," burst out as he scrambled to his knees. The woman the eyes belonged to grinned. Dave knew her. "Skid?"

She pushed herself to her feet and rested hands on hips and turned her weight onto her right leg like nothing unusual had just happened. "Bud Light Dave," she said, then spoke over his head. "Brick?"

Brick? "What's a Brick?"

Massive hairy hands grasped Dave's shoulders and lifted him into the air.

"Hey," he shouted. "*Hey.*"

Whoever, or whatever, had grabbed Dave walked into a kitchen and sat him in a chair.

"Did you see that?" Skid asked. "It was just like at the bar, except the other way."

"No," Cord said. "In this house, it was exactly that way."

Skid and Brick turned toward him.

"He just, pop, fell out of the air and landed on the stain in the hallway. He landed in exactly the same spot."

Dave pointed a finger at Cord. "I've seen you before." He moved his head toward Brick. "But not you. I don't know you."

"This your Oilyman?" Skid asked Brick.

"No." He grabbed Dave's chair and leaned it backward to inspect him, ignoring Dave's shout. "And yes. He's not hurt, he's not covered in oil, but this is the guy I saw near the bathrooms at Slap Happy's. He's also not the guy."

"You're not making any sense," Cord said. "Either this is or is not the guy. He's the man *I* saw."

Brick relaxed and allowed the chair to rest on all four legs. He scratched his beard more out of habit than need. "I know it sounds ridiculous, but this guy just fell out of nowhere, remember? What I mean is he's not the Oilyman I saw, but maybe he will be. Like my guy is the future this guy, but even dirtier. If that makes any sense."

"It does," Skid said. "But first, let's all call him Dave."

"Why?" Brick asked.

"Because that's his name." She sniffed Dave, but all she could smell was beer and rotten fish sandwiches. She cringed. "From what you said, the guy you saw is Dave, but not Dave. It's Dave—possibly from the future—dressed in the same clothing, but somehow injured and covered with oil."

"Where are you going with this?"

Skid exhaled slowly. "I'm just trying to make this less confusing. Is it working?"

Bud Light Dave cleared his throat and the three of them turned their attention to him. He sat at the table, his shoulders slumped, leaning his bruised face on the palm of his left hand.

"From a purely textbook physics perspective, what you're suggesting—that you both saw different timeline versions of me—is theoretically possible, but technically impossible." He paused to let this sink in. "But in a that's-exactly-what-my-boss-was-working-on perspective, yep. You pretty much nailed it."

"So," Cord said. "You're from the future?"

Dave drummed his fingers on his bruised cheek. "Were you even listening to the conversation?" he said, his voice dripped with defeat. "Hey, could one of you bring the beer from the hallway? I've just flown here from 1982, and boy, are my arms tired."

9

Dave finished his story from the moment he fell from the bar to the moment he saw his own grandfather at the farm. Then he looked around the kitchen table of the Sanderson Murder House. His eyes landed on Skid.

"I know people usually preface something like this with, 'No offense,'" Skid said, staring at Dave from across the table. "But I won't. You stink. You smell terrible. Like beer and rotting fish sandwiches from All-National Burger."

Dave shook his head. "I've gotten used to it." He pulled the last beer from the six-pack ring and waved it at Brick. Skid already had a Miller Lite from ı yll? ı111 the table in front of her. Cord held one as he paced from the wall near the hallway to the back door and back again, stopping occasionally to take a drink. "You want one?"

"No," Brick said. "It's 10:30 in the morning."

Cord stopped pacing across the bad linoleum and barked a laugh. "You're kidding, right? Did you hear him? After what he told us and all the shit that's happened to you personally, you're worried about having a beer too early in the day? Hell, I think I'll start drinking even earlier and legitimize it by saying it's 10:30 a.m. somewhere."

"What I want to know," Brick said, leaning forward on his elbows toward Dave, the table groaning under his weight, "is why all this is happening."

The crack of the beer opening seemed loud in the kitchen. Dave fumbled with pulling the tab off the can. "I don't know the logical scientific explanation—"

"But isn't that what you do?" Cord blurted, dropping into the chair between Brick and Skid. "You're a physicist, right? You—"

Skid slipped a hand behind Cord's neck and pulled his face close to hers. "Shhhh," she whispered, then nodded to Dave. "Please continue."

The moment seemed to have gone, Dave's attention drifted over the kitchen. "I've been here before," he said, then took a sip of beer. "A long time ago. The light fixture was different, and Cecilia would have hated those curtains over the sink."

He paused and looked around the table, his eyes wide. "Oh, shit. This is all my fault."

10

A wet David limped from the cattle tank to the dusty pickup, the farmer out in the field oblivious to him. Pain lanced through David's left leg as the knife ripped at the muscles of his thigh with each small step. *Goddamned Skid.* His right hand hit the bed behind the cab door; his left lifted the handle and pulled it open. He bit his bottom lip to muffle a scream as he pulled himself onto the driver's seat.

"Plan, Davey boy, you need a plan," he said through his teeth.

He had to pull out the knife, he knew, but there would be blood, and lots of it. *What if she hit an artery?* But at that moment, he didn't care. He had work to do. Skid was a menace; he had to stop her.

"Okay, buddy," he said, his voice shaky. "You can do this."

David looked around the cab of the truck. Empty gun rack in the back window, oily T-shirt. He pulled the shirt toward him and held it up; a clean spot ringed the center. *This will have to do.*

The interior of the cab started to swim in his vision. David closed his eyes to steady himself, sucking air in and blowing it out through his teeth. "Come on. Come on, man."

The collider was out there and in danger. The attack would happen, if not now, soon. If Skid got to the lab, everything would be over. Kaput. Boom. No matter what, he had to protect the collider.

David slid his eyes open and reached for the glove box, trying to choke back another scream. He screamed anyway. A lighter, leather gloves, insurance card, pens with seed company logos, pliers, a half-empty box of ammo. If the farmer were anything like Grandpa Sam, this glove compartment would hold something else he needed.

He squeezed the compartment release. *Jackpot.* David reached in and pulled out a half-empty pint bottle of Windsor Canadian Whisky.

"Hello, farmer's friend," he said as he unscrewed the lid. "You're going to keep me from having my leg amputated." He took a swig from the bottle, the whisky burning as it went down, then gently tipped it on either side of the knife.

"Shiiiit," he moaned into the cab as the amber liquid seeped into the knife wound. The cattle that had gathered near the open door of the truck backed up a few steps.

"Sorry, ladies," he wheezed, "but this is going to get even louder."

He capped the bottle, set it on the seat and grabbed one of the leather gloves from the glove box.

Sticking the glove into his mouth and biting down, his breath coming fast and hard around the leather, which smelled of manure, he took the handle of the throwing knife in two shaky hands and closed his eyes. "It's the end of the world as we know it," he mumbled through the leather between his teeth, "and I feel fucked."

He pulled.

11

"Your fault?" Cord snapped and began to stand. "What do you mean it's your fault?"

Brick's hand landed on Cord's shoulder and pushed him back onto the wooden chair. "There's no need to get excited—"

Cord slipped under Brick's meat hook and backed from the table. "When would be a good time to get excited, Brick? And what kind of name is Brick, anyway?"

"Well, I used to be a bricklayer—"

"Well, I used to be a bricklayer," Cord mocked, putting the table between him and the giant. He'd just met these people and he was already tired of their shit.

"That's cool," Dave said underneath it all, although no one heard him.

Skid stood. Brick stood. Dave took a drink of beer and set the can on the table. "I'm the calmest person here," he said, "and I just time-traveled to the day my foster grandfather died." He pulled two Ziploc bags from his Dockers pockets and laid them gently on the table. "I have summer sausage and sharp cheddar cheese from 1982. They're kind of smashed from me falling on them, but I'm willing to share if you have more beer."

Jesus, Cord thought. *I should be charging these people. This is gold.*

Skid sat next to Dave and pulled open the Ziploc that contained the sausage. "What did you mean when you said this was your fault?"

"Do you know who I am?" He looked around the table and laughed. "Wow. That sounded really Kardashian. Do you know who I am? I'm so sorry."

Something in the air had changed. Cord sniffed, but only the smell of summer sausage wafted around the table. Brick pulled a slice from the bag.

"Beer?" Skid said, looking up at him.

Goddamnit. Cord stomped from the refrigerator and put a Boulevard Pale Ale in front of Dave.

"Hey, thanks." Dave's eyebrows furrowed slightly like he tried to remember something he couldn't. "I don't think I got your name."

"Cord."

Dave smiled. "Hey. Skid, Brick, Cord, and I got stuck with Dave. I think it's—"

Cord opened his mouth, but Skid cut him off.

"You're David Collison, Ph.D.," she said over hands gripped into a single fist atop the table. "You're a theoretical physicist at Lemaître Labs near Peculiar, Missouri, where you've worked on weapons for the government. You grew up around Kansas City, got your doctorate from Stanford, and your only surviving relative is a foster sister named Susan."

"Hey," Cord said, but everyone ignored him.

Dave tried not to look directly at anyone as he took a drink of beer, Skid and Brick remained silent in the murder house kitchen.

"Hey," Cord said again.

"That's impressive," Dave said, ignoring Cord again. "But what about Susan? Do you know her last name?"

"It started with an M, I think," Skid said. "Mink? Monk?"

"Meek." Brick drummed his fingers on the table. "I'm pretty sure it was Meek. We read about her in the newspaper story on your disappearance."

Dave started to speak, but Cord cut him off. "Hey," he said, the word coming out like it had way more syllables than it did. "Meek is her married name. She's a Sanderson."

Skid and Brick looked at him.

"I'm not an idiot." Cord turned toward Dave. "You used to live here, didn't you?"

Dave took a long pull of the bottle before setting it back onto the table. "I did. The foster system moved me to a new house in 1984 after Delbert killed Cecilia and Tommy. I was staying the night with a friend." Dave took a long breath before speaking again. "I never saw Susan again after that."

"Oh, wow." Brick took another piece of nearly-brand-new-40-year-old sausage and leaned back in his chair.

Skid stood and stepped closer to Dave. "And you don't work on weapons." She bent close to his ear and whispered. "You work on something that can disrupt space-time, don't you?"

He turned. Her brown eyes burned into his. "Yes," he said, his voice equally as soft. "But I can't talk about it. My work is as classified as the Roswell crash."

"What?" erupted from Cord.

Dave winced. "I've said too much. I'll go to prison if anyone finds out. Not just don't-bend-over-in-the-shower prison, but Leavenworth Federal Penitentiary. That's serious."

Skid grabbed the back of Dave's chair and turned him to face her.

"It's not just you. Reality is changing. Things we know to be true are now false. It's like we're in a choose-your-story book and some idiot is reading it."

His eyes dropped from hers. "You're right. Lemaître Labs doesn't design weapons. We have a supercollider the size of CERN's underground."

"Holy shit," she said. "You're crashing the building blocks of the universe together practically under our feet? You're looking for the God Particle?"

Cord had no idea what they were talking about. He tapped the fingers of his left hand into the open palm of his right. "Hey, time out."

Nobody listened.

"No," Dave said to Skid. "We're not."

"That's a good thing." Skid looked at Brick and Cord. "They could be creating black holes out by Peculiar. Black holes in Peculiar. Heh. Sounds like a punk band, but it could really mess with... every... thing. Oh, no."

"I'm sorry, Skid," Dave said. "But we're looking for what's beyond the God Particle. We're looking for the walls that keep dimensions from meeting and the magic that makes time appear to flow in a straight line. I followed my foster father's work into physics to develop time travel. Don't hit me."

Cord picked up the beer in front of Dave and took a drink. "I think I saw this on *Doctor Who*," he said.

"I left work Friday," Dave said to no one and everyone. "Our boss Karl was pissed at me and ordered everyone on the project to leave. I'd found some problems with his math. As in, intersecting-dimensions problems. And I left."

"So?" Brick asked.

Dave became as grave as a tombstone. "I never logged out of the system. It takes at least two people to log in for the machine to work. Karl must have used it after I left. For some reason I can't pin down, he knowingly used it with the bad math." He stopped for long enough to pry his beer from Cord's fist. Everyone sat quietly and watched him chug the rest of the bottle. "He wouldn't have been able to do this if he was the only person logged in."

Brick frowned. "Well, if this Karl used the machine, it should have affected him, too, right?"

Dave stood and walked to the refrigerator for another beer. He drank half of it before turning back to the group at the table. "Yeah. No. I don't know. Maybe."

Cord pulled out a chair and sank into it. All he wanted to do was make money in an innocent enough con then these people showed up.

"But why are you the one popping in and out of reality and not him?" Skid asked.

"A number of reasons. Karl's equations totally screwed things up," Dave said, then looked around the table. "By 'things,' I mean colliding realities and intersecting moments in time. If we were looking for the God Particle, we'd have sucked the Earth into a black hole of our own creation and wouldn't be having this conversation, but what Karl did is shredding our physical existence."

"But why you?" Skid asked. "That still doesn't explain why you're vanishing and reappearing, and why we recognize reality is changing when no one else seems to notice. Why has this brought us all to this house?"

The smile on Dave's bruised face had no humor behind it. "I guess you haven't been in the basement." He nodded toward Cord. "Is the equipment still down there?"

Cord swallowed hard. "Yeah."

Dave stood and walked across the kitchen floor to the basement door he hadn't opened in more than thirty years.

CHAPTER FIVE

SEPTEMBER IV: THE VOYAGE HOME

1

THE VENDING MACHINE across from the first-floor bathrooms was out of Cheetos. Karl scanned the rows of foil packages arranged inside corkscrews that moved the snacks onto a ledge and dropped them into the delivery tray like so many sacrifices to the god of saturated fat. Except on the first floor next to HR; there was no real fat. This machine held Baked Doritos, Baked Ruffles, Popchips, power bars, roasted edamame and things so void of saturated fat Karl wouldn't put them in his mouth. The jerks in human resources were too healthy for their own good. It didn't matter anymore since the employees of that department hunkered low in their cubicles in the open office space chittering angrily to themselves. They didn't like the light that poured from the hallway ceiling.

The dollar he'd slowly pulled from his wallet and smoothed on his slacks still looked iffy, especially the corner to the left of the all-seeing eye. He pressed the folded corner between his index finger and thumb to try and hold it down before feeding the bill into the money slot. The machine hummed as hidden pinch rollers grabbed the bill and pulled it in, then pushed it back out.

"Damn it."

Something large rustled in the dark recesses of HR. He told himself that was a perfectly normal, human-sized sound, although he realized he might be lying. *Come on, Karl.* He'd intended the trip through the lab complex to be quiet. That's why he ditched his hard-soled Oxfords for the pair of Adidas he wore when he went to the gym down by the loading docks, which was never. The Adidas were brand new.

Come on. Come on. Karl turned the bill over and fed it into the slot the other way. The hum kicked on; this time the dollar disappeared.

He'd lived in the lab since Friday. Oh, that wonderful Friday when the physicists and engineers went home and left him alone with the supercollider. The Karl Colossal Collider. At least that's what he wanted to name it. The loudmouths in engineering were pushing for BAB-C. Big-Assed Bastard Collider. Not professional, but the government loves a catchy acronym.

That idiot Dave Collison didn't like the name either. He wanted to go with something a little more scientific, but he also wanted to put off the machine's launch because of some "anomalies" in Karl's computations. Prick. Karl laughed when he discovered Collison had never logged out of the system and he could launch the project alone. That was poetry. Beautiful karmic poetry. *You'll see, Collison. The experiment worked. I found the secret to everything.*

But Dave Collison didn't come to work Monday for Karl to rub it in. Karl didn't know if Collison was still alive. He also didn't care; Collison was the last tie to his former life of servitude, not of his current life of conquest, the kind of conquest that would put him in a comfy office in D.C. after, only after, he gave the military what it had asked for. But all Karl cared about right now was eating Cheetos and the building was out of them. Not a bag of Cheetos in the place. If

Lemaître Labs survived the next few days, things were going to change around here.

Change. That was funny.

Karl went back through the selections. *Crunchy and cheesy. Crunchy and cheesy. Crunchy and cheesy.* The Baked Doritos were nacho cheese, but the Baked Ruffles were sour cream and cheddar. The Popchips—*No. No Popchips.* Karl punched E-4. Nacho Cheese Baked Doritos. They weren't Cheetos, but they'd do. The corkscrew slowly turned and the underfilled bag of chips moved toward the edge and stopped.

"Are you kidding me?" he said, his voice no more than a whisper. He pushed the machine and the thing wobbled slightly on its short leg, but the bag held. "Come on."

The chittering from HR grew louder, and Karl realized he might not be the only one hungry. He didn't want to be around when those jerks came looking for munchies. *No, no, no.* He grabbed the 670-pound vending machine with both hands and shook, just like the sign on the side told him not to. It rocked forward and back, forward and back, the Doritos hanging on for one, two, three—then the bag dropped.

Something big scuttled behind him from one cubicle wall to the next, and Karl froze. Most people—except that stupid David Collison—had reported to work today and none of them had left. They were all probably in a foul mood. Fear began to grow in him like a tumor. Karl reached into the metal flap near the bottom of the machine, grabbed his chips and turned toward the elevator. That was when a roar he felt in his own chest bellowed throughout HR.

As Karl leaned against the vending machine, a light at the far end of the hall popped on and a massive hairy leg appeared from around a corner. Oscar was loose.

He ran.

2

The stairs seemed to move slowly beneath Dave's feet, like an escalator going the wrong way. A step moaned under his sock, the step that was always loose. He paused, but only for a moment. He didn't want Brick to trip and fall on him.

But Dave's mind wasn't fully here. The dim hole of the basement stairway had sucked his thoughts somewhere else.

"Come on down, Davey," Delbert Sanderson said from his workbench around 1980 or '81, soldering gun in hand, computer hardware and wires strewn in front of him. Dave had snuck down the stairs as quietly as he could, but that one stupid, stupid step groaned under his slight weight.

"I'm sorry, Daddy D," came out in a soft voice, his mouth pointed toward his chest.

Delbert Sanderson pulled off his black, horn-rimmed glasses. "Don't be." He waved. "Come on, son. Let me show you what I'm doing."

Dave took a deep breath and went down the rest of the steps. No one was supposed to interrupt Delbert Sanderson when he worked in the basement. His project was secret, so secret not Momma C, Susan nor Tommy knew what he did there at night, except drink a lot. But Delbert hadn't had too much to drink tonight, at least not yet. The smile on his face was kind.

"I guess you want to know what I do down here." Delbert laughed and stood from a barstool in front of his work bench. He grabbed a glass half-filled with an amber liquid and walked toward a pile of machinery and wires in the middle of the basement that looked like the robot from *Lost in Space* inside out.

Little Dave shuffled toward him. "Is it some kind of experiment?"

Delbert lifted the glass to his mouth and took a long drink before bringing it back down and setting it on a stack of crates. "I'm a physicist. That means I deal with gravity and how it reacts to other things."

His smile faded for a moment, only a moment, before it returned. "I also try to find out what gravity can do. Things we don't know yet."

Dave stared into Daddy D's tired eyes. "Like time travel?"

It took a few seconds for the words to catch in Delbert's mind, but when they did, he reached out and mussed Dave's hair. "Exactly. You read that book I gave you, right?"

Dave nodded. "Yes, sir. But is that stuff real? Really real?"

Delbert didn't hear Dave's words; his eyes were fixed on the vertical ring he'd built in the middle of the basement floor. Wires hung from it like jungle vines. "I've wanted to travel in time all my life, kiddo," he said, voice near yet as far away as his eyes. "Ever since I read the book I gave you."

The book was H. G. Wells' *The Time Machine*. Dave winced at the weight of Delbert's hand coming down on his shoulder.

"The answer's out there," Delbert said, pointing to a pin board filled with papers, mathematical equations scribbled across them. His voice was starting to scare Dave. "I can reach out and grab it. I know how. I'm going to go back in time and rid the world of the likes of Ray, Hitler, Judas, Oswald, Sirhan. There's so much evil out there." His wide eyes bore into Dave's as the pain from his grip bit into Dave's arms. "Then I need to travel forward and bring home cures for diabetes, cancer, all addictions."

Dave didn't remember whatever else Delbert might have said. He had fled upstairs as soon as his foster father let go of him. Now, his hand went to the light switch at the bottom of the stairs and hesitated before flipping it up and flooding the basement in a yellow glow. The machine was there; the big ring still sat in the middle of the floor, more complete than Dave remembered. Tight loops of insulated wire wrapped tightly around its metal body. A control panel next to the workbench looked operational, but the lights and gauges were dead, the machine empty of power.

"Whoa," Brick whispered from behind him. "What's this? Coffee maker?"

Dave stepped onto the floor, the concrete cold under his sock feet. "Delbert Sanderson was trying to build a time machine."

"This makes better sense," Skid said, stepping next to him. "This is all his fault."

No. Not even close. Dave stepped to the pin board, still covered in Delbert's equations. "His math was wrong. All this machine would have done is waste electricity."

"Then what—?"

Dave cut her off. "Delbert Sanderson was a civilian in charge of a top-secret military project; this was his way of working on it after hours." He brushed his hand over the pinned-in equations. "By the time he went crazy and—" Dave paused and swallowed. "You know the rest. Before that, he'd already hired my boss, Karl. Delbert was nowhere close to doing what Karl and our team did. This is Karl's fault."

"What do we do?" Cord asked from his seat on the fourth step.

They all looked at Dave.

"We have to stop this. Karl's experiment could rip apart the foundation of every conceivable universe and—" He stopped, mulling over his next words.

"And what?" Skid asked. "Come on."

"If we ever want a chance at things going back to normal," he said, "we have to destroy Delbert's work, Karl's work, and everything I've done in my whole career."

3

Skid followed Cord as he made his pre-ghost tour rounds. Hidden stereo system, on. Upstairs murder closet refrigeration unit, on. Pulling a nail from the wall so a family picture of the smiling Sanderson family on a beach vacation hung precariously enough vibrations from foot traffic would drop it to the floor, done. They walked in silence. It was like they hadn't just heard a potentially-mad scientist talk about black holes and dimensional shifts.

Skid sighed. She knew this game. She thought about Constantinople Phargus, the operator of the Polar Ring Toss on The Roe Bros. Traveling Circus midway. "What are you doing?" she'd asked when he dropped a set of metal rings into a blue Coleman cooler decorated with icebergs and shaky lettering that read *sub-zero*. She was ten years old and had long suspected Constantinople Phargus was really Gary Schmidt because that was the name on his checks. She also suspected Gary Schmidt was hiding from something, but she couldn't think of what. She was just a kid.

"Metal expands in the cold," he told her.

Her thoughts ground against each other. "If it's supposed to be hard for the people to toss the rings onto the jugs, why are you making it easier for them?"

Constantinople smiled. Skid liked to see him smile. His beard was gray, his fingers and mustache yellowed from cigarettes, and when he smiled his wrinkles made him look like a pug dog. His voice was deep like Darth Vader's, but way friendlier. "You got your dad's smarts, that's for sure."

She'd heard that more than once. "That still doesn't tell me why."

Constantinople looked down the midway, but no one was near. It was still too early in the day for the teenagers to be milling around thinking their parents didn't know what they were doing, and most of the young families had already worked their way inside the big tent for the first show. He lifted the cooler lid and pulled out a cold ring. "You see this?"

Skid nodded, pigtails flopping everywhere.

Constantinople leaned forward in his metal folding chair and picked a ring from the ground. He held it against the cold one. "See the difference?"

She didn't. "No, but Daddy said—"

The smile came back, the lines forming a topographical map on his face. "And your daddy's right. Cold makes metal get bigger, but here the difference is so small it don't matter." He tapped his forehead. "It's what people think that matters." Constantinople waved his hand over the five-foot square table of wide-mouth jugs. "The warm rings barely fit over the rim," he said, pausing to turn his head back down the row of games that made up the midway. A twentysomething father and his wife stood four booths down at the card game, their baby son in a stroller. The father tossed a dart toward the cards racked to the back wall and mouthed when he missed the Queen. They always missed the Queen.

Constantinople lowered his voice. "The people know the rings are too small. They also know cold makes metal grow. What they don't know is how much."

Skid's eyes grew wide. "Are you cheating people?"

Constantinople laughed, the sound as low and comforting as a wise Disney character. "No, honey. This game is just giving them what they expect. They know the cold don't make a damn bit of difference, but it gives them hope. Life is about believing in something, and if you give the people something to believe in, they'll keep on hoping."

He tossed one of the rings toward the table of jugs. It bounced off a jug on the first row and came to rest on a thick jug neck on the third. "Hey. Would you look at that. Everybody gets lucky once in a while."

Skid followed Cord into the master bedroom, where he turned off lights that were on a dimmer switch. The 1980s decor went nearly black as the dimmer clicked. A small sliver of sunlight sliced from between the thick maroon drapes and seemed to cut the bed in half.

"You're a thief." Skid stood in the doorway, leaning against the frame.

Cord stood his ground by the light switch and Spocked an eyebrow. "Interesting accusation," he said. "How do you figure?"

"The stereo, the cold closet, the falling picture and whatever else I didn't see—"

"There's a step I keep loose on the way to the basement. It creaks something fierce."

She nodded. "Impressive grift. You've designed the game so you always win."

"No," Cord said shaking his head. "Not at all. I've designed the game so everybody wins. My customers get what they want, and I get what I want. It's not just a win, it's a win-win."

She stood straight and crossed her arms. "Then you're a conman."

"That's the nicest thing you've said to me so far," Cord said, stepping a foot closer. Only a foot. He was still out of her reach. "I can live with that. I'm giving the customer what they want to believe. I'm giving them entertainment. What's the difference between this and a movie?"

"The people paying for the movie know it's a movie." Skid's eyes moved to the ceiling before dropping back down to Cord. She was with him alone. Brick had gone to check on Manic Muffins, and Dave had crawled onto a couch. "I can't believe I'm saying this, but I can't wait for Brick to get back."

Cord's car salesman smile grew effortlessly on his face. He moved a thumb to point at the bed. "You know, he'll probably be gone at least an hour and the science guy is asleep downstairs."

"It's been a while," she said. "But I have ex-boyfriend issues. I'd hate to kill you out of spite." Skid grinned and patted his cheek before she turned and walked from the room.

A breath slowly escaped Cord's lungs as he watched her leave. "Hey, can I at least have my phone back?"

4

The keys were in the ignition. Of course, because this was farm country. No one would steal Farmer Jim's pickup, and if they happened by his field and drove off in it, they must need the vehicle and would bring it back when they were finished. The windows were rolled down, too, because in the country, who needs a working air conditioner?

David winced as he pulled his injured leg into position under the dash, thanking God or whomever was responsible for the rarity of standard transmissions in today's world; he didn't have enough working legs for a clutch. The farmer's T-shirt he'd wrapped around the wound had stopped the bleeding somewhat, the constant throb from the pressure better than bleeding out. The whisky didn't do anything for the pain, but he took another swig before starting the engine just to be sure.

Nope. His leg still hurt. He pulled the door shut, dust kicking up at the motion.

"Moo."

A cow, about 1,200 pounds of between-two-slices-of-bread goodness, stood near the open driver's side window and regarded David with soft brown eyes. He turned the key and started the engine. Bossie would just have to move.

"Moo."

The cow took a clumsy step closer, her face now less than two feet from David's.

"Sorry, Bossie," he said. "I—"

The great, lowing beast opened its slobbery mouth and a foot-long belt-like black tongue shot toward David's face, the forked ends crawled over each other as they fought to get close enough to touch him.

The fall, the knife, the truck he was stealing all shot from his brain. He'd traveled too far. He was no longer on his Earth.

A scream caught in David's throat as he lurched to the right and threw the transmission into drive. He didn't look back.

5

Brick never intended to return to the murder house. He was with Skid when they went to question Cord. He was with Skid when they questioned the guy who wasn't the guy he'd seen in the bar; but Manic Muffins had been closed for hours and it was almost time for the after-work crowd. At least he'd get to talk to Tanner about Dungeon and Dragons; the boy's mother, Serenity, usually stopped by for an afternoon coffee. Skid could take care of herself.

Walking up Gerry Avenue toward Binnall Whatever felt good. The sun shone, the day was not too hot, the cars that drove past looked normal, and there were no velociraptors hiding in the tall grass. Each step left behind the nightmare of vanishing people and brought him closer to a slightly less frightening nightmare of ceilings that changed from copper to tin and back again.

He turned onto Binnall. *Back to Boulevard now. Nice. Maybe this thing fixed itself.* Tanner and Serenity already stood in front of his store. There was something wrong with Manic Muffins, but he couldn't take his eyes off Serenity's; they blazed with anger. He shoved a fist into his right front pocket and pulled out his keys. Tanner saw him and waved.

"Brick," he shouted, swinging an arm over his head. "Hey, Brick." His mother looked at Brick coming toward them and dropped a hand on Tanner's shoulder, drawing him closer to her.

"Hey, Tanner," Brick said, walking toward them. "Sorry I'm late. I—"

"What is going on here?" Serenity's voice was cold, harsh. "And how do you know my son?"

This stopped Brick like he'd walked into a wall.

"I'm sorry?" he said, looking at the two closely. The boy was definitely Tanner and the woman his mother. "You come into my shop all the time. You came in this morning."

"This muffin shop Tanner keeps talking about? This muffin shop that doesn't exist?" There was no confusion in her face.

"I had a chocolate muffin Brick," Tanner said, his face pinched in uncertainty. "Tell her. Tell her I had a chocolate muffin."

What the hell is going on?

"Here," he said, holding up the key. A vehicle pulled to a slow stop on the street behind them, but Brick's eyes never left Serenity. She was serious.

"Stop it," she said, anger now in her voice. "We came down here because Tanner wouldn't stop talking about you and muffins and that stupid dragons game all morning." She took a step backward, pulling Tanner with her. "I had to show him there was no muffin shop."

No shop? "I'm sorry, but I've owned Manic Muffins for the past five years." He jiggled the keys. "Let me show you."

Brick turned toward his store front. Amy's bright hand-painted *Muffin Monday All Week Long!* was gone. The awning, the tables and chairs on the sidewalk, gone. The words Tammy's Tanning Oasis peeked through the thick dust on the window, and a Closed sign hung in the door. His knees threatened to buckle.

"This is wrong," he mumbled.

"You bet your ass it's wrong, Brick." The *Brick* came out thick with spite. "I need your real name, Brick, so I can do a sex offender search on you."

This isn't happening. "Chauncey," he said, his voice weak. "Chauncey Hall." He stepped forward and leaned into the dirty front window. A lone desk and posters of bikini models on beaches he'd never been to dotted the interior of the front room he'd torn down five years ago along with the drop ceiling and black and white floor tiles.

"I just want you to know, I'm alerting the police," she said as she pulled Tanner away, but her words barely registered. Tanner's did.

"Mom. *Mom*," he screamed although she pinned him tightly to her side and pulled him toward a silver Toyota across the street from a dusty pickup that hadn't been there when Brick walked up. "You *know* him. It's Brick, the muffin man."

6

The young mother and little boy left Brick standing alone and slump-shouldered on the sidewalk, staring at a long-closed storefront. It would have made a touching scene in a movie, David thought, if the mother hadn't accused Brick of being a child molester.

The farm of the devil cows where David fell from the sky had only been about twenty miles east of Kansas City, at least the part of Kansas City where Brick told him he worked, although David didn't remember if Brick had told him that yesterday or tomorrow; some part of him didn't even remember knowing Brick, but that was crazy. David didn't expect to find Brick quickly, or even alone. Seeing him standing on the street talking with a kid and a young mom in yoga pants meant one thing; the strength of the waves must be increasing.

How else could you explain the cow? It wasn't because of time travel, or it wasn't just because of time travel. Karl's experiment smashed dimensions into each other. It was the waves. Karl's Miller waves were getting bigger and David's reality was getting weirder. *What kind of hell place did that thing come from?*

But the cow was twenty miles behind him, and so was the farmer who might one day get a call from police reporting they'd found his truck with an empty whisky bottle and David Collison, Ph.D's blood all over the place.

"Hey, Muffin Man," David shouted out the open passenger window of the borrowed pickup, and then gritted his teeth at the sudden movement. A person doesn't know how much strain yelling puts on the entire body until they've been stabbed with a throwing knife.

Brick's shoulders rolled back at the sound and he turned around slowly. "Holy shit," he said, closing the gap from the storefront to the truck in a couple of steps.

"You're not Dave." Brick pointed a thick finger at the open window. "You're the guy I saw in the bathroom hallway at Slap Happy's. You're David Collison."

Something was happening here, something David wasn't in control of, and he had to be in control. He had to. "Yes. I'm David Collison."

Brick leaned into the window, his bulk casting the cab in shadow. The wound was there, the greasy rag around the left leg, but there were no oil stains on the man's clothes. "No. It's not you. Not yet."

This is getting off track. Concentrate, Davey boy. Focus.

"I need you to do something, Brick." Everything was a jumble. David had met Brick at Manic Muffins months ago, but now he'd apparently met Brick at a bar. "I need you to do something, not for me, for everyone."

He pulled a lanyard from inside his shirt and held it out to Brick. "Come on. Take it."

Brick took it gently, looking at it like it might bite him.

"It's my key card to get into the lab. It will get you through the front gate, into the building and into the collider's bridge." A pain almost as bad as pulling out the knife lanced through David's leg. "You have to—" He stopped, sucking in air. "You have to stop Skid."

Brick stood back. "Why? Why's Skid so important in all this?"

He doesn't know. Bless him, he doesn't know. "Because she wants to turn off the collider. She wants to stop the experiment."

"But you said she should."

A realization jumped into David's mind; this Brick might not be the Brick he'd met. This might be a different Brick; from the past, or from somewhere else.

"That wasn't me, at least not-now me." As the words left his mouth David knew they sounded like bad middle school poetry. "Look, you have to stop Skid."

Brick took another step back from the truck. "What if I can't stop her?"

"Then," David said, putting the truck in drive, "she's going to kill us all."

In the rearview mirror, he watched Brick push the key card and lanyard into his shirt pocket and glare at him until he turned left at the stoplight. David had to keep the collider on, even if he had to kill these idiots to do it.

7

People started arriving at the Sanderson Murder House at 6 p.m. for the 7 p.m. tour. Some milled in the yard trading stories and comparing ghost-hunting tools while others walked around the house taking pictures. One guy, Phil Preston from Pine Bluff, Arkansas, came inside to buy a Pepsi jacked up by Cord to $2.50 a bottle.

"When does the magic start?" Skid asked, sitting on the kitchen counter and flipping a meat cleaver in the air.

Cord gave Phil his change and motioned another man in a Razor-backs polo to the hallway and back toward the front of the house.

"The tour starts soon," he said, looking around. Two heads bobbed past an open kitchen window. "Although paranormal events can happen at any time," his voice raised just enough to carry outside, "the ghosts seem to like it better at night."

Skid caught the blade as Cord stepped closer.

"This is my livelihood. Don't try to ruin this for me," he whispered. "What do you do for a living, anyway?"

"I work security at concerts and occasionally have to tackle violent drunks."

He reached an open hand toward her. "Figures. Now, give me the knife before you hurt me with it."

She ignored his hand and slipped the heavy blade into the type of wooden cutlery rack everyone had in 1982.

"I grew up in the circus," she said, now fingering the handle of the butcher knife. "We had a midway. Most circuses don't have those." She pulled the knife halfway from its slot and absentmindedly slid it back in. "When my father took over the business, there weren't any brothers left in Roe Bros. All his uncles and great uncles had gone to whatever afterlife circus people go to. He wanted to offer something different. A circus, a zoo and a carnival, all for the price of admission."

Cord lifted the cutlery rack and moved it across the room. "Businesses adapt to demand or they die." He turned and looked at her. "Or they give the public something it didn't know it wanted."

Skid put a finger to the side of her nose. "I learned a lot from the old guys who ran grifts on the midway," she continued, leaning forward on the counter. "One of the things was not to oversell the grift."

Cord's forehead creased. "Are you trying to help me?"

Skid dropped off the counter, her Hello Kitty shoes making little sound as they hit the linoleum. "I'm just pointing out your little—" She stopped and looked around. No one was close enough to hear. "—gimmicks might be overselling it."

He smiled, honestly for the first time today. "Is this your apology for threatening to kill me?"

The paring knife Cord didn't even know was missing from the rack suddenly appeared in Skid's hand. With a flick of her wrist, the knife flew past him and stuck into the wooden rack millimeters from its slot.

"Don't flatter yourself," she said, pulling her ponytail tight and walking into the hallway.

8

The elevator door didn't budge.

"Come on. Come on. Come on."

Another roar bellowed from somewhere on the floor, too close for Karl to hold his bowels steady for long. Scream-like squalls from things that could no longer scream had chased him from HR, followed by thumping, specifically the thumping of heavy feet on a metal floor. Karl had stopped that thumping, locked it tight in engineering because he no longer needed engineers. They'd all screamed, too. Then they stopped. Now the thumping was in HR. Oscar was in HR.

He swiped the key card closer and harder to the elevator door sensor. No beep.

"Come on," he whispered, then winced at what sounded like a desk slamming into a wall.

"Mirrrooooo," Oscar howled, the sound of its voice echoing down the hallway.

"No, no, no," the words barely moved past Karl's tongue as he swiped the card again and again.

Thump.

"No." Karl didn't register if this word came out. It didn't matter. Oscar was closer.

He pinched the card in a fist and swiped it again across the sensor, his breath coming in pants.

"Mirrrooooo."

He's yelling for me. He's yelling Miller. No, no, no. Swipe. Swipe. Swipe.

"Beep." The light on the sensor turned from red to green. The world around Karl Miller stopped, the silence as pure as what Karl expected death to be like. The key card activated the door.

"Mirrrooooo."

The doors slid open and Karl fell into the elevator. His world shook as Dr. Oscar Montouez's slab-like feet slammed again and again onto the hallway floor.

I left him in engineering. He can't be here. He ca—

"Mirrrooooo."

Karl rose to his knees and pounded the keys with a fist. "Close. Damn you. Close."

The elevator doors began to slide shut as the enormous shadow of the engineer Karl had hired loomed close. Karl did not turn around to look at him.

"Igeyou Mirrrooooo," it bellowed, the force of the sound throwing Karl backward.

"No," the word came out in a sob.

The doors slid shut and the elevator began to move. Oscar slammed against the metal. As the elevator car shook, Karl hugged the floor.

"Mirrrooooo," Oscar howled again, but music began to play in the elevator and Karl pretended he didn't hear it.

9

A crowd of people stood in the front yard of the Sanderson Murder House. Brick checked his phone. It was 6:45 p.m. He opened the gate, which felt more familiar than the rest of his life at the moment even though he'd only first opened it late this morning. It certainly felt more familiar than the apartment he'd walked to after David's truck chugged away from what had once been his storefront. It turned out his apartment wasn't his anymore either. At least the nice Tunisian family who now lived there, the Bejaouis, hadn't called the police when he walked in. They'd insisted he eat some freshly made kefta before he left. This reality, he hoped, was close to his own; his key still worked.

Brick could sense the excitement in the group, no doubt fueled by the article in *The Star*, or *The Times*, or whatever. He was sick of the coincidences, the changes. He just wanted his muffin shop back. *Then why the secrecy?* tiptoed across his noggin. The second warning? The key card? Brick didn't know exactly why he held back this information. It was just something in his gut. *I'll tell them when I need to.* But he didn't know when that was.

"Chauncey?" a woman's voice spoke from somewhere in the gathering.

A total of five people outside his graduating class knew Brick's real name, and the only one here in that club was Skid. It wasn't her. He kept walking; people moved aside without really seeing him.

"Chauncey," the voice said again.

This time he stopped and hoped to hell it was no one from high school. A woman pressed through the group with much more difficulty than Brick. Her shoulder-length hair bobbed as she weaved. She did a side-step dance around a young woman dressed in dark grays and blacks.

Beverly. Beverly Gibson, the one who abandoned Brick in the bathroom at Slap Happy's the night this shitshow hit the fan. She approached him smiling, resting a warm hand on his hairy forearm. In the other hand, she held a reporter's notebook.

"I am *so* happy to see you." The emphasis on 'so' drew the tiny word out by at least three extra letters. "I had so many calls Friday night, your number got knocked off my phone."

"Wha—" He stopped and coughed. "What happened to you?" Brick's tongue felt heavy, the words hard to get out. Sure, he'd only known her for an hour and a half, but still, not cool.

Her grip tightened. "I am *so* sorry about that. I got a call from my editor about a fire; I had to go." She held the notebook up. *Beverly Gibson, Reporter: The Kansas City Times* was handwritten on the cover. "I just figured I'd call when it was over, but then I got calls about something that happened at the murder house, and by then—"

"My number got knocked off your phone," he finished for her, his voice trailing off when he realized he'd seen her name already today; it was the byline on the Sanderson Murder House story. *She didn't say she worked for the paper.* But the signs had been there. Her first "like" on the Turbodate.com profile was journalism, then there were all the pens she'd pulled from her purse at the restaurant.

She smiled. It was a nice smile. An honest smile. "Yeah." She slipped the notebook in her back pocket and grabbed his other arm. "I felt so bad. I was having a good time on our date."

"You could have called my store in the morning," Brick said.

Her smile widened. "Yes, but you never told me the name. You just said you make muffins. Do you know how many places in the metro area make muffins?"

"Lots?"

A laugh, loud and honest, burst out. "Yeah, lots." She released his arm and pulled her cell phone from her pocket. "I shouldn't have agreed to a date when I was on call, but I really wanted to meet you." She held up the phone for Brick to see and dialed the ringtone volume to off. "I'm not on call tonight." Beverly looked up at him. "So, Chauncey, are you into ghosts?"

Maybe this coincidence stuff isn't bad after all.

"Everyone calls me Brick."

10

The tour began precisely at 7 p.m. with a ghost story to set the mood. Cord worked the crowd, making everyone feel like he was telling them the story personally. *He'd be a good ringmaster,* Skid thought as Cord stopped to build to the proper crescendo next to a particularly pretty young woman in a pink blouse. *Dad would like him.* The thought sent a shiver down her back.

Brick motioned to her. He stood well behind the tour next to a woman she recognized but wasn't sure why. Something was different about Brick. The way he stood? No. Dressed? No. Then she realized what was different. He wore a smile.

Skid made her way through the group Cord led into the front room of the Sanderson Murder House and walked up to Brick.

"What's the status?" Brick asked. Skid shrugged.

"Dave's still sacked out on the couch in Cord's office," she said, looking the woman over. "You look familiar. Have we met?"

Just as the woman opened her mouth to respond, Skid knew. "You're Beverly Gibson, the reporter."

Beverly nodded, a faux-shy smile on her face. "Guilty. And you are?"

"Suspicious. Of everything." Her attention rose to meet Brick. "I didn't know you had a girlfriend."

"Well, it was just the one date on—" He stopped, a look of revelation swept across his face. "Friday."

"Friday?" Skid pointed toward Beverly's chest. "Then she's part of it."

"Wait a second." Beverly held up her hands to form a T. "Time out. I feel like I'm missing something."

"Friday," Skid said, ignoring them. "Things started to go wrong Friday. Have you noticed anything strange?"

Beverly looked up at Brick, whose gentle face seemed to calm her. Then her gaze drifted back to Skid.

"I don't know. Maybe. Well, yeah. There is this one thing." Pink washed across her light complexion. "I didn't want to tell anybody. It sounds like I've lost my mind, or something."

"It's okay," Brick said, his voice soft and comforting.

She swallowed and took her hand back, nervously pulling at her shirt.

"I had to leave our date early." She leaned into Brick maybe, Skid suspected, so she didn't fall over. Beverly had gone from normal to scared shitless faster than Scooby and Shaggy. "I didn't want to. I was having a really good time, but my editor called me to a house fire. It was a big one, too. A total loss. It was one of those big 1920s mansions on Independence Avenue. The thing is—" She stopped again, her voice starting to shake. "I drove by the house on the way here tonight, and it was there. It was still there. The whole thing. There weren't even signs of a fire."

Brick put an arm around her shoulders. He winced as if worried she'd shrink away, but she didn't. Beverly melted into him.

"Are you sure it was the same house?" he asked.

"I'm positive. I'd be a pretty shitty reporter if I couldn't get details like that right."

The day grew darker, just for a moment, as a cloud drifted over the early evening sun. A chill crept through Skid. She didn't like it. Not one bit.

"There's more," Beverly said, her voice stronger. "I checked the paper's website when I pulled in here tonight, and the story I wrote was missing. I logged a story Friday night, but it was about an armed standoff with police at a QuikTrip not far from that house. I didn't write that story."

A whistle turned them toward the front steps of the Sanderson Murder House, where Cord stood, holding open the door.

"Are you coming?"

11

The sound of people walking outside the door pulled Dave from sleep. He now hated waking up; he never knew when someone would steal his shoes. He wiggled his toes on the opposite end of the couch. They moved in filthy socks.

"I don't have any shoes."

Reality sifted through his brain, pushing out sleep and leaving things he didn't want to remember. The super collider. The machine shed. Nineteen-eighty-two. Grandpa Sam. The Sanderson house. A weight lay across him. Nothing physical, just the weight of the universes. It was the plural part that got to him.

Karl's equations were the cause; they had to be. When Dave saw Karl's final report Friday, he'd known the danger of dimensions intersecting. Multiple universes connected as Miller Waves ripped temporary paths through them could cause anything to jump through. Anything. A side effect were time slips. He'd already experienced that. But what of other Daves? Other Karls? Good God, another Skid? They were out there, somewhere.

Standing seemed harder than he remembered as he forced himself to his sock feet. His mouth seemed dirtier, but that could be because of all the beer, or the time travel, or not brushing his teeth. He steadied himself on the desk next to the couch and took in the room. The guy who now owned the house had taken him to an office in the back of the building and put him on a modern leather sofa that didn't go with the '80s decor at all.

"This is my office," Cord had told him. "Someone will be back to check on you. Don't vanish. Unless you want to vanish and reappear in the hallway at about 8:25 tonight, then that'd be great."

Windows filled the walls, and a four-bladed fan hung from the ceiling. *This was the Sandersons' sunroom.* Tommy had a TV and Atari 2600 in the corner across from the chair where Cecilia liked to drink screwdrivers and read Jackie Collins novels late in the afternoon. The Atari and the chair, and Tommy and Cecilia, were long since gone.

"I gotta stop this," he said aloud in the room.

The air suddenly changed, growing thick like Dave had just stepped underwater. A smell, the smell of fresh air flooded his nostrils. He grabbed the desk to brace himself as the windows buckled without breaking, flowing outward in impact waves as if a T-Rex were nearby. "Oh, no," he whispered. "This is a big one."

12

The lights weren't on because there was no need; the sun would still be up for two hours. But when the tour needed them, every light fixture in the house was ready to offer 60 soft-white watts of ghost-hunting illumination. When the Sandersons lived in the house, they probably used 100-watt bulbs like normal people, but Cord felt 60 watts provided just the right amount of mood lighting to get the proper feel of the place. It's the little things that count.

"And here," Cord said, car salesman mode in full gear, "is the kitchen where Cecelia Sanderson made her award-winning pies."

Skid leaned against the counter, arms crossed. "What kind of pies?"

Annoyance flashed across Cord's face for a second, only a second. "She was particularly fond of berries." The salesman smile returned. "And this," he said, stepping to the sink, "is where Delbert Sanderson came to wash off the blood of his family."

The woman in the pink shirt raised her hand.

"Yes, Danielle."

Already got her name, Skid thought. *This guy is smooth.*

"If this is where he washed off the blood," she said, pausing to bite her lower lip. Skid made barf face behind her. "Aren't we going through the tour backward?"

Skid watched for any crack in Cord's armor. No chance.

"Why yes we are," he said, then addressed the entire tour packed into the kitchen like a boring family dinner. The smile he wore would sell anyone a car.

Yep. My father would hire you in a second.

"Would you all like to see where it began?" A few murmurs of *yes* came from the group. "Would you like to start with the first murder?" The murmurs turned into a smattering of applause.

Brick didn't clap, but Beverly did.

"Okay then." He motioned for everyone to follow and started to walk toward the hallway when the walls began to swim.

Skid's hand shot out and grabbed the cabinet. Her eyes flashed to Brick. "You feel that?"

He nodded.

"Yeah." Beverly grabbed Brick's arm.

An air freshener smell grew thick in the kitchen, the same smell that had accompanied Dave's fall into the hallway.

"Brick?"

"Yeah, Skid."

"Do you see the walls moving?"

"Yeah, Skid."

Beverly tugged Brick's arm. "What's happening?"

He gently rested a hand over hers. "I don't know. I—"

A wall of what felt like water pushed past, engulfing them, then moved on, leaving them standing quietly in the still kitchen.

Beverly's nails bit into Brick's arm as she tugged. "I don't want to be here anymore. Can we go?"

"That was weird," Brick said, then closed his mouth. *We?* A dog barked from somewhere upstairs.

"Oh, no." It came from Skid.

He turned toward her. Beverly no longer pulled at him; her hands now clutched his. "What?"

"The curtains are different," she said, her voice shaking. She pointed to the thin green drapes at the window over the sink. Guernsey cows formed its border. "Dave said Mrs. Sanderson wouldn't like Cord's curtains."

Someone laughed from the hallway and conversations began, quietly at first.

"Whoa." Brick released Beverly's hands and leaned back into the refrigerator door. The blocky harvest wheat-colored unit leaned with him. "Do you think we're there? Do you think this is the night the murders happened?"

"No." Beverly had stepped away from them, her arms folded across her chest. "No. That's not possible."

Skid resisted an urge to look outside; she didn't want to know what was out there. "Neither is a burned house that never burned."

The dog barked again. "What—" A yelp stopped her, then the dog fell silent.

"The Sanderson guy killed the dog, too," Brick said, standing up. The refrigerator thunked back into place. "He's going to murder his family. Tonight. Now. We gotta stop him."

Skid stepped in front of Brick. "We can't do that."

"He's going to kill two people," Brick shouted. Someone from the hallway cheered.

"No. He *killed* two people. Past tense." Skid held her hands in front of her. "We can't change what's happened. He already killed them"

Brick's meathooks grew into fists. "No, he hasn't. They're still here. They're alive."

A woman screamed from upstairs.

"Okay," he continued. "Maybe he has. But there's still Tommy. We have to try and save him."

Someone in the hall screamed as footsteps thundered down the stairs. Skid, Brick and Beverly stepped toward the scream.

"Tommy," a man shouted from upstairs. "This is why I never got your teeth straightened."

"No," came from a different voice as feet landed in the hallway. "Get out of my way."

A light flashed as someone in the hall took a picture of 32-year-old Thomas Sanderson, squat and cushy, his wet eyes seeming to see nothing. Tommy pushed through the ghost tour as he moved toward the kitchen.

"Hey, it's Tommy," someone shouted.

"Why are you people in my house?" Delbert Sanderson had reached the hallway, the blood of his wife and dog Muffit glinting in 100-watt light off the samurai blade he held. "Tommy," he bellowed and ran past the tour members, who pressed themselves against the walls while still hissing delightedly at one another, *Can you believe how real this is?*

Tommy reached the kitchen seconds before his father.

Skid stepped in front of Brick. *This is wrong. The whackjob killed*

Tommy in the hallway.

Tommy looked at Skid. Confusion filled his face before he turned toward his father.

"Dad, please," escaped his mouth before the blade came down on his neck, blood spraying the refrigerator and cow curtains. Delbert Sanderson pulled the sword back and struck again, sinking it into his son's chest. Tommy dropped to the floor gurgling. The cold Japanese steel slid out effortlessly, like Delbert had cut a sandwich.

Cord yelled, "Holy shit," from somewhere down the hall. Someone else cheered.

"Get out of my house," Delbert screamed, his eyes wide and jiggly, like a cheap doll's. He lunged toward Skid, who jumped out of the way. Beverly screamed behind her.

Skid's body tensed. Her body on full-automatic. She kicked Delbert's left knee out from under him as a giant fist flew from above her head and crashed into the madman's face. Delbert flew backward and crumpled into a pile; the sword clinked on the linoleum.

Cord appeared in the kitchen. "Holy shit," he said again. "This just happened. This *just* happened. Holy shit."

"We could have stopped this," Brick barked at Skid. "We could have—" Then his voice dropped to a whisper. "Oh, no. No."

Skid turned. Beverly sat on the floor, grasping her arm. Blood ran from between her fingers. *No. No. No.*

"Beverly?" The word came out of Brick like it didn't want to.

"Come on." Skid grabbed a dish towel from the counter and dropped to her knees. The sword had barely nicked Beverly. Skid wrapped the towel around her arm. "She's going to be okay." She smiled at Beverly. "You're going to be okay. It's just a surface wound."

"We could have stopped this," Brick said again.

A weight seemed to drop on Skid. "I need you to be here with me, big guy," Skid said, popping to her feet, pulling Beverly up by her good arm. She reached up and grabbed Brick's hairy chin, turning his face to meet hers. "I can't do this alone."

"Uh, guys." Cord stood looking out the window over the sink. A man stood in the window of the house next door holding a telephone receiver to his ear, the pigtail of wire trailed behind him. The man had dialed "o," Cord knew, because on Friday that man told him so. Cord held up a hand and waved at a decades-younger Olan Wanker.

"Uh, guys. Somebody get the scientist," Cord said. "We gotta get out of here."

"What's the matter?" Skid asked.

"That guy over there," he said, pointing. "He's calling the cops."

CHAPTER SIX

SEPTEMBER IV: THE QUEST FOR PEACE

1

"MY PHONE DOESN'T HAVE any bars," someone said from the hallway.

Skid ignored him and moved away from the cabinets, skirting the bloody corpse of Tommy Sanderson.

"Excuse me, ladies and gentlemen," she tried to say to those on the ghost tour who had wandered toward the kitchen, but her voice caught in her throat. She coughed, trying to clear it. "Excuse me, ladies and gentlemen," she said again, louder. "We've had a—" She stopped, the faces from the hallway filled with excitement, or horror. Her voice caught again.

Cord stepped next to her. "We've experienced a major temporal anomaly," he said, his voice calm, steady, comforting. "This is the kind of thing you paid for, folks. Just please move down the hall to the front room. I'll be there in a moment to discuss what happened." He pulled his phone from his pocket and held it up for them to see. "The anomaly disrupted cell service, so you may be out of contact with loved ones or your favorite pizza place until the universe normalizes."

He walked into the hallway, herding the ghost tour away from the carnage. A man in the back took a picture of the bloody mess before Cord rested a hand on his shoulder and turned him toward the living room.

"Also," he said into the crowd. "If anyone's thirsty, the Sanderson Murder House offers whatever pop is in the fridge for only $2.50 a can."

"He's incorrigible," Beverly said, holding onto her wounded arm.

Skid went to the sink and turned on the cold water, splashing it on her face. When she looked up, Olen Wanker was staring at her. She pulled the cow curtains closed, shutting him out; the neighbor was still on the phone. The darkening sky and tungsten lights had intensified the bloody painting of the kitchen to a vivid red.

"Okay," she said, her normally tight-fitting mental armor beginning to unravel. "There's been a double homicide here tonight and, according to Cord, the Gladys Kravitz type over there has called the cops." She focused on Brick. "We need a plan."

"We need to leave before the police show up," Brick said. "How do we explain this, us, everything?"

"We can't leave." Dave stood outside the open door to the sunroom, a hand on the frame to steady his unsteady legs. The bodies of Delbert and Tommy Sanderson drew his attention. "The sad thing is, this might not be the worst day of my life."

"Who is this?" Beverly asked.

"David Collison, Ph.D.," Skid whispered. "And why can't we leave?"

"The missing scientist?" Beverly stepped away from everyone and moved closer to the back door. "Did you kidnap him?"

Dave laughed a dull "ha," his expression lifeless, like he'd just woke up from a bad dream and realized he was still in it. "I wish. That would be a heck of a lot more fun than this."

"Why can't—"

Dave released the door frame and walked to the table, plopping into a chair. He used his heel to roll Delbert onto his side and out of his way, then paused to consider Beverly. "I don't know you, but you look like a nice person. Would you please get me a beer from the fridge? There should be at least half a case of Old Milwaukee on the bottom shelf."

Not knowing what else to do, she moved to the refrigerator.

"I am aware we're stuck in a house with three dead bodies," Dave continued. Delbert moaned; his body shifted slightly. "Two dead bodies. But the thing you all need to understand is that what we did on the BAB-C was run quantum physics experiments. Cord called it a major temporal anomaly, which is surprisingly accurate."

Beverly stepped over Delbert and set a beer on the table in front of Dave.

"Thank you." The crack of a pull-tab was unusually loud in the kitchen. "You look confused."

"Dave, this is Beverly, and I'll catch her up," Brick said, resting a hand on her shoulder. "Keep talking."

"On Friday, our project leader Karl Miller ran an unauthorized experiment that has ripped open every conceivable dimension and point in time. Those are now slamming together at random speeds." Dave took a swig and set his drink down, holding it in both hands. "Every insane thing any of us can think of not only can happen, it probably will. When we get home, or as close to home as it matters, we have to get to my lab. We have to shut off the Big-Assed Bastard."

"But why can't we leave right now?" Skid asked.

"Because when the next Miller Wave crashes," Dave said, "if we're not in the same place we were when the last wave crashed, we may never get home."

2

David threw the empty whisky bottle across the bench seat and out the open passenger window of the farmer's pickup. It hit the dry, brown grass on the shoulder and skidded into a ditch. Nope, officer. No whisky bottles here.

Dusk descended on the day hard and fast like an ambush when the tall sign for the Flying J Travel Center appeared on the horizon. There might not be more whisky there, but there would be a telephone. He had to call Karl, to warn him of the visitors who'd be coming sometime soon.

He put on his right turn signal out of habit, not necessity. Traffic on U.S. 71, both ways, had dried up. *Where is everybody?* he wondered, but really, he knew. It was Monday night in the Midwest. Everyone was home having family dinner or watching football. But that didn't explain the lack of trucks. Maybe the missing vehicles were his fault, too.

He slowed as he pulled the pickup onto the off-ramp and stopped at the bottom, the dusty stop sign riddled with bullet holes.

"Owww," he shouted to no one, his wounded leg screaming in pain.

He considered calling 9-1-1 at the truck stop but quickly pushed that thought from his head. Police would come, and they might be looking for a stolen pickup, one with his fingerprints, his blood. *There's a facility at the lab, Davey boy. You're close. So close.* County routes J and C intersected under the highway. C ran into East State Route YY that led to the lab, but he couldn't just show up at the lab unannounced. He'd given Brick his card key.

The signal tock-tocked when David turned left and pushed the accelerator, gritting his teeth at the pain he knew was coming. The speedometer grew to 25 mph by the time the truck reached Route J, the lights of Flying J already flooding its parking lot.

Almost there. Just gotta call Karl, tell him to get Med Services ready. Tell him—

The air inside the cab became still, static. David's eyes shot to the rearview mirror. A ripple bent the rural highway behind him, twisting the asphalt out of shape and dropping it back in place behind it.

"Oh, no."

The electric connections to contract David's muscles enough to mash his foot into the accelerator began to fire when the wave slammed into the truck and David's world melted around him.

He no longer drove a truck.

Oh god never had the chance to escape his mouth. His shoulder hit the grassy ground, not like an action hero throwing himself into a shoulder roll and coming up swinging, more like when a Chevrolet Suburban hits a deer.

He didn't know how far he rolled and didn't care. He was still alive. David lay on his face in the grass. When he moved his fingers and toes, new pain flared through the knife wound in his leg. He was sure it had started to bleed again. The side of his face throbbed, but he could still move his jaw.

I'm okay, he lied to himself, then opened his eyes.

He lay in a field, the buzz of traffic on U.S. 71 behind him, and started to laugh. *I was in a truck. My body is caught in a temporal, possibly dimensional, shift cycle and I'm stupid enough to be inside a moving truck.* "Unbelievable."

Wherever he was, the light from the truck stop didn't exist. Day was swiftly dropping out of sight. *Let's go, Davey boy. Now you can call an ambulance.* He took in his surroundings. He lay in a field, yes, but it wouldn't be one for long. A yellow bulldozer rested about thirty yards away, awaiting its role in the work on what would one day be the Flying J's parking lot. A dump truck was also parked in front of a crumbling sign identifying the ruins around it as the "Highway 71 Motel: Best sleep in the Midwest." But the loader grabbed his attention. It stood right where the entrance to the truck stop would be. David had rolled to within a foot of the front tire.

Get up. You need a doctor. As David pushed himself to his knees, the searing pain in his leg almost dropped him back on his face. *Suck it up.* His left hand reached above him for something, anything to grab. It fell on some kind of tube covered in rubber. *A cord? A cable?* Or it might have been a hose. At this point he didn't care. David tightened his grip and pulled. Whatever it was, it held.

He reached out with his right hand and found the wheel hub. He pushed, dragging both legs beneath him. *You got this. You got this.* His breath came in quick bursts through his teeth as he regained his feet. *Yeah. I got it.*

Then something snapped and the cord came loose. He thrust himself forward, throwing both hands onto the tire to keep his feet as a thick, cold liquid poured over his shirt, the smell that attacked his nostrils familiar. Hydraulic fluid.

3

Laughter and applause echoed from the front room. Cord was starting to impress Skid and she didn't like it. Not at all. "We may never get back to our exact timeline, but there's always a chance we'll get to a timeline close enough it won't really matter," she said, moving from the table to the hallway, her Hello Kitty sneakers all but silent. She turned back to the people gathered in the kitchen. "But this will be irrelevant when the cops show up. Police of any time don't look kindly on people at a murder scene. They tend to call us 'suspects.'"

"I knew there was a reason I sat by you Friday." Dave had finished his beer. He asked for another, but nobody moved closer to the refrigerator, so he got up and did it himself. "But we don't have to worry about the police, because the next Miller Wave should put us somewhere we won't have been arrested."

Skid rested fists on her hips. "Miller Wave?"

"I didn't name them, Karl Miller did."

Brick had moved away from Beverly to loom over Delbert, who was slowly regaining consciousness. Beverly now sat on the counter where Skid had perched earlier. She'd found Cecelia's pitcher of screwdrivers in the refrigerator and drained two Care Bears Pizza Hut Funshine Bear glasses of it. She was on her third.

"And what," Skid said, "did good ol' Karl do to us?"

"The universe, or universes, are normally static, by which I mean they stay separate and don't intersect," Dave said. "At least not often. But now they're like a bar jukebox on random. We have to suffer through some god-awful pop songs, but the juke box will eventually play the tune we like. But to enjoy it, we have to be in the same bar when it plays."

Beverly laughed. To Skid, it sounded like the annoying laugh of a sitcom neighbor. "Unless it's 'Don't Stop Believin'.' Am I right?"

Skid's jaws clenched. *I like 'Don't Stop Believin'.*

"And we have all those unsuspecting ghost-hunters to think about," Dave added, ignoring her. "They have no clue what's going on. It will serve them best if they never know."

Delbert moaned again. "I wonder if the abusive asshole knows someone is drinking his beer," Dave muttered.

"So, the juke box is on random," Skid interrupted, "but songs aren't the same length." Her eyes grew wide, and she dropped back into her chair. "Wait a second. These waves are random. Brick and I saw the last one coming, we felt it move through us, but you're still here. You didn't vanish this time."

"Oh, I did," Dave said. "You didn't notice because you vanished with me. We're becoming more and more tied together."

Brick leaned on the table. It tipped enough some of Dave's beer sloshed onto the Formica surface. "I hate not being able to do anything."

"It's the Miller Waves, Brick." Dave stuck a finger in the spilled beer and stirred. Despite the nap, he looked tired. "The waves emitting from the BAB-C are at varying strengths at varying intervals. This makes their effects, and their timing, as random and unpredictable as possible." He lifted his finger to his mouth and licked the beer. "A wave is coming, one that will probably drop us back in the house we left. We just have to wait for it."

"Why are they so random?" Skid asked. "If your lab successfully initiated these time, dimension, whatever waves, why can't you control them?"

A laugh jumped from Dave. "You haven't read much on quantum indeterminacy, have you? It's math with a bit of guesswork to fill in the blanks. It's the randomness in Karl's equations that are dangerous."

"What's that mean?" Brick asked.

"It means some people may be sucked into the next Miller wave but not into the one after that. There's no predicting how the next wave will work, or when."

The sound of police sirens seeped into the kitchen through the open window. The unmistakable wail must have hit the living room, as well. Some clown yelled, "busted," which got more laughs than it should.

"Visitors are on their way," Skid said, her strength coming back. "We might not have that long to wait."

"No, we don't."

They turned toward Brick, who stood at the open back door.

"Beverly's gone."

4

There were a lot of things Skid wanted right then, and to be home in a hot bath topped the list. The thing she didn't want was a piece of missing luggage at baggage claim.

Brick tensed to move, but she stepped in his way.

"Whoa. If we're going to stay together, we can't leave the house. Bud Light Dave said so."

The sound of an empty can clattering across the table came from behind them. "I don't think I like that name."

Brick flexed, the muscles of his arms rolled under the fabric of his flannel shirt. "I have to go get her. She'll be stranded here."

Come on, Skid. What are you doing? What are you doing?

"Then so will you." She swallowed and pushed his arms down. For some reason, he let her. "I'll go. I'm faster than you."

"But—"

She waved and bolted out the door before he could protest, leaping down the steps and through the open gate in the chain-link fence. *This is stupid, Skid. Stupid, stupid, stupid.* But she also knew she'd want someone to do the same for her if she lost her shit.

There were things Randall Roe wouldn't allow his daughter to do at Roe Bros. Circus: tightrope walking, high diving and lion taming. She may have spent most of her life up to her armpits in elephant poo, but she had never had her head in the mouth of a 400-pound cat. Knife throwing and driving a motorcycle under a Russian bear dancing on top of a ramp-jumping clown car were fine, but what took up most of her time was running. Running messages, running bandages, running pizza money. Just running.

She ran now.

A figure moved clumsily under a streetlamp up the block, the old yellow lights eerie in the night. Beverly. Skid was in full sprint as a police car, an old Plymouth Fury with lights flashing, buzzed past her.

The car slowed and somebody shouted, "Hey."

"Damn it," she hissed under her breath and tried to keep away from the pools of yellow light, her stomach clamped in a vise.

Beverly stumbled ahead of her. Three screwdrivers in a different temporal plane will do that to a person, kind of like jet lag on Krypton. Skid caught up to her in seconds, Beverly limping on the sidewalk between a bush and a 1979 AMC Pacer. Skid didn't try to talk with her, there was no time. She bumped Beverly like a NASCAR driver, sending the woman crashing through the bush into a shadowed yard. She slid to a stop and doubled back.

"Hey," Beverly said, her breath coming in vodka wheezes. Skid didn't breathe heavily at all.

"Shhh," Skid hissed, her voice low. She grabbed Beverly's arm.

"Ouch. Hey, stop it."

Skid pressed a hand over Beverly's mouth and leaned close, nose-to-nose. "You've put us all in danger."

Beverly tried to shake loose but couldn't. Skid's arms were hammered iron.

"Do you know who it you are?"

Beverly nodded.

"Really?" Skid's grip over Beverly's mouth never loosened, the weakness, the fear she'd felt now buried deeply, back where she liked it. Beverly pinched her eyes tight and when she opened them, they were hazy with tears.

"Do you know where you are?" Skid repeated. This time Beverly shook her head.

"You are in 1984 and if you ever want to get back to where you're supposed to be—" She paused, choosing her next words carefully. "If you ever want to see Brick again, we have to get back to that house. Do you understand?"

Beverly's eyes grew wide.

"Yes?"

Beverly drunkenly nodded.

"Good. Keep quiet and come with me." Skid slowly released Beverly's mouth and stood, pulling her to her feet. "Let's go."

They kept to the back yards that separated them from the Sanderson house, Skid holding Beverly's hand so she couldn't get away. Drunk people were unpredictable.

"How can we be in 1984?" Beverly asked, her voice as quiet as three screwdrivers would allow. "This isn't the movies. We can't do this kind of thing."

Skid shushed her as they stopped at the fence of the Sanderson yard and she squatted behind a thin veil of decorative plants. She pulled Beverly down with her.

"Now," Skid whispered, pointing toward the back door. A police officer stood in the yard, thumbs in his belt, looking over the street. "—we need to get over this fence. I'll take care of the cop—"

"But it's a police officer," Beverly said in a drunk whisper.

Skid paused and took in Beverly. Past the confusion, past the annoyance, she could see kindness in Beverly's face. Maybe that's why Brick liked her. She helped Beverly to her feet.

"Come on. Please don't pull this crap again."

5

Officer Poulson had a hard time getting the handcuffs shut over Brick's thick wrists.

"That really isn't necessary," Brick said, holding his arms behind his back simply because the officer told him to.

"Shut your mouth, Dan Haggerty," Officer Poulson said as he tried again. Officer Davis had already helped Delbert Sanderson into a chair and cuffed Dave, who sat in a chair in front of a beer he could no longer reach. "And don't step in that blood. It's evidence."

Tommy Sanderson had bled as much as Tommy Sanderson would bleed, leaking a pool of sticky, dark fluid staining the linoleum of dead Cecilia Sanderson's once spotless kitchen floor.

"We didn't do anything," Brick said, shuffling a step to his left as Officer Poulson finally clicked the cuffs closed.

"Ouch. That hurt."

"Don't, Brick." Dave sat back and relaxed. "It doesn't matter. Do you smell that?"

The room was suddenly awash in the odor of a giant air purifier that had just clicked on. Someone protested from the front room. Probably more handcuffs. Police were everywhere.

Dave's eyes bore into Brick's. "It's coming."

6

"I don't feel comfortable running from the police," Beverly said, attempting sobriety.

Skid tried to ignore her as she glanced at the back door. Officer Thumbs-in-His-Belt hadn't moved. "Can you get over this fence?"

Beverly shrugged, gazing toward Skid with glassy eyes. "I think so."

Skid. "I want to go to a bar with you."

The sky, tinted in the flashing reds and blues of police lights, wavered in the distance. Houses in at the far reaches of Skid's vision swelled then bowed as if they were made of sound.

"Oh, no."

She turned to the lost, confused woman next to her. "If you ever want to see Brick, or your family, or 'Queer Eye for the Straight Guy' again, you'll get over that fence, and you'll do it the moment I signal. Now, get ready."

In a fluid motion Skid shot up, setting a hand on the top metal bar of the fence for support and launched herself over. She landed silently on the Sanderson lawn. The officer, about twenty yards away, didn't move. Skid stuck a hand in Beverly's direction without looking and snapped it open and shut three times fast before taking off in a dead sprint.

Chain links rattled behind her as Beverly fell into the yard. The cop heard it too, but it didn't matter. By the time he'd turned halfway toward Beverly's jingle, Skid dropped into a baseball slide and took the man's legs out from under him. The officer landed awkwardly, his face planting in the grass.

"I'm sorry. I'm so, so sorry," Skid whispered as she ripped the handcuffs off the officer's belt like she'd done it before and slapped one side on a wrist, dragging the surprised man's arms behind his back and pushing the second cuff closed on the other wrist by the time Beverly had made it to her, huffing.

"How ... did ... ?"

"Come on," Skid said, grabbing the woman's hand and dragging her up the steps.

The policemen in the kitchen may have heard their man drop outside but didn't show it. The Miller Wave had made it to the house, sweeping through the front room to the hallway. Brick's eyes grew wide as it engulfed the kitchen, he and Dave dissolving into nothingness before Skid's eyes.

She pressed Beverly's hand more tightly in hers as they passed the threshold of the kitchen and leapt into the Miller Wave.

7

The day had melted into darkness by the time David decided he couldn't stay at the construction site any longer. Not because of the humming, chirping, buzzing insects he was certain wanted to drink his blood, but because his leg and the side of his face throbbed. He wished he'd saved some whisky—not to drink but to pour into his leg wound, *then* to drink. He pictured the leg red and swollen under the thin material of his slacks, but he wasn't going to look. It was probably even worse.

A vehicle, just one, had driven by during the time he'd leaned against the loader's tire. A pickup with stock racks in the back and two Yorkshire pigs looking at him over dirty, wet noses. He raised his arm and waved at the farmer, who raised an index finger off the steering wheel and kept driving.

David needed help now; he knew it. A warm flush spread across his face, but whether it was from an infection fever or all the skin he'd rubbed off dropping out of the air at 25 mph, he wasn't sure. The loader didn't have a magic farmer's glove compartment like the pickup he'd borrowed. A lighter would have been nice. People tend to show up when things get set on fire, even at this spot in whenever.

The highway traffic had slowed, only one, maybe two cars zipped by every few minutes on their way to and from Kansas City, but the darkness gave him something he hadn't expected. Stars blazed in the sky this far in the country; David picked out the constellations Andromeda and Triangulum in the northeast. He hadn't seen stars like this since college, since the night he and—

His body sensed something was wrong before his brain could catch up. Gooseflesh grew on his forearms even though the night had to be in the low 80s.

"What " he started to say, but the realization hit him. The insects had stopped humming, chirping and buzzing; the night birds were silent. Except for the car that drove south from KC on the highway that seemed so far away, the night had fallen silent, dead. David's guts clenched like he'd taken a punch. *I'm not alone.*

"Hello," he said, his voice louder than he'd expected.

Something moved at the corner of the loader, emerging from the tall grass, something like a dog, but not a dog. The fur may have been gray, or maybe tan, but he couldn't tell in the darkness. The beast, at least fifty pounds, bared its teeth and growled.

"Good bo—" David started to say, but a crunching in the tall drying grass to his right destroyed the moment. He slowly turned his head toward the sound. Another dog-thing, slightly smaller than the first, crouched at the other edge of the loader.

Coyotes, he thought. *Those are coyotes.*

Outside the Roadrunner cartoons and nature programs, David had never seen a coyote. These lean, angry beasts, their muscles rolling beneath their fur, didn't look anything like the ACME mail-order junkie or even like the lone creatures that roamed the American West, avoiding humans. They looked too big, too dangerous.

These aren't regular coyotes. These are super-coyotes—I'm not home.

Another coyote appeared next to the second. It began to slink forward, low to the ground, almost obscured in the grass. *No, no, no.*

David turned back to the first, which hadn't moved, then back to his right.

I'm going to die. A shiver ran through his body. *No. I've traveled through time and space. I've been stabbed. I fell out of the sky. And I lived. I am not going to be killed by a cartoon character.*

"Shoo," he shouted.

The beast froze for a second, only a second, before it started creeping forward slowly again. David knew what would happen. He'd seen enough nature programs to understand coyote number three was probably a distraction. With the other coyote coming toward him, the big one on his left would leap at David's back and take him down.

He stuck his hand in his pants pocket and grabbed the only thing there, pivoted on his good leg and threw overhand. The ring, with keys to his apartment, the laundry room, Toyota Camry, his parent's house and the office of a company he hadn't worked for in eight years, flew from his fingers and spun through the air. The jingling metal mass smashed into the coyote's forehead. It yelped and scampered backward. The grass to his right rustled as the other wolf wannabes vanished into the darkness.

"Yeah. You better run," David hollered into the night before he dropped backward onto the tire, his heart hammering like a drum solo.

"What the heck, man?" He pulled the sleeve of his Oxford shirt across his forehead, wiping off sweat and replacing it with hydraulic fluid. "Coyotes? What else does the universe have to throw at me?"

Another set of headlights appeared on Route C and continued under the highway to Route J; straight toward David.

"Yes," he screamed into the night. "Yes. Come on, baby." Not that the volume disturbed the flies that had begun to crawl on his leg and face like on those poor starving kids on the late-night Save the Children commercials.

The headlights wavered in what could have been a heat mirage if this had been Death Valley in September instead of Missouri. But this wasn't Death Valley, and that wasn't a heat mirage. The Miller Wave hit David, and the field, the loader and the headlights dropped out of his reality, the night peeled away and revealed a white room bathed in fluorescent light.

His stomach lurched and almost found its way out. *A bathroom? I'm in a bathroom.* Wherever he was, it was better than coyote ugly. He reached a hand behind him and felt the cool porcelain of a sink. "It's a public bathroom." Darting looks all over the room, he identified a spring-powered door next. "There's got to be a telephone out there."

He released the sink and limped forward. The pain in his leg sent tears down his dirty face. A sound reached his ears, a rhythmic thumping. Music pounded through the pain. *Music?* David's hand, now shaking from fear, lack of sleep, lack of food, adrenalin, it didn't matter, gripped the door handle and opened it. He threw himself into the hallway and slammed into the wall opposite the door.

"Hey," said a soft, deep voice from farther into a hallway full of music, the kind of thump-thump dance music that gave him a headache.

"That was some dump, huh?" said the deep voice as somewhere a door shut, lessening the pounding of the repetitive beat.

David twisted his neck to stare up at the man, the big, big man. His mouth dropped. *It can't be,* although he knew that it sure as hell could be. David planted both hands on the wall and shoved himself toward the giant.

"Brick," David wheezed.

Brick stepped away from him. "Hey, back off, now."

He doesn't know me, David thought. He took another step toward Brick, planting his weight on the wrong foot.

"Ooooh." The pain doubled him over. *Leg's bleeding again, Davey boy. Bloody footprints all over this nice tiled floor.* Black spots swam before his eyes, so he shut them.

"Holy shit," Brick whispered. "What happened to you?"

I gotta warn him. I can stop it. David tried hard to swallow but there wasn't enough spit in his throat. He grasped wads of Brick's red flannel shirt in both hands.

"Hey—"

"Watch her, Brick," David wheezed. "Watch out for Skid. She's not what she seems."

Brick didn't move. David knew the big man could have ripped him off his shirt and tossed him into the corner. He could have punched David back into 1994, but he didn't. Confusion draped Brick's face.

"I don't know you," Brick said, "but I do know you need a doctor." He reached toward his pocket for his cell phone. David pulled harder on the man's shirt.

He doesn't understand. He has to understand. "Skid's going to kill us all," he said, trying to shout, but his voice couldn't do it anymore.

"Who's Sk—"

The hallway door slammed into the wall, and the dance music grew louder momentarily. Three drunk girls nearly fell into the hallway laughing before they tripped over each other and stumbled into the bathroom marked "Hookers."

From the three seconds the door that led to the bar stayed open, he understood it was Slap Happy's Dance Club. He saw a three-days younger David Collison sitting at the bar laughing with a woman—without a knife wound in his leg, not drenched in hydraulic fluid, still blissfully ignorant of the words Dr. Karl Miller shouted at him in anger—and he had no memory of it. David still wasn't sure if he was in his universe, or a similar one. He also didn't think it mattered. Everything seemed connected—somehow. The picture wavered and the air freshener smell flooded the hallway. David closed his eyes and unfolded alone into the darkness.

8

There's a point during a stunt, any stunt, where something gets broken. Sometimes, like motorcycle daredevil Evel Knievel who suffered 433 bone fractures during the first ten years of his career, it's obvious. Crashing a motorcycle while attempting to jump 13 buses on national television will do that. And sometimes, like illusionist Harry Houdini silently breaking three bones in his left wrist filming a movie, it's subtle. A film's stunt involving a dancing bear, a motorcycle and a clown car fit somewhere in between.

This stunt only broke a table.

Skid, her hand still locked on Beverly's hand, came first, appearing to leap from a hole in the air. She and Beverly hit the tabletop in the Sanderson Murder House kitchen just as Cord and his ghost tour came through the hallway. The table legs buckled, and wood snapped, crashing them onto the clean linoleum. People on the tour leaned around each other to click pictures.

"Beverly," Brick shouted.

He and Dave stood over the women, hands still cuffed behind their backs.

"You didn't have to jump," Dave said.

"What happened?" Cord asked. "I mean, that was awesome, but really, what happened?"

Skid pulled herself to her feet, dragging Beverly with her. She frowned at Dave. "Well, Brainiac?"

He ignored her and walked to the refrigerator that was the exact model from Cecelia Sanderson's kitchen, except for the color. "You traveled in time to September 19, 1984, to witness the actual murders of the Sanderson family." Dave's voice was flat, like an amusement park ride operator who followed the same script one hundred times a day for an entire season. He opened the door with his foot and scooted a beer onto the floor. It rolled away from him. "Now we're back, I think. Somebody want to get that?"

"I've got bars," the My Phone Doesn't Have Any Bars guy said. "This is great." He nudged Cord. "How much for the overnight stay?"

"Oh, yeah," the particularly pretty young woman in the pink blouse said. "I'm not going anywhere."

Cord nodded to Skid and turned toward what was once the door to the Sanderson's sunroom. "Anyone who wants to extend their stay, please come into my office." Everyone on the tour followed.

Except Beverly. She stood near the back door. "I'm sorry guys." Her voice steadier than it was in 1984. "But my car's outside. Before it was a Ford Pinto. I, uh, I gotta go."

"Beverly?" Brick started to move toward her.

Beverly paused, eyes wet, but not from drunkenness. Tears fell slowly down her cheeks. "I'm sorry," she whispered. "I like you. I really, really do." Beverly raised her right hand, thumb next to her ear, pinky by her mouth. *Call me*, she mouthed and walked into the night.

Brick stood still, his big chest moving in and out like a bellows. "I've lost her three times in the past four days."

"And you'll lose her again, big guy. Don't worry," Skid said, patting his chest. "Let's get these cuffs off."

Dave was easy enough. Skid poured a can of Coke into the sink and, after rummaging through drawers for a pair of scissors, cut a slim rectangle out of the can and bent it into a U.

"What do I do?" Dave asked as she stepped behind him. A click, and the left cuff came loose.

"Nothing," she said, then released the right.

Brick stood over her, watching. "Should I be worried you know how to do that?"

"Nope. I picked this up from the circus escape artist. She was pretty cool until she married an accountant and left to live in the suburbs. Somewhere in Ohio, I think." Skid held up the piece of aluminum. "This fits between the locking mechanism and the teeth.

Just tighten the cuffs while pushing on this and the teeth have nowhere to lock. The cuffs slide right open."

"But my cuffs are already as tight as they go," Brick said.

"Then this is going to hurt."

9

The Baked Nacho Cheese Doritos weren't as satisfying as Karl had hoped. They crunched, sure, and the cheese was there, but it was the greasy film Cheetos left on the inside of his mouth he really wanted. He wadded the empty foil bag and threw it on the floor of his office. Karl hated littering—so senseless, so random—but his trash can had already spilled onto the floor, and custodial kept phasing in and out of reality. He figured he didn't have much choice.

He exhaled in relief. His office was safe, his office smelled like home. It was one of three places in this lab he knew he was safe. He picked up a pen and jotted down a note: *Move vending machine from HR to Admin.*

The computer on Karl's desk beeped, drawing his attention from the growing mess on his normally spotless floor. The waves. *The Miller Waves.* Karl was proud to have named after himself because they were only getting stronger. That much was certain. The computer chimed each time the BAB-C emitted a Miller Wave, and the graph reflected a steady growth. Sure, there were smaller fluctuations, the Collison Effect, he called them, but they were only blips on the chart. They—

His office phone rang. Karl jumped in his space-age Aeron Chair complete with built-in hemorrhoid cushion. The motion sent it rolling back on its wheels. "What the heck?"

Line One on the sleek, black business phone blinked. No name on the soft blue readout to tip him off, and no number. Only one word: UNKNOWN. His phone hadn't made a sound since 9:32 a.m.

Saturday when he'd checked his voicemail. Gillian had called to tell him Collison would be late.

The phone rang again.

He wheeled his chair closer to the desk. The call had to be from outside the facility, and Karl had no idea what things were like on the outside.

Ring.

He moved a hand and gently picked up the receiver, a slight tremor in his arm shook like he'd had too much caffeine, which he hadn't. Karl Miller loathed coffee and thought tea too stuffy and presumptuous.

Ring.

He timidly reached his other hand toward the phone and hit the button for Line One then slid the receiver to his ear. "Hello."

Heavy breathing met his ear. *Gross.*

"Hello," he said, his voice louder. Karl Miller had little patience. "I can hear you."

A gurgle rattled through the line. Karl began to move the receiver from his ear to slam it onto the phone base, but then someone spoke, voice raspy.

"Karl."

A feeling crept inside him, a feeling he didn't like.

"Karl?" the man on the phone said again.

Karl knew that voice and didn't like the person it belonged to. In a facility full of people under his control, Karl felt nothing toward David Collison but contempt, no matter how sound the guy's mathematical mind was. That was one of the reasons Karl hired him, the other to repay an old debt. But here he was, on the phone. *It's about time you showed up.*

"What do you want, Collison?"

"They're *hss, crack,* Karl."

What? "What did you say?"

The man on the other end inhaled deeply before he spoke again. "I said *crack, pop* coming."

"You're breaking up." He was. The connection to the International Space Station was better than this. "You're not at work. Where are you?"

The speaker in the receiver screeched and Karl yanked it from his ear. When he put it back, Collison was already talking. "—in a truck. I time *hsss* —aveled *hsss, crack.* —most eaten *crack, hsss ⌐ ⌐ ⌐ ⌐ ⌐ ⌐.*"

Karl's world suddenly looked better. Collison was on the outside, which meant he was inside the experiment. If Karl was right, his experiment wasn't just doing anything—it was doing everything. He hoped the soldiers he'd sent through the Miller Ring were doing well.

"I'm sorry, Collison," Karl said, mashing the receiver to his ear. "Did you just say you traveled through time?"

"Yes *hsss.*"

"And were almost eaten by coyotes?"

"*Crack—*es."

Suddenly, all his anxieties washed away. The employees in HR, the serious lack of Cheetos in the facility, his ex-wife, Oscar, everything. *I'm still in control. I never lost it.* "That's marvelous."

The phone squealed again. When Karl put it back to his ear, the line had cleared.

"Where are you, Collison?"

The phone fell silent. *Oh, no. I lost him.*

"I don't know. *Click, crack.* I had to break into somebody's house to find a phone." Collison's voice trailed off. "I called 9-1-1," he said, the gurgling in his voice louder. "I'm hurt bad. I think my leg's infected, and I probably have internal bleeding from when the truck disappeared. I need an ambulance."

No, no, no. "Collison. I need you to keep it together. No ambulance. No authorities. This experiment is classified. You signed a

129

contract. If you go under some kind of drug, you may talk and mess up this whole thing. No—"

"You told me not to shut off the BAB-C," Collison said.

It was Karl's turn to fall silent. "I never told you that."

Sirens began to creep through the phone lines. The police, and Collison's ambulance, were getting closer. "Well," Collison said heavily, "whenever I show up, make sure you do."

CHAPTER SEVEN

SEPTEMBER 5

1

SKID WOKE in her own bed, yesterday as foggy as dusk in a summer camp slasher movie. *We have to turn off the BAB-C*, Dave had told them as they sat around the ruins of the murder house kitchen table while someone from the ghost tour screamed upstairs. "Although this is an amazingly simplistic answer, once the power's cut, the machine stops producing Miller Waves. Once the Miller Waves are gone, the universes stop colliding and—"

"And everything goes back to normal?" Brick asked.

"I don't know, maybe. It's the best shot we have to fix things."

Cord stood behind them with arms crossed. "Officially, I'm totally against this plan. It's going to seriously damage my income stream."

"So, when are we going?" Brick asked, his low voice pulled tight. "This is the closest I've ever come to an adventure."

Cord snorted. "A what? Listen to me. We can't do this. No, wait. I don't care what you do. *I* can't do this."

Brick flexed and looked down at the haunted house owner.

"We're going on an adventure. An honest-to-Eru Bilbo Baggins adventure." His smile looked like a mad grimace. "I'm ready to slay some orcs."

Skid, ignoring Brick and Cord, did something she had never envisioned herself doing. She wrote her address on the back of Dave's hand with a Sharpie from a notepad on Cord's fridge and told him to come get her in the morning. She needed a good night's sleep before saving the world. Skid handed the Sharpie to Brick, who swung it like a sword making "clang-clang" noises as she walked out the back door.

That was last night. This morning, well—?

It must be early, she thought, her brain still heavy with Melatonin. Mee Noi and Sirikit hadn't started yelling at each other as they prepped the Dumpling King for the early lunch crowd. Skid yawned and stretched. Maybe the WABAC or whatever stupid acronym these highly educated 14-year-old boys named the supercollider, had been shut off by someone with more sense than the idiot who turned it on. She could use more sleep.

But the poster on the wall above her bed bothered her. A kitten hung from a branch, the words *Hang In There* across the bottom. Skid liked kittens, and always felt sorry for this one, but she didn't have that poster in her bedroom. She had one wall decoration, a photo of Audrey Hepburn from *Breakfast at Tiffany's*. Anything more seemed too permanent.

"Damn it," she said aloud and hoped the sunlight that forced its way through the slits in the blinds were from her sun.

She rolled over and fell back to sleep.

2

The competition for what woke her was fierce. The speaker next to her front door buzzed to the tune of "Don't Stop Believin'" while down in the restaurant someone shouted. Usually it was Sirikit's high-pitched "You are a shitty cook" in Thai that reached all the way through the floor, but this morning's scream was different, guttural.

Skid's muscles didn't fight as she left the warm, clean sheets, her morning-after-crashing-into-a-table body not as sore as she'd feared.

"Beep-beep, Be-beee-beep."

"I'm coming," she mumbled and slid her bare feet across the clean, wood floors. The *Hang in There* poster was now a map of Middle-Earth stuck in place with masking tape. At least one Miller Wave had hit during the night. Skid wondered what else had happened.

She reached the living room. She now had different plants. A fern and peace lily instead of her dracaena and spider plant, a hanging tomato vine with three not-quite-ripe tomatoes instead of arugula, and what appeared to be a miniature rubber tree. The window curtains had been laid wide for maximum sunlight. She was concerned alternate-dimension Skid also had issues with stress.

"Beep-beep, Be-beee—"

She walked past the wall where her belt of throwing knives still hung and hit the speaker button. "What. The. Hell."

"We're here." The voice belonged to Dave.

"Who else is 'we'?"

"Me," Brick said.

"What about Cord?"

"Beeeeeep."

"Hey." Skid pounded on the speaker.

"Sorry."

"I told you it was the other button," Dave said in the background.

"Shut up," Brick said away from the microphone, then he must have turned toward it because the volume increased. "Cord still had people at his house. He said they'd be gone by noon."

Noon? She looked at the microwave oven; the time read 10:42. *We should have left hours ago.*

"All right, all right, all right." She flicked one of the tomatoes with a finger; it swung a few times then stopped. "We're late, but I'm going to take a shower. Go in the Thai place and get some dumplings. They may not be open. Tell them Skid sent you. I'll be down in a minute."

She pulled the knife belt from the wall as she walked toward the bathroom. She felt it might come in handy.

3

When Skid stepped outside, her knife belt obscured by a light jacket tied around her waist, Brick and Dave stood by her door like slackers in a Kevin Smith movie. Dave now wore shoes. A heavy backpack hung from Brick's shoulders, but Skid didn't care about that. She cared more that their hands were empty.

"Where are the dumplings? I'm starving."

"Uh," Dave started, but Brick cut him off.

"What kind of restaurant did you say that was?" He shoved a thumb at the building.

She frowned. "Thai. It's run by Mee Noi and Sirikit. They're a nice couple. Sort of."

"The place is full of Klingons," Dave shouted, then slapped a hand over his mouth.

Skid glanced in his direction, but the sign over the restaurant doors caught her eyes; the name 'The Dumpling King' had been replaced with 'Gagh wItlhutlhbej 'ej Qe'.' "What is *that*?"

"It's Klingonese." Brick stuck one hand in his jeans pocket, the other he waved around like he was delivering a lecture. "It means Gagh and Bloodwine Restaurant."

"What's gagh?" Skid asked.

"You don't want to know."

"You're awfully calm about this," Dave said, his voice ratcheted high.

Skid leaned on her left hip to look even calmer, but she wasn't. Not at all.

"So?"

"So?" Dave started pacing and Skid got a better look at his shoes, old tennis shoes someone used for yardwork.

"So," he continued. "There are Klingons in that restaurant. Not cosplay Klingons, actual Klingons. We walked in to ask for dumplings, and you know what they said? They said, 'DeKH delv gobeh quack naDEV oh,' then laughed. You ever hear a Klingon laugh? It's terrifying."

Sho stepped closer to Brick as Dave stomped around the sidewalk, never getting near the restaurant door.

"DeKH del what? What does that mean?"

"My Klingon's a little rusty, but I'm pretty sure they told us Federation credits are no good here."

"Damn it," she said, her voice tight with tension. "I need coffee." Skid started walking down Baltimore Avenue.

4

Sunlight didn't willingly shine through the dusty front windows of Dan's Daylight Donuts as much as it showed up for work because it had to. Dan sold them coffee and crullers in the shadowy shop interior and came from behind the counter later to top off their cups with mediocre coffee. He took no special notice of Brick; the big man just another customer.

"Dan and I don't get along," Brick said.

Skid's eyes followed Dan as he walked behind the counter to fish out two jelly doughnuts for a new customer, his face all smiles. "I don't think he knows you."

Brick sipped his coffee from a Styrofoam cup. "No, he doesn't. But whatever dimension we're in, he still makes shitty coffee."

Dave had calmed somewhat. He took a long, probably uncomfortably hot drink of his coffee and sat the cup down next to his cruller. "I can't get over those Klingons back there."

Skid took a bite of the doughnut. Bits of sugar glaze broke off and fell onto her napkin. "We need to focus. You said we need to turn off this BAB thing, right?"

Dave rested an elbow on the table and rubbed his temple. "Yeah. It's going to be difficult. It's a government facility, so there's security everywhere."

"But you have a key?" Brick pointed his half-eaten cruller at Dave, who reached a hand into his shirt and pulled out a key card on a lanyard.

Brick brushed off the bits of glaze. He wanted to know if that exact key card on that exact lanyard, the one the other Dave gave him in front of Tammy's Tanning Oasis, was still in his pocket. His fingers grazed the metal lanyard hook and hard plastic underneath.

"This will get us in," Dave said. "But—" He bit off a quarter of his doughnut and chased it with coffee.

"But?" Skid asked.

"But," he said. "I'm not exactly stable, am I? I keep popping in and out. Here." He tossed the key toward Skid. She didn't move. It slapped against the table. "You were supposed to catch that."

"Can we get in without you?"

He nodded. "Normally no. No chance in hell, but now, maybe. The lab is the launching portal of the Miller Waves. Things are probably more messed up there than anywhere else. We may see soldiers with machine guns or we may see sunflowers, and if we see soldiers, we just wait for the Miller Wave that turns them into sunflowers. I don't know. It's just—"

Dave shoved more fried, sugary dough into his mouth as Dan made his way to their table with a coffee pot.

"Anyone need more coffee?" he asked, a smile still on his face.

Skid motioned toward hers and he topped it off.

"Say," Dan said, nodding toward Brick's backpack on the floor next to the table. "You going camping?"

Brick didn't look at him. "No. It's a standard explorer's pack with a bedroll, mess kit, tinderbox, ten torches, ten days of simple rations, a full water skin and fifty feet of hempen rope."

Skid buried her face in her hand.

Dan stood next to Brick for a moment, rocking back and forth from his heels to the balls of his feet. "Weh-ell," he said, his laugh forced. "Good luck with that." He turned and took coffee to the next table.

Skid slapped Brick's arm, the back of her hand striking a bicep like a rock. "A full water skin and fifty feet of hempen rope? Seriously? Where does anyone get that?"

He hefted the backpack and bedroll. "It's standard equipment for Dungeons and Dragons Fifth Edition."

She opened her mouth to say something, then closed it. Then opened it again and closed it.

"We're getting off track." Dave waved at Dan and motioned toward his empty napkin. Dan grinned and moved toward the counter for more doughnuts. "If everything's normal, I'm going in myself, but in case I don't make it there—" He plucked the key card and lanyard from the table and tossed it toward Skid again. This time she caught it. "—you have to get into the lab and complete the mission."

Skid didn't look at the key card; she shoved it into her pocket. "Mission? *Mission?* Is this—"

Brick's hand fell on Skid's arm, and her eyes went to his. "Yes. It's a mission, Skid. It's an adventure, it's a dungeon, it's a campaign."

"Are there going to be dragons?" she asked, her voice not nearly as sarcastic as she'd planned.

"I freaking hope so." Brick handed Dave the Sharpie from Cord's fridge across his sugar flake-covered napkin. "Draw the map," Brick said, with the excited voice of a fourteen-year-old. "Draw the goddamned map."

The layout of Lemaître Labs seemed simple enough. It was a long low building set 100 yards off a rural highway south of Belton and west of Peculiar. Skid called BS on the name of the small town but dragged out her phone and Googled it. Peculiar, Missouri, population 4,979 as of the last census.

"That's so odd." Skid started to slide the phone back into her pocket but stopped and typed in 'Sanderson Murder House.'

"And that's even before the BAB-C went online," Dave said. "I used to go to Johnny's American Tavern there for lunch once a week. The pork tenderloin's worth it. Wing night's not too shabby either."

Skid ignored him while she texted the murder house phoneline. *We're at Dan's Daylight Donuts. Be here.* She set the phone on the table.

Brick's finger traced a dotted line Dave had drawn a good distance around the building. "What's this?"

"This," Dave said, "is the three-and-a-half meter-tall perimeter fence. It is 11-gauge chain link, the links 3.8 centimeters square with a top guard strung with 12-guage barbed wire. A security camera is stationed every six meters. There are roving patrol guards inside the fence that are always visible to one another."

Skid set aside her phone. Sitting back in her chair, she gripped her coffee cup in both hands. "If this building's so well protected, why's the fence so far away from it?"

"Explosives," Dave said. "There's a 60-meter buffer zone between the fence and the building in case someone tosses a bomb."

"That building's not the lab." Brick rocked back and forth in his chair. The energy wasn't from coffee. His nerd level had spiked. "Where's the lab?"

Dave moved Skid's napkin in front of him and started to draw. "You're right. The surface structure is reception, a conference room, human resources, accounting and a warehouse accessible only through Area 51-level security in the back. Now this—" He pressed the Sharpie to the napkin and drew a much larger structure. "—is underground. We have three layers. The first holds offices and a cafeteria."

"I thought you said you went out for lunch?"

Dave shrugged at Skid. "I didn't say the cafeteria was any good."
He sectioned off the level. "Here's my office, Karl Miller's office, the
offices of three other physicists, conference room and lunchroom. If
Miller's still there, he will give us trouble."

"Will he be armed?" Brick asked.

"I don't know," Dave said. "Maybe. He angers quickly and this is
his baby. Now—" He took Brick's napkin, unfolded it, and drew on
both halves. "The second level is engineering labs and the infirmary.
A lot of sensitive stuff happens in engineering, so it can be locked up
tight. You probably won't have to go there, so don't sweat it. However
—" He made an X in the hallway down from Human Resources.
"These are elevators. If the elevator in the hall is disabled, no way
you'll get to the one in engineering. It goes to a section sealed off from
the rest of the lab with one exit—into the Bridge. You'll have to use
the stairs." He marked the stairwell entrance with an O. "But you
probably don't want to do that."

Skid leaned toward the table to get a better look at the map.
"Why not?"

Dave twisted the Sharpie in his fingers. "Security. If the complex
is compromised, one switch shuts down the elevators forcing
unwanted elements to take the stairs. Once the invaders are in the
stairwell, another switch locks the doors and floods the three-story
chamber with chlorobenzylidene malononitrile—tear gas."

"What's that do?" Brick asked through the last of his cruller.

"Best case scenario: you cough a lot. Worst case: you die vomiting
blood."

"You government types don't mess around." Skid tapped the
clean section of napkin. "What's left?"

The Sharpie scraped across the napkin to create a shape the same
as the second floor. "We're getting closer to the BAB-C. It's three
more stories below the second floor, but nothing's in that space but
concrete. Enough concrete to withstand a MOAB."

"Wha—" Skid started.

"Mother of all bombs. I told you the government likes acronyms." He started sketching again. "The MOAB is the biggest explosive shy of an atomic bomb."

"Your BOBBIT is that important?" Skid asked.

Dave looked at her for a second before he spoke. "We conduct experiments that can tear the fabric of time and space. Yeah. It's that important. The Bridge is in the center of the collider, which itself is in a twenty-seven-kilometer-long circular tunnel 170 meters underneath the entire town of Peculiar and then some."

"Holy shit," Skid whispered.

"What I don't understand," Brick said, "is why you'd want to tear the fabric of time and space in the first place. I mean, don't you guys watch movies? This never ends well."

Daylight Dan stopped at the table with a tray of crullers, a basket of doughnut holes, and a stack of napkins. He winked at Skid. "The holes are on me," he said.

"Thank you." She grinned at the round, balding man as he walked to attend another table, and Brick wondered why she'd never smiled when she went to Manic Muffins.

Her phone chirped; she keyed in a few more words and sat it back down. Brick and Dave stared at her.

"It was Cord. He said he wasn't coming."

"And?" Brick asked.

"And I told him if he didn't, I'd travel back before he was born and kill his parents."

"Would you?" Brick asked, the words of Not-Dave echoing in his head. He picked up another cruller.

"I'm skilled in self-defense," Skid said, meeting his gaze, her eyes soft. "I'm no killer."

Brick took a bite of doughnut and chewed through a thought. No one knew he'd met Dave. Another Dave. He opened his mouth to speak—

Dave coughed, dragging their attention back to him. "The BAB-C," he continued, "is behind heavily fortified blast doors that you can get into with the card key. Once you get to this floor—" He drew an X by the elevator and O by the stairs and made arrows to a door. "—go to this room. It's the Bridge. It'll look like the command room of the Death Star." He pulled napkins from the tray and drew a board with lights and switches. "This is the master key, it's on the far-left portion of the board; right next to it is a big red button. Turn the key and mash the button."

Skid glared at Dave, who shifted a little in his seat. "And the machine will, what? Just turn off? What's going to happen when we hit the red button?"

The table fell silent, the murmur of other conversations seeping in. "Well," Dave said, "best case scenario—"

Skid slapped her hand on the table and the rest of the shop fell silent. She looked around at the faces staring back at her and mouthed "sorry."

"Please stop saying that," she said to Dave. "Just tell us what happens when we push the button."

The physicist stretched a hand to the back of his neck and rubbed, his face clenched in verbal constipation.

"One of two things. First—and this would be awesome—the power goes off and everything's back to normal." He paused and leaned forward on his elbows. "Second—and this is the sinker—hit that button and whomever is on that floor will probably be sucked into the hole in the universe they just created."

"Is there a third option?" Skid asked.

Dave took a long drink of his mediocre coffee and set the empty Styrofoam cup on the table. The bell over the door chimed, but no one at the table seemed to notice.

"Yes," he said. "We could choose to do nothing, allow Karl Miller's experiment to run its course and watch everything we've ever known and loved disappear and reappear again and again and again."

They were still sitting there in silence at Dave's words when the chair next to Skid pulled away from the table and Cord dropped into it. He grabbed a doughnut hole and pointed it at Skid.

"You," he said, taking a bite, "are a charmer. What did I miss?"

5

The darkness was complete. David woke on a cold, hard floor, his body beaten and ragged as an old sock. *Am I dead?* The words pushed from the deep recesses of his mind before consciousness pulled it back. David was in too much pain to be dead. Besides, he had to go to the bathroom. If he were dead, nature would have taken care of that for him. The small room smelled awful, a combination of ammonia and rot. He thought the rot might be him.

The ambulance had been so close to the farmhouse. The flashing lights of the emergency vehicle and sheriff's department Crown Vic had bathed the yard in reds and blues. The Miller Wave came next, engulfing the scene David watched from the kitchen window. He was the only one there who saw it; then the wave swept him away.

"Where am I?" he said. His voice, rough as a smoker's, shrank the room he was in considerably. David started to reach out a hand to feel around him when something moved outside the darkness.

A skittering, quiet at first, grew louder as something outside approached what David could only assume was a door. The footsteps clicked and shuffled as they grew closer, like tap dancers that couldn't decide between a shuffle and ball change. David laid his hands flat and pushed himself backward, away from the sound. His elbow hit a mop bucket, the impact sloshing dirty water onto the floor. It soaked into his pants, but he didn't notice.

"Cree?"

The sound from outside the door almost sounded like a rusty hinge, but it didn't come from anything mechanical; it came from something alive.

"Cree? Krrkrrrkrrrkrrrk, cree?"

David's bladder went, the warm urine mixing with the dirty mop water on the floor. *Oh shit. It's talking to me.*

The handle clicked and the door swung open a crack, the bright white light of a bright white room stabbed into the darkness. Then the door opened wide and David screamed. A bright green praying mantis filled the doorway. David screamed again.

The monster hissed and skittered backward, bumping against a hospital bed in the lab's infirmary.

David tried to push himself further into the wall, but couldn't because, well, physics. The insect, at least six feet tall, picked itself off the bed and rubbed its triangular head with the backs of its hooked front legs, smoothing out its antenna. Then it straightened its clean, white lab coat.

"Cree? Krrkrrrkrrrkrrrk, cree?" it said again, stepping cautiously closer.

David's bowels threatened to go next.

"Cree?

The monster's jagged feet clicked on the tiles. A nametag pinned to its coat read *Chet*. David's heartbeat began to slow, his breath deepened.

"Dr. Hahn?"

Then a memory, a brief mention, filled David's head. *Oh, shit. This is what they warned me about.*

His scream was deafening.

6

"No. Nope. Not happening." Cord walked on the outside of the sidewalk as they made their way back to the Sanderson Murder House. Because if anyone was going to get hit by a car, he hoped it would be him. "This is dangerous, this is not well thought out, this is illegal and it's—it's—did I say it's dangerous?" He shoved his hands in his pockets in case someone wanted to grab one. "I get why you're doing it, Skid. You're a control freak and all this ooga-booga stuff has made you uncomfortable. Or, or maybe it's a family issue."

Skid ignored him.

"Okay, maybe not." He turned to Brick, taking in his explorer's pack. "But you, your business is gone, your girlfriend is gone, and you hope this is all over by the time you get finished camping." Brick started to say something but didn't. "No. That's all wrong." Cord pointed at Dave. "*You* smell like rotting fish sandwiches from All-National Burger and—hey, why are you wearing my yard shoes?"

"You don't understand," Skid said, her eyes never leaving the sidewalk before her. Cord's house was half a block away.

"But me? I have something to lose," Cord continued. "Whatever this BAB thing is, it's caused my business to explode. The past two nights I've run tours, I made $1,400 a night. That's high-end stripper money. I feel like Bill Gates with a better haircut. But this? This is insane." He pulled his hands from his pockets and waved them around his head. "You people actually think it's a good idea to try and break into a heavily-guarded secret government facility? Fine. I'll read about your trial in the paper."

Brick stepped in front of everyone and stopped in the middle of the sidewalk. He turned around and loomed over Cord.

"You're part of this," he said, his voice too gentle for a man that big and hairy. "You went to 1984 and profited, you profited from the murder of a wife, a son and their dog. Even though you did nothing to start the destruction of multiple universes, if you do nothing now, you're as complicit as those who caused it." He leaned toward Dave and whispered, "No offense."

A frown creased Cord's normally smile-afflicted face. "That is a dick move," he said. "I've prided myself on a clean police record, my life post-car salesman is close to making me feel as cool as I felt in high school, and Tamara Hooper's already paid for tonight while her hot vampire boyfriend is too scared to come. But overall, what you're suggesting we do might not get us arrested. We may be shot first. We can't do this. I wish someone would listen to me."

"My dad was a jackass," Skid said, her words abrupt.

Cord stopped. "What?"

"My dad," she repeated. "Was a jackass. But he was right some of the time. One of his favorite lines was, 'If something needs done, do it.'"

"Sounds like something Andy Griffith would say, but—"

"But that wasn't all," she said over Cord. "It was, 'If something needs done, do it. Most people won't.'"

Cord frowned. "So? What does that have to do with me?"

"Don't you get it? We're the only ones who know about this. Nobody else is going to fix the universe." Skid stared down Cord. "Do you have a car?"

"Yeah."

She walked past him and stopped at his gate. "You're driving."

7

The stark terror of a 1950s horror flick in a lab coat subsided once the mantis injected midazolam and David started to relax. The insect with Dr. Chet Hahn's name tag at least seemed to know what it was doing. A thought nagged at David. A warning, or some damn thing that had seemed important just a few minutes ago. But in the haze of the drug, it was gone.

The creature helped David off the custodial closet floor by grabbing his shoulders in its hooked front arms and lifting him effortlessly. David winced as his bloody, infected leg dangled below him.

"Krrkrrrkrrrkrrrk?" it asked, laying him gently atop the clean white sheets of the hospital bed. "Cree? Cree?" It thumped a hypodermic needle and injected something into David's arm.

"No. I'm not all right," David said, worry bleeding from him. "I think my leg's infected."

"Cht, cht, cht."

Dr. Hahn plucked surgical scissors from an instrument tray using surprisingly agile chitinous forelegs and sliced David's slacks, gently peeling them from his leg like it was a banana. A putrid stench wafted up to David's nostrils.

"Creet, creet?"

"Yeah, it's infected all right," David slurred. "Can you fix it?"

"Cht, cht, cht." Dr. Hahn skittered to a sink and washed his claws, returning to the table with a bowl of liquid and a jar of long cotton swabs. "Krrkrrrkrrrkrrrk?"

The mantis washed the infected knife wound and cleaned inside it with the cotton swabs. The pain was there, but also far away.

"You know," David said, his words oozing out long and slow. "You had me worried with the whole praying ma—" A yawn broke his thoughts. He didn't remember what he was saying. David tried to focus heavy eyes on the doctor, but the damn mantis wouldn't stand still. The room began to waver like a heat mirage. "So, how's your golf game? Those tibial spines must play hell with your back swing." David thought he asked before his brain dropped off a cliff and everything turned black.

8

The road south was dead. Cord's Toyota hummed alone down Interstate 435, a beltway that encircled Kansas City and would eventually intersect with the US 71, which would then take them to the junction of Routes J and C south of Belton. The lab was on one of those rural highways to the west.

"Hey, guys," Cord said, pointing toward a sign that read, *Kansas City Zoo: Next right.* "Instead of committing a federal crime, how about we go to the zoo? We can take pictures of the elephants, feed the penguins and play chess with the orangutans because they can probably fucking talk by now."

Dave laughed from the back seat. "That would be pretty cool."

Cord pounded the steering wheel with the heel of his hand. "No," he said between gritted teeth. "It would not. I can't believe that with a scientist, a baker and a—" he paused and looked at Skid in the rearview mirror "—a potentially dangerous felon, that I'm the voice of reason. And I cheat honest, hard-working suckers for a living. In no way should we be doing this."

It was the college road trip to White Castle all over again. You drive, Cord. You're a great D.D., Cord. Hey, you wouldn't mind if me and Melanie made out in the back seat, would you? Just put on some tunes so you can't hear it.

"Melanie was *my* girlfriend," he said under his breath.

Brick leaned over and whispered loudly enough everyone could hear. "Who's Melanie?"

"Whoa." Dave leaned closer to the front seat and tapped Cord's shoulder. "Stop the car."

"What?"

He fell back into his seat. "Do I not speak loudly enough? None of you seem to hear me the first time." He coughed into a closed fist and yelled. "Stop the car."

The Toyota screeched to a halt.

"What?" Cord repeated, but Dave had already released his seat belt and stepped onto the highway. Cord turned toward Brick, who'd opened the passenger door and lifted his bulk onto the Interstate, dragging his explorer's pack with him.

"Skid?" Cord asked, but her seat was already empty. "Shit." He flicked the door handle and followed them outside. "This is surprisingly worse than the road trip to White Castle."

Dave stood on the concrete shoulder and stared south. A Quik-Trip sat at the bottom of a nearby off-ramp, and an apartment and office buildings lined the highway. Dave stretched, his dirty shirt rippling in a soft breeze that blew from the west.

"What is it?" Skid asked, hands resting on her knife belt.

The scientist pointed. "Do you see the spot that looks like a storm?"

She nodded; part of the southern sky had turned dark purple. "Yeah. It's a thunderstorm."

"No," Dave said. "It's not."

Brick threw his pack over his shoulders and stepped next to the scientist. A mass of clouds on the near horizon curved over themselves like a fist. It looked like a weather front, but if it were a storm, the wind that brushed his beard came from the wrong direction. "What is it?"

"A Miller Wave," Dave said. "The biggest one I've seen."

Cord slammed both hands onto the hood of his car. "Hey, Bill Nye. Does size matter? Do we need to scratch out wills on the McDonald's napkins in the glove compartment?"

Brick considered him from across the roof of the Toyota. "You don't have a will?"

"What?" Cord asked.

"He doesn't seem to be able to hear you either, Brick," Dave said. "Maybe he has a hearing problem." Dave looked at Cord. "Do you have a hearing problem?"

Cord leaned against the car on his elbows and rubbed his temples with both hands. "No. I don't have a hearing problem and I don't have a will."

"That's awfully short-sighted of you." Brick had a thumb hooked in a strap of his explorer's pack and looked like a guy taking a break from grad school to backpack across Narnia. "Think of your family."

"I don't have a—"

"Stop it," Skid said, but she might as well have shouted. It had the same effect. "It's coming in fast."

The green-rimmed, undulating clouds rolled onto the highway, its center a deep twisting chasm.

"Do we need to get back in the car?" Cord asked. "We could try to outrun it."

"No." Dave stood on the shoulder, his hands at his sides, watching the incoming interdimensional tempest sweep across southern Kansas City. "Trying to outrun it would be futile."

"Resistance is futile," Brick echoed him. The oncoming wave was even larger now, reality folding in on itself as the wave approached.

Dave swung his head toward Brick and grinned. "Let's hope it's not Locutus of Borg. Am I right?"

"You two can nerd-bond later," Skid said, walking to the front of the car. "Can we do anything about what's about to happen to us?"

The wave had reached a juncture where the highway merged with the US 350, maybe two miles away. "No," Dave said. His gaze landed on the QuikTrip. "Wait. Yes, we can. I'm going for beer. Anybody coming with?"

Everyone stood watching the anomaly crash toward them as Dave trudged down the thick, weedy grass of the embankment toward the convenience store. The green-tinged storm grew a deeper violet. Thunderless lightning crackled in the chaos.

"Hey, Dave," Brick called down the slope. "You watching this?"

Dave shoved a hand into the air and waved as the storm reached them, sweeping across the landscape, obscuring the world in a Saran Wrap haze. Then the Miller Wave hit, this time with force, like being slapped with a laundry sack of Jell-O. The push knocked Skid backward onto Cord and they both went down. Brick stood through the onslaught of one dimension crashing into another. Then the wave was gone, cascading past them to the north.

"Don't touch anything you'll regret touching later," Skid said, pushing herself off Cord.

"You guys okay?" Brick asked, then his eyes hit the landscape around them. "Oh, wow."

The world had changed. Fields of prairie grass rippled like ocean waves in every direction, punctuated by occasional patches of deciduous trees. The apartment buildings, the business centers, and the QuikTrip had vanished, replaced by great, jagged lumps of rock.

"Dave?" Brick called.

No answer.

"He disappeared again." Skid walked around a boulder to stand next to Brick.

"Yeah," Brick said. "He went all Gandalf. One minute he's here, the next minute he's off dealing with the Necromancer."

Skid ignored him, scanning the prairie. "It looks like Europeans haven't shown up to pour concrete over everything yet."

"Yeah," Brick agreed. "I wonder what else happened."

"Hey," Cord said behind her. "Where's my car?"

9

The white ceiling over the land of white floors seemed too far away to be in the same room as David. His eyes rolled as he tried to focus. Green. Something green stood in the room. *Oh, yeah. My doctor.*

"Ha," David may have yelled, although he couldn't hear himself. At least, he thought his mouth moved.

Dr. Chet Hahn pulled a stitch through David's leg with the green things it used for hands. At David's shout, it raised one limb to its insecty face and hissed before slipping the needle back into David's leg and tightening another stitch.

He's shushing me? The midazolam still had him, although his brain was starting to shake it off. David tried to give a thumbs up but the most he could do was a smile.

The mantis doctor threaded another stitch and tied it off, clipping off the surgical filament with his mandibles. *Whoa,* tried to push itself into the small part of David's brain that still cared, but failed. Those jaws were sharp, but Chet was a doctor, right?

Dr. Hahn dabbed David's stitches with a saline solution and peeled the sterilized protection strips from a large adhesive bandage, stretching it across the wound before leaning back on its four powerful rear legs to admire the work.

"Chhhhttt. Cht. Chit."

Yeah, doc. It's great, David wanted to say, but he just mouthed like a fish.

"Chhhttt. Krrrkrrrkrrreeee?"

The mantis loomed over the bed, and David's world turned dark. Its triangular head moved closer, its enormous eyes moving independently of each other. *Stop it,* David thought, his pulse starting to race despite the drug in his system. *Stop it. Stop moving, please.*

Dr. Hahn shook his head and rubbed it with a forearm before lifting another hypodermic off the stainless-steel instrument table to insert into David's arm.

"Chhhttt. Krrrkrrrkrrreeee?" it repeated.

"Whaaa—" wheezed out of David as the mantis lifted his arm and bit off one of his fingers.

10

The prom dress was uncomfortable. Skid pulled at the parts that gripped her in places tighter than she liked and tried to shift them to the places that were too loose. It was impossible. Jimmy Nikola sat in the back seat with her, a comfortable enough distance away, Skid's pink corsage between them in the kind of clear plastic box convenience stores put breakfast sandwiches in. Randall R. Roe drove. He insisted. It was his baby girl's first school dance with a date, so hell yes, he insisted. The circus spent the winter months in Prescott, Arizona, where Randall sent his daughter to public school, 'to be around some normal people,' but that and the wisdom of Constantinople Phargus weren't her only education. During the business year, a teacher traveled with them to make sure the circus kids weren't getting shortchanged by their parent's choices.

Randall had picked up Jimmy at his house in an aged Chrysler New Yorker, smiled as he introduced himself to Jimmy's parents, Jimmy Sr. and Caroline, who already seemed two or three Cuba

Libres into the evening, and promised to take good care of their boy. No hanky panky. Nope. Not on Randall R. Roe's watch.

A few miles later, the New Yorker ran out of gas and Randall pulled a dented metal gas can and rubber hose from the trunk. He handed it to Skid.

"Why do *I* have to do it?" she'd asked.

"Because I promised Jimmy's parents I'd make sure nothing happened to him."

"I'll be okay," Jimmy said.

Randall rounded on him. "You shut up, son, and lock that door. I don't like the looks of this neighborhood."

"But what about me?" Skid asked, finding it hard to believe—but only superficially—that her father was sending her to siphon gas in a bad neighborhood on prom night. She stood next to the crumbling curb in the pastel ankle-length dress, her face now as pink as the corsage she hadn't put on.

Randall smiled. Skid remembered that. He smiled that *I can sell anyone anything* smile and said, "You can take care of yourself, kiddo." Then he slid back into the car and locked his door.

Skid walked nearly six blocks before she found a car in a dark, shaded spot far enough from the street no one driving by would see her siphoning gas. On the way back to the New Yorker and her date, tears streaking the makeup Randall finally let her wear, a young guy in an Anthrax T-shirt, already missing his front teeth, asked if she wanted to go someplace and get funky. He still may not have the use of his right knee, but that wasn't her worry. Her worry was walking six blocks in meth town in a prom dress carrying five gallons of gasoline. Randal's worry of hanky-panky would never happen anyway. She doubted she could find enough gum to remove the taste of regular unleaded from her mouth.

She never again asked her father if she could go to a school dance.

"You're not suggesting we walk," Skid said to Brick, no question in her voice. "I hate walking. It's just like prom night."

The grin across Brick's face had pulled so tight, it probably hurt. "Of course we're walking," his voice loud, not yelling, booming. "We have to walk, just like the Fellowship, just like Thorin and Company, just like young Spock when he ventured into the Vulcan's Forge mountain range to look for his lost shelat."

Cord turned to Skid. "What's he talking about?"

"Don't ask." She shouted at Brick's broad back, "Hey, Mortimer Nerd. Do you have a plan?"

"A walking stick," Brick said like he hadn't heard her. He'd already started hiking south on the path of the last Miller Wave. "I need to find a good walking stick. Everybody needs a good walking stick. Bilbo liked walking sticks."

"But," Cord said, his voice not reaching far enough for anyone to care, "I have a ghost tour tonight."

Skid increased her pace and touched Brick's hairy arm. "Brick," she said. "Do you have a plan?"

He stopped with and expression like he hadn't known she was with him. "Yes, walk."

She held back the frustration—and, if she was admitting it, the fear—from her voice. "Okay, yes. Walk. But how far?"

He licked a finger and held it up to test the breeze for no apparent reason.

"It was about twenty miles to the lab when we started," Brick said, "and we drove at least five of that. According to Dungeons and Dragons 5e rules, a party traveling at fast speed can go thirty miles per day; slow is eighteen. For us? We should be ready for battle or whatever by tomorrow afternoon." He took a deep breath and began to sing as he started to walk again, his voice low and mournful. "Roads go ever, ever on. Over rock and under tree, by caves where never—"

Skid pushed past him. "I swear to God, Brick, you are not going to make this any worse for me."

"You keep thinking that, Skid of the Black Gloom," Brick said, "but before this is over, some lady warrior is going to wish she had 50 feet of hempen rope and a full water skin."

She slapped her thigh. "Let's just get this over with," she said, marching through prairie grass that came to her waist. "Keep up, Cord, and watch for anything that might want to eat us. That's all we need."

CHAPTER EIGHT

MORE SEPTEMBER 5

1

THE DIM LIGHT WAS DISORIENTING. The Miller wave hit just as Dave opened the glass door of the convenience store, the undulating purple storm enveloping him and the whole damn place. He stepped out of the wave into a long room filled with shiny furniture and said, "shit." Karl Miller stomped in moments later, grinning like an idiot.

I'm in the lab conference room. Then he said, "Shit" again.

"Why's it so dark in here?" Dave asked, casually dropping into a comfy office chair and slapping the heels of Cord's yard shoes onto the conference table, the same table where Friday he had told Karl his math might do exactly what it was now doing. "And do you have any beer squirreled away in this joint? I think I'm going to need some."

Karl smiled. Dave made that out by a glint in the darkness. "We have some imported beer for the brass. Alcohol seems to make them a little more agreeable when we tell them something they don't want to hear."

Dave joined his hands and formed his index fingers into a steeple, then he opened the doors to see all the people. "You can fetch me one. I'll wait."

Karl pushed back the rolling office chair and slowly stood, whatever effect he was trying totally lost on Dave.

"I'm actually glad you showed up, Collison," he said, sitting on the corner of the table, his tacky J. C. Penney slacks stretched across his thigh. "I have a little problem."

"Slamming dimensions together through black holes cooked up in our little Easy-Bake Oven isn't going the way you'd hoped?"

This time, Karl barked a laugh in the gray haze. He was playing this one well. "Yes, and no," the man who smelled like Cheetos said. He wheeled his chair next to Dave and dropped into it. "There have been some, um, complications in the experiment, but we never planned on finding the particle behind the God Particle."

This wasn't right. That was the plan. That had always been the plan.

"But—"

Karl leaned close to Dave. "Come on, Collison. Think about it. Why would the United States government give a rip about discovering the building blocks of the universe?"

That had never occurred to him. "I'll take one of those beers now."

Karl pushed his chair even closer. Dave could make out his eyes; he didn't like it.

"The United States government cares about three things," Karl continued. "Keeping its citizens complacent, keeping its enemies distracted, and looking for anything—anything—to have the upper hand." He moved back enough that his crazy eyes were in the shadows again. "That was our purpose the whole time, to find a hand so high the rest of the world couldn't see it until we slapped it down."

Cord's yard shoes hit the floor as Dave pushed back, putting a few feet between him and his most probably former shit-house-rat crazy boss. "No," he said. "The team would have known. Dana, Marcus, Oscar—"

Karl's head moved side-to-side like a bobblehead. "Compartmentalization. That's how the government works, Collison." He held up his hands and waved them out of sync. "Right one doesn't know what the left one is doing. I'm the only one who did."

"And my foster father. How did he fit into this?"

"He started it all," Karl said, spinning in his chair. "The project germinated from his idea. He may have even been the one to see it to completion if he hadn't sliced and diced his family." He paused, waiting for Dave's countenance to change. It didn't.

Things began to fall into place inside Dave's head. He never knew what the guys in engineering were doing, not really. *And Oscar? Dana? Marcus?* They had their niches. *Just like me.* "Why did you show us your figures in Friday's meeting?"

The scientist leaned forward and patted Dave's leg before he stood and walked toward the sleek metal lectern at the head of the conference table. "I was the only one who'd gone over them." He pushed a section of wall, which sprang toward him, revealing a refrigerator filled with bottles and cans of everything from water to beer to Pepsi Ice Cucumber imported from Japan. He plucked out two bottles of Harps and an Ozarka water.

"I needed somebody with brains to tell me I was right." He opened both beer bottles with a church key from inside the refrigerator and walked them over to Dave, setting the beers on the table before opening the water and taking a drink.

Dave took one of the beers. "So, the government was looking for a way into other dimensions," he said to himself. "And eras." He looked at Karl. "I went back in time—twice."

"I know." The grin on the Cheetos-smelling cocksucker was huge. "That was something I'd suspected might happen, but you actually doing it?" He lifted his arms for a touchdown. "Score."

Goddamnit.

Karl went behind the lectern and flicked a few switches. Panels on a large screen at the opposite end of the table lighted. One showed the hallway that went through HR, where man-sized lumps shifted in the shadows just outside the lights of the hall. One screen revealed a section of engineering that led to the Bridge, the heavily reinforced door dented.

"What's thi—"

A figured jumped at the camera, filling the lens, its body covered in hair, its knife-like teeth the last thing Dave saw before that panel went blank.

"Holy shit," Dave yelled.

"That was Dr. Oscar Montouez."

The bottom of Dave's beer thudded against the table. "No," he whispered. Oscar, Marcus and lab physician Chet Hahn came over to Dave's place for cards every couple of weeks, and Oscar usually joined Dave at Johnny's American Tavern for wing night. "It can't be."

"This is fun," Karl said.

Dave started to rise from the plush office chair and punch that Cheetos-smelling Karl Miller right in his smug face, but Karl clicked another button and something appeared on the screen that froze Dave in his seat.

Dr. David Collison, a three-day growth of beard, was lying unconscious on a hospital bed. This David wore the same shirt Dave wore, although dirtier, and the same pants, although the left leg had been cut and a wound in the thigh treated. A scrape across his cheek glistened with salve. "That, that's me."

Karl stood behind the lectern, the water bottle hovering at his lips. Something came into the frame, its movement smooth and jittery at the same time. It hovered over the David on the hospital bed, cleaning its horrible jagged mandibles with the backs of its forelegs.

"What's that thing?" Dave demanded, swinging toward Karl. "What's it doing?"

Karl lowered the water bottle, a grin shined on his face. "You showed up out of nowhere earlier. You were pretty banged up. Looks like a puncture wound in your leg became infected." He waved his bottle at Dave. "That's not *you*, you, of course. You're here and he is there. He must be you from somewhere else."

Dave sank deeply into the chair. He'd figured out that much on his own, but—"What the hell is that thing?"

"Oh, that? That's Dr. Chet Hahn, our lab physician. You know Chet. You guys used to go to that place in Peculiar for lunch. He's a giant praying mantis now."

On any normal day before last Friday, Dave's brain would have locked up like the engine of an old Dodge. He may have dropped to the floor drooling, or he may have run screaming toward the door, only to pound on it futilely because he'd given a woman named Skid his key, but not today. A giant praying mantis in a lab coat wasn't his greatest worry.

"Where'd he come from?"

Karl took a slow drink of bottled water. "I don't know, but isn't he magnificent?" he said. "That's Dr. Chet Hahn from some other dimension, and he's exactly what the government hired me to find. Can you imagine a dimensional collision that would leave the United States Army with a division of soldiers that looked like that monster? The enemy would run away thinking that Hell itself was upon them. That guy's terrifying—and he's a doctor. Imagine what a professional wrestler, or a biker, would look like."

The mantis rubbed its head and slipped a sock off the David-on-the-table's foot.

"What's he doing?" Dave asked.

"He's got you doped up on something," Karl said. His eyes gleamed in the darkness. "Good old Chet's been eating you alive for the past couple of hours. It's hypnotic, isn't it?"

2

They walked until nearly sunset. The topography of wherever they were consisted of brown prairie grass dotted with an occasional boulder and patch of trees, the world looking like an enormous sausage and broccoli pizza. Brick found a walking stick, a crooked six-foot-long dead branch he'd plucked from the leaf-covered floor of a small wooded grove. He started humming after that; Skid didn't know how much longer she could stand it.

She also didn't know how many miles they'd pushed through the grass. Brick threw out some "party traveling at fast speed can go blah-blah-blah miles per day" bullshit. Was that miles on a flat, even surface? Miles in the mountains? Miles walking across the foreshore holding a daiquiri? *Life isn't Dungeons and Dragons, Brick. I can't believe I just said that to myself.* Skid did know exhaustion kept taking experimental jabs at her. Not physically—she could keep up this pace all day—but mentally. Her soul felt tired, like one of the universes they kept intersecting with had descended onto her head and nested there.

Brick walked in front because of "initiative marching order" or something else Skid, and she expected Cord, didn't care about. She wasn't going to argue, partly because Brick had taken control of their little group like a mad knight, and partly because it didn't matter which one of them got to the lab four feet ahead of the other. They were all going to get there. At least, she hoped. They topped a small rise in the gently sloping prairie and Brick stopped, not suddenly and without a reason, but slowly, bending his knees as if he didn't expect to stand still for long. He raised his arm level with his head, his hand in a fist.

"We need to make camp," Brick said swinging his thick arm toward an expanse of trees at the floor of the slope. "We can hide there."

"From what?" Cord asked. "We've been walking all day, and the only things I've seen are butterflies. They're pretty, I'll give you that, but I doubt they'll smother me in my sleep."

The big man's head moved slightly in disapproval. "You don't know that."

Skid stood straight, cupping her elbows in her hands and ignoring the men, which she figured was for the best. The woods below seemed harmless enough, and the orange, yellow, and pink clouds that spread across the darkening blue in careful streaks looked like finger paints. She wanted to sit someplace soft, eat a sandwich and drink water, none of which she realized might exist in this reality except inside Brick's explorer's pack.

"Come on," she said, starting the march down the rise. "Let's make camp like the dungeon master suggested."

Cord followed, but Brick stayed, stuck in place. "You're breaking initiative marching order."

She waved at him from over her head, not looking back. "I rolled a twenty."

"Natural or with your dex modifier?"

I wish babysitting the universe came with a salary so I could say I'm not getting paid enough for this, bounced around her head. "Natural. Everything about me is natural. Now start moving before one of Cord's butterflies straight-up kills you."

3

The mantis started with the semi-conscious man's toes and worked itself up to his ankle before stopping to apply a tourniquet and elevate the leg in a traction apparatus. The man who looked like Dave moaned, but didn't call out. If he was on the type of drug Dave thought he was on, the man might need to scream but couldn't. The giant insect pulled a blood-stained white handkerchief from its lab coat pocket and dabbed the blood from its mandibles before scraping out of camera range. It obviously wanted to keep this other Dave alive while it devoured him.

The crack of a beer bottle opening came from Dave's left, but he didn't look. His eyes were fixed on the man on the table. Karl took Dave's empty bottle, his second still half full, and placed a full bottle on the table.

"You make a hell of a bartender, Karl," Dave said, not turning his head. There was something wrong with this picture, besides the giant sentient mantis and his dying Doppelgänger. Something he couldn't latch onto.

Karl pulled out a chair and sat next to him. "You seem to be holding up well, Collison. I'm surprised and, I hate to admit it, a little impressed. I thought you were weaker than this."

The beer in the second bottle had begun to warm. Dave drained it and set it in front of Karl. "So, this was always the plan," he said. "Not looking for the particle beyond the God Particle but looking for a way into other dimensions."

"Yes." Karl picked up Dave's empty and turned it in his hands. "Don't be upset that I lied to you. I lied to everybody. It was the best way to get the job done."

Dave nodded because he knew it was true. Compartmentalization was common for top secret projects because it worked. If no one knew what anyone else was doing, the chance of them talking no longer mattered.

The man on the screen moaned, although Dave couldn't hear him. The other David turned his head slightly, facing away from the security camera, which was all he could do under the medication; his arms and left leg strapped to the table to keep them stable. Not at the wrists or ankles, of course, because he no longer had them. There was something wrong with the man's head, though. *But what?*

"Where did he come from?" Dave asked.

Karl stood back up. The man never had been able to sit still long, even in the meetings he conducted. Dave's boss tended to wander around the room and wave his arms as if delivering a lecture on Italian stereotypes.

"The mantis?" He stopped and eyed Dave before a grin crept across his face. "No. You. Where did you come from? The buffet you, am I right?"

Dave shrugged, toying with the bottle in front of him. "Yeah, sure. There are two David Collisons in this facility. Aren't you a bit curious?"

The room fell silent for a moment. The other David Collison appeared to moan again, and Dave was happy the security camera didn't have audio.

"I am." Karl started walking toward the screen then changed direction. "Or, I was. When he showed up in the infirmary, I thought he was you, obviously."

"Obviously."

The Cheetos-smelling scientist walked toward the screen and tapped Infirmary David with a finger.

"But then you showed up, and there he is. He looks, hmm, different from you, don't you think? Beaten, worn down, even filthier than you are—and do you see his face? The beard growth? Yours is just a few days, but his? He looks like he hasn't shaved in a week." He moved from the screen and placed his palms on the table. "However, that is you, Collison. You from the future, or somewhere else. It doesn't really matter."

Could that be possible? Dave wondered. The image of his grandfather alive just a few days before dragged itself into his thoughts. *Of course, it could.*

"How about we test that hypothesis." Karl jumped up again, marching to the head of the table. Dave took another drink of Harps. "What day is it?"

"September 4, maybe? Things have been kind of jumbled lately," Dave said, picking at the label on the bottle. "No. It's the fifth. It's September 5."

Karl smiled. "That is correct. If I asked Mr. NoFeet Dave, I bet he'd tell me it was September 9, or September 10." He looked back at the screen, sweeping an arm like a game show model presenting a new car. "You're you. He's probably future you."

The David on the screen's eyes fluttered and he moved his head again, slightly, beginning to fully wake.

"I don't think I want to watch this anymore," Dave said. "Isn't there a game on, or something?"

A laugh erupted from Karl, a deep-down fuck you laugh. "No. No, no. I'm having way too much fun." He pointed toward the screen. The mantis had shuffled back into view holding a hypodermic. "Looks like our friend Dr. Hahn is back."

Then Dave saw it. The thing that had bothered him. The thing that wasn't right. It was the David on the hospital bed's facial hair. Sure, it was just growth the man would shave off if he lived through being eaten by a giant insect and got prosthetic hands, but it wasn't the beard that caught Dave's attention. The man had sideburns, short ones, but definite sideburns. Dave had never worn sideburns—ever. *That's different-dimension me.*

Dave leaned backward in his chair, placing his borrowed shoes back onto the conference tabletop, and drained the bottle in his hand. He waved it toward Karl. "Hey, get me another beer, will you?"

4

Afternoon began its ritual flirt with dusk, the golden hour fading, the sky transitioning from azure to cornflower to whatever hue of blue Crayola chose to put in a box. Tamara Hooper sat on the front steps of the Sanderson Murder House staring at the nineteen other people who'd paid good money to tour a certified piece of Kansas City history. Whether the murder house was actually certified, and if so, who had certified it, none of the people standing in Cordrey Bellamy's yard knew or cared. Cord had thrown those words onto the website now bustling with reservations because they sounded good. The sale is, of course, all about the presentation.

Tamara recognized a few of them, like the nurse who'd been on Friday's tour, and the woman with her son. The rest were new faces. The guy in the KCFD T-shirt, the goth woman in gray and black, and the tall somber woman. She wore her dark hair streaked naturally with silver, and stood alone in the back of the group not talking to anyone, looking at the house like it might bite her.

Tamara regretted coming tonight. *But there are reasons,* she reminded herself. Friday, she'd seen a ghost. A real live ghost, although Roman would correct her on that, but screw him. She also came because she thought Cord was cute. Roman—

Pfft. Roman.

Roman was pretty. *You know, like those vampires on TV,* as she'd told her friends, and decent in the sack, but he couldn't hold a conversation that didn't include protein shakes, how many reps he did at the gym, and how stupid the people in his office were because they didn't recognize Justin Beiber's artistic genius. Cord, on the other hand, was cute and funny. Tamara wanted to talk to him, you know, just talk, all night long. Then maybe have sex in the morning—and pancakes. Definitely pancakes.

"Our tour was supposed to start half an hour ago," said a forty-something guy in a business suit who'd probably come straight from work. He'd pulled his blue and green paisley tie loose and undone his top button, but still looked uncomfortable. "Anybody have this guy's phone number?"

The faces went from bored to the-hell-with-this.

Business-suit guy threw his hands up. "I'm not waiting anymore. Nothing's worth this bullshit. Anybody with me?" A few people murmured in agreement. Someone gave a half-hearted cheer and the group began to disperse.

Tamara did something she didn't quite understand. She stood and faced the group. She didn't know why, but she thought of these people as her group. She'd been there/done that. "Wait. I know you paid for a ghost tour and Cord's not here to give you one, but there must be a good reason."

She bit her bottom lip as conflicting thoughts collided in her head. She pushed apart the bushes around the front door but didn't find what she was looking for.

"I have to go around back." She raised her hands. "Wait. Just a minute."

She scuttled past a green water hose hanging in loops around a tin rack next to a faucet and a garden gnome grinning at her from beneath a bush. She bent down, searching. Still nothing.

The back door sat silent, locked and unwelcoming.

"You gotta be here," she mumbled, poking through the bushes growing on either side of the four-step back entrance. Then she saw it —a rock that wasn't a rock. She picked up the fist-sized lighter-than-advertised faux stone and turned it over, opening a sliding door with her thumb. "Bingo."

Thirty seconds later, Tamara Hooper opened the front door of the Sanderson Murder House and let everyone in.

5

The trees looked normal enough. Brick said they were elm, hickory and maple with an occasional fir thrown in just to keep things interesting. Skid was just happy the tops were green, the bottoms were brown and not one tried to attack them like those asshole trees in *The Wizard of Oz*. Cord gathered firewood as Brick cleared a spot down to the dirt and made a ring of fist-sized stones he pulled from a nearby creek.

"Were you a Boy Scout?" Skid asked as she sat, leaning into a tree and hugging her knees.

Brick shook his shaggy head, gently piling dried moss and last fall's leaves into the center of the stones.

"No. I just read a lot." Small sticks the size of chopsticks came next, followed by pencil-sized, then pieces as thick as Brick's thumb.

"I've been thinking about the Klingons," he said, not looking up from his task.

Skid picked up a stick from the base of the tree and tossed it into the woods before she realized they could have used it.

"I haven't," she said. Brick's demeanor had changed since Dave had gone waltzing off into time and space. He'd become excited, jittery, like he knew something was coming. Something big.

Cord walked into the small clearing under the shade of an ancient tree none of them knew the name of. He knelt and stacked his armload of branches next to the ring of stones.

"Klingons?" he said, holding up a branch like a pistol. "You mean, 'You are without honor,' 'Pew, pew' Klingons? Like from *Star Trek*?"

Brick stopped arranging the tinder and glared at Skid, her face unreadable. "You haven't given any thought to them?" He swung a stick like a baton. "You should. Why would fictional creatures, as real as you or me, suddenly show up to run a restaurant under your apartment?"

Skid waved him off. "Many people need a second job these days."

"Klingons?" Cord said, dropping to the ground, legs crossed, his head pivoting from Brick to Skid. "You're not kidding, are you?"

"That's it exactly," Brick said to Skid, gently placing the stick he held into the fire pit before rummaging in his explorer's pack. "Why would Klingons need a second job? They don't exist. Or do they?"

"They don't," Skid said through a grimace. The simple act of building a campfire in this strange place was somewhat comforting. She didn't want to talk about Klingons.

"Right." Brick was really building steam now. He pulled out a small tin box and slid it open, removing pieces of flint and steel. "In our reality, they don't exist, but what if they do in some other reality? What if the writers who think up things like Klingons, murderous clowns, killer robots from the future, or pixies that poop magical fairy dust, didn't come up with these monsters out of whole cloth? What if creative types unknowingly see into other dimensions, thinking it's just their imagination, but they really copy monsters that are already real?"

Cord pushed himself closer to Skid. "Shut up, dude."

"But now," Brick continued, eyes blazing in the fading sunlight as he clicked the flint and steel together, a few pitiful sparks dancing from the friction, "thanks to Dave and that Karl guy, those dimensions can touch, and things from there can bleed through to here. There might really be Klingons in your apartment building and a Predator may out there—" he waved an arm toward the deeper part of the shallow woods "—watching us right now."

"I do not like this conversation," Cord said, taking a Bic lighter from his pocket and setting the leaves and moss on fire. "It's making me uncomfortable."

The tinder blazed. Sticks, small and large, crackled in the heat.

"Goddammit," Brick said, then laid a few of the dry branches Cord had collected atop the growing fire.

6

The David on the monitor now only had one leg. Dr. Chet Hahn from Dimension Nightmare had slowly, methodically, surgically, sliced the meat from the bones. The monster's clipping at the flesh surrounding the tibia and fibula reminded Dave of wing night at the bar in Peculiar. He laughed when that point worked its way into his head, but by then he'd consumed a lot of beer.

"Got anything to eat around this joint?" Dave said, his words louder than he intended. "I'm hungry enough to eat all the way up to my femur."

He could see the disappointment in Karl's face. The lead scientist at Lemaître Labs wanted to break Dave, to make him weep, maybe. To make him beg, definitely. But Dave wasn't having any of it.

Karl stood, his shoulders square and stiff, and walked to a panel next to the refrigerator. He reached inside, pulled out a bag of something and threw it overhand at Dave. A sack the size of a baseball hit him in the chest with a crinkly whack before falling into his lap.

"Hey, peanuts," Dave said, picking up the packet and fighting to open it with his beer-clumsy fingers. "You know, if this whole scientist thing doesn't work out, you could always vend at Kauffman Stadium. Royals fans would just love you. Peanuts. Pretzels, Psychopath, Peanuts Pretzels. Psychopath."

Karl stomped toward Dave, who didn't move, and slapped his feet off the table.

"You know what your problem is, Collison? You never take anything seriously. Nothing." The man's hands were pinched into fists Dave was sure he'd never used before, and he pushed air through his nose like a bull ready to gore a matador.

"You mean like Friday when I told you flat out, flat the hell out, that your equations would result in the insane catastrophic bullshit that's happening now?" He finished the bottle of beer he held and stood, pulled his arm back, and threw it into the giant television screen. The bottle shattered, some of the shards clacked as they rattled across the top of the desk, foam leaked down the monitor, but didn't fog the picture.

"Generals come in here who don't like it when they don't get their way," Karl said, his voice more under control. "Anything expensive to replace is shielded by bulletproof glass." He paused for a moment, regarding Dave with cold eyes. "You told me what I hoped to hear. I needed this to happen. What you call 'catastrophic bullshit,' I call a presidential cabinet position."

"You did what you were instructed to do," Dave said over the top of him. "Open portals to other dimensions, other times, maybe even the women's shower room on the second floor." He stopped, hoping to get more anger from Karl. It wasn't enough. "What happens now? What happens when everything cycles through, and these temporal and dimensional shifts don't stop. What then, Mr. I Got My Ph.D. From A Directional University?"

Karl retucked his shirt, shoving the tail in the back with a flat hand and yanking at his belt before coughing and holding his head up, chin high.

"First, fuck you. Second, fuck you. And third, fuck you." He picked up the full beer bottle Dave hadn't gotten to and threw it against the bulletproof glass that covered the screen. The bottle, spraying beer, hit with a thunk and dropped to the floor whole, vomiting foamy liquid over the tight, gray carpet. On the screen, the mantis began to work on the other David's right arm.

"Hey, I was still drinking th—"

"What happens," Karl said, walking calmly back to the refrigerator to pull out another beer, cracking off the cap and taking it to Dave, "is nothing. It's going to work. This experiment has revealed to me that there aren't just the ten dimensions, or eleven dimensions, or twenty-six dimensions, or whatever number string theory mathematicians predict. There's an infinite number. Infinite. And now—" He grabbed the arms of Dave's chair. "Now? Our people. Ours, are going to have the power to reach into those dimensions and pluck out what they want. And if that doesn't work, they can go back a day, a week, a year, one hundred years, and try again. We're the masters of space and time." A grin, the grin of a horror movie clown, crossed his face. "*I'm* the master of space and time."

It took effort for Dave to pry Karl's fingers from his chair, but when Karl realized his face was inches from Dave's, he let go anyway and walked back to the lectern.

"That is impressive," Dave said. "Now I know your motivation, your goal, the—" he sniffed. "Wait, have you eaten Cheetos today?"

This took Karl off guard. "No."

"Right, as I was saying, now that I know the reason you don't smell like Cheetos, and that you enjoy watching me being eaten by a boss from a 1950s sci-fi movie—" he stood, his legs wobbly from all the beer—"could you let me go? There are some people I was hanging out with on the outside, and they may be in trouble. I'd like to find them. One was this really cute girl who wants to kill me."

"She can't be the first."

7

The mantel clock in the living room of the Sanderson Murder House ticked away and Cord hadn't returned.

"This sucks," the guy in the KCFD T-shirt said.

Most of the people who'd paid for the tour stayed. At about 8:15, the man in the business suit announced he was going to get his "damn money back" and stormed out of the house, trying to slam the screen door behind him. It didn't work. Two people agreed immediately and followed him out. Two more waited about five minutes before leaving. The rest stayed. The mother and her son, the nurse, and the tall woman who never smiled, among them. The guy in the fire department shirt just thought things sucked.

"Do you know when he's going to get here?" he asked Tamara.

Tamara resigned herself to the fact that she hadn't gotten Cord's phone number, and she'd been the one to let them all in. It was now her tour. "I don't know," she said, standing and walking to the window, the sun gone, the glow of the streetlights and neighboring houses painting the night outside gray. "I'm sure he'll be here soon. And it's worth it. Believe me, I'll never forget Friday night, ever."

"Is that when Tommy Sanderson appeared in the hallway?" a plump young man asked. He leaned against the wall drinking a Pepsi Tamara was sure he'd taken from Cord's refrigerator and hadn't paid for.

"Yes. The lights on the EMP, EMCEE, EMF, whatever meter went all crazy, the hallway made a crackling sound and smelled like someone had just sprayed Febreze." Tamara stopped, realizing everyone in the room was now staring at her. "Then Tommy Sanderson fell right out of the air and landed in the hallway."

An 'ooooh' came from somewhere in the room.

"Here," Tamara said, pulling out an icebreaker from every college class she'd ever taken. "While we wait, let's introduce ourselves. When I point to you, please give us your name, where you're from, and why you're here." She almost asked what year they were in but caught herself. She pointed at the guy in the KCFD shirt, who smiled and nodded.

"Garry Hawkins, originally from Orrick, Missouri," he said, his voice deep, but friendly. "I watch all those ghost shows on cable. I just wanted to see one for myself."

The nurse was next. "Carrie Franklin. I was here on Friday when the fireworks happened, like Tamara." She waved at Tamara and mouthed 'hi.' "I'm from Independence, and I saw the most amazing thing I've ever seen in my life right in this house. I haven't been able to think about anything else since that night."

Tamara smiled at her. The nurse's testimony the sort of thing a witness says to convince a jury. *They'll stay.* She pointed at the tall woman next, whose frown deepened.

"I'm Susan Meek," the woman said, the reluctance to talk clearly audible. She crossed her arms and glared at Tamara. "My last name was Sanderson in 1984. I was away at college on September 19 when my father killed the rest of my family in this house."

8

The lights under the big top had the same pull on Skid as a bug zapper had to a moth. The glare, the crowd, the heat, the tension in the air. Skid could do without the smell of elephant poop but knew it was part of the package. She straddled her motorcycle, a small one, a Honda CS90, propping it up with her leg as a kickstand. Her heart pounded as if she'd sprinted across the midway, but all she'd done for the past five minutes was sit.

Randall R. Roe smiled his ringmaster smile as he walked toward her, his top hat in hand, dressed in a sleek, black tuxedo that had begun to shine from wear, although the audience couldn't tell from a distance.

I can't do this. I can't do this. I can't do this, ran through her head at a speed too fast to clock. She couldn't look at her father as he approached, her wide eyes superglued to the scene before her. Two ramps sat in the middle ring, just high enough for her to drive under if she bent low over the handlebars. On either side of the ramps were runways that stretched outside the tent, the big canvas flaps pulled back and held in place by bungees. Outside the tent to her right was Jimm-Jimm the Daredevil Clown. His real name was Patrick Moon from Steamboat Springs, Colorado, but that didn't matter. He always went by Jimm-Jimm whether he was in makeup or not. The clown sat in his miniature VW Beetle, the roof reinforced to hold the weight of Svetlana, the Roe Bros.' dancing Siberian brown bear. The runways were for Jimm-Jimm to pick up enough speed for the little car to launch through the air with a bear on the roof and land, the momentum carrying the spectacle out of sight. The Beetle wasn't supposed to take a header on top of the motorcycle because the weight of the engine was in the back, but she didn't care. She was scared shitless.

"You can do this, honey," Randall said, calm and soft, his microphone switched off and behind his back for good measure. "Just like in practice."

"But—"

He rested a white-gloved index finger on her lips and smiled again, but this smile wasn't real, she knew. She'd seen his real smile before, and this wasn't it. "Just like in practice. I know the stands were empty then, but that doesn't matter. You're on the same bike in the same ring with the same car with the same bear. You can do this."

He pointed behind him, his eyes never leaving hers. "These people paid to watch you drive this motorcycle."

"But—"

The smile that was not a smile faded. "The success of this night is all up to you, kiddo," he said, then patted her back and walked away, raising his arms to the crowd. The ring erupted in applause.

But I don't want it to be all up to me.

That night followed her everywhere, even into other dimensions.

She never moved, still sitting with her back to the tree. She'd dozed some, but now watched as the wood Cord had gathered burned down to embers, the red glow hypnotizing. Cord lay on a bed of dried leaves Brick had inadvertently made when he cleared a spot for the fire pit. Brick slept on his bedroll, the explorer's pack more practical now than it had seemed yesterday on the floor of Dan's Daylight Donuts.

She hadn't thought of the crash that hard in years.

"Hey."

Skid looked. Brick's eyes were open, and he was studying her.

"You okay?" he asked.

No. She wiped the short sleeve of her shirt across her eyes and snorted, sucking back her runny nose before hocking it onto the embers. "Fine. I'd rather be home watching a baking show with a couple of people and a bottle of wine that would help me ignore them."

Brick sat up, his hairy face awash with concern.

Stop it, Brick. Just stop it. Don't care for me.

"Are you crying?" he asked, but his voice didn't sound accusatory like she'd expected. *The strong don't cry,* Randall Roe had told her when she broke her favorite doll, when she laid the CS90 flat on the elephant poo-covered middle ring of the circus as Svetlana and Jimm-Jimm sailed overhead and landed perfectly, when her mother ran off into the night and didn't even leave a note.

"No," she said flatly, then wiped her sleeve across her face again. "Yes, I am. I'm allowed."

"Of course you are." Brick leaned his elbows on his knees. "Do you need a hug?"

Skid took in a deep breath and cracked her shoulders. "I wouldn't recommend it."

"It's okay to have emotions, Skid."

This brought a slight grin. "Tell that to my father."

Brick smiled. Not a Randall Roe smile, but a real smile, an honest smile. She relaxed. A thin reed of breath escaped her lips.

"From the day I met you, you've seemed guarded, like you didn't want to let anyone into your life," he said.

"That's accurate."

"I felt like that toward Beverly, for a while." He paused, closed his right hand over his left. "We met through a dating site. I didn't know anything about her except from her profile and picture, and those are usually lies. I once went on a date from one of those sites with a girl named Jayna who told me she ate her sister's placenta."

"What?"

His head bobbed. "But, Beverly and I, it was like we knew each other when we met. We joked, she laughed. And a good laugh, too. Not some cursory thing. A belly laugh. Then we had a nice dinner and she wanted to dance so we went across the street—"

"To Slap Happy's Dance Club," Skid finished for him. "On Friday night."

"Yeah, bad timing. She had to go to the bathroom and just disappeared." The smile he'd been carrying melted into a look Skid didn't want to see. "I cried when I got home because that hurt. I'm not ashamed to say it."

Skid picked up a stick and tossed it onto the embers. Bright orange specks flew into the darkness and died. "You going to call her when you get back?

He raised an eyebrow. "Not if?"

She shook her head. "No, when. This thing isn't all up to me. I got you and Cord, and Bud Light Dave's out there somewhere. We're all going to set this straight." She tossed another stick into the fire pit.

Brick grabbed a branch and stirred the coals; he leaned forward and blew slowly on them. Fire jumped, then caught.

"When we realized something weird was going on," he said, "I wanted to make everything go back to normal. Now I just want to get back and see Beverly." He took the branch in both hands and snapped it more easily than Skid thought possible. "And I won't let anything stop that, you know. I mean anything."

She leaned back into the tree, sleep nagging at her again, but something else nagged harder. She wanted to know where Dave was and if they could do this without him.

"I want to do something else, too," Brick said. "There's this older woman named Katie, and she looks like I should know her. Some déjà vu stuff. She comes into my shop a few times a week and orders a large cup of black coffee and a chocolate muffin."

"Sounds like my kinda gal," Skid said through a yawn.

"She told me something the last time I saw her." He fumbled with his hands, trying to form some kind of shape but looked like he was trying to hand-bra some boobs. "She said I should offer a muffin, red velvet baked in a mini-loaf pan to at least sort of look like a brick because—"

"Yeah, you go by Brick, I get it."

"Well, that's a good idea, but she also said I should fill them with cream." He looked up, his hands still at hand-bra level. "You think that's because she thinks I'm soft?"

Skid laughed, only a short, quiet laugh, but a laugh all the same.

"I've never heard you laugh before," he said.

"It happens sometimes," she said, trying to wipe off her smile. "This Katie didn't mean you're soft, Brick. She meant you're sweet. You seem like a good guy, I'm sure that's all she meant. I think that's why Beverly likes you."

Brick flinched at the sound of her name and something flamed across his face.

"I—" Skid started, but a third voice made her jump. Brick looked over at Cord.

"Would you guys shut up," Cord said. He lay by the glowing embers, propped up on his elbows.

"I'm sorry our bonding moment was too much for you," Skid told him.

"That's not it," Cord whispered. "Can't you hear?"

Skid and Brick fell silent, their moment gone. Then she heard it, in the distance. Drums.

CHAPTER NINE

SEPTEMBER 6

1

BRICK THREW dirt on the coals, damping the fire they'd just revived, but this didn't throw the small flat spot where they'd camped into darkness. A bright moon that seemed larger than their own sent buttermilk light soaking through the thin canopy of trees. The drumbeats didn't grow louder, at least they didn't think so, but their ears became more attuned to the rhythmic pounding coming from beyond this small patch of woods. The drummers played a single steady beat, like the cadence on a rowing team.

"I didn't sign up for this," Cord said, his voice high and tight as a guitar string. "I wanted to stay home. I feel like I need to be on record about my position on this."

"Why bother?" Brick said, tying his bedroll onto his explorer's pack. "So we can feel guilty when you die?"

"Screw you, Brick."

Skid brushed dust from her pants. "Live in the now, Cord," she said, giving her right thigh another swipe before resting her hands atop two of the throwing knife hilts peeking beneath the jacket around her waist. "I'm terrified. I don't want to be here either, but the world might be coming to an end and someone had to do something. We're someone." She faced Brick who turned and frowned at her, the pack now slung over his shoulders. "I expect better from you, Chauncey."

The big man's eyes flared.

"Chauncey?" Cord barked, then slapped a hand over his own mouth when he realized the word had been too loud.

The broken camp dropped silent, Brick's thick, angry breathing the only thing they could hear over the drumming. Skid shook her head and started walking south, toward the drums.

"We're in a different universe, and boys are still stupid," she said. Brick huffed, then followed. "You going to be okay, Brick?"

"No," he growled behind her. "I feel like I did playing football. I'm going snap and take out the next guy that jumps in front of me."

"You played football?" Skid shrugged but didn't turn around. "You seem like more of a Home Ec guy."

Cord hurried to catch up. "Nice moment you've got going here," he said, his voice a forced whisper. "But let me get this right. We're moving *toward* the drums? We're in an alien—literally alien—world, we don't know what we're facing, we're armed with four throwing knives and fifty feet of pot rope, and we're walking toward potential danger? Hell, I need a drag off that rope."

Brick reached over his shoulder and pulled loose the leather thong that tied shut one of the side pockets of his pack. He slowly pulled out a steel blade at least a foot long, the guard curved upward on both sides in a Jokeresque smile.

"I have this."

"And what's that?" Cord asked. "A can opener?"

"It's a tekpi." Brick flipped his wrist, the blade shone in the moonlight.

"A what?"

"It's Raphael's weapon in *Teenage Mutant Ninja Turtles*."

A look of recognition crossed Cord's face, but quickly fell back to defeat. "Oh. Okay. That makes me feel great—if we run into Shredder. We're as safe as if we had abso-fucking-lutely nothing to defend ourselves."

Brick held the weapon up as if it were his middle finger.

"Awesome. That's just awesome. This is what you're doing now?"

"We're going south because that's the direction we need to go to get to the lab." Skid reached behind her head and pulled her ponytail tighter. She'd hate for it to come loose in a fight. "We—"

Distant machine gun fire filled the night, the sound nailing the group's feet to the forest floor. The rat-a-tats came in dozens of short bursts, then in a couple of long streams, then the world grew silent.

Skid started walking south again. "That should make you feel better, Cord," she said over her shoulder. "The drums have stopped."

2

Everyone stared at Susan, her arms still crossed, her face stern. She stood against the wall of what had been the back of the room when the ghost-hunting group filed in but, because of her, was now the front. They looked, mostly in awe, like they expected her to deliver a speech, or bless them, or kick them out of the house, or something.

"You're Tommy Sanderson's sister?" Tamara said. "I saw... I saw your brother."

Susan shook her head. "No, you didn't." Her words were flat. "If Tommy's ghost is doing anything, it's still mooching off my mother. Like I told the lady from the newspaper, even his ghost would be too lazy to haunt a house."

"But—"

Susan waved her off.

"I read the article in the paper," the plump young man with the Pepsi said to Susan. "It didn't sound like you wanted anything to do with this house. Why did you come back?"

"It was my father," she said flatly.

A hush fell on the group.

"Your father?" a woman asked. It was the nurse, Carol. "Do you still—"

"Speak to him?" Susan started to laugh but thought better of it. "Heaven's no. That psychotic bastard killed my family, and since I was an adult at the time, I no longer had a home to go to. The house was mine, but I certainly couldn't live here." She took a long breath, like the discussion had already exhausted her. "I was watching television, a true crime program called *The Slasher Files* or something ridiculous like that. My family's murder was one of the segments, not that they bothered to contact me."

Susan gripped the back of an overstuffed chair where the firefighter sat, knuckles turning white.

"I saw him. He was older, of course, much older. I hadn't seen him since 1984. He talked about that night, about the anger that gripped him, about storming down to the basement to retrieve his sword from atop the workbench, the sword my grandfather brought back from World War II. He talked about marching up the stairs to the bedroom. He claimed the experiments he did in the basement had driven him mad—" She stopped, the words momentarily caught in her throat. Susan coughed into her shoulder before continuing. "He could have received the death sentence, but the jury felt this was a crime of passion, not planning. He got life in prison, but it was something he said right before the first commercial break that got to me. He said when he came back downstairs, chasing Tommy after killing my mother and our dog, that the house was full of people. That isn't true."

"What do you mean?" asked a young woman by the fireplace. "I did a report on this case in my Intro to Criminal Justice class at college. That's exactly what happened."

Susan frowned, a look that seemed more natural on her than anything else. "I'm sure that's what your research found. Haven't you all noticed things are different now?" She slowly dragged her eyes around the room, the faces blank, at least mostly. "Product names are wrong? Actors you've never heard of are playing parts in your favorite movies? The national animal of Canada is now the moose."

"Yeah," the fireman said, turning in the chair to look up at her. "Poptarts is one word. Didn't they used to have a hyphen?"

"Maybe?" she said. "But the national animal of Canada is the beaver."

"That doesn't sound right," the plump young man said. "Who would pick a beaver as a national animal?"

"Canadians, I suppose," Susan said. "The point is that the madman on the video claimed the house was filled with strange people and that when he got to the kitchen, a giant in a red flannel shirt beat him unconscious. I know this story better than anyone on this planet, and that is wrong."

The goth woman in dark grays and blacks stood in a corner by herself, her hand raised tentatively over her head. When she spoke, her voice was soft, like she wasn't used to using it. "Did he say the man had a big, black beard?"

Susan nodded. "Yes, he did."

"And did he say if there were women in the kitchen?" Goth lady wrapped her arms across her chest as tightly as they would go and glanced at Susan through her bangs.

"Two," Susan said. "One he stabbed in the arm. The other, with dark hair and a ponytail, looked ready to hit him too. When he regained consciousness, everyone was gone but the police."

"Well, I was there," the woman said, the words came out fast. "I'd signed up for the tour and things happened. Weird things." Her eyes darted nervously underneath those black bangs. "We were all there. The whole ghost tour. When the police came, the big man and a smaller man in khakis got arrested, then it felt like a bubble burst and we were back here. Now. I think—" She stopped and seemed to try and shrink into the wall. "I think we actually were there; I mean here, when it occurred. We were here in the house in 1984 when the murders happened."

A smile, or something like a smile, worked its way onto Susan's lips. "That's what I'd hoped," she said. "I'm here because I want that to happen again. I need to see my father."

3

The woods where they'd briefly camped had been at the bottom of two gently sloping hills, the trees at its boundary not thinning so much as giving way abruptly to another expanse of knee-high grass that rippled in the night breeze. The moon, which had looked so large through the thin roof of leaves at their campsite, seemed smaller in the wide-open space, small enough that Skid confessed it was probably their same moon. Brick pointed out a few constellations they all recognized. Cord complained. This was Earth, apparently, just a different Earth, with more whining.

"We could go around," Cord whispered loudly. "Nothing's stopping us from going around."

"Go around what?" Skid asked, never slowing her pace. "We don't know where the drums and gunfire came from." She pointed to the east, west, south. "It could have come from there, there, or the way we're headed. We're not going to find out until we get there."

Brick, who'd insisted on reinstating initiative marching order, stopped suddenly and went down on one knee. Cord dropped behind him. Skid didn't need to guess that Cord was the kind of guy who understood hiding behind the big man was a nice place to be in a fight.

"What is it?" she asked, looking across the limited horizon available. The crest of the hill was close, an orange light glowing beyond it, but they weren't close enough to see where the glow came from.

Brick lay the palm of his hand on a ten-inch-wide depression in the grass. It, and a matching one, came parallel from the west then turned up and over the hill.

"Tire tracks," he said with a tenseness Skid had never heard in his voice. It wasn't fear. "Some kind of truck, big and far apart."

"Where—" Cord tried to say, but Brick cut him off with an index finger in front of his mouth.

Brick stood and started back up the hill. "Whatever we see here," he said as they neared the top. "Don't freak out."

Skid jogged up the rise in front of the men, their man-nonsense too much for her. *The success of this night is all up to you, kiddo,* ran through her mind. *To hell with you, Dad.* But she realized that although Randall R. Roe wasn't right much, those words were. She took a deep breath, hands gripping the knife handles at her belt tightly so Brick and Cord wouldn't see them shake, and walked over the rise secure in the knowledge that whatever was on the other side, she wasn't ready.

The world over the crest seemed to be on fire, at least in bits and pieces. Orange flames crackled from what used to be small, round, thatch-roofed houses. Some still stood, with people roaming between them. The tire tracks stopped at a military Humvee tilted onto its side about halfway toward the burning village. Multiple Humvees lay in ruins farther down the hill.

Dear lord.

"What happened?" Cord asked.

Skid took in a deep breath and exhaled before answering. "It looks like we're not the only ones from home." Not for the first time, she wondered what happened to Dave. Was he sitting back, having a beer, while they did the dirty work?

"There are bodies." Brick held the tekpi tightly in his fist and looked out over the field. "Lots of bodies."

Then the breeze shifted and brought with it a smell—smoke saturated with oil and something they couldn't identify but had a pretty good guess as to what it was. A few of the figures below tossed limp, bloody corpses onto a bonfire. Cord gagged. Skid gently grabbed his shoulders.

"Come on, keep it together."

"Something's happening," Brick said, paying them no attention. He pointed toward a Humvee that was still relatively intact, although the driver's side roof was dented like it had been hit with a giant's fist. The milling people were closer to the village. A few formed a circle, one of them gesticulating wildly. Brick leaned forward on his thick left leg, his right one behind it, then switched, stretching his hamstrings. "I'm going in for a closer look."

"We can just go around," Skid said, but Brick was already off, running low with his back bent, like it made any difference. Maybe the villagers would think this dark, hulking figure was simply a bear. But people killed bears, too. Brick reached the vehicle and stopped. No one in the village noticed, or if they did, they decided this shadow on the hill wasn't a threat.

"We can just go around? That's what I said in the first place."

"Shhh," Skid said and followed Brick to the second Humvee, staying low.

"Damn it, nobody ever listens to me." Cord ran after her.

The sickening smell of burning flesh grew thick closer to the village, and voices reached their ears. The words were strange, their delivery thick, like growls. If they lived through this, Skid would have to tell Cord he was right; they should have gone a different way. Brick held a hand toward them as they approached, palm first, his other hand up to his mouth. The orange firelight, now closer, blazed in his wide eyes. His mouth set in a grin with no humor behind it.

"Don't scream," he said, his voice soft, but hard at the same time. "Whatever you do, Cord, don't scream."

Cord shrugged. "Why me? Why did you say that to *me*?"

"There's something at the front of the Humvee. It's a body." His grin didn't falter.

"Hey, Brick," Skid said, slow and soft. "I think you're getting overly excited. Maybe we just need to go back over the hill and take a little break, okay? Maybe have some cookies. Did you bring cookies?"

"It had this in its hand." He pulled something about three-feet-long from the tall grass; it was a sword, the blade curved like in *Aladdin*. "It's a scimitar."

Brick held the tekpi out to Skid, who took it. A cold feeling grew in her gut. "What's on the other side of this truck?"

"It's not a tr—"

Her eyes sliced his sentence off before he could get it all out. "I don't care, Brick. What's on the other side of this truck?"

His grin pulled across his face even tighter; firelight flickered in his slightly crazy eyes. "Just remember, I told you not to freak out."

The drums found their beat again, the pounding not as loud, the rhythm not as urgent. Skid had read once that Mexican restaurants played up-tempo music to encourage patrons to eat faster so the tables could empty and refill. The earlier drums were at Mexican-restaurant pace; they were for battle. These drums were more at the pace of an Italian restaurant playing Sinatra's "It Was a Very Good Year."

They won, Skid thought. *They're celebrating. No.* The sound was all wrong. *They're mourning.*

"What's on the other side of this truck?" she said through clenched teeth, each word hard and sharp.

Brick leaned back to give Skid and Cord room to slink around and look. Cord lurched back and vomited near the back wheel of Humvee.

"You're freaking out, Cord," he said. "I told you not to."

The light from the full moon showed Skid more than she wanted to see. The cold feeling burrowed deeper. The body, thick at the shoulders, narrow at the waist, with arms like back deck supports, was clad in a hardened leather shirt studded with rough iron bolts. Whatever the clothing, it couldn't stop bullets. But it was the face that chilled her. She buried her hands into the grass, grabbed fistfuls and held them as tightly as she could to keep herself from falling over. The thing that lay in the stench of its own blood wasn't human.

Deep, scarred lines crisscrossed the creature's face, as if someone had tried to sew something back together it had never seen before. A piggish nose covered more of the face than it should, its ears pointed. But the still-open eyes nearly sent her running. The pupils, visible in the bright light of the moon, were horizontal rectangles, like the eyes of a goat.

"What the hell is this?" she asked, her voice weak, lost.

"It's an orc," Brick said from behind her.

Skid sat in the grass and leaned her back against the Humvee's front tire, the corpse of the dead orc and fiery scene below now far away. *But not far enough.* Brick loomed over her, the scimitar in his fist. She didn't like the look on his face.

"An orc. A sure-as-shit, *Lord of the Rings*, Dungeons and Dragons orc." He pushed his muscular arms behind his back, cracking his shoulders, the blood-stained, chipped sword terrifying in his hand. "Listen, this is it. This, right here, is the reason my friend Mitch and I planned a trip into the sewers with machetes and flashlights during sophomore year. It's the reason I didn't go to prom senior year because it fell on D&D night. Orcs, guys. *Real live orcs.*"

Skid was pretty sure the amount of adrenalin pumping through Brick's system right now would worry his doctor.

"This is what I dream about," Brick said with a wink for her. "This is my time."

The big man stepped over Cord, who sat by a puddle of vomit at the back of the vehicle, and unslung his explorer's pack, dropping it onto Cord's lap before he disappeared around the side. Skid leaned forward, trying to keep her eyes off the corpse of the orc, or whatever it was, and watched Brick. He darted through the grass and ducked as he reached the next Humvee. He looked back and gave thumbs up.

"He took the sword from the dead guy," Cord said from behind her.

"So?"

"So, I played D&D in high school and I never understood why everyone was so eager to pillage bodies." He'd crawled close and sat next to her, his back propped against the big tire. "I mean, whatever armor or magic ring or scimitar the dead guy had, it didn't do him any good."

Skid sat silently and watched Brick spring from the shadow of the overturned Humvee and rush the circle of orcs.

Damn it.

4

The Sanderson living room exploded into a cacophony of chatter. Some questions bounced around the room; others were thrown directly at Susan.

"What was it like living with a psycho?"

"What would you have done if you were here?"

"Do you bake pies?"

"Come on, people," Tamara said, her words buried beneath the questions that had turned to shouts. She stepped into the middle of the room, her fingers pressing into her scalp. "Quiet," she shouted, the room shushing to a series of unintelligible grumbles. "She didn't come here to be attacked or make pies." Tamara lowered her arms and faced Susan.

"I have only one question, Mrs. Meek," Tamara asked. "Is that all right?"

Susan's shoulders raised and dropped like they were pulled by a string. "I suppose."

Tamara took a step toward her. "What are you going to do if you see him?"

The smile that grew on Susan Meek's face sent a chill through Tamara. "That's easy," Susan said. "I'm going to kill him."

5

"What's he doing now?" Cord asked through what sounded to Skid like a mouthful of food. She turned her head away from the bloody scene on the other side of the truck to find Brick's pack unzipped and open in Cord's lap. Cord was eating something that looked like a piece of old boot.

"Look for yourself." Skid crossed her arms and frowned at him. He ripped off another chunk and chewed the food like it didn't want him to. "Didn't you just throw up?"

"I don't want to look for myself. I want you to tell me. I'm just waiting for the world to change again." He moved the dried food to the other side of his mouth; Skid thought he looked like a dog with a strip of rawhide. "And yes, I just threw up. That's why I'm hungry."

He held the boot food toward Skid, who took it without hesitation.

"I got this out of Brick's magic backpack. I think it's jerky." He dug through the open pack. "There's also dried fruit in here and a box of Ding-Dongs. You want?"

Yeah, she did; all of it. She hadn't realized how hungry she was. "Later."

Skid ripped a strip of jerky off with her teeth. The dried, seasoned meat was tough to chew but tasted semi-normal. She sat back against the Humvee, closed her eyes and chewed slowly, focusing on the act of eating. The drums, the monster, the world around her, the Adventure, none of it as important as the act of eating.

Cord ruined the moment. She figured he was probably good at that.

"Skid." His voice shook, the tenor urgent. It didn't sound like he'd found those Ding-Dongs. Cord slapped at her arm with the back of his hand. "Skid."

Her eyes slid open. The orange glow from beyond the Humvee

and the yellow glow from the mostly full moon bathed the world in soft light. Except in front of her, where a shadow loomed. *Brick's back.*

"Hey, Brick," she said before she saw what stood before her. Tall, metal-shod boots gave way to leather pants and a leather jerkin. The dried beef in Skid's mouth dropped onto her shirt. This wasn't Brick. The pig nose of the orc snorted, and the beast reared back, swinging a six-foot-long mattock.

Oh, no, she thought, then self-defense training kicked in.

Skid rolled and popped to her feet in one seamless motion, Brick's tekpi in her left hand. The blunt side of the mattock thudded into the ground where she'd just been. A great divot of grass and sod flew up as the beast yanked the weapon back into the air. The monster bent low and roared, spittle and mucus spraying the grass.

A knife appeared in Skid's right hand and she threw. It spun and struck the orc's chest, the blade glancing off an iron peg in its leather mail. The knife disappeared into the darkness.

"Damn it."

The orc roared and swung the mattock again. The great overhead arc came at her in slow motion. She hit the ground in another roll and popped up a few steps from the monster just as the head of the weapon hit the ground in a blow that would have crushed her. She waved her hands over her head as it started to lift the enormous bladed hammer again.

"Hey, hey, hey," she shouted. *Come on, Skid,* she thought. *What are you doing?*

The orc snorted and glared at her, dropping the head of the mattock onto the ground, the blade side glowed orange in the nearby firelight. A grunt escaped the cruel, V-shape in its face; tusks protruded from either side.

"Hundur, mat nalt," it said, the words vaguely Slavic. Then it grunted again, trailing off into a snort. It was laughing at her.

"Sure. You bet, asshole."

All up to you, kiddo. The words kept playing themselves in her head like a bad song she couldn't shake. *All up to you.* She started to reach for another knife when Cord's voice reached her.

"Use the Ninja Turtle thingy," he whispered from his huddle by the Humvee. The rest of his body apparently wasn't interested in answering what his brain should have been telling him, which was to run.

Ninja Turtle thingy? The tekpi. *All up to you. Yeah. It is.*

She stood upright slowly. She didn't want to give the orc a reason to raise its mattock again. It cocked its head like a dog as it watched her pull another throwing knife from her belt and aim it at Cord.

"That's not what I meant," Cord said, his voice sounding far away.

The orc's head tilted the other way. *It wants to know what I'm doing,* Skid thought.

It's what people think that matters, said the voice of Constantinople Phargus, operator of the Polar Ring Toss on The Roe Bros. Traveling Circus midway. *This game is just giving them what they expect.*

She hoped the old drunk was right.

Skid smiled as she hadn't the night at the bar of Slap Happy's Dance Club, the night she'd met Bud Light Dave and entered this nightmare. She turned to the side and, with the tekpi still in her right hand, whipped the throwing knife toward Cord. The point sank into the government rubber of the Humvee's tire right next to Cord's ear. He whimpered and closed his eyes.

I'm sorry. Skid bit her lower lip to hold in a scream.

The orc barked and slapped its leg with its free hand. *This game is just giving them what they expect.* Skid curtsied, feeling the beast's eyes on her back, knowing it might want another show. *You got it.*

She planted her weight on her right foot and sprang upward. The orc, not realizing she'd moved, stood stupidly over her. The tekpi, tight in her grip, entered the thing's skull under its thick, knotted chin with a pop. Hot, sticky blood gushed over her hand and down her arm. A gurgle escaped the orc, the tip of the tekpi emerging from crown of its skull, and the gurgle turned into a wheeze. Then all sound from the beast stopped.

Skid pulled the blade to the left, and the orc fell lifeless to the grass.

She tried to regain her breath, heart pounding like Mexican-restaurant music. She nudged Cord's leg with the tip of a Hello Kitty shoe, and his eyes sprang open like a broken toy. He looked from Skid to the dead orc and back again.

"Does Brick have any Purell in there?"

"Yeah, I think so." Cord dug into the pack and pulled out a handful of white packets the size of condom wrappers. "How about an alcohol-based moist towelette instead?"

She didn't respond.

"Skid?"

She fell to her knees in the grass beside the dead orc, her head in her hands, body racked with sobs.

"Oh no, don't cry." Cord fought with the moist towelettes as if freeing one of them would wipe this whole problem away. "If *you're* crying, what chance do *I* have? Come on, Skid, tell me we can make it through this."

A bellow, from what seemed like the other side of nowhere, split the night. The bellow had erupted from Brick. Did that mean he was gone?

"This is bad," Cord reiterated, but Skid couldn't find the words to calm him down.

Cord threw up again.

6

The group fell silent. Susan's words hung in the air as if a storm had moved into the house, the atmosphere charged and heavy. The firefighter shifted in his chair, and the nurse coughed. The plump man opened his mouth to say something but thought better of it and looked at his shoes instead.

The woman dressed in blacks and dark grays raised her hand slightly, then lowered it. "How are you going to do it?" she asked.

Someone whispered in the back. Someone else told them to shut up.

"I've had close to forty years to think that over," Susan said, looking around to take in all the faces. "I could poison him, but there's a big margin for error. Bigger than I want. I could use something sharp and slice him up like he did my mother. You know, chop him right to bits." Some gazes remained fixed on her as she said this, while others danced between each other and the floor. "But I might not be able to reach the sword before he does, so that's not a good option. Or—"

The sentence stopped as Susan took in the room, the room where she'd spent the first quarter of her life watching TV, having Saturday night popcorn-and-a-movie, the first place she'd kissed a boy, praying her crazy-assed father didn't walk in on them. A lump grew in her throat.

The woman with the long black bangs stepped from her position against the wall, hands buried into the deep pockets of the long, thin dark gray cardigan she wore. "Well?"

"I think," Susan said, moving away from the chair and toward the stairs that lead to the second floor. "I think I will wait for him upstairs before he gets a chance to kill my mother. Then I plan to shoot that psychotic monster in the face."

7

The screams. If he survived the night, Cord knew he would always remember the screams. Brick launched himself from behind the nearby Humvee howling like an Icelandic berserker. The orcs in the rough circle howled back, their voices starting deep and guttural then rising to pig-like squeals when they turned and ran toward the guy in the red flannel shirt.

Cord took back that last thought—Brick had shed his red shirt before launching himself toward the cast of *Lord of the Rings*. The muscles of his shoulders rippled, scimitar held high as he closed in and met the first leather-clad creature with a downswing of his blade. The thing lifted its own sword and the two blades clashed and sparks flew. The orc grunted and crumbled as Brick's foot came up and caught it in the midsection.

"Not seeing this," Cord whispered. "Nope."

The scimitar flew in a backswing and caught the next orc across the face, slicing through its brow and ruining its eyes. It dropped, squealing. Its limbs thrashed mindlessly with pain. Brick slammed his scimitar into the grass where the first orc had fallen. A spray of blood followed when he whipped it up and thrust it through the throat of the third.

"Oh, do you know the Muffin Man," came from somewhere deep in the recesses of Cord's brain, a brain quickly losing track of itself. The words made their way to his lips and ventured out soft, singsong into the night to join the sounds of battle.

A long knife flew by Brick's ear. It might have nicked it, but Cord couldn't tell. The big man reached out and grabbed an orc by the throat and brought the pommel of his scimitar down atop its bald, misshapen skull. The crack reached Cord's ears.

"The Muffin Man, the Muffin Man." The song stuck now, his brain on autopilot.

An orc, one as large as Brick, appeared from the doorway of one of the few round houses that still stood. It squeaked a piggy sound and rushed toward Brick, who had lifted the last living creature from the broken circle and thrown it into the nearby bonfire. His sword had disappeared into the grass.

"Oh, do you know the Muffin Man—"

The night was suddenly strangely silent, save for the crackling fire, Skid's sobs, the heartbeat in Cord's ears, and the screeching orc closing quickly on Brick, a knotted club in its knotted hand. The club pulled back to deliver a blow to Brick's head, but it didn't land. Brick shifted weight onto his back foot and threw an uppercut at the monster that connected with its scabby chin, sending the creature's head back farther than it was allowed to go. A sickening crunch dominated Cord's universe for a second. Then the orc dropped lifeless onto the ground.

The last words dropped when Brick threw his shoulders back and screamed to the moon and stars. "That lives on Drury Lane?"

Cord's song died as surely as an orc when Brick's bellow vanished into the sky. "No. You do not know the Muffin Man at all."

Brick stood in the ruined village, the sword back in his hand, and surveyed his surroundings. No orc charged him, no weapons flew. He heaved in heavy breaths. Cord could see the Muffin Man's muscles twitch. He stood and waved at Brick. Brick waved back.

"Hey," Cord shouted, his mind somewhat back in his control, still intact, but a bit loose. "How'd you know how to do that stuff?"

Brick put a bloody hand to his mouth and shouted back. "I've seen 'Conan the Barbarian' forty-six times."

"Oh, yeah," Cord mumbled, turning his back to Brick. He moved toward Skid, who had risen to sitting sometime during Brick's battle.

She wiped the tears her cheeks with her shirttail and raised her face toward Cord, eyes swollen. "I killed that guy. I flat-out killed that guy." Her shirttail came back up and went away with the contents of her blown nose.

Orcs, swords, Humvees, ghosts, time-traveling scientists, dimension-hopping and Tamara quite probably at his house wondering where he was tonight. It all came and went. His mind was suddenly clear, as clear the one time in college he dropped acid and ate "Smells Like Teen Spirit" as it flowed from his stereo like spaghetti.

A smile appeared on his face. Not a sales-seeking grin, but an honest smile. Skid balked like she couldn't believe he was capable of it. He reached out a hand and pulled her onto shaky legs. "When the orc came around the truck, what did it have in its hands?"

"That great big mallet."

"Right, the mallet he tried to kill you with, Skiddo. You were defending yourself. But you weren't just defending yourself, you were defending me. Thank you." He held out his arms. "Now, come in here."

Skid, with that disbelieving look still plastered on her face, allowed Cord to wrap her in his arms. He kissed her forehead like a parent and patted her back. "You're not alone, you know?"

She planted a hand in his chest and gently pushed him away. "Thank you, Cord. I needed that, but if you call me Skiddo again—"

Brick appeared, his shirt back on but unbuttoned, chest splattered with black blood. He stood at the head of the slain orc, the tip of the tekpi still sticking out from its skull.

"Nice." He walked past Skid, pulling a pistol from his back pocket, and handed it grip-first to Cord. "Here. You might need this."

Cord looked at it as if it were a strange, poisonous reptile. "Where'd you get it?"

"Our friends were in a circle around a soldier." He stared off toward the fire. "A soldier of the United States Army. There are lots of them out there, dead in the grass."

Skid wiped at the last of the tears. "Was he still alive?"

"Yeah."

"Did he say anything?" Cord asked, the smile gone. He took the sidearm but didn't look at it.

Brick's shaggy head fell forward slightly. "He said, 'negotiations failed.' What do you think that means?"

"Dave would know," Skid said. "We need to find hi—"

She stopped; something snapped in the night. They all turned south to find the crawling storm of a Miller Wave nearly upon them.

Before Cord could grab her, Skid ran to intercept the rolling purple clouds, ready for once to welcome it.

8

Susan walked through the twenty people scattered throughout her family's former living room, the darkness outside now complete, their faces grim in the harsh shadows of Tungsten lamps. No florescent or LEDs for the Murder House, oh no. Everything was authentic 1984. Tamara stood and followed the last surviving Sanderson into the hallway, the memory of Tommy falling from thin air sent a chill through her when she stepped over the bloodstain in the floor. She knew nothing of Cord's artwork; to her, the stain was real.

"Mrs. Meek?" she said. The older woman turned, a strange smile on her face.

"Yes, dear?"

Tamara twisted her fingers nervously. "I'm so sorry about what happened to your family."

Susan's smile waned but didn't disappear. "That was a long time ago. I was sad for a long, long time, but I found anger is a good replacement for sorrow." She turned back toward the stairs, but Tamara stopped her before she took a step.

"Are you—are you really going to kill your father?" she asked, her voice shaking.

"I don't know." The remaining whisper of a smile drifted away; her brows pinched. "No," she said. "That is what I came here to do. That's why I have a Glock 19 in my purse. But, now that I'm here, it all seems silly. No one can travel backward in time, and I'm too frightened to shoot anyone." Her eyes fell on Tamara. "Even the person who robbed me of a normal life. My mother, my brother, a place to call home. If it wasn't for him, I could bring my children here, to this house, to play with Grandma." Her voice trailed off and she wiped a tear from her eye before looking up to Tamara. "But Grandma's dead."

Tamara resisted the urge to hug this woman. She didn't seem the hugging type. "Then what are you going to do?"

"Ask that Cordrey fellow for my money back, if everything I just said doesn't happen."

She turned for the final time and ascended the stairs to the second floor.

9

As Cord and Brick—holding onto his pack with one hand, gripping the sword in the other—ran to catch Skid, the Miller Wave engulfed them. Their tired limbs struggled forward until the wave passed and they spilled onto another grassy plain, the same moon, the same dusting of stars overhead.

"Goddamnit," Cord shouted, then realized that had been stupid and lowered his voice. "Where are we? We'd better not be in another orc world, because that would really not be fun."

"I don't know," Brick said, lifting his pack, shoulders slumped. "It doesn't look much different from—" His words trailed off. "Oh, my god. That is beautiful."

"What?"

He held out a beefy arm and pointed. A light, an electric light, shone in the darkness. "That's an outdoor light, my friends. We're back."

Skid stood behind them, looking in the opposite direction. "Boys, turn around."

They did and Cord let out another shout. They hadn't gone straight south in Orcland. They'd veered to the east. Skid faced the US 71, or at least a highway. About a half-mile away a tall sign stood in the air like a beacon in a lighted court.

"That looks like a motel," she said.

"Yeah, out of a 1960s biker movie." Cord stood next to her, pistol held lightly in his hand because that's what people did in movies.

She pushed him, a friendly push, then started walking across the grass field toward the far-away lights.

"I need a shower," was all she said until they reached the Highway 71 Motel, the bug-infested marquee telling them they'd soon get the "Best sleep in the Midwest." A diner was attached to the line of doors facing the parking lot, windows dark this early in the morning. Four motorcycles, three Harley Davidson Sportsters and an Indian Chief Black Hawk rested in front of motel rooms along with two cars, the makes and models strangely out of place. One car was a two-door Studebaker, the other a DeSoto with Nebraska plates.

"I hope one of you has cash," Skid said through a yawn, walking to the office door, which bled the only light in the place. They were all tired. So tired no one felt the tremor that shook the floor when they stepped into the office of the Highway 71 Motel and woke the night clerk asleep behind the desk. The man wore a plaid button-down, short-sleeve shirt and horn-rimmed glasses. He almost knocked over the full ash tray at his elbow when Skid hit the call bell. A print painting of a sailing ship was tacked behind him on the wall. The frame shook, but not enough for anyone to notice.

10

Darkness draped the top of the stairs. Susan Meek, Susan Sanderson Meek, the last surviving member of Delbert Sanderson's family, took each step slowly. Dread gripped her as a river of memories flowed. The last time she'd stepped into this house was days after the murders, after police removed the bodies of her family, mopped up the blood and pulled down all the crime scene tape. She'd come to take her belongings and remove anything she may want to keep; she didn't want to keep much. It was no longer her home, and the possessions no longer belonged to her family. Her family was dead. Police had arrested her father just days before as he stood in the yard covered in red screaming at their neighbor. Mr. Wanker simply stood in his kitchen with the telephone receiver to his ear frantically talking to the police as he watched Delbert wave the sword stained by his family's blood. That's not how the story read now. Delbert had been knocked unconscious by a giant of a man Susan was sure didn't exist.

The stairs were the same, the refrigerator was the same, the carpeting in the living room was the same. Only Delbert Sanderson had changed. Or had he always been a pressure cooker waiting to explode? It was hard to see her childhood through adult eyes. She turned and sat at the top of the stairs, the bathroom door behind her. Her parents' room and the twin bedrooms where she'd grown up next to Tommy were on either side of the staircase.

A sigh escaped. *What are you doing here, Susan?* She looked around the upstairs through the darkness and, for the first time since she'd stepped into this house tonight, it looked like home. The gray shapes of closed doors, a picture on the wall, the table in the corner Mother had loved—they had stayed put all these years. *This is crazy. Go home.* Susan huffed, feeling silly for having come here at all. She prepared to grab the bannister rail and pull herself up, when a scream of surprise hiccupped from downstairs.

A ripple, the moment in a science fiction movie when everything is about to go to hell, spread through the hall and up the stairs. A picture fell in the hallway near the bedroom where Delbert Sanderson had murdered her mother. Susan slapped a hand on the rail and held on when the ripple washed over her and was gone. She sat, eyes pinched shut, but nothing happened, not really.

"What in the world?" she whispered.

The sound of people downstairs chattering, saying things like, "What was that?" "Did you feel it?" "Was that real?" rose toward her. As Susan sat with her eyes closed, another sound drifted into her ears. A television. A television that hadn't been on before played from somewhere nearby and—

What is that? Snoring?

Something, something alive, moved nearby. Her eyes sprang open as a brown and white cocker spaniel put its paws on her shoulders and licked her face, its tongue warm, wet, real.

"Hey," she said, reaching toward the dog to hold it back. She didn't know there was a dog in the house. Then she saw it and her world dropped from under her.

"Oh, my God. Muffit? Is it Muffit?" Susan gently took the dog's wet chin in her hand. It was the family dog. Her stomach fluttered. "Who's a good boy, Muffit?"

The dog leapt again, trying to lick her nose, docked tail beating back and forth. A chill shook her core. *This can't be Muffit.* Muffit was Delbert Sanderson's first victim.

The bottom step moaned under a great weight. Susan swallowed dryly and she glanced tenuously toward the bottom of the stairs. The next step groaned. A large, heavy man came up the stairs, a long slim sword in his right hand. He took another step, then another. In the darkness, the man hadn't noticed Susan sitting at the top. She gave up trying to keep Muffit off her.

Dad? Fingers fumbled with the latch of her purse then her hand dug in, feeling the cold steel of the Glock 19.

The man with the weapon took another cautious step upward, then another, then another. He was halfway up the stairs when Susan broke the silence.

"Hello, Father."

CHAPTER TEN

SEPTEMBER 7

1

BUD LIGHT DAVE woke in the gray world of twilight, the hallway that ran past the conference room dimmed to mimic the night of the outside world. He didn't know what time it was, but it wasn't morning. Not yet. Or had he missed morning? *I had too much beer.* The bottles were gone, even the one he broke by throwing it at the monitor where the B-horror movie starring an enormous praying mantis and Alternate Universe David had played out. Dave slowly rolled his sore head toward the feed from the infirmary. Other David was dead. No one outside Virginia Leith in *The Brain That Wouldn't Die* could survive with only a head.

He sat up slowly, expecting his own head to start pounding, but it didn't. Dave gave it a slight shake. Nothing. Just a hint of a headache hung back amongst the cobwebs. He could handle that. His legs swung over the table where he'd slept and dropped his feet onto the floor. Karl was gone, and he cleaned up nicely.

The world took a slight tilt as Dave made his way down the table, running his fingertips across it for balance. "Whoa." He almost stumbled but caught himself. "That was some par-tay, amIright?"

Something moved in his periphery, or not. He refused to turn his head before he plucked a bottle of juice and a bag of peanuts from the Magic Wall of Food. The cabinet revealed apple, apple, apple, grape, watermelon, tomato and finally orange. Dave grabbed the orange and leaned against the refrigerator door, his attention directed at the hall. He didn't have the stomach for Other David's severed head this morning.

Something moved again.

"What now?"

He struggled with the cap, but finally got it off and tossed it on the floor before draining half the bottle. The sharp citrus burned his mouth, which tasted like beer and the rotting fish sandwiches he'd slept on in the alley behind All-National Burger.

Whatever moved outside kept just below the frame of the long window that gave the conference room a clean view into the hallway. Then, on cue, something pressed onto the glass that his hangover-addled brain couldn't identify. He only knew it couldn't be Oscar, because Karl had showed his friend in the monitor and Oscar didn't have scissors-like mandibles.

The thing moved again, and he jumped. For the first time since he'd met Dr. Karl Miller Ph.Dickwad, Dave wished they were in the same room.

"What the hell are you?" The movement outside the window grew more agitated. *How thick is that glass?* he wondered. Whatever was out there, there were more than one.

Dave walked toward the head of the conference room. He finished the juice and left the empty bottle on the table before approaching the door. All he had to do was open the sleek metal door a crack and the hall lights would turn on. Then he could see whatever was out there. The handle turned easily in his hand.

"This is stupid," he said, and pulled the door open anyway, just a few millimeters, enough for the hall lights to pop on, when he discovered he was right.

What the unholy hell? The light, emulating daylight as its engineers intended, flooded the hallway, and Dave screamed.

Cockroaches the size of Galapagos tortoises froze for a moment before pounding over each other and scattering from the light. They disappeared into the open area of HR, leaving black droppings strewn across the once-spotless complex floor like ice cream sprinkles from hell.

Dave vomited over the tiles.

2

Delbert Sanderson stopped halfway up the stairs. "Who the hell are you?" he asked, his words slurred. Daddy'd been heavy on the Old Milwaukee tonight. Muffit stopped licking Susan and turned toward Delbert, a growl in his throat.

Her body shook. *Dear God, this is real.* The strength washed out of her and she nearly dropped her purse. *This is actually happening. This is my father. This is the night.*

Susan had so many questions for the man who murdered her mother, her brother, her dog, and left her to face life alone. Grandpa's heart attack had erased the rest of the family. All that was left was David, a foster brother who was gone. The agency had taken him; she had no idea where he was.

Why did you do it? she wanted to ask. *Why did you kill my family? Why did you slice open Muffit like a tomato? Did you lose your mind that night? Or did you really want this? Were we really that awful?* And the one question that lived through the years like a bad dream, a black cloak that hung in the closet of her memories, haunting her for nearly forty years. *If I hadn't been away at college, would you have killed me too?*

"It's me, Dad. It's Susan."

Delbert stopped, his face in shadow. She couldn't see his expression; his only movement was the sword twisting in his hand. "You can't be Susan," he said, his tone flat and dead. "Susan isn't here."

The hand in her purse slipped around the handle of the Glock and gripped it as deftly as she would a gardening tool.

"It's me, Dad." Her voice shook, but only slightly. If Delbert noticed, he didn't care. "I know what you're about to do, and I can't let you."

Her brilliant father, whose experiment in the basement had something to do with this, swayed enough to rest his hand on the wall to keep from falling down the stairs.

"You sound like Susan, but you don't sound like Susan." He raised the sword. "Please, don't be Susan."

He took another step and stopped.

Please, don't be Susan? "Why are you doing this?"

Delbert turned his head. The thoughts running through it must have scattered like the break on a pool table. *I've confused him.*

"Because," he growled, the word turning into a yell. "They're leeches. They're demons. They won't let me work. They—" He paused, waiting for his brain to catch up. "They beg me to kill them. It's a blessing. A blessing."

Her grip tightened on the pistol. "What about me, Dad?"

Delbert's free hand moved from the wall, slapped the crown of his head and rubbed in rough circles. Curses flew from his mouth. When he looked back up, he was dangerous. "You're Susan, but you can't be Susan. Susan isn't here."

At that moment, she knew the man who pushed her on the swing set at the park down the street, the man who drove her to softball practice, the man who brought roses to her eighth-grade graduation wasn't there, either. It was the man who repeatedly told Tommy he was a disappointment and called her mother a worthless drunken fool. It was the man who kept the family terrified for the last four years of their lives. That's who was slowly marching up the steps.

205

"Tommy," Delbert shouted past Susan like she wasn't there. "Get your lazy ass out here."

Someone on the ghost tour laughed downstairs, but Delbert didn't notice. He started back up the stairs, his eyes full of crazy, when Tommy's bedroom door opened, and light flooded the dark stairway. Muffit tensed to spring, barking as Delbert reached striking distance of Susan.

"Delbert, Tommy, what's going on?" came from down the hall.

Mother. Oh, my God. Mother.

Muffit sprang at Delbert, who was close enough Susan could smell the cheap beer oozing from him.

"Goddamned dog," he grunted and swung the sword to slice into the cocker spaniel, but Susan shoved a foot against her father's chest and pushed hard. Delbert's eyes sprang wide when he realized what was about to happen. His arms waved almost comically, and the sword flew from his hand, clanging against the stairs. The force of Susan's foot tipped his drunken balance, and he teetered backward.

Delbert Sanderson fell, head hitting the wooden steps with a crack before he tumbled into the hallway and landed in a pile of limbs. He didn't move again.

"Delbert honey? Are you okay?" Cecilia Sanderson asked, her voice closer now.

Oh, no.

3

Karl came in at 6:30 in the morning. Dave knew this because Karl shouted it.

"It's 6:30 a.m., sleepy boy." Dave's boss stepped into the conference room like he'd had a great night's sleep and set a cup of coffee on the table in front of Dave. The vomit on Dave's shirt didn't seem to bother him. "Drink up to celebrate. The Army sent a squad into a wave yesterday to recruit some new non-human soldiers. They should be back today."

Dave took a sip of coffee. It was stronger than he liked, but whatever.

"There were cockroaches in the hall," he said, "Big ones." The words sounded strange to him because they were. "They were like bears with exoskeletons."

Karl lifted his own cup, a picture of Lex Luthor next to the words "World's Second-Best Boss" painfully visible.

"That's HR. They turned like that in the first wave. I find them loathsome, but then again, I always did. They can stay that way for all I care." He sipped from Lex, the slurp too loud to be accidental.

"I'm not hung over," Dave said, then shook his head again. "That doesn't bother me."

"Pity," Karl said. "Would you like to leave?"

Well, yeah. Who wouldn't? "My breath's awful. Got any gum?"

Karl's right hand waved in front of his face. "No, and I don't care." His eyes focused on Dave's, and they were bat shit. "Would. You. Like. To. Leave?"

He's going to kill me. If I say 'yes' he's going to kill me. I have to get to the Bridge and shut this thing off. "No." He forced a natural smile. "I would like some more peanuts."

4

A crowd of ghost hunters had gathered around Delbert's unmoving body by the time Cecilia made it out of her room.

"What happened?"

"Who's this?"

"Oh, my God. Call an ambulance."

"I don't have any bars."

Susan's mother stepped into the hallway tying the waist of her purple robe, her long, auburn hair disheveled. "Del—" she started, then saw Susan. Susan's stomach lurched. Those were the clothes Cecilia had worn the day she died, hacked to death by the dead man in the downstairs hallway.

Cecilia stopped, her hands still on either end of the terrycloth belt, her face awash in confusion. "Susan?"

"Hey, Mom," Susan said.

"But—"

"It's me, Mom." *My mother is alive.* Muffit bounded back up the stairs and licked Susan's hand. The volume of Tommy's television increased to drown out the noise.

Cecilia's eyes grew wide. Her head involuntarily shook. "No. No, you can't be Susan." She took a step back toward the bedroom she shared with Delbert. "You're old. Older than me." Cecilia glanced at the stairs but didn't dare look down them. "What did you do to my husband?"

Susan opened her mouth to speak, but someone screamed downstairs, cutting her off. The people had moved away from Delbert's body like death was a disease they could catch, all but the nurse, Connie. She hovered over the body of Susan's father, trying to find a pulse in the man's neck.

"He's dead," said the woman who'd brought her son. "He's—oh my god, he's dead."

When Susan turned back toward her mother, she was gone.

"She's calling the police," Susan mumbled. The police. *The police are coming, and I'll be arrested.*

She stood and calmly walked past Tommy's door and stopped at hers, pushing it open and flipping on the light switch without looking. Posters of Wang Chung, Wham! and Culture Club covered the walls.

"Hi, guys," she whispered and shut the door, but it didn't shut out the screams.

5

"For a dollar, I can get fruit, three eggs, boiled, fried, scrambled or poached, or dry cereal with cream, and toast. Not milk, cream. My drink choices are tea, Postum, coffee, matte or milk." Cord held the menu for the Highway 71 Diner attached to the Highway 71 Motel where they'd spent the past six hours wrestling with sleep. Cord, Brick and Skid sat at a booth on maroon vinyl seats, their elbows on a white table dotted with cigarette burns, a stainless-steel napkin dispenser, salt and pepper shakers, and a chipped glass ash tray pressed against the wall under a long, plate-glass window. Brick's explorer's pack leaned against the booth. He'd left his sword outside.

"What's Postum?" Brick asked, looking at his own menu, type-written in Pica on an 8x10 slice of poster board stained with coffee. "Or that other one."

"Matte?"

"I think you're pronouncing it wrong."

Skid stared through the window that overlooked a dusty gravel parking lot. The Studebaker was still parked in front of a motel door, but the family in the DeSoto had taken off before any of them woke. The motorcycles in front of two rooms leaned on their kickstands like the cool kids in a 1950s teenybopper movie. Skid took them in and quickly looked away, past the lot and out over a cornfield that grew on the other side of the highway; a gravel road intersected it and continued west.

"How are you supposed to pronounce it?" Cord asked.

"I don't know," Brick said. "I don't even know what it is."

Skid hadn't slept when she stumbled into her room, at least not right away. She peeled off her sweat-stained clothing, the blood-splatter not visible on the black material, and washed each article one-by-one in the sink, hanging them wet in front of the open bath-room window. The world changes had been a tough to make sense of, but then again everything was. The time slips and dimensional jumps were just new twists in a life full of fuckupery. She'd handled the little changes, like Bud Light Dave disappearing, the street names, and the annoying synchronicity of Brick. But the orc she'd faced in the Otherworld, that was different. She'd killed it. It would never come back. For the first time, she wondered if the monster with the pig nose and six-foot hammer had children. Skid cried as she sat in the rust-stained bathtub, and again later, naked and dripping in the darkly decorated room with a tacky painting over the bed. Then she cried herself to sleep.

Now these people were arguing about tea.

"It's pronounced MAH-teh," she said, her gaze never leaving the parking lot. A sudden breeze sent a dust devil careening toward the highway.

"I think it's MAY-Tuh," Brick said.

Cord slapped his menu onto the table. "How do you know?"

The big man batted his eyes. "I'm not just a pretty face."

"It's pronounced MAH-teh," Skid said again, louder this time. She picked her menu off the table studied it. "And it's spelled wrong on the menu. There's only one 'T'. It's a type of South American tea."

She frowned at Brick and Cord, who sat opposite her, and lifted her menu.

"I'm getting the omelet with cream minced chicken, the chilled grapefruit, bacon, rye toast with orange marmalade and a pot of coffee." She ticked off each choice on her fingers. "That totals one dollar and twenty-five cents. You got that covered, Cord?"

When they woke the night desk clerk and he told them two rooms, one single and a double, would be thirty dollars, Brick pulled out two twenties and the man laughed. "What you tryin' to pull here, captain? That's play money." Cord quickly took out his wallet and flashed a thick stack of ones, making a joke about the bills Brick held. "That's funny, right?" he said, flashing the car salesman smile. "My friend's hilarious." Cord plucked a twenty from Brick's hand and ripped it in half, then counted off thirty one-dollar bills, the only style of bill that hadn't changed since 1957.

"Yeah. Just like the rooms, miss 'I need my privacy'," Cord said. "I can cover breakfast, and Flo's tip."

"Why do you have so many one-dollar bills, Cord?" Brick asked. "I mean, I know it's for strip joints. I just think you should clarify things for our lady friend."

Cord cleared his throat. "What you call a strip joint I call my ongoing effort to support young mothers and college students."

A truck drove by on the highway, the flatbed covered in wire cages, feathers from the chickens inside drifting in its wake.

"Just stop," Skid said. "What are we going to do?"

"I say those motorcycles are a nice option," Cord said. "Slip the friendly bikers some cash and we'll be at the lab in no time, then we can forget this every happened."

The thought of getting back on a bike—even without Jimm-Jimm and Svetlana flying overheard—sent a shiver through her.

"No motorcycles," she said, her tone hard and unmoving.

Cord lifted his menu again. "Then I don't care. I'm ready for breakfast," he said, wincing as Brick jabbed his ribs with an elbow.

The waitress, an attractive woman with sad eyes, approached the table with glasses of ice water to set in front of them. She pasted on a smile. "What can I get you folks?"

Brick slowly spread his menu on the table in front of him. "One of everything."

"Oh, come on," Cord said.

The woman, whose nametag read *Carla*, scratched it down on her order pad without looking back at Brick. She turned to Cord. "And you, hun?"

"Uh, sausage, a short stack and coffee." He looked at Brick then back to Carla. "How much does 'one of everything' cost?"

"Deal with it, Cord," Skid said and told Carla her order.

"I'll be back with your coffee in a jif—"

A *thum* sounded from somewhere outside, sending a ripple across the surface of the water glasses. Carla grabbed the back of the booth seat over Skid's shoulder, the fake smile dropped from her face.

"What the hell was that?" shot from Cord.

"Oh, don't worry about that. It's just one of the monsters," escaped Carla in a strained, awkward giggle. "I'll have that coffee right out."

6

Karl left almost as soon as he'd come. "Get your own damn peanuts," he said, and stomped into the hallway, trying to slam the door behind him, but the pneumatic dashpot wouldn't let him. The door closed slowly and quietly. Dave watched his boss disappear down the hall, slipping and almost falling, probably because of a piece of giant cockroach shit. Dave knew he should have followed Karl out the door and run. Freedom was just down the hall, but he was close to the Bridge and he knew he'd get closer. That Cheetos-smelling bastard would take him there himself. His ego was too big not to.

What did Karl want from him? The man had watched with almost lusty enthusiasm as the praying mantis he called Dr. Hahn ate the other David inch by inch. He wanted Dave to have a breakdown, and he wanted to be there to watch. Dave laughed and went to the refrigerator to grab another juice. Karl wouldn't see a breakdown, because it had already happened.

What did he say? Soldiers had gone into a wave to bring something back? What they hell could they bring back? Then he remembered what Karl had said. Giant praying mantis and Bigfoot.

"That's mad scientist kind of stuff," he said into the empty room, knowing full well Karl probably heard every word he said.

What if the soldiers didn't do what they were supposed to? Or worse, what if they did? Karl's muffler was already tied on with loose wire. One more bump, and it would fall off. And when that happens—

I'm dead. I have to go, today, now.

Dave Collison walked into the bathroom connected to the conference room by a short hall. He wanted to clean up before the next Miller Wave hit or Karl shot him with one of the guns that had to be lying around the lab complex. It was a military instillation after all. "It's important to be clean. You never know who'll see you in your underwear, Davey," Cecilia Sanderson had told him in the short time she was his foster mother.

You had that right, Momma C.

7

The coffee was black, strong and hot.

"This is better than the coffee at Dan's Daylight Donuts," Cord said, setting his cup back on the table filled with plates, some empty, some not. Brick had made his way through half the menu and didn't look like his pace was slowing.

"Dan's Daylight Donuts coffee sucks," Brick said through a mouthful of scrambled eggs.

Skid toyed with her omelet, the cream minced chicken not as odd as she'd hoped. The impact tremors from whatever Carla's "monster" was came at regular intervals. *Like steps. Something's walking out there. Something big.* Then the tremors stopped for a while before starting again. The monster must have had an itch or was just really out of shape.

"We're not home," she said. "This isn't even the same reality as ours. It's close, but you know, monsters."

Brick looked up from the plate of breakfast fish and fried potatoes, a piece of cod flopping on his fork. "How bad could it be?" he asked. "Our waitress talked like it was no big deal."

Skid's personal pot of coffee filled her thick American white porcelain cup about halfway before it emptied, drips slowly falling as she held it steady, staring at the waves the droplets made across the surface. Then the *thums* began again and the impact waves grew bigger. A pull, one that started in her stomach, threatened to bring the tears back. Skid took a deep breath and held it for a few seconds before letting it out through pursed lips.

"It's not a big deal to her," she said slowly, softly. "She lives here. But she's frightened of it, too. Didn't you see her face when she told us about the monsters? She laughed, but she didn't mean it."

Cord and Brick glanced at each other. Brick shook his head, and Cord said, "No."

Skid sat her cup heavily on the table. "Boys are dumb."

Carla brought their ticket after Brick had finished his last plate and stretched as far back as the booth allowed. The impact tremors were heavier now, Brick's stack of plates and silverware rattled with each step.

"Thank, you," Carla said, laying the bill down and topping off coffees. "You folks here long?"

"We could be," Cord said, his voice as smooth as Colt 45 malt liquor claimed to be in the '70s. "It really depends on when you get off wor—"

"No." Skid cut him off with a word, then turned to Carla. "We're not. We're going to Peculiar. Are we close?"

Carla's face dropped; she shifted her feet but didn't move. "You can't do that," she whispered, trying not to look at any one of them directly. "It's—it's—it's—" Her eyes pinched shut for a moment. When she opened them, the concern had vanished, her smile was back. "It's gone," she said flatly, then pointed out the plate-glass window down the gravel road to the west. "It used to be over there, but Gorgo stomped it flat back in—"

Carla shouted over her shoulder. "Hey, Martin. When did Gorgo eat all those people in Peculiar?"

"Fifty-five," Martin called from the kitchen. "No, no. Wait. It was '54. Linda was still in high school. Yeah, '54."

Carla lifted more of the plates from the table. "You folks can't even have friends or relatives from around here if you don't know that. Why do you want to go to Peculiar?"

Before Cord could answer, his stupid mouth sliding open to say something Skid knew he'd regret, the floor beneath them shook, and a chair fell over.

"Oh, no," Carla hissed. "He's coming this way."

8

The wooden handle unscrewed from the broom head easily. It took Dave twelve hits against the bathroom sink to realize he didn't need to break the handle to take it off. The tiny janitor's closet in the restroom held some interesting choices for self-defense. The aerosol cans would make a decent fire deterrent for the giant insects, but Lemaître Labs was a "smoke-free zone" except for the military brass whose rank was so high they only cared about what they wanted to care about, so they smoked in the conference room. If the janitors smoked, they kept their Bic lighters in their pockets instead of storing them with the supplies. The cans of furniture polish and air freshener wouldn't do much to keep the cockroaches off him without fire. He didn't know how Karl was able to stroll out into Roachville, but Dave wasn't stepping into that hallway without something deadly, or at least annoying. The broom was the only viable striking weapon. He briefly considered sharpening the end to a point, but he couldn't find anything to sharpen it with, and he didn't think he had the heart to stab a living creature anyway. Even if it was icky.

Dave walked from the bathroom using the broom handle like a staff, his face and hair washed, dirty underwear in the trash bin, teeth brushed with a paper towel and liquid soap, and shirt armpits blasted with lavender air freshener. *Date night in Roachville. The girl cock-roaches will be lining up for sure.*

The ambient light from the hallway had brightened some, but not much. He took a deep breath, walked to the door and tried the handle. It moved. *Still not locked. What's your scheme, Cheetosman?* Dave pulled on the door and it swung slowly open.

Any sign of the man-sized cockroaches from earlier was gone.

Did I dream that? No. He knew he hadn't. There were enormous insects capable of surviving an atomic holocaust loose in the lab. He'd seen them, and Karl had said it was the human resources department. The people who handled his health insurance and conducted irrelevant programs about civility in the workplace were now cockroaches. The face of the creature that slammed into the glass in the night flashed across his mind. *Eww.*

The hallway was empty. The white walls must reflect the ceiling fluorescents effectively enough to ward off the roaches. He knew he wouldn't have to worry about them with the motion-activated lights. Dave stepped out of the conference room, looking left and right like a cop in a 1970s TV show. Still nothing. Zombie-apocalypse silence engulfed Dave as he made his way toward the elevator. He'd told Skid and Brick at that doughnut shop with the terrible coffee not to use the stairs. The stairs were booby-trapped. Use the elevator, and that's damn well what he was going to do.

Halfway to the elevator, the lights went out.

9

The footsteps had become thunderous, sending Norman Rockwell prints and pictures of the stars of *Leave It to Beaver* and *Father Knows Best* crashing to the black-and-white tiled diner floor. The cigarette machine rocked back and forth, but it and the jukebox were fastened to the wall studs by metal cables. This wasn't Highway 71 Diner's first rodeo.

"That's not good," Brick said, an understatement, the word *good* coming out with a belch.

The thing outside came from the east, the part of the diner that backed up against the motel, so there were no windows. Their first look at the monster Carla called Gorgo was through the south window, when a dark and hulking figure the height of an office building parted a patch of trees and stepped through. Tall elms and cottonwoods shattered at the trunk and fell to the ground. No one screamed. Carla stood against the counter, grabbing a red vinyl-topped barstool in each hand. Marvin said something unintelligible from the back that sounded to Cord like, "Cheese and rice."

"What is that?" Skid croaked as she stood, sliding from the booth and falling against the counter next to Carla. She turned toward the waitress, the woman's face white as a vampire's. "Where'd that come from?"

Carla swallowed as the next tremor knocked her elbow into the pie display, throwing the door open and dumping a fat slice of coconut cream onto the floor. The monster moved into the parking lot, and a scaled, three-toed foot slammed atop the Studebaker, smashing it flat.

It's a—it's a—

"Dinosaur," Carla said as if she said that word every day to describe whatever passed by on the highway. Buick Roadmaster, Ford truck, International Harvester tractor, dinosaur. "The A-bomb tests. These things started coming back to life. That's Gorgo."

The monster paused to scratch under its chin with its little forearm before it roared. The windows vibrated. The shaker at their table tipped over, grains of salt bouncing over the Formica surface.

Something quick and sure as a bear trap snapped in Skid's head. It was her sanity.

"We're in a goddamned 1950s atomic warning science-fiction movie?" she screamed, throwing herself to her feet. "I want to go home."

"Skid," Cord said, his voice tense. "Don't do anything stu—"

Before he could finish, she threw open the diner door. The bell on a wire above it rang as she launched herself outside and sprinted toward the monster.

10

Andrew Ridgeley leaned into the Wham! poster from the left, smiling like he didn't mean it. Susan remembered tacking that poster over the head of her bed with pastel blue and pink thumbtacks that matched the splashes of 1980s colors surrounding the black and white photo of Ridgeley and George Michael. She lay with her head at the foot of the bed staring at the British pop duo, a bed she'd last occupied on August 22, 1984, the night before she drove herself to college because, "come on, Mom, I'm grown up now." Twenty-eight days later, her father killed her family.

No, I wasn't grown up, Mom. Nothing happened like it should.

"Sorry, Andrew," she said, her voice nearly silent over 'The A-Team' blaring through the thin walls from Tommy's room. "You were cute. But you were no George Michael."

A light rap sounded at the door. She sat up and swung her feet to the floor, the momentary flashback to eighteen gone. She now felt the sixty-something she was.

Come in? Can I say that? Is it really my room anymore?

She started to speak, to give someone permission to enter a place that felt familiar but was not home, when the knuckles rapped again. The door creaked open, and Muffit dashed in. The spaniel sprung onto the bed and jumped into Susan's lap, licking her face, the short, wet darts of its tongue the most comforting thing she'd experienced all day. Tommy stuck his head into the room, keeping the rest of himself safely in the hall.

"Hey," he said, staring at Susan.

"Hey," Susan responded. Although she'd loved Tommy when

she was a girl, that had changed as she grew older. He lived at home into his thirties, holding shit job after shit job, spending nights playing video games and mornings sleeping off whatever he'd drunk the night before. But now, seeing his sad, weak face looking into her high school bedroom, the anger melted. He was as lost as Dr. David Livingstone. *Mom and Dad didn't do him any favors.*

He stepped into the room, gaze still averted to the awful shag carpeting.

"You're Susan, aren't you?" he asked, his voice shaking. He looked up at her. "You're old. You're like, older than Mom." Tommy clenched his fists before speaking again. "But you have that scar on your chin from that time you fell off the swing. You have the same ears that don't have the parts that hang down."

"Lobes," she said, a hand instinctively reached to her ears. Her lobes were attached, Tommy's weren't, Mom's weren't. It was one of the few traits she shared with Delbert.

"You have the same eyes as Susan," he continued. "They're nice. How did you get here? You're from the future, right? If you occupied the same space as the Susan here, would the universe explode?"

"I guess I am from the future, or something like it," she said, the words sounding like a lie, but they had to be true. "And I know Dad was going to kill you, and Mother, and Muffit." This time she looked away. "I don't know about the explosion, though. Maybe it would."

Tommy nodded. "Yeah, maybe." His hands, which had been fidgeting around his shirt tail, found their way into his jeans pockets. "You killed Dad."

"Yes, I did." The words escaped her easily.

He nodded again. "He said he was going to kill me, you know. He told me that a lot. He told me that's why he didn't fix my teeth. He wasn't going to pay all that money when he was just going to kill me anyway. I saw him at the bottom of the stairs with all those people you brought. He had his sword."

A tear ran down his cheek. Tommy was still a lost little boy. Susan grabbed the pink comforter on her bed and squeezed.

"If you're from the future, then you didn't know me after tonight," he said. "I didn't live. I didn't get married or have kids. Now I get to do all that stuff."

Gasps came from the first floor, followed by a shout. Police sirens had made it into the house. The cars were maybe a few blocks away, but would be here soon.

"Mom called the cops. You should hide."

11

Cord sat in shock watching Skid run across the gravel, little tufts of dust appearing in the wake of her pink sneakers. The gargantuan creature stood on the outskirts of the lot, turning its blockish head full of sharp teeth, the thing's body covered in green scales. But the monster didn't see Skid, or if it did, it didn't care. She was too small.

"What the hell, Skid?" *This isn't happening, right? She's not actually running across a parking lot in 1957 screaming at a radioactive dinosaur, is she?* "Brick?" he said, but Brick had already gone. The bell above the door rang and Brick was outside, following Skid, the orc sword he'd leaned against the side of the building high above his head.

"What on earth are your friends doing?" Carla shouted, her tone not fear, not anger, but disbelief that anyone would do something as stupid as what she was watching.

Cord lifted Brick's explorer's pack and hefted it onto his shoulders. It was heavy. "Making my life even more difficult." He turned toward the door but stopped and nodded at Carla just as Brick reached Gorgo and swung the scimitar. "Hey, if we make it through this, you want to go out for drink later?"

Carla fished an unfiltered cigarette from her white vinyl purse and flipped open a Zippo lighter. "Sure," she said, grinding the flint wheel and sucking down nicotine and tar the surgeon general was still eight years from warning caused cancer. She blew out a puff of smoke. "Why the hell not. My husband was in Peculiar when Gorgo attacked. Bring me a toe."

A grin flashed across Cord's face before he dashed out the door.

This is stupid, Cord, whipped across his brain. *Stupid, stupid, stupid.* The self-defense mechanism in his skull, the one that had kept him alive and largely intact the past thirty-five years, sat silent. Duck, run from trouble, tell the authorities, don't jump off the bridge into the river like that moron Mike Miller did in high school even though Cord knew Miller would call him a pussy later (he did). Yeah, he'd done fine in life. So why didn't he stop running, even when the pack threatened to slide off and give him a second to think about what he was doing? Cord pulled the straps tighter and kept his feet pumping. Skid worked the giant lizard's left leg like Rocky on a side of beef in the Shamrock Meats freezer. Brick slammed the orc sword into the monster's right leg, giving it no more than a paper cut. Gorgo didn't seem to care, its eyes moved east, west and north in search of something worth eating.

Dust flew when Cord slid to a stop near the beast's tail, his heart pounding, his breath heavy. Skid and Brick took as little notice of him as the giant lizard.

"What are you doing, Skid?" he managed to spit out, leaning on the monster's tail for support while he tried to catch his breath. The radioactive flesh beneath the beast's scaly skin was oddly warm and tingly.

"I'm pissed," she said, matter-of-factly and delivered a right to Gorgo's leg.

Cord turned to Brick. "What about you?" Brick kept hacking. "Hey, Brick," he barked, the level of his voice surprising even him. "What are you doing?"

The Muffin Man Cord had seen in the field of orcs paused for a moment, his eyes nearly as dark and berserker as last night. Brick shrugged and hit the monster again. "Skid ran out so, you know, I thought we were attacking it."

"Attacking it? Attacking it?" Skid had lost it. At least, that's what he thought. Killing another living thing had taken something out of her; she was just trying to cope in her weird messed-up-childhood kind of way. But Brick? *That bastard's having fun.*

"This isn't a boss fight," Cord shouted, taking off the explorer's pack and throwing it at Brick's feet. "Exactly which vital internal organ were you planning to hit from down here? This isn't Bowser. Good ol' Gorgo doesn't even need a Band-Aid, *Brick.*"

The big man lowered his sword and looked at the pack lying in the dust. "But I thought we were attacking it," he repeated, picking up the pack and slipping it over his shoulders. "I was knocking down hit points."

Gorgo's tail twitched and Cord leapt out of the way. The bikers had decided they'd had enough. The roar of motorcycles buzzed like giant angry insects away from the diner, shooting onto the highway. The dinosaur screeched, high-pitched, whiny and nothing like in the movies, then tensed its legs to move toward the bikers racing north on the US 71.

"Grab her." Cord pointed at Skid as his feet churned on the gravel. Gorgo's massive leg clipped Cord and he flew across the gravel, landing on one knee. A scream caught in his chest as the monster's tail swept past, the tip slashing him across the belly.

Skid screamed when Brick wrapped a thick arm around her waist and slung her over his shoulder, but she didn't fight back. They had reached the gravel road Carla pointed out as the way to Peculiar when Gorgo blew a beam of nuclear fire from its mouth and lit the cornfields to their north on fire, chasing the bikers like a big, stupid dog.

Cord pulled the pistol from his pants pocket and held it sideways like street thugs did in the movies. He snapped back the slide and fired the gun until he'd emptied the clip. The bullets never came close to Gorgo, but it sure as hell made him feel better. He lowered the empty pistol and dropped it onto the dusty ground before looking down at the slash in his shirt. Gorgo had barely left a scratch.

"You're lucky," Brick said, his breath heaving as he swallowed his rage, the sudden loss of adrenaline causing his hands to shake. "You're okay."

A small, controlled voice cut the air. "I'm not," Skid said as Brick set her down. Her eyes were hazy with tears. "I want to go home."

Brick pointed west. "Then we have to make up time."

"Sure thing," Skid said, her voice shaky. "I always wanted to go to Fordor."

"Mordor."

"Whatever."

About a half-mile later, Skid and Brick passed a rusted, scorched sign that read "Peculiar," and realized Cord wasn't with them.

CHAPTER ELEVEN

STILL SEPTEMBER 7

1

SKID RAN through the shadows of circus tents carefully arranged along the southern outskirts of a small town in North Dakota; she didn't know the name and it didn't matter. All small towns looked the same after a while. The big canvas mountains shook as the men and women inside pulled down the giant wooden poles. They were animal handlers, performers and a few locals who were desperate enough to take forty bucks for an afternoon of sweat. The big top that trumpeted "Roe Bros. Traveling Circus" in big red letters would fall first, as it always did, the first tent to be packed away on the biggest tractor-trailer in the fleet. That wasn't part of Skid's job. Randall R. Roe told seven-year-old Skid her job was to stay out of the way. When she arrived at the traveling zoo exhibit, far away from the circus tear down, a noise pulled her to a stop. Bandy, the baby chimp, sat in small cage crying. Animal handlers had already loaded her mother onto the animal truck.

"Hey, there Bandy baby," Skid said, squatting next to the cage, holding onto it with her fingers. Bandy looked up at her with intelligent brown eyes and touched Skid's fingers, the ape's own were warm and soft. She whined. The noise, much too human, dragged tears into Skid's eyes. "I'm sad your momma is away, but I'm sorry. I can't let you out."

The small chimp, only about ten months old, released Skid's fingers and gently grabbed the door to the kennel and shook, her moist eyes never leaving Skid's. Bandy rapped the door to the little cage with her knuckles.

A feeling grabbed Skid, tying her stomach like a necklace thrown into a drawer. "Oh, come on Bandy, I can't. I really, really can't," she wailed. The knot in Skid's stomach pulled tighter. "Will you promise to be good?"

The chimp didn't move but locked mournful eyes with Skid.

Skid reached toward the gate latch. *It's okay. She'll play with me, then go back in her cage. No one will know.* "Dad would say you're manip, manip, manip-u-la-tive," she said as she released the latch and the cage door swung open.

Bandy sniffed and lifted herself onto her hands. Skid gently waved the little ape closer. "Come on, baby." Bandy did, knuckle-walking out of the cage and onto the grass, looking around her as if everything was new.

Skid reached out her arms for Bandy to melt into as she had before, but that had been when circus vet Doc Caldwell squatted next to her, helping Bandy along. This time Bandy didn't melt into Skid's arms. She silently dashed past the little girl and disappeared into the cornfield.

Oh, no. "Bandy," Skid screamed after her, springing to her feet and running into the corn after the ape. Too many steps later for Skid to count, she froze. Bandy had vanished into the sea of evenly placed green stalks that loomed over Skid's head, the bright Maya-blue sky occasionally peeking through like it couldn't find its way in. She didn't hear the little chimpanzee anymore; its hoots had vanished into the distance.

She turned in a circle and realized she was lost.

Cornfields had only held horror for her since.

"Hey, Skid," Brick said. He dropped a heavy hand on her shoulder. "What's the matter?"

She stood still, staring out over the cornfields that lined the road on either side. Her stomach didn't feel so good. "Bandy never came back," she said, her voice far away.

"Who?"

"Bandy, the chimp." That was the last time she saw the chimpanzee, and she'd told the Doc she'd seen townies near Bandy's cage. "I let her loose, and she disappeared into the corn. Everything is my fault."

The sword made a muffled zipper sound as Brick stuck it point-first into the dirt. He grabbed both her shoulders as gently as he could. "I know you're going through something here, but you've got to focus. What does Bandy the chimp have to do with Cord?"

"Nothing." She shook off his hands. "Let's go find him."

Cord sat on the side of the road to Peculiar in the shade of the corn, not twenty feet from where it intersected with the US 71. In the distance, the field Gorgo had lit ablaze still smoldered, fingers of black smoke wound into the sky.

"Hey, guys," Cord said as they approached, his pants leg soaked in blood.

2

Dave stopped the moment the lights blinked out, the broomstick clenched in both hands, his heart threatening to jump out of his chest. *You're a bitch, Karl. A little bitch.* The elevator, its door strangely dented, had only been about thirty yards down the first-floor hallway when Dave's feet failed him, but now, he might as well be on Europa. A curtain of black fell over him, and he couldn't pull it off.

Come on, he thought, the words of reassurance weak, even for his standards. *Keep moving. Keep moving. There's nothing here. Keep—*

A noise from behind knocked his brain off track. *A click? A crack? No. A scuttle.* Something hard hit the tiles, moving across the floor from near the conference room. He tried to swallow but didn't have enough spit.

The scuttle echoed down the empty hall again, tap-tap-tap, scrape. Dave loosened his grip on the broomstick and realized his hands shook. The cockroaches, the man-sized cockroaches that had sniffed around the conference room windows, could smell him. Last time, he'd been tucked away nice and safe. Not anymore.

Damn it.

The scuttling began again. *Oh, god. There's more of them.* The tarsus of the creature clicked behind him in the void. Dave stood frozen. *Come on. Come on, man.*

A hiss, metallic and alien, spat behind him and to his left, pushing him forward. His legs began to move ever so slowly. He'd read somewhere that when confronted by a predator in the wild, a person needs to try and make themselves appear bigger than they are. The animal might not attack if the strategy went off right—especially if the person didn't run—but these things weren't mountain lions or wolves. Dave thought he could deal with those. They were mammals, he was a mammal. Solidarity. The roaches might as well have stepped from a spaceship. Every molecule in Dave's body told him to run.

I can run. I can run and open the elevator, and this will all be over. I'll just run. He stuck the stick in the crook of his right arm and felt in his shirt for the card key. The card key he'd given it to Skid.

"Shit," he screamed.

His voice echoed down the hall, and the roaches scattered. One must have tried to go down the stairs and slammed into the metal door. Dave stood, his breathing hard and slow. *Keep moving,* his mind said, but he didn't know why. There were offices down this hallway he could hide in, but there was no way out of this hall except through the elevator, and he couldn't open the door.

Ten feet, ten yards, ten miles. It didn't really matter in real terms how far he'd traveled, sliding his feet forward in this dark, suffocating world. The scuttling, and worse, the chittering, from behind him crept closer. The roaches were regrouping. He could almost feel their presence edging into his personal space—the clicking mandibles, the antenna reaching out to feel him, the huge, bulging eyes groping for a sight of him through the darkness, black acidic ichor dripping from their jagged mouths. He tapped his forehead with the palm of one hand to shake out the thoughts, but that never worked like it did in the cartoons. In his mind, the roaches crept at his heels, along the walls and on the ceiling above waiting for the first chitinous monster to pounce. Then they would all feast. *On my flesh. I'm going to die right here like the other Dave. Right the hell here.*

He leaned to the right until his fingers brushed the wall, his heart trying to beat itself from his chest. Then his fingers hit it. A door. He gasped, and a hiss split the darkness from only feet away. "Ahhh," Dave screamed and spun, gripping the broomstick like a baseball bat, swinging at waist level. The wood connected with something hard and snapped in two. A piece flew into the black void and clicked down the hallway. The thing hissed again, but the harsh alien noise was farther away now. Sweat soaked Dave's shirt, a drop snaking down his butt crack.

"There's more where you found that, pal," he shouted in a shaky voice.

An electronic chime sounded from somewhere that was now behind him. A crack, tiny at first, slowly grew in the wall and spilled light into the hallway. The skittering resumed, faster this time, as a door slammed against the wall and the sound of the roaches disappeared.

Dave ran forward and jumped into the elevator.

3

"What happened to you?" Skid cut at Cord's pantleg as Brick knelt and dug through his explorer's pack. A hiss blew from clenched teeth when she yanked at the material and it didn't come free.

"I fell," he said, waving a hand toward the motel and diner parking lot. "My knee is screwed."

Skid cut the rest of the pantleg off, revealing a deep gash. The blood had already begun to clot but still oozed from the ragged, dirt-covered flesh studded with pieces of gravel.

"Oh, it's not bad," she lied.

"Here," Brick said, dropping a small leather satchel on the grass at the side of the road. "Found it."

"A purse?" Cord wheezed, pinching off a wave of pain.

The big man ignored him and took out a package bound with a leather strap. His fingers untied the knot with more deftness than digits that large should, and unfolded the package revealing a strip of white linen. He handed the bandage to Skid and pulled a small leather flask from the satchel.

"What's that?" she asked.

"Whisky."

Cord grunted as he lay down in the grass, his head shaded by cornstalks. "You've been holding out on me. Hand it over."

The lid came off with a pop. "Hold his legs," Brick said, eyes directed at Skid before he dumped the liquor over the wound.

A scream that may have started somewhere near Cord's testicles shot from him. Brick kept a hand on his chest and held him to the ground. The leather flask, capped, hit the grass and Brick used a short, thin blade from the medical kit to pick gravel from the wound.

"Now Cord," he said, taking the bandage from Skid. "This may sting a bit."

"Sting? A bit? Fuck you, Brick. Fuck you."

Two minutes later, Cord's cleansed wound lay tightly bound in a bandage. Brick tied the ends together and lowered the leg gently onto the ground.

"There," he said, leaning back to inspect the dressing. "I've just cured you of up to 2d4 of piercing or slashing damage. You're welcome."

Sweat dotted Cord's forehead and began to show on his shirt. He tried to sit, but let out a strangled scream. Skid held his shoulder to keep him from falling backward.

"I'll make sure to give you a review on Yelp." Cord adjusted himself and leaned back on his hands, a lie of a smile growing on his face. "I'll be okay. You guys go ahead. I can't walk much farther than back to the diner motel thingy anyway. You have to finish this."

Great. The ponytail that had started to come undone during the attack on Gorgo fluttered behind her as Skid shook her head. "This isn't some macho war movie 'go on without me' garbage, is it?"

"Pfft. From me? Not on your life. It's just, I'm as helpful as Bud Light Dave right now," he said, nodding toward the diner. "Besides, I have a date."

Skid stood and watched Carla jog toward them, a cigarette pinched between her lips. She didn't wait for the waitress to reach them.

"That's just great," Skid said and started the march back toward Peculiar.

4

The hand looked soft. It had to be; it hadn't done much work in its owner's life. Tommy held it out for Susan to grab. She didn't.

"Come on," he said. "You don't have much time."

Yes, I do. Delbert Sanderson's screams at Tommy, her leg moving, her foot planting itself in her father's chest, the push, the expression that sprang onto his face as the man who had stolen her family fell backward and broke his neck on the stairs. Those moments were all tattooed onto her memory. They would be there forever, and she welcomed them.

"I killed him, Tommy. I have to face that. I want to."

"But—"

Muffit leapt off the bed and stood in front of the door, growling. The people downstairs shouted when a knock came at the front door. Susan stood.

"The police are here. I'm sorry. I have to go."

Muffit jumped at Susan's legs, yelping as she made it to the door. She patted the dog's head and gave Tommy a tight hug before pulling the door completely open.

"Good-bye, Tommy," she said, then stopped and stared, the other things she wanted to say—*I love you*, and *take care of Mom*—stuck in her throat. Then a shimmer rippled through the walls of the house, and a Miller Wave washed over her.

The next moment, the wallpaper in the hall was the same, but dingier, yellowed. Susan stepped back into her room. Tommy was gone, George Michael and Andrew Ridgeley's black and white faces were gone. Her bed was gone. A toddler's plastic kitchen rested against the wall where her headboard had been, and boxes of games lined bookshelves. Mom's hope chest, lid removed, was in the middle of the room overflowing with toys, some old, some new, all broken in.

"Oh my god," Susan said, covering her mouth. Then she realized Muffit wasn't there.

"Who are you people?" came from downstairs, followed by the murmurs of the ghost group, who didn't know what had happened to them.

"Mom?" Susan stepped through the door and into the hallway. The body of her dead father no longer lay in a crumpled heap on the floor. Cecilia, wearing a pale blue terrycloth robe, stepped into view and stared up at her through pink cat-eye glasses, her silver hair tied into a bun. *I've never seen anything so beautiful.* "Mom? It's okay, they're with me."

"What are you doing here, Susan? Dinner's not until six." She frowned. "Is everything okay? Who are all these people? They're not staying for dinner, are they? The roast is just big enough for you, Dan and the kids and Tommy."

Susan smiled. She couldn't help it. She stood in her house talking with her mother, who had never seen a day after 8:50 p.m. on September 19, 1984. She started down the steps, wiping tears from her face with the back of her sleeve.

"Everyone's leaving, Mom. I can't wait for supper. What else are we having?"

5

The Miller Wave crashed into Skid and Brick in Atomic Monster Crazyworld as they approached Peculiar, Missouri. The undulating bubble of quantumwhatsit from the nearby lab appeared stronger, angrier than it had before. It rolled upon them, and a Shark Week of thrashing engulfed the ruins of the tiny town, washing over the cornfields, leaving buildings, trees, stoplights and banners over the street welcoming visitors to the 12th Annual Peculiarfest. A bright, shiny Midwest townscape replaced the scorched streets and skeletal buildings in a video wipe that spat out a world with modern cars in driveways and not a radioactive dinosaur in sight. Nope. Not one.

They weren't surrounded by cornfields on the outskirts of Peculiar anymore, they stood near the center of town; Peculiar had grown since 1957.

"I think I need a cigarette after that," Skid said, hands on her knife belt.

"I didn't think you smoked," Brick said, walking again.

"I don't. It's a figure of speech." She started after him.

A bright blue sky was dotted with fluffy, cumulus, "The Simpsons" clouds overhead. Skid listened, but everything in Peculiar seemed strangely quiet.

"We could ask somebody for a ride, you know," Skid said, pushing to keep up with Brick's long strides. "Or maybe Countryville has an Uber, or something. It would be faster."

He didn't stop; he didn't even look at her. "This is a quest, Skid. We didn't ask to be on it. We were dropped into it the moment Dave disappeared from Slap Happy's."

"Pffft, because I punched him." She gripped her knife handles in both hands. "That's not something I'd normally do. He just hit the wrong button."

"Don't blame yourself. Don't blame Dave. All of this, the dimensional shifts, the street names, the orcs and radioactive dinosaur, all of it, is the fault of some guy named Karl." He pulled a sheaf of napkins from Dan's Daylight Donuts out of his pants pocket. "The button that can shut this all down is in this lab," he said, scanning the napkin. "Our quest ends at that button."

He unfolded the napkins and pulled out the first, a map to the lab. "This is a noble quest. This quest will get me back to my muffin shop. It will give me an honest shot with Beverly. A noble quest doesn't have shortcuts."

"What about when Luke left his Jedi training early to go to Cloud City and rescue everybody from Darth Vader?"

Skid froze. The voice was Cord's.

"Well, yeah, but—" Brick began, then stopped himself and turned around. Cord stood five feet behind them.

"I thought you had a date?" Skid asked.

Cord laughed. "Date? That's funny. We're tramping through dimensions and you think I have a date."

Brick started to speak, but Skid grabbed his thick wrist to silence him. They all started down the empty asphalt street, passing a Sonic Drive-In to their left. The fast food joint stood quiet, no cars under the eaves, no carhops carrying trays, the electricity to the marquis off. The outside clock of the Community Bank of Peculiar across the street read 10:42 a.m./82 degrees, but its parking spots was empty.

"Hey, Cord," Skid said, pointing toward the drive-in. "Would you hop over there and see if it's open. I could use some tots."

"Sure," he said, his face as eager as preschooler. Cord broke into a jog and crossed the street toward the Sonic.

"What's going on, Skid?" Brick asked watching Cord run.

"I don't know," she said. "But that's not Cord."

"Yeah. You see his leg? It's fine."

Cord scampered down a ditch and up onto a patch of grass that sat in front of the restaurant before approaching the building and pressing his face against the window.

Skid slid her right hand onto her belt and wrapped her fingers around the hilt of a throwing knife. "But it is Cord, maybe Cord from a dimension where we didn't run into old Gorgo."

Brick's muscles tensed. "He's like Spock with a beard. We should keep an eye on him."

They continued on. By the time they reached the Tollbooth Coffee Company, its lights dark, its parking spots empty, Skid didn't think Cord was the only problem.

"Something's wrong," she said. "There's nobody here."

Small town ranch-style houses with silent wind chimes and black metal silhouettes of a cowboy smoking, pickups in the driveways, stood among the occasional businesses, a café here, another bank there. They stood silently.

"There's no sound here. There aren't even birds," Brick said. "There should be machinery, dogs barking, somebody mowing their lawn."

"Somebody running us down for walking in the middle of the town's main drag." The *Twilight Zone* vibe of this town gave Skid the jitters. "Or cops arresting us for vagrancy. We must look homeless." Her eyes ran up and down Brick. "Especially you with that stained shirt. That crappy backpack doesn't help."

"It's an explorer's pack," he said, hitching it higher up on his shoulders, the hilt of the orc sword stuck from the flap. "And I noticed that, too. It'll be lunchtime in a little while. Even if we just caught everyone at the wrong time, the streets should be busy. This is odd. It's really, really—"

"Don't you dare say it."

"—peculiar."

"What do you think, Cord?" Skid said, turning around to an empty street. "Cord's gone again."

"It's for the best." Brick glanced at Dave's map to Lemaître Labs and pointed toward a convenience store down the street before carefully folding the napkins and sliding them back into his pocket.

"We take North Street to Peculiar Drive then west on the YY. We'll be to the lab by early afternoon." He rested a hand on Skid's shoulder. "Our quest is almost at an end."

She walked from under his hand. "That's great, Lancelot."

A black pickup sat at a gas pump in front of the brown brick Casey's General Store. The store signage read, "Donuts. Sandwiches. Pizza." A poster of two slices of pepperoni pizza and a large Coke for "$3.75 Limited Time" looked at them from behind a sheet of Plexiglas. The food Skid left on her plate at the Highway 71 Diner in 1957 came back to taunt her.

"I really wanted those tots. Pizza wouldn't be bad either," she said. Brick didn't answer. She turned; he had stopped in the street a few feet behind her. "What are you—"

His arm lifted into a pointed finger and she followed it. The driver's side door of the pickup, a black Ford F-150, swung open and a man in a sweat-stained blue and gold NAPA Auto Parts cap and mirrored sunglasses pulled himself out. Although they couldn't see his eyes, Skid felt him staring. The man waved as he lifted the nozzle from the pump, an aw-shucks smile on his face.

"You folks look lost."

6

The elevator at Lemaître Labs didn't play its usual music, and Dave didn't mind at all. Everyone's musical tastes sucked because no one listened to Oingo Boingo anymore.

The scientist sat on the floor of the elevator in his dirty slacks and someone else's shoes; his beard growth had started to itch. The broken broom handle was still gripped in his fist, the splintered end resting against the *door close* button. The bell rang and he pushed the broken stick against the button again. The door started to open, revealing the Bridge, the control room to the supercollider, but it swiftly slid shut again, protecting Dave inside a six-and-a-half by six-foot box which he was more than happy to stay in. There weren't any monsters in the elevator. He wondered if there were any in the Bridge, but it didn't matter, he had to go there. He also had to use the bathroom.

Get up. Get out of here. The red button was out there, behind the door to the Bridge. A terrible thought crept into his mind. It would be easier to get to the supercollider itself without his card key than it would be to get inside the control room. He could stop the madness from there; he could shut off the machine manually, stopping the experiment, stopping the Miller Waves and setting everything back to normal. Probably. It would also shred every atom that made up Dave Collison, shooting the electrons, protons and neutrons into an uncountable number of directions to float forever in space, but he *could* do it.

There's gotta be an easier way.

The bell dinged again, and the doors slid open. Dave's muscles tensed to push the button again, but he let out a stifled scream instead. Karl Miller stood in front of the elevator. Dave's boss pressed his right hand against the butt of the retractable door until it moved to close, struck his hand, and remained open. Dave jabbed the button again and again. It didn't budge. Then his eyes noticed the Army-issued pistol tucked in the front of Karl Miller's pants.

"Glad you could join me, Collison," Karl said, his face blanketed in oddly sharp shadows.

"A gun, Karl?" Dave said in his best Bud Light Dave voice. "Could you be any more cliché?"

"Shut up."

But he couldn't shut up. His brain seemed to be on auto-smartass "You know you're supposed to put the gun in the back of your pants. If it discharges in the front you might shoot off your dick."

Something big pounded down a nearby hallway, slamming again and again into a wall, or a door, or the thick sheets of bulletproof glass that filled every window frame. Whatever it was, each strike sent tremors through the lab.

A vibration, a shimmer separate from the pounding, came from underneath them and seemed to turn the floor into water, though Karl's feet didn't sink into it. Then the Miller Wave burst through and swept over them both, disappearing through the ceiling and out into the universes. Dave looked around. He still sat on the elevator floor pushing the broken broom handle into the *door close* button while Karl remained outside holding the door open, the gun in his pants. The vicious striking continued down the hall. *Nothing changed. Nothing.*

"You're an ass, Collison," Karl said and motioned for Dave to stand. "Come with me. There's a friend I'd like you to get reacquainted with."

7

Skid had a bad feeling about the man with the black truck, but she had a bad feeling about everyone, even before the United States government won the goddamned eighth-grade science fair and sent them careening through time and dimensional space. Now she didn't even trust the look of herself in a mirror because the one at the motel showed a strand of gray.

With a click, the guy in the NAPA hat pulled the nozzle from the filler neck and snapped it back into place on the pump. A receipt crept out near the credit card slot, but he left it there to ripple in a slight breeze. The man did this all on autopilot, those mirrored sunglasses never leaving them.

"You're not from around here," NAPA Man said through a mouthful of white teeth. It wasn't a question. Skid didn't know what she'd expected him to sound like, but not this. The farmer sounded like he was about ready to step into a boardroom, not a dusty pickup with an I ♥ BEEF bumper sticker. He moved away from the pump and around to the driver's side door.

"Can I give you a lift somewhere?" he asked. "There's not a whole lot west of here but Kansas wheat fields. They're pretty but get kinda stale after a while."

Where is everybody? Skid wanted to ask but didn't. This cattle farmer in FBI shades sent claxons ringing in her head. She no longer wanted a ride. She just wanted this over.

A hand gently grabbed her elbow and jump-started her feet into motion.

"Keep moving," Brick said from the corner of his mouth, not loud enough for the farmer to hear. "We're not home yet."

The door to the pickup moaned as NAPA Man swung it back open and pulled himself into the driver's seat. "Suit yourself," he said, their backs now to him as they made their way to North Street toward Peculiar Drive, heat from the sun beginning to make the late morning uncomfortable.

"Hey, circus is in town," NAPA Man called after them. "Maybe you folks'll come join us. I hear the motorcycle bear trick will make you slide off your seat."

Skid felt her legs stiffen, but Brick didn't let her stop.

8

Something translucent and gooey covered the thick, bullet-proof glass set in the steel door that separated the Bridge from engineering. It could have been saliva, or Vaseline, or gelatin. Whatever, it was wrong.

"I figured this would be the last place you'd take me, Karl," Dave said, still clutching his broken broom handle but now out in the hall.

Karl asked him to leave it, and after numerous hand gestures toward his pants and a few pelvic thrusts to drive home the point that Karl did indeed have a gun, Dave dropped the stick on the tiles. Karl swiped his key card across the sensor, and they stepped into the control room.

The scientist looked smug. Pricks looked smug. Dave shoved his hands in his pockets and fumbled with his keys and ChapStick.

"What's so funny?" Karl asked.

Dave didn't know he'd been smiling, but yes, he had. "I was just wondering what the company head shrinker would make of you."

Karl set his key card on a bank of computer monitors and shut the door to the hall behind Dave. He motioned Dave toward a wall with a heavy set of sliding doors, far from the control panel.

"I'm doing my job, Collison. I'm doing what Uncle Sam is paying me to do." He shoved his fists into his love handles. "I've found a gateway to other realities. What have you done today?"

Not waiting for a reply, Karl shifted out of his normal slouch and yelled into the room, empty except for a control panel, computer monitors and a couple of swivel chairs, "Hey, guys. Who's the Dimension King? What? It's me? Why yes, it is." He pulled out the gun and pointed it limply toward the floor. "You tried to stop me, you know. On Friday. You tried to get every scientist in the lab to go against the very plan we were all here to accomplish."

Dave slowly raised his hand. "Yeah, excuse me there, Chief. Nobody but you knew the plan. We only knew our little puzzle piece. You filled us in on Friday and when I put the puzzle together, I knew this was going to happen. This catastrophic blending of the timelines. This travesty of nature. This, this—"

"Brilliance."

"Yeah, okay. I was going to say fuckupery, but brilliance works, too, I guess."

Karl growled, but Dave kept talking.

"Reality has changed." He almost waved his hands, but the gun Karl held kept them down. "Let me repeat. Re-al-it-ee has changed. It *changed*, Karl. Everything's the same, but everything's different. Buildings look like they always did, but their names are wrong. People I knew, I didn't know anymore. History—history, Karl— history is different. I saw my grandfather. He died when I was a kid, but you know what? I saw myself standing next to him the day he died in 1984."

"So?"

"I relived that day, and it's your fault." Dave pulled one of the office chairs toward him and sat down. "You're either a raving loony or an asshole. I haven't decided which."

The gun pulled level with Dave's face.

"Okay," Dave said. "I'll go with both. Can I log out of the system? I kind of forgot to when I left work Friday."

9

The arena under the great tent of The Roe Bros. Traveling Circus reeked of elephant shit and sorrow. A circus tried to mask all that with lights and music, sequins and misdirection, but down on the floor, the smell was impossible to miss. The night Skid woke in the hospital, the metallic scent of industrial strength antiseptic covering everything, she could still smell the circus. It was in her nostrils. She feared it was ingrained too deeply in her psyche to get free of. That night, while she suffered through stitches and the nurses stopping by to make sure her concussion wouldn't kill her in her sleep, was the night she decided the circus was her past.

"Circus?" The word tasted like a ghost pepper dipped in the blood of a serial killer. "You're not getting me within a mile of that thing."

The black truck pulled out of the convenience store parking lot behind them and drove past, NAPA Man watching them instead of the road the way they did in movies. He pulled onto North Street, then west.

"We might not have a choice," Brick said, releasing her elbow as he continued walking. "He's going our way."

She stomped ahead of him. Of course he was going their way. Their trip, their twenty-mile trip from Dan's Daylight Donuts in Kansas City to Peculiar, just kept getting harder, like the levels of a video game.

Evenly spaced white and yellow houses gave way to larger brick ones set back farther from the street, which quickly dissolved into a smattering of crappy "I only care about the dog I leave outside on a chain year-round" houses with overgrown yards. By the time they reached the highway, the houses were gone. Cornfields ran on either side of the chip-and-seal asphalt road. It was as if the town of Peculiar was an island in an ocean of unsustainable agriculture. About a mile down the road, the crown of an enormous canvas tent rose above the fields.

"No," Skid shouted, throwing her body around looking for something heavy to grab and heft as a weapon. She didn't see anything, so pushed her hands into her belt.

"I almost didn't see it," Brick said, slowing his pace.

"The tent?"

Brick nudged his big head toward the north side of the rural highway. The nose of the black F-150 from the gas station stuck out from between cornfields on a gravel road Skid would have missed until they were upon it. A chill, like she'd sucked down a slushy too fast, clamped her stomach into a knot and traveled up her body until her shoulders shook.

"He's waiting for us," she whispered, knowing she was Miss Obvious, but she couldn't help it, her guts where in a slushy ball.

Brick turned her toward him, his face warm and uncomfortably confident. "We can go into the corn and lose him."

"Cord can't do that," a feminine voice said behind them. "Not with his leg in this condition."

Skid and Brick slowly turned to find Cord behind them, an arm slung around Carla the waitress' shoulders. A cigarette hung from the corner of her mouth; Cord's leg was wrapped in a blood-stained bandage.

"Well, obviously," Brick said like the two had been behind them all along. "Then we march on. You guys okay with that?"

At that moment, Skid understood something. Brick really was the leader. He would take care of her whether she wanted him to or not. He was the hero of her story. Some of the weight that sagged her shoulders fell away.

Carla the waitress took a deep inhale of filterless smoke and blew it out. "Are we getting on with this or not," she said. "This guy owes me a drink."

Brick released Skid and turned west. "Okay, then. We keep going."

The farmer watched them through the cab window as they approached, the sun glinting off his mirrored sunglasses. He didn't move; he might as well have been a mannequin, except for that smile. That toothy, Jimmy Carter mouthful of piano keys seemed to follow them more than the man's mirrored eyes as they approached the gravel road and walked across its twelve-foot width before losing the truck behind them, hidden by corn.

Moments later, the slight grinding clunk of the truck slipping into gear, followed by the crunch of tires on gravel. Then the truck hit the blacktop and all they heard was the subtle growl of the big engine.

"He's behind us," Brick said. "I don't think he'll hit us. But don't turn around."

NAPA Man was herding them toward the circus. That much, to Skid, was obvious. She stuck a fist in the air, middle finger extended.

"Who is that guy?" Carla asked, because Cord's smart mouth was clenched in too much pain.

Brick opened his mouth to speak but Skid cut him off.

"Evil," she said.

"Well, that's a cheery thought," Carla said through a mouthful of smoke.

Skid turned and nodded to her. "I'm glad you're here. Do you know how difficult it's been not having another woman to talk to in this sausage fest?"

Brick snorted. "I've been talking with you."

"It's not the same." Skid turned back toward the highway and kicked a loose piece of asphalt that bounced into a weed-filled ditch.

"Why not?"

"What you know about women could fit in the front pocket of these jeans," she said.

"How big is the pocket?"

An audible sigh escaped Skid. "There isn't one, right, Carla?" Carla didn't answer and Skid didn't turn around because she knew the waitress and Cord were gone.

The truck crawled along the asphalt at least thirty yards behind them as they walked, their pace never changing. As the big tent grew closer and closer, the fist in Skid's gut grew bigger and bigger. The tent, the lights, the noise, the crowd, the heat, the smell she knew festered under all that canvas. *Blech.* She never thought she'd ever experience it again, any of it; now a circus tent loomed over her.

"I don't care what he wants. We're just going to walk right past—" Brick's voice cut off mid-sentence. Skid didn't stop; she didn't dare to.

The corn shook on both sides of the road and Skid's legs faltered but didn't stop. Visions of hundreds of angry chimps behind those stalks scraped across her mind. Maybe the imaginary locals she'd blamed for Bandy's disappearance were out there, too, with chains to capture her and drag her back to the circus. She inhaled sharply, not realizing she'd been holding her breath. Brick put an arm around her and kept walking.

Figures, dark at first, bled from the field as the corn parted. People drifted from the field and onto the road in steady, even steps, all heading toward the circus tent.

"The whole town's here," Skid whispered.

Brick turned his shoulders and looked behind them, but there was no escape route. The townspeople melted from the field there, too, forming a barrier behind the truck and the NAPA Man, his John Elway teeth gleaming from behind the truck's safety glass. Brick knew they could get through them but didn't know where they'd go. That group could easily chase them down and overwhelm them with sheer numbers.

"They want us to go to the tent," he said, the townspeople taking a collective step toward them to narrow their lane as if choreographed. "I don't think we have much choice."

"Nope." She pulled the sleeves of her jacket around her waist to hide the knife belt and cinched it tighter. "Let's get this over with."

10

Karl shook his head, the grin, for once, not stained orange from Cheetos. "I'm not letting you close to the control panel. I'm not stupid."

Dave knew the man wasn't stupid, but that didn't mean anything at the end of the world. Karl had brought the person who wanted to stop his insane experiment to the one place in the universe it could happen—the Bridge.

"Then why am I here?" There was no question in Dave's mind that Karl was in over his head. He just didn't know it. Yet. Dave pointed toward the big red button, next to the door to engineering. "I'm here to push that button."

Confusion spread over Karl's his face. He didn't know why Dave wasn't scared out of his mind. He lifted the pistol, not like he intended to use it. More like he'd brought it for show-and-tell.

"But I have a gun."

"That you're not going to use." This might have been a bluff—it certainly seemed like one—but something about Karl's body language told Dave it wasn't. "And you're a monologue machine."

Dave paused, his attention solely on his boss's eyes. He thought for a moment Karl might cry.

"You're a walking cliché," Dave continued. "The government hired you to break the universe, which you did, so congratulations there." Anger seethed close to the surface, waiting for the last straw. Karl had engineered the most insane, most destructive force since Oppenheimer, Szilard, Bethe, Lawrence, Fuchs and the rest of the brilliant madmen in the Manhattan Project had developed the atomic bomb, and he was too Fuchsing blinded by achieving it he couldn't see how Fuchsing stupid it was. "Now you're walking around with a pistol you don't know how to use and getting ready to monologue your ass off like a poor excuse for a Bond villain."

He jerked the pistol up to his waist and pointed it at Dave. "I know how to use this," he said, aiming like they did in 1970s cop shows.

Dave's eyes narrowed as he wondered when he'd finally grown a pair. "Show me."

The air conditioner kicked on, blowing cold air over Karl. His hair fluttered. He reached up and tried to smooth it back into place. It didn't work. "Okay, I will."

"No, you won't."

His eyes narrowed. "Yes, I will."

Dave leaned forward in the chair, his hands on his knees. "No. You won't."

"Yes, I—"

Dave shot out of the chair and gave him the finger. "Then do it. I'm right here."

The pistol, dull in the florescent lighting of the lab, swung away from Dave. Karl wasn't ready to shoot him. His hand tensed around the handle, but nothing at all happened.

"What?" Karl gripped it harder, and when that didn't work, he hit it with his other hand. "Shoot. Just shoot you stupid thing."

A shadow grew in engineering. Dave could make it out in the corner of his eye, but Karl's back was to the door.

"That was awesome, Dr. Nope."

Karl swung the barrel toward Dave just as the shadow came to life, slamming into the door. A face full of sharp white teeth chewed the glass. A scream tore from Karl, and he lurched away from the Bigfoot-thing that used to be Dr. Oscar Montouez, his arms pinwheeling comically. The pistol flew from the scientist's hand and clattered across the floor.

The sound that began as laughter deep inside Dave caught in his throat when the floor began to shake. Another Miller Wave was coming.

It didn't occur to Dave to pick up the gun.

11

The entrance to the Big Top loomed in front of them, its flaps tied back with rope, the interior as black as a vacation photo from Tromsø, Norway, in contrast to the high late-morning sun. Townspeople lined the path in front of a pasture flattened by trampling feet and the countless cars and pickups from town around the circus tent.

"Have you noticed something odd about these people?" Brick asked, hands wrapped in the straps of his backpack, voice betraying nothing. Skid thought he might be enjoying this.

"You mean other than everything?" she said.

"No. More specific than that." He pointed toward his right to the high school marching band that formed the front line of the human fence. "They're all wearing sunglasses."

"So?"

Brick shook his big head. "I don't know yet," he said, walking into the tent with long, sure strides. Skid followed. The smell was something solid.

"Dear god," she wheezed, her breath snatched from her. There was no stench of manure, sweat, or depression. It was death. A wall of people forced Skid and Brick forward, and they stepped into the first ring of this three-ring clusterfuck to get out of their way. Sunlight pushing through the canvas overhead was the only light in the tent. In minutes, the residents of Peculiar filled the metal stands with pine boards for seats; they'd made no noise, thrown no elbows. They simply filed in and sat down, save for the ones who blocked the exit.

"What the hell's that smell?" Brick asked, leaning in close.

"Death. It might be us in a few minutes."

"Huh?"

The audience sat still and silent. Skid loosened the knot on the sleeves around her waist. "Get ready for anything," she said aloud, not caring who heard her.

The silence grew as if the audience anticipated the show and held its collective breath.

"Ladies and gentlemen," a voice echoed in the dim light and golf claps rose from audience. "Welcome to Paradise."

The golf claps became a full-on come-on-KISS-we-need-an-encore madness. The noise, nearly deafening, stopped as quickly as it started.

Lights high up on poles snapped on, flooding the tent in bright yellow, and Skid almost fell into Brick.

A man, or what could have been a man, stood in the center ring, a microphone in his bony hand. His tuxedo, similar to what Randall Roe wore when he whipped up a crowd, was torn and stained with mold.

A huge false handlebar mustache rested under his nose, held in place by a strip of stained elastic. But his face almost knocked Skid to the floor of the tent; strips of rotted flesh dangled from bleach-white bone.

"Don't look at the floor." The words were close, but she had a hard time hearing them. She thought they'd come from Brick.

"What?"

"Don't look at the floor," he repeated, his face inches from her ear.

She looked at the floor. Scraps and pieces of flesh scattered the ground, and human skulls lined the ring. "I think I'm going to throw up."

Something moved in her periphery. Her head instinctively turned toward it. Human-shaped figures melted from the harsh shadows cast by the spotlights, some with tattered circus costumes, others nude, bones showing through holes in their flesh.

"What kind of hell is this?" fell from Skid's slack, dry lips.

A sound, the Gregorian chant of the damned, started low through the stands and grew in pitch until Skid nearly threw her hands to her ears. Then it stopped. The townspeople lifted their hands to their sunglasses and pulled them off as if they were of one mind. A swallow caught in Skid's throat. She saw what kind of hell this was. The eyes that had been hidden by those dark glasses were black, solid black. No iris, no sclera. Just black—sharks' eyes.

"We gotta leave." Brick sounded panicked. "Like, right now."

"Let's give it up for our guests," the dead man in the tuxedo shouted, the microphone booming his hollow voice over the audience. His emaciated arm and fleshless hand picked them out, as if the audience didn't know who he was talking about. The golf claps returned. "They're the next brave souls—" The thing's voice drew *souls* out for seconds "—to try the Ride of Death."

Someone shouted from the distance, but Skid couldn't make out from whom, or where it came from. In the stillness of the thousands of things that looked like people sitting on bleachers in this tent of death, this one flaw, this one outburst, felt wrong.

Brick reached down and took her hand. She let him.

"Aaaand," the emcee boomed. "What happens if the motorcycle —" He paused, and another spotlight sprang to life, revealing a Laverda American Eagle 750cc not ten feet from them. "—fails to clear the ring of fire?"

On the opposite side of the center ring, a hoop much too small to fit the motorcycle through, suspended by means they could not see, sprang to life. Fire erupted from it in a loud, low whoosh.

Another chant started in the crowd, low at first, then pounding like a drumbeat. "Eat them. Eat them. Eat them."

The smell, the heat, those dark black eyes hit Skid with fists. "You're right, we gotta leave." She grabbed Brick's sleeve and yanked. "Now."

"Who's ready for some action?" the emcee bellowed, and the stands exploded into applause. Two of the skeletal beings shuffled toward the center of the ring pushing a ramp for the motorcycle. There wasn't another ramp on the other side of the flames to absorb the blow of the landing.

The emcee stepped toward them, its thin body momentarily blocked out a spotlight, throwing it into silhouette as it donned a top hat. For a moment, it could have been Randall Roe.

But she knew it couldn't be Randall. She wasn't that cursed.

"It doesn't hurt that much, does it?" Randall asked Skid as he pushed her wheelchair down the hospital hallway toward the front glass doors. "I mean, you can walk, can't you?"

"It's procedure," the gruff nurse beside him said. She hadn't been gruff to Skid, just to the man whose motorcycle trick had put a sixteen-year-old girl into the hospital with a concussion, stitches, and broken bones.

"I'm not very good with motorcycles," Skid said.

Randall nodded, his grin too merry for her tastes. *You're supposed to be sorry, Dad.*

"I saw that, kiddo. But you need to do something. You're old enough now you need to hold a real job because—"

"Responsibility is what keeps the trains running," she finished for him. "I know."

The nurse grunted.

Randall glanced at the nurse then snapped his attention back to the hall before him. "What are you good at?" he asked. "You know, circus-wise."

Circus-wise. Skid knew at that moment in just two years she'd never have to do anything circus-wise ever again. She'd get her GED and drive into the sunset—on anything as long as it wasn't a motorcycle.

"I'm pretty good with knives," she said.

CHAPTER TWELVE

SEPT-GLITCH-IN-THE-MATRIX-EMBER 7

1

THE PISTOL LAY on the floor between the two men. Bud Light Dave ignored it and sat casually back on the office chair. Karl lifted himself from the hard, cold floor, his whole body shaking as Oscar pounded the door from engineering, screaming something over and over. Dave couldn't tell what his chicken wing–eating friend said. The door and window were designed for noise dampening, and lipreading a Sasquatch was hard. Dave also didn't know where all this was going, but Karl wasn't nearly as in control as he thought.

"You looked like a pinwheel," Dave said, smirking. "You gotta admit that was pretty funny."

"Shut up, Collison." Karl flashed him a pained look and moved in a wide arc away from the door to the opposite side of the room, a slight limp in his step. Karl didn't move toward the pistol; he didn't seem to remember it was there.

"You're in no position to be a smart-ass." Karl reached for a bank of computer terminals and leaned against a monitor, his face drained white by Oscar's outburst. The hatred from Oscar was palpable even through the thick ballistic glass. "I'm in command here," Karl shouted, holding up his right hand, index finger out. "I have a—" He looked down. "Dang it."

It was at this point Dave realized there were two options open to him. Karl would either kill him and this shit show would be over, or Karl's head would explode on its own. Then he could turn off the machine at his leisure.

"You still haven't told me why you brought me here," Dave said, nodding toward the master control panel across the room. "I could just hit the big red button and, boop, this is all over. You're not yourself, you know? Have you finally contemplated the possibility your actions could strand you in a universe that never invented Cheetos?"

The rage on his boss's face returned. His skin glowed red as his hands shot out to pull the monitor right off the desk. The government-purchased computer crashed onto the floor in a shattered mess that would require quite a bit of paperwork to replace.

"Stop it." The words came out in a controlled burn. "I know what you're doing." He stood straight and tucked his shirt back in as well as he could. "We're here for two reasons." He waved a hand dismissively before starting again. "One, I thought the cockroaches in HR would eat you, but apparently I can't trust HR to do anything right. Two, since you're still alive, I want you to see this experiment—my experiment—through to the end. Besides—" He reached into his front pocket and pulled out a large brass key, the key to the control panel. No one could hit the button without that key. "—it's not like you can just walk over and boop."

Karl threw his shoulders back and tried to walk like he owned the place, but he'd hurt his leg jumping away from Oscar and instead resembled a drunken sidekick in a 1960s western.

"I really wish you'd look at this from any perspective other than your own," Dave said, leaning back in the chair and lacing his fingers behind his head. "You've altered—" The room wavered and fell in on itself for a moment before reality popped back in an elastic snap. He didn't flinch. "—the flow of time and have intersected dimensions. These aren't just paradoxes and temporal causality loops we're dealing with here. These are—"

A man who hadn't been there before stepped into Dave's line of sight. Dave shot out of his chair, sending it wheeling back into the wall.

"Wha—?"

Dave had to give himself a moment to understand what his eyes told him. This handsome man was a clean and freshly shaven version of him except for his short but noticeable sideburns. He also still wore the shoes taken by the homeless guy. An urge to tackle the man just to get his shoes surged through Dave, but he didn't move; his head was too jumbled.

"You're me," he said.

Clean-David ignored Bud Light Dave as he bent and picked up Karl's pistol from the floor.

"She's coming," he told Karl, his voice calm, serious. "We have to be ready."

Karl leaned toward him over a computer monitor, wincing at the pain in his leg. "Who's coming?"

"Skid," Clean-David said. "She'll be here soon."

"Who's Skid?"

Dave sat back down. "Oh, you'll like her, Karl. She's a real people person." He eyed Clean-David, who held the gun like he knew what he was doing. "This is really exciting and all, but you never mentioned I'd meet myself from another dimension when you hired me. I'm going to have to ask for a raise."

2

The smell of death inside the circus tent was nearly overwhelming in the late-summer heat. Skid swallowed, trying to keep her stomach down where it belonged. The circus master stepped closer and grinned, but she couldn't tell if it was a real grin. The thing no longer had lips.

"But before we watch our guest daredevils brave the ring of fire, let's hear it for Madame Zorelda and her amazing chimps." The crowd burst into eerily synchronized applause as a flap in the tent whipped open and a zombie in bright gypsy clothing lurched into the center ring dragging a chain.

No.

Two hulking, stoop-shouldered figures appeared in the tent flap, emerging from some dank, dark enclosure that had hid them from the audience. Madame Zorelda took two more steps, and the chain grew taut. The gypsy pulled and the pair of male chimpanzees followed her into the ring, swaying back and forth on their knuckles. Swaths of fur were missing from their torsos, and the ribs of one showed through a rip in its gray flesh.

The ring master waved a hand, and the metallic tick-tick-tick of a winch came from somewhere behind the stands.

"As a warm-up for the main event, who wants to see Madame Zorelda's magnificent beasts, creatures so much like ourselves—" He paused, raising a hand above his head as two human figures were lowered from the darkness. "—tear this nice couple from Wisconsin to ribbons?"

The audience clapped in a drum-like cadence. The couple, their arms held above their heads by ropes, screamed from the sudden movement of the wench, either from the shredding of their muscles or the goddamned horror of it all. The chimps started hooting, a dry, hollow sound from rotting throats. Brick took a step forward.

The chimps, far removed from the beautiful Bandy, shifted their weight on their short, thick, decaying legs, rocking back and forth like a wave. Skid's own legs had grown weak. She stepped past Brick, wobbly as a drunk. "Hey," she tried to shout at the ring master, but it came out as a squeak. "Me first."

The zombie circus master glared at her, yellowed teeth gleaming in the spotlight.

"Yes?" Its voice jagged as rusty steel. It turned toward the audience, spinning slowly on impossibly thin legs to take everyone in. "Who's hungry?"

The Gregorian chant started again, and Skid realized finally that, like the applause, these people were cheering as one. She felt small. *I'm going to die here.* The circus zombie snapped its fingers, and the motorcycle roared to life, then the spindly rotting ringmaster stepped from behind the spotlight, face ragged, one cheek hanging in a fold like lunchmeat. Skid flinched. Flies buzzed everywhere.

"I'm sorry, dear, but you'll just have to wait your turn," it said, too low for the audience to hear. "Bobo and Bandy need to eat."

Bandy? Memories of the baby chimpanzee, small, sweet, soft, clinging to her shirt, holding her index finger tightly in its fist like a human infant would as Doc Caldwell smiled at them both. *She likes you,* Doc had said as Bandy's momma watched from a nearby cage. Skid looked at the monsters in the middle ring. Neither of them was Bandy.

"You bastard," she whispered.

Brick bellowed like a bull and shot forward past the ringmaster, pulling the orc sword from his backpack as he went. The master's top hat slid to one side as it swung at Brick, its bony hand missing him by a foot. Brick rushed the first naked circus zombie and swung, hewing through its chest with the rough blade, its upper half sliding off its lower like in a cartoon. The big man leapt between the chimps and caught one of them in the temple, sheering off its thick skull cap.

The ringmaster stepped in front of Skid, hiding Brick behind its sunken ribcage, its face in a grinning rage. She tried to step back, but her legs wouldn't let her. The zombie's face wavered as the bone, the rot, and the flap of skin swirled and smoothed.

"No," Skid whispered, the strength starting to melt from her knees. "You can't."

Before her, in a moldy tuxedo, stood Randall Roe. Her legs buckled, and she dropped to her knees on the rancid, bloody floor.

"Dad?"

The man in the tuxedo chuckled, low and powerful. "Yes, my child," it said in Randall's voice.

A sweat broke over her face. Skid hadn't seen Randall Roe in years, and he didn't look any different. A wave of doubt crashed against her. *Daddy? Are you here to help me?* She shook her head to clear it. A fly crawled across Randall's cheek and disappeared up his left nostril; he didn't notice.

When she first left home, working her way across the Southwest, waitressing, cleaning motel rooms, late-night clerking, she kept up on the circus, spending free time in public libraries where cards were sometimes free and internet time was short. Then she went north into a part of the Midwest that didn't intersect with Randall's schedule. She found comfort, and quiet, and a job where nobody asked questions. She lost track of him. But this—He was here. Her father was here, smiling at her, flies crawling over him. *Does he forgive me for running away?*

"My child," the thing said in a voice that was no longer Randall's and held out its skeletal right hand. A centipede fell from the creature's sleeve.

She clenched her eyes tight. Motorcycles, clowns, fixed games, living in a trailer, prom, bears. Her eyes popped open, but the illusion remained. Randall R. Roe stood before her, arm held out in welcome.

You're not my dad. The thought small, weak, suffocated in a cloudy mental haze.

"Come to Daddy," it said.

Her right leg twitched, and she began to rise. The circus master's grin grew and a strip of its cheek broke and fell to the bloody, shit-stained ground, shredding the illusion of Randall.

It's in my head. A voice from deep within her barked, ripping away the cloud that had formed in her brain. *That zombie monster is*

IN MY HEAD. She sucked in breath through her teeth, anger bubbling inside her.

Skid took a deep breath, ignoring the stench in the air. Strength began to flow back into her legs, her arms. A humorless smirk tugged at her face to match the monster who no longer looked like Randall Roe.

"My turn," she hissed through gritted teeth and pulled the sleeves of the jacket at her waist. It fell to the foul tent floor. The monster's expression didn't change when Skid shot to her feet, hands falling to the belt. They came up with her last two four-inch Browning Black Label stainless steel throwing knives. She flipped them into the air and caught both by their tips.

"This shit show ends now."

With a simultaneous flick, the knives flew from her fingers and twirled in the stifling hot death-filled air. The circus master's mouth dropped right before the blades buried themselves in its eyes. The Randall Roe face vanished, and the thing crumbled to the ground like someone had dropped its strings.

A scream split the air, but not from the ringmaster, whose muscles had fallen from its bones. A man in the audience stood, tearing at his own eyes. The big top exploded in shrieks. The residents of Peculiar, Missouri, tumbled from the stands over one another, shredding their faces with their fingernails.

"Nooo," the man from Wisconsin shrieked as the remaining chimp sprang toward his wife, its chain trailing behind it. Brick leaped out of its way, twirling. He brought the great sword down on the monster's shoulder, severing its long, hideous arm. The zombie chimp dropped and tried to get up, but Brick was there and lopped its head from its thick shoulders before throwing back his own shoulders and howling like an animal. The Wisconsin woman screamed again, or maybe it was her husband. Skid couldn't tell.

The last circus zombie fell on its own, its limbs dropping from its body like an overbuild chicken. It hadn't rested there long before the people of Peculiar stomped it flat as they ran screaming, some eyeless, blood streaming down their faces.

"Brick," Skid yelled toward him, but he couldn't hear her.

Damn it.

The motorcycle, the same model bike daredevil Evel Knievel once drove, purred not ten feet from her. She stomped the ground. *Double damn it.*

She ran to the bike and hopped on. The seat vibrated beneath her.

"I hate this," she said, grabbing the handlebars and revving the throttle. The motor roared. "I haven't met you, but I hate you, Karl Miller." A Peculiar native ran past her, his eyes gone. "And Dad, I don't like you much, either."

The motorcycle felt familiar beneath her. She hadn't been on one since the day of the trick, the day she woke up in the hospital, when she swore she'd never get on the back another bike again, ever. Seriously fucking ever. Skid spat on the ground and popped the bike in gear. Dirt and blood spun under the rear wheel, and the American Eagle shot toward Brick.

The Wisconsin couple sat on the blood-soaked ground, rubbing numb arms freed from their bonds by Brick. He tried to talk to them, but with the sword in his hand and the gore splattered across his face, he looked like a madman.

The bike slid to a stop closer to the Wisconsin couple than Skid would have liked.

"Brick."

He didn't turn around, too focused on the husband, whose face was frozen in terror. Skid reached out and slapped Brick's shoulder. "Hey."

Brick's head turned slowly. "What?"

"We gotta get out of here," she said, holding out the hand she'd used to hit him.

He ignored it. "You need to leave," he told the couple. A woman in a pleated skirt ran screeching toward Brick, the flesh ripped from her cheeks, teeth showing red and white through the dangling shreds of meat. He grabbed the bloody woman's shoulders and spun like a discus thrower, heaving her into an oncoming man who had ripped skin off his own face. "Now."

The Wisconsin woman nodded and shook her man. He didn't move.

"Brick," Skid screamed.

Brick stood slowly, wiping the blood and strips of flesh from his sword before sliding it into his backpack. "Okay."

Skid jerked her head behind her. Brick didn't look like he understood, so she did it again.

"You want me to ride Wookie?" he asked.

"What?"

"Pillion," he said, laying his hand on the small patch of leather at the end of the seat. "You want me to ride pillion."

"Yeah, I guess." More frantic townspeople had poured into the center ring; a man slammed into Brick's shoulder and fell backward. Brick didn't act like he noticed. "No one calls it that," she said. "Get your ass on the bike."

He ran his blood-streaked fingers through his hair and climbed onto the seat behind her. The bike frame groaned in protest.

"Bitch," she said.

"What did you call me?"

She put the bike in gear and swung the nose around toward the open flap the townspeople had herded them through only minutes earlier. The couple from Wisconsin ran toward the opposite flap in the tent.

"It's called riding bitch," she shouted over her shoulder.

"That's patently offensive," Brick said into her ear.

"You're telling me." Skid gunned the throttle, and they shot through the howling mass. "Bitch."

3

The motorcycle died two miles later, the once clean and shiny machine sickening beneath them. Bits of rust flecked off in the breeze as Skid drove. The American Eagle coughed and sputtered, slowing to a crawl before the engine stopped entirely and the rear tire blew under Brick's weight. Brick now stood on the rural highway facing west as Skid used the bike for balance, its tires weather-cracked, the front one hissing as it sank toward the asphalt.

"Should you really be doing that right now?" he asked.

"Girls have to pee, too," she said behind him.

"I know. I have a sister. She had to go at weird times." He pointed toward the western horizon, but Skid wasn't looking. "Another wave is coming. Are they more frequent now? Or is it just me?" A movement behind him and a zip told Brick it was okay to turn around. He didn't.

Skid stepped next to him. "I haven't been keeping track, Poindexter." These weren't the rolling, purple, lighting-filled clouds they'd watched roll over them in Orland and 1957 Atomic Dinosaurville. The green wave cascading toward them more resembled a clumsy puppy than a storm. "Weird. It's actually kind of cute."

A thick, hairy forearm extended itself protectively over her chest, but Brick still hadn't looked at her. "I think we should hide in the ditch," he said, taking a step back. Skid stood her ground until Brick's arm hit her shoulders.

"This isn't a torna—"

The wave threw out what looked like a tentacle that slammed into the highway, digging through the asphalt and concrete, pinching it to find a purchase before pulling itself forward. Brick dove, wrapping his arms around Skid in a textbook tackle and they dropped into the weed- and beer can–filled ditch. The Miller Wave rolled over them, lashing out with tendrils of solid smoke that fell like a net.

"Oh, no," squeaked from Skid as the cloud dragged them into darkness.

4

Skid's air shot from her when she hit the ground, sandwiched between concrete and Brick. Black specks swam in her eyes as she tried to focus, the world around her dim. It took a few seconds to figure out why, the sun had dipped behind the buildings.

The cornfields were gone, the highway was gone, the rusting motorcycle was gone. A dirty alley and concrete had taken their place, and a taller skyline loomed in the distance. The place looked familiar, but it sure wasn't Peculiar.

"Get off," she tried to say, but nothing came out.

"Skid?" Brick asked. "Skid, you okay?"

He shifted slightly and some wind found its way back into her lungs. "Get off," she wheezed.

He rolled to one side and grunted, his backpack bumping against a wall. "Where are we?" he asked.

She sucked in and pushed out air, her chest ached.

"We survived a fire-breathing dinosaur, and your ass almost crushed me." She lifted herself onto her elbows. The shadow Brick lay in was filled with dented beer cans and a couple of greasy pizza boxes. "Why now? We were almost there, Brick."

He pulled himself to his feet and held out a hand. She took it, her legs still wobbly, either from the horror circus or Brick's weight.

"Maybe we still are," he said.

"What?" She pointed to a nearby door to a cheesy nightclub. "This obviously isn't a cornfield in the middle of BFE. Do you know where the lab is? In a cornfield in the middle of BFE."

He waved his hand in front of him. "I know. You're right. But every place and every time these Miller Waves have taken us has been somewhere we needed to be. To hook up with Dave at the ax murder house, to the D&D world to see what Karl had done, to 1957 to—"

"Something weird happened to Cord in 1957."

Brick's face grew serious. "Maybe something weird was supposed to happen to Cord in 1957. This is you and me, Skid, and sometimes Cord, and sometimes Cord and the waitress, and someti—"

"You've lost your mind," she said.

A car door shut from somewhere down the alley, and the high-pitched sounds of drunken girls spilled out.

"No. I haven't. There's a reason we're here. We're connected to this on a—I don't know—dimensional level? Spiritual level? Molecular level? But the night you met David Collison and I met the guy who wasn't him at Slap Happy's Dance Club, we became part of it." He stopped and looked around. "Hey, I know where we are."

A door creaked open on a spring from down the alley and snapped shut, a woman stepped out. "Jesus, Lou, you're making me abandon my date for this," she said into a mobile phone. "A house fire? It better be a damn important house. I was having a good time. I hope he understands when I call him later."

Oh, shit. Skid felt Brick's body tense behind her. She turned and slammed both hands into his chest, catching him off guard and sending him into the wall. He started to speak, but she slapped a hand over his hairy mouth and pressed hard.

"That's Beverly," she said, her voice low and sharp. "But it's not our Beverly. I think it's last Friday's Beverly."

Beverly walked by them on her way to a parking lot at the end of the alley, her unnecessarily large smartphone over the left side of her face, obscuring the two filth-smeared crazy people in the shadows.

"Shit," she said, moving the phone in front of her face. "I lost his number. Goddamnit, Lou."

Brick relaxed as he watched the girl he thought had dumped him walk to the end of the alley and disappear behind the side of the building, dressed in the first thing he'd ever seen her in. Skid released her hand.

"She told me she left because her boss called while she was in the bathroom. Some kind of emergency." The big man's voice sounded far away. "She said she didn't have time to say good-bye. This proves it. She was having a good time, Skid. You heard it. She didn't ditch me."

Skid slapped his chest. "Focus, Brick. You said we were here for a reason, and that reason is not to stalk your girlfriend, Ish, thingy." She dropped her hands to her hips. "You've only known her a couple of hours. You're aware of that, right?"

"Yeah, but it seems longer."

A thought crossed Skid's mind. "We're in an alley behind Slap Happy's, right?"

Brick nodded. "Yeah."

"Where the past seven days of hell started, right?"

"Yeah."

She stepped away from Brick, walking backward toward the rear door of Slap Happy's. "Then we're here to warn ourselves. That has to be it."

Brick seemed to snap out of his Beverly haze. "No. That might not be it. We could be here to intercept Dave in the murder house; it's only a couple blocks away. Or we could be here to talk him into going back to the lab before everything goes crazy, or I might be wrong. This could all be random, and the past week was for nothing."

Skid slapped her bicep with an open palm and shot her fist into the air before she strode toward the back door to Slap Happy's.

5

"She will be here soon, Karl," Clean-David said, waving the pistol in no particular direction. Dave shifted in his seat each time the barrel ventured anywhere close to him. "We have to be ready."

"For what?" He leaned against the wall, trying to look calm and cool instead of constipated. "For a person to break into this high-security facility, make it through a hallway teaming with hungry Human Resources cockroaches, walk down stairs for which worst-case-scenario safety protocols have been activated, and into this locked room where I have a gun?"

"I have the gun," Clean-David said, holding it up.

"Where New Collison has a gun," Karl finished. "I'm shaking."

"You should be," both David Collisons said in unison.

Karl ignored them and looked at his watch. "The unit that went into the void yesterday at 1300 hours should be reporting back in about three hours. At that point, you can go screw yourself, Collison."

Dave knew he shouldn't, but he smiled anyway. "Were those the Army guys who usually guard the fence?"

"Yes," Karl said. "Why?"

Then they won't be there to stop Skid.

"Oh, nothing," he said. "Nothing at all."

6

The hallway smelled of ozone and vomit. The spring-controlled door smacked closed behind Skid then opened almost immediately. Brick stepped through.

"I remember that smell," he said.

The door labeled "Hookers" swung open, and three drunken college-aged girls walked out. One's face was pale, her eyes nearly closed.

"Oh my god," one of the girls said, looking Brick and Skid up and down. "Homeless. Eww." She put her arm around her friend and walked away. Her foot slid on the floor outside the "Johns" door. Skid was disappointed the girl didn't fall. The third Barbie held the door to the dance club, music pounding down the hall, and as they left, the two who hadn't drunk themselves sick giggled.

"Watch out for the blood," Brick said, nodding toward the floor. "That's where Not-David stopped me. He had a knife wound in his leg and bled everywhere."

Knife? Did I? She wondered, because she knew she probably did, or someone very much like her.

The spots on the floor were shaped like a man's shoes, except the one the drunken girl had slipped in.

Something on the floor did not belong. A cigarette butt or fragment of glass from a broken beer bottle she would expect in a classy joint like Slap Happy's. But there, on the floor, was a key on a short fob. She squatted and picked it up, the blade thin and wide, the tip square, its teeth rectangular.

"What did you find?" Brick asked, looming over her shoulder.

"Maybe something." She stood, shoving it into her rear pants pocket. "Maybe nothing." Skid stepped over the blood spots and walked to the door back to the club. "Why the hell did I ever come to this place?" she said as she opened it, her voice drowned by "Old Town Road."

"What?" Brick shouted.

She waved him off. Everything was irrelevant except the scene before her, where last week's Brick started toward the dance floor. He stood at least a head above everyone. His attention was focused across the room, where last week's Skid sat with last week's Dave. Most of the people around them were oblivious to everything, but the few standing nearby gawked at last week's Skid as she pulled absolutely the wrong knife from the bar and nailed the beer poster model across the room right between the baby blues. A few people clapped, but not a sixty-something woman with graying hair pulled back in a ponytail. She stood a couple of people away from last week's Skid and Dave, just staring. On the other side of the woman stood Cord and Carla. *What?*

Last week's Dave said something she could in no way hear and last week's Skid punched him in the face. The scientist fell backward and vanished.

"We're too late," Skid breathed. Then she disappeared too.

7

Brick didn't like this. He didn't like this at all. If they were at Slap Happy's Dance Club on the night of September 1 to warn themselves not do something, they'd gotten there too late. They'd already missed intercepting Not-David. Last week's Skid had already done her knife trick. Dave was about to disappear any second, and—

Oh, wait. He's gone.

But nobody seemed to notice, or care, except for an older athletic woman whose dark hair was streaked with white. She stepped away from the bar, gaze fixed on the spot where Dave had vanished. She'd seen it.

"Hey," he said aloud, although no one heard him. "I know her." The other Brick stepped forward, blocking his view. Brick shuffled to the side, exactly where he'd stood one week ago for twenty minutes waiting for Beverly to come out of the bathroom.

The woman was Katie, who came into Manic Muffins after her morning jog to order a black coffee and chocolate muffin. The same Katie who suggested he create a rectangular red velvet cream-filled muffin and call it The Brick. "What is Katie doing in a crappy place like this?" Then he saw Cord and Carla.

"Skid," he said, but Skid wasn't next to him anymore. A millisecond later, neither was he.

8

The forest was thin and orderly. Skid stood alone in the shadow of a large hoary oak surrounded by younger, evenly spaced trees—land that should have been choked with brambles and the rotted remains of older trees, but had been cleared. This wasn't a raw forest. It might have been a park, if not for the soldiers.

Brick appeared behind her and stumbled before catching himself on the oak.

"Whoa," he said, too loudly.

"Shhh," she hissed and pointed past the tree. About ten yards through the woods lay a flat strip of land about twenty yards wide, bare but for the short-cropped grass and a metal signpost. The lawn ended at a high concrete wall. Next to a post that read "Das Hinterland" on one side and "Nue Merica" on the other, four soldiers stood in field gray uniforms and caps, assault rifles over their shoulders. They didn't seem to realize Skid and Brick had just stepped out of nothingness and were gawking at them with open mouths.

"What the hell?" Brick said, quieter this time.

"I'm not sure your hypothesis about being somewhere for a reason pans out," she whispered.

The Miller Wave had washed them into this world in the middle of the soldiers' conversation. One of them held up a finger and said, "Er sagte, ich weiß nicht, fragen Sie den Metzger," and the other three laughed.

Brick sucked in his breath and leaned closer to the tree, putting it in front of as much of himself as he could. "What the hell?" he repeated, bending close to Skid's ear. "Did we go back to the 1940s? Those are Germans in Nazi uniforms."

Whatever Skid might have said was interrupted by the ringing of a cell phone. One of the soldiers pulled a sleek silver rectangle from his pocket.

"Entschuldigen Sie mich," the soldier said, looking down at the screen. A frown grew over the smile. He made a talking motion with his hand as he put the mobile up to his ear, then cupped the hand close to the microphone to mask the other soldiers' laughter.

"That's an iPhone," Skid said, her voice almost too soft for Brick to pick up. "This isn't the 1940s."

"But what are they? Reenactors? Neo-Nazis? Is somebody shooting a movie?"

The soldier said something else Skid couldn't understand, and the other soldiers laughed again, quieter this time, their hands over their mouths.

"I don't think so." Skid reached behind her and tightened her ponytail. "What are these assholes saying?"

Brick shrugged.

"You don't speak German?"

"No," he said. The soldier disconnected the call and pocketed the iPhone. One of his buddies mimed a man in terror as another flicked an imaginary whip. The third ignored them all and lit a cigarette.

She turned toward Brick, her eyes as narrow as Clint Eastwood's. "So, you speak Klingon, but you can't speak something useful like German?"

"Hey," he said, pointing a finger at her. "Ha'DIbaH."

Her eyes were slits. "I'd better never find out what that means."

The forest, or what there was of a forest, fell silent. Skid's head swiveled slowly from Brick back to the wall. One of the soldiers was gone.

Skid's "Oh, shit" was instantly followed by a gun hammer click from behind them. "Goddamned German soldiers."

"Wer bist du?" asked a voice, the accent heavy.

Skid instinctively raised her hands above her head because that's what people always did when someone held a gun behind them. Brick didn't move at all.

The German soldier's tone grew more urgent, verging on angry. He took a step toward Skid and yelled.

The men near the wall began to walk toward them. The one with the cigarette took a long drag and dropped it into the grass, crushing it under the toe of his boot. The soldier with the most insignias reached them first, the smiles and laughter gone from his face. "Was ist los?" he asked.

The man with the pistol on Skid brought it level with her forehead.

The man in charge smirked and waved the soldier off. "Nein." He reached out a finger and tapped Skid's nose.

Brick hit the man hard enough he flipped before landing on his face, cap flying into the trees. Skid dropped and swept a leg across the ankles of the soldier with the gun. He went down hard on his back.

Before Skid could jump the other soldier with an open palm to the bridge of his nose like she'd planned, a purple storm engulfed them, and the soldiers disappeared.

9

"I think you're right," Skid said, walking west as they weaved through a field of enormous mushrooms, some as tall as Brick. The thick gray stalks were topped with sickly yellow caps, the gills beneath gently moving in and out. She wondered, not for the first time, if the things were breathing. *This is too much,* she thought, then stiffened her shoulders. *Keep your shit together, Skid.* "The Miller Waves are coming more often, and I don't know where they're taking us. I just want another one to show up quick and take us the hell out of here. This place is an H. P. Lovecraft story."

Brick sidestepped a fat mushroom he swore moved toward him when he got close. Drawing the orc sword from his explorer's pack, he said, "I preferred facing the Germans. They had less personality, but at least they were supposed to move."

"I know. Gross."

They stopped and turned toward a healthy Cord. Carla the waitress wasn't with him.

"Where have you been?" Skid asked.

"What? I've been with you the whole ti—"

"Whatever," Skid said, and started walking.

The remains of a highway ran under their feet, bits and pieces of the cracked gray asphalt showing under a scant layer of topsoil. A few ruined structures leaned sadly on the horizon. Skid thought they'd once been grain silos.

"What do you think happened here?" she asked. "These mushrooms aren't normal."

"Aliens," Cord said without hesitation. "Totally aliens."

Skid started to speak, then decided better of it.

"That makes sense," Brick said. "Space aliens. I mean, we've seen everything else, right? Orcs, Klingons, Baby Godzilla, zombies, Nazi soldiers with cell phones. What else is left?"

Skid walked around a mushroom the size of a sedan she was sure hadn't been that close to her a moment before. "Those talking orangutans Cord mentioned."

"Orangutans?" Cord asked. Skid ignored him. The whoosh of air in and out of the wide gills of the enormous fungus definitely sounded like breathing. She shivered. The caps, glistening with moisture, undulated like Jell-O. "What you're saying, Brick, is that we're playing out a movie script."

"What I'm saying is the world is a weird place. Why wouldn't multiple worlds be even weirder?"

Skid rounded the fungus and stopped. A pile of rusted metal stuck half out of the dirt on the other side. "Oh my god."

Brick stopped next to her, clenching the sword in his fist. "What? It's junk."

She bent to brush dirt away from what could have been a kind of tank. She wet a thumb on her tongue and rubbed it over a raised round logo. Bits of green, white and red showed through, the word *Laverda* barely visible. "It's our motorcycle from the circus." She stood and looked out over the remains of the road, but couldn't see far over the mushrooms. "We're close."

"But that can't be the motorcycle. It doesn't make any—"

A shadow passed overhead, and Skid screamed, "Holy shit."

She grabbed Brick's arm and reached for Cord, but he had

already dropped to the ground. Skid followed him, bringing Brick with her, and pointed up at a rectangle, black and big as a Carnival cruise ship, slowly moving through the sky. White lights, bright even in the midday sun, dotted its surface. The thing was silent as a thought.

"Cord was right," Brick pushed through his teeth. "Space aliens. What are we going to do?"

"You could kill me," a voice beside them wheezed. "That'd be nice."

They froze and looked toward the trunk of a gigantic mushroom. A gray human face leered at them, fingers protruding from the fungus where hands would be if—

"It ate you?" Brick's mouth hung open, but he didn't know it.

The flying rectangle slowed. Long, spindly arms lowered into the mushroom field, and pincers clamped onto the stems of the darker mushrooms to rock them back and forth gently until each fungus broke from its weak purchase in the thin soil. Then the arms, each gripping a mushroom, retracted into the craft.

"What happened?" Skid asked the face. She turned, scanning the mushroom field around them. Bits and pieces of people, a foot here, a knee there, stuck from every stem, the human body parts covered in a thin fuzzy mold.

"You don't know?" the face asked. "I was hoping you did. It might be just an accident. The alien guys stopped by for a picnic and stayed." He stuck out an index finger. "But he—"

Skid turned her head and cringed at a yellowish face half swallowed in a tall mushroom behind her. It winked.

"He thinks it's that government lab outside town. It called these things, brought them down here. Turns out our planet is great for growing what they eat." He stopped, out of breath.

"People?" she asked. "They eat people?"

The face considered her, no emotion showing as it sucked in air. "They don't have people in space, idiot. It's the fungus. The

271

fungus eats us, and the aliens eat the fungus." He tried to cock his head, but it was held tightly in the giant stem. "Why are you two free?"

"Two?" Brick asked. He turned toward Cord, who wasn't there.

Skid elbowed Brick's arm. "We have to leave. Now. I am not going to be one of these guys." She turned back toward the gray man in the mushroom. "No offense."

"None taken," he said. "I don't want to be me either. Now, are you going to kill me, or not?"

They didn't kill the man. They didn't have it in them.

10

A Miller Wave swept Skid and Brick from the moldering floor of the alien landscape and left them in a field of flowers—Missouri primrose, purple prairie clover, New England aster, button snakeroot, and Columbine. A breeze swept through the natural prairie, tickling the flowers into a dance. A kaleidoscope of butterflies fluttered across the tops of the wild prairie flowers. American ladies, eastern tiger swallowtails, pearl crescents and monarchs landed, only to take back to the air in a flurry of color.

The sky stretched above, clear and peaceful. No clouds, no contrails, no birds, no multi-armed mushroom-picking alien spacecraft.

"This place is nice," Brick said, lying on his side, staring up at the sky. "I wonder what's here that wants to kill us."

Skid pushed herself to her feet and brushed dust from her pants. "It's pretty, but it's not home. I want to go home. I just—" She froze. "Are you kidding me?"

Brick rose and followed Skid's gaze toward the west. A low, square building sat in a greenish-yellow field in the center of a tall chain-link fence, designed to protect the building from a bomb attack, just as Bud Light Dave had told them over bad coffee in Dan's

Daylight Donut's. A sign stood well away from the building, a small, glass-lined building next to it.

"We were close in Zombietown. We just couldn't see it over the corn," he said, pulling out his sheaf of napkins and holding the first one up so Skid could see. "It fits Bud Light Dave's drawing."

Butterflies flitted around them. A common buckeye, with orange, black, and blue spots on brown wings designed to look like eyes, landed on Brick's shoulder. The thousands of insects in the field didn't compare to what was flipping around Skid's stomach. *This is it. We're finally here.*

Brick's sword made a slight shhssh as he slid it back into his pack. Napkins folded and replaced in his pocket, he waved a hand in front of Skid's wide-eyed face.

"Let's go before another wave hits and turns us into My Little Ponies."

He took three steps toward the building when he discovered they were too late.

11

This wave seemed less threatening than the wild, purple, undulating monsters that swallowed the countryside. The white, spinning vortex looked as planned as a toilet flush and just as delicate.

Brick barely uttered a "Wha—" before the world opened and sucked him into darkness, only to reappear seconds later in a cluttered bright room with shadowed corners. Skid stood beside him. Brick threw his arms out and grabbed the wire-wrapped metal ring surrounding them. He instinctively pushed as if he were Samson trying to drop the Philistine temple.

"Hey," a male voice shouted. "Hey, you. Stop that."

A man in his mid-forties holding a can of Old Milwaukee stood before a control panel, a workbench filled with electronic components behind him.

"Come on, stop it," the man said again.

Brick did, relaxing his arms and releasing the ring.

"Where are we?" Skid asked.

"Kansas City," the man with the Old Milwaukee said.

Skid turned her head, taking in more of the room. She knew this place. She'd been there only three days before. And she knew this man; Brick had punched him unconscious.

"You're Delbert Sanderson," she said.

Old Milwaukee Man nodded. "I am," he said, a touch of suspicion in his voice. "You're the second person I don't know who's said that to me today."

Second?

"Who's the first?" Brick asked, not willing to step outside the ring. He didn't know where he'd end up.

Footsteps thudded down the stairs. Skid's eyes grew wide, taking in Cordrey Bellamy holding a cup of tea, waitress Carla what's-her-name beside him. Cord braced himself against the wall as he descended, a new bandage on his leg; Carla helped hold him up, an unfiltered cigarette dangled from the corner of her mouth.

"Him," Delbert said.

"Cord," Skid shouted. "What are you doing here?"

An honest, non-car-salesman smile broke across Cord's face, and he continued his slow downward walk. "Oh my god, Skid, Brick. This is awesome."

Carla went ahead of Cord and helped him down the last few steps.

"The machine in my basement worked," Cord said, draping an arm around Carla's shoulders. "At least, the machine in Delbert's basement worked. Carla and I were helping Brick fight giant cockroaches when the ground opened up and, boom, here we are."

Carla sucked in a lungful of smoke and blew it into the room. "It wasn't cool. I peed a little."

Skid ignored her. *Cockroaches?* "Okay, okay. Focus. We need to finish this." She turned toward Delbert. "Can you send us back where you got us?" she asked. "All of us?"

Delbert started to answer but didn't get the chance.

"Uh, no," Cord said.

Skid turned to him. "What do you mean, no?"

The car salesman smile returned. "I'm not going anywhere," he said. "Carla and I already talked about this." He held up his cup, a Lipton tea tag hung over the side. "She's from the past, I'm from the future January 1984 a right in the middle. It makes things fair."

"But—"

Cord waved her off. "Just look us up when you get home. I plan on being a rich guy with silver hair and a Porsche."

"There's too much power build-up," Delbert said, looking at his digital watch, the other hand now empty of beer and hovering over a big yellow button. "I can't tell you what's going to happen when I hit this, but if I don't, it's going to electrocute you." He looked at them through hazy eyes. "You okay with that?"

Brick held up an index finger. "The electrocution part?"

"The button," Skid shouted. "Hit it."

Cord reached behind him and pulled something from his back pocket.

"Catch," he shouted over the humming equipment and tossed a small, dark object toward the ring. Less than a second later, the white toilet flush wiped Skid and Brick from 1984, leaving their friend and the waitress behind.

12

They landed on the spot they'd left, at the entrance of the facility grounds in the field of native flowers and butterflies, in front of a sign that read, "Lemaître Labs: Property of the United States Government. Authorized Personnel Only. Trespassers will be shot." Not as welcoming as they'd hoped. The paint on the sign looked fresh and well maintained, as did the small building next to it, the empty guard shack clean, as if it had just been built.

The black thing Cord threw went over Skid's head and thudded in the tall grass behind her.

"What was that?" Brick asked.

"I think it was one of my knives," she said, her voice drifting.

She dropped into the tall grass. *My knife?* Skid combed her hands through the prairie flowers and weeds. *How did—?* Then she knew. Orcland. She'd distracted the orc by throwing a knife at Cord, burying it in the tire inches from his face. She hadn't seen Cord take the knife from the tire, but he must have. Her hands swiped the ground with more urgency.

"What are you doing?"

It has to be here. It has to be.

"You're never going to find it," Brick said.

Come on, come on. She spread her arms wide as she crawled, sweeping the ground; pollen and butterflies launched into the air. Then her fingertips touched something familiar. She lifted the throwing blade so Brick could see it.

"I'm not sure if I should be impressed or terrified," he said.

Skid headed toward the lab through the grass and butterflies. Brick watched her march across the prairie before hurrying to catch up.

"Why would the lab be in this world?" she asked like he'd been beside her all along. "There doesn't seem to be anything else here but nature."

"All this hopping around in time and space is caused by that place," Brick said, "And apparently Delbert Sanderson. Dave said he started experimenting on time travel at home, so maybe, at least while the super collider is on, this place and maybe the Sanderson house, is in every dimension at once."

Dave was never around when they needed him. Skid stared past the sign toward the depressing gray building.

"Are you ready?" she asked, sliding the knife into the empty sheath below her right hand. "Let's get ourselves home. I need a long, hot bath."

The weight of it all, every emotion she'd tried to ignore for the past week began to sweep away. A smile replaced what she almost felt. They'd beaten everything. *Screw the universe. What the hell else can it throw at us?*

She took a few steps forward into the dull yellow flowers that had been slowly overtaking the prairie on their march west. Brick didn't follow. She turned and found him kneeling in front of his explorer's pack, digging near the bottom.

"What are you doing?" she asked.

"Getting my Fluticasone." He pulled out a bottle with a green lid which he removed, revealing a nasal sprayer. "I knew there was something wrong here. The lab's surrounded by ragweed."

He sprayed the allergy medicine twice up each nostril and replaced it in his bag. "Okay," he said. "I'm good."

"What a hero." Skid started walking toward the lab. "Frodo and Sam never used an antihistamine."

Brick slung the pack over his shoulders and followed her. "That's because ragweed doesn't grow in Mordor, Skid. Don't you read?"

12

The next wave didn't so much hit the Bridge as it swallowed it. A purple maelstrom opened in the floor and seemed to stretch the room, 1980s-horror movie style, into a vast pit. Dave held onto his office chair with both hands expecting to roll into the storm, but the wheels never moved. Clean-David casually pulled out a tube of ChapStick—cherry, not real-Dave's first choice—and applied it to his lips. The floor disappeared beneath Karl, and their boss fell into the ether.

Clean-David grabbed a rolling office chair and wheeled it over to Dave. He sat in it backward, resting his arms over the headrest. The pistol hung limply in his hand. The man's eyes, so much like his own —*no, exactly like my own*—stared into Dave's. Clean-David smiled. A small chip in his lower left permanent lateral incisor blemished a perfectly good smile. "Let's talk."

"We're not exactly alike," Dave said. "What happened to your tooth?"

Clean-David ran his tongue over the tops of his front teeth. "Hmm. Yeah. I fell out of a tree on Grandpa's farm. I was trying to pick an apple off the Fork Branch, and it snapped. I'm lucky I just chipped a tooth."

The Fork Branch, ten feet off the ground over what was once a rock garden. It had a spray that looked like tines.

"You broke the Fork Branch?" Dave rested his elbows on his knees, lacing his fingers. "Last time I was on the farm, the Fork Branch was still there."

The pistol in Clean-David's hand hung so close to Dave he could reach out and take it. He didn't.

"I wasn't happy about it either. I was going to build a—"

"Treehouse," Dave finished for him. "Me, too. Then Grandpa died and my priorities changed."

A sad smile touched Clean-David. "I was there when Grandpa had the heart attack. Were you?"

Dave nodded. *I was almost there twice.*

"Now, what are we going to do about—" Clean-David waved the gun around the Bridge. "—all this?"

The exhaustion of the last week lifted for a moment, only a moment. *Is it going to be this easy?*

"We're going to turn off the supercollider. Intersecting dimensions and times is madness. Irreparable damage has probably been done to the timelines and cohesion of every world Karl's bullshit idea touched. We have to stop it before it gets any worse."

Clean-David frowned, resembling a teacher who'd just gotten the wrong answer to a question he'd asked a dozen times.

"I was afraid you were going to say that." He stood and grabbed the headrest, spinning the chair as he walked away. He casually examined the room, looking at monitors and control panels like he was bored.

"Karl—not your dimension's Karl, my dimension's Karl—explained everything to the team. This is a matter of our survival. The world is in chaos. By equipping the government with as much non-human cannon-fodder as we can drag into our dimensions, we stand a chance of setting things right." Clean-David talked with his hands, waving them as if he were swatting mosquitos. "Fill a battle-field with orcs, enormous sentient insects, nine-foot-tall non-human primates, fire-breathing radioactive dinosaurs, and whatever else we find out there, and no enemy can face us. It will bring about a peace the world has never known."

Any hope Dave had melted from him. This man who looked like him wasn't him. Something had happened to Clean-David long before Karl Miller got his crazy-hooks into him.

"Where did you go to live after Grandpa died?"

Clean-David sat on the table that used to hold the monitors smashed by Karl. "What do you mean? I went home to the Sandersons."

"The Sandersons?" *Oh, shit.* "Cecilia and Delbert?"

The man nodded. "Yeah. Who else?"

"Cecilia and *Delbert* raised you? How long did you live with them?"

The man waved the pistol absentmindedly. "Until I graduated from Stanford. I still have lunch with them after church on most Sundays. Dad and I usually watch the noon football game before I head home."

Dad? A short bark of a laugh erupted from Dave.

"That explains a lot. Okay, douche nozzle, in a few days you're going to be eaten by a giant praying mantis from another dimension, and don't expect that Cheetos-smelling bastard Karl to do anything about it," he said. "He's going to watch it happen and enjoy every second. Let that sink in while you're getting all high and mighty about this plan to give peace a chance through radioactive dinosaurs. Oh, and the praying mantis is named Chet. He'll be wearing a lab coat."

"The Sandersons are great—" Clean-David cut the sentence short. "Wait. What did you say?"

13

Brick was right, the prairie was thick with ragweed. The pollen stuck to their clothes like stripper glitter. As they waded into the weeds, he took a big red handkerchief from his pocket, something like what John Wayne would pull from a saddlebag and use to wipe someone else's blood from his face. He tied it around his nose and mouth just in case his nasal spray wasn't cowboy enough.

It was well after noon when they reached the fence, a twelve-foot-high chain-link cage designed to keep out intruders who weren't driving a vehicle. Waist-high steel posts set in concrete every three feet would dissuade those who were. Motion-sensor security cameras mounted atop the fence every six meters moved with them as they approached.

"Power's still on," Brick said through a mouthful of jerky. "I thought this part was going to be easy."

Skid bit down on her jerky and took Bud Light Dave's key card from her front pocket. "I gah iss overed." She spat out the seasoned dried beef. "I got this covered."

The card slipped into a reader to the left of the gate, level to the height of a car window. A light on the reader went from red to green and a motor churned from somewhere; the gate began to retract.

"Easy peasy." She ripped off another piece of jerky and chewed, walking onto the lab grounds. "You make this yourself?"

Brick smiled. "Yeah, I did."

"Better stick to muffins."

They couldn't follow the road, because it didn't exist in this dimension. They dragged their legs through the tall prairie grass and weeds and walked directly toward what looked like the front door, a glass and metal rectangle that resembled the entrance to a grocery store. The ground rippled as they approached it.

"Hold on," Brick said, reaching out to Skid. She took his hand, which no longer even fazed her. She didn't like touching people, but Brick and Cord and Dave didn't seem like people anymore. She knew she'd only met them a week ago, but they already seemed more like family than any member of her own. *Maybe Brick and Beverly really do have something.*

Skid closed her eyes as the Miller Wave swept through the glass of the front door and pushed through them. She didn't want to know where they were going. *We're here. We're here. We're here,* ran through her head, her hand pinching Brick's in a steel grip. *Please, don't make us go away.*

"Skid." Brick's voice was soft with relief. She opened her eyes. The building remained unchanged, the sign over the card reader read *Lemaître Labs.* "We're still here."

The weight in her stomach lifted. She swiped the card and the weight dropped again. Nothing happened. She ran it one more time. The machine beeped, but the light stayed red. "Something's wrong."

"Maybe not," Brick said behind her, his big arm moved over her shoulder holding a key card identical to the one she held. He swiped it and the light turned green, the door opened with a 'woosh.' "That time I went back to my store, the other David showed up. He gave me this."

What? "Why didn't you tell me?" she asked, turning to face him.

"I didn't think you'd want to hear what he said."

"Let me guess." She tossed the remaining bite of beef onto the now neatly trimmed grass. "I'm going to kill everybody."

"Well—" Brick began.

A cough came from behind him. An intentional cough, the kind of *hey, pay attention to me* cough people use when they think they're important. Skid couldn't see the source because Brick's giant chest covered her field of vision in filthy, blood-stained plaid. She flicked the last knife into her hand. "I might have to."

CHAPTER THIRTEEN

SEPT-DEJA-VU-ALL-OVER-AGAIN-EMBER 7

1

THE GRADUATION PARTY had everything a graduation party was supposed to have. Seniors counting down sixteen hours until they walked across the stage, chips and dip, a ridiculous amount of mostly empty cheap liquor bottles, a keg, annoying dance music no one danced to because they were all playing Quarters, and a gate-crasher throwing up in the bathroom. Karl stood against the wall of Marty McClure's rented house feeling incredibly uncomfortable.

"And I'm telling you, Karl," drunk Marty said, a red Solo cup of cheap light beer in his fist, "there's no sense staying here. You're fucking brilliant. You could be the next Bill Gates, and that Microsoft-founding son of a bitch didn't even graduate college." He paused only to take a drink. The next words came out in a slight spray. "Or, what's that other guy? The one that makes the Apple stuff?"

"You mean Steve Jobs?" Karl asked, swirling Diet Coke around his own red plastic cup, the bubbles mostly gone. "Or Hostess Fruit Pie?"

Marty stared at Karl with glassy eyes before he realized his friend was being a smart-ass. "Jobs," he said, patting Karl's cheek before grabbing his chin. "He didn't graduate college either. Both of those guys are making money. Why do you need to go to grad school?"

Karl brushed his friend's hand from his face and started to lift the cup to his lips, but the diet soda had gone warm as well. He didn't want it anymore.

"Because computers aren't my thing. I'm going to get my master's in quantum physics, maybe even my doctorate. Dr. Sanderson, the man who hired me for my summer internship, said he's toying with time travel at home. I may one day roam the universe and not even leave my house."

"Where are you going, Karl?" Marty's girlfriend Suzie Watters appeared next to them and leaned into Marty.

Marty sneered. "Nowhere, honey. Our good friend Karl is going nowhere."

Suzie pulled back and shoved her boyfriend's arm, not hard, not even hard enough to spill his beer, just enough to get her point across. "Leave him alone," she said, turning to Karl, pointing a finger at him. "Our wedding, you're a groomsman, two months, be there. Just don't let this asshole do anything to make you say no."

Marty ignored her, his drunken attention on Karl. The irony of the Simple Minds' song "Don't You Forget About Me" playing in the room was not wasted on Karl.

"I love you, man," Marty told his friend, "but sometimes you can be such a twat waffle. Why don't you cut loose for once? You'll never have this day again." His gaze dropped to Karl's wingtip shoes and climbed up past his button-down shirt to his parted-on-the-right hair-cut. "You're the same as you were the day we met at freshman orientation. It's too bad this is our last night instead of our first. It would have been fun to have called you Twat Waffle for the past four years."

Marty laughed before draining his cup and dropping it on the floor. It landed with a hollow tink. A beery smile leaked over his face, and he gave Karl a hug before draping an arm over Suzie's shoulders and leaving to join the people having fun.

"You're wrong, Marty," Karl said as his friend filled a new Solo cup at the keg across the room. "I might just have this day again."

Marty flipped him off.

Karl didn't say good-bye. He just went home because it was almost 10 p.m., and he had to be fresh for graduation. Not that he was going anywhere after graduation. Summer classes started in a while.

The heavy front door of the rental house shut with a thump behind him and cut the blare of some of the music, but not enough. Karl could still hear it and the sound of laughter for the next two blocks before he reached his apartment building and locked himself in tight.

That night was a long time ago, decades before he grabbed the job of chief scientist of Lemaître Labs. From that moment, Karl was the man. He was the boss. He was in control.

That didn't keep him from peeing just a little when the floor swallowed him. Not enough for anyone to notice if they were around —which they weren't, since Dave 1 and Dave 2 were still back on the Bridge—as it was just a squirt, but he could feel it in his underpants. There was no shame. His body dropped through the tiled surface of the floor, through the steel-reinforced supports and into the supercollider tunnel to the Miller Ring before a visible violet wind swept him back up through the bedrock, the substratum, the subsoil and topsoil, pushing him onto the ground outside the lab as if it were a growing plant blooming a fully-grown human with no social skills. When the wave passed and Karl stood in the waist-high grass near the back fence, he thought he'd handled everything well considering the fact being dragged ethereally through solid objects wasn't something he made a habit of. The spot of urine was understandable.

"So," he said, stretching his arms, wincing at his uncomfortably loud voice in the silent air. "This is what Collison's fuss is all about?"

A butterfly landed on his forearm. He smiled before slapping it dead and brushing the broken, dusty wings off his sleeve. Karl took in the flowers, the clouds of butterflies, the sharp electric blue sky that stretched to the Kármán line sixty-two miles over his head and 24,901.461 miles across the surface of the earth from his extended right hand to his left. Most people who think about such things would probably say "infinity," but Karl knew better. Nothing was infinite but space and time, and Karl controlled them both. He was the Dimension King.

He breathed deeply. This air was uncorrupted by human pollution. He didn't know this world, but he did know he wasn't outside Peculiar, Missouri; there were too many flowers and too few field crops. Karl had started back toward the lab when an unmistakably human noise broke the pristine silence and nailed his feet to the ground.

"Power's still on," a deep male voice said in the distance. "I thought this part was going to be easy."

Two people stood outside the fence. From this distance, it was either a normal-sized man and a ten-year-old girl, or a normal-sized woman and Bluto from *Popeye*. "She's coming," one, or both, of the Collisons had said. "We have to be ready." *Is this her?* he wondered. *Is this Skid? She doesn't look so tough.* Bluto, on the other hand, did. He seemed like a hairy house with teeth.

"Easy peasy," the woman said as the gate rumbled open and they walked through. Karl marveled at how far a voice traveled when there was no other sound but his awkwardly drumming heart to compete with it.

He stood as still as he could. There was nothing that could hide him without creating a sudden movement and giving himself away— no trees, no outbuildings, no cars. Just the weeds, some of which were topped with colorful flowers. Karl was glad he didn't suffer from hay fever.

The two strangers marched through the prairie grass at an angle away from him. They didn't seem to notice him, exactly like at college parties. As they approached the lab, the big man strode with his shoulders back, but the woman walked with an air of purpose mixed with not giving a damn, which was tough to pull off. *She's in charge.* It was that moment Karl realized that, yes, this had to be the woman the Collisons had warned him about. Skid.

The world began to shake without shaking, more like heat wavering over a highway. A Miller wave—something Karl had named himself, without help, nope, none at all—sprang from the building, washing over these interlopers, and flew toward him in rolling silence. His eyes slammed shut, but if the wave struck him, he felt nothing. When he finally looked, the grass was neat and well-trimmed, cars dotted the parking lot. A few contrails crisscrossed the sky. A smile broke across his face. *I'm home. This is my place.* And he had a plan. He'd just watch the two go inside the lab, wait long enough for the cockroaches in HR to eat them, assuming they didn't die from the poison in the stairwells. Then he'd go back inside, his back straight, his shirt tucked in.

The woman tried a key card on the door. It didn't move.

It didn't move? "Oh, no," Karl whispered, shoving a hand inside his right pants pocket. He felt car keys and nail clippers. His left hand slid into his other front pocket only to wrap around loose change. His own key card, the one that would have let him into the building, the elevator, and the BAB-C control room was gone. "I left it in the Bridge."

Think, Karl. You have three master's degrees and a Ph.D. Fricking think. He rushed behind Gillian the receptionist's Camry and squatted, leaning out to watch the woman. The giant man pulled another key card from his shirt. *How do they have two?*

Then Dr. Karl Miller Ph.D. knew what he had to do. He slammed his face into the front left quarter panel of Gillian's car and stifled a scream. He was no Twat Waffle.

2

"A giant sentient praying mantis named Chet," Dave said, getting some satisfaction from the fact his smug doppelganger looked as if he'd just swallowed a cat. "It seemed nice. I mean, it fixed that festering knife wound in your leg."

Clean-David's hands instinctively dropped to his thighs and felt to make sure they were there.

"I thought you said it ate me." His voice was slightly panicked, but mostly confused.

"Oh, it did, right after it cleaned your leg and sewed up the wound." Dave absentmindedly picked at a fingernail before looking back up. "I think it did so partly out of loyalty to the Hippocratic Oath, but mostly because oozing puss doesn't do much for anyone's appetite." He pulled off a bit of nail and flicked it onto the floor. "Karl didn't care. He just wanted my will to break while I watched that monster eat someone who looked exactly like me."

"Did you?" Clean-David asked. "Did you break?"

"No." Dave leaned back in the office chair and rested his heels on a nearby table. "I had a couple bags of peanuts and drank six or seven beers. Your slow, anesthesia-numbed death was on a big monitor, so it was like a Saturday night at home watching the Syfy Channel."

All the air seemed to come out of Clean-David as he slumped into a chair. "I've never been eaten before."

Dave's eyebrows rose. "A pity. Now, suck it up. Karl's going to come back through the door, and we can put a stop to all this. Just turn off the BAB-C, and we see what happens. Either everything goes back to normal, or you get eaten by the lab physician."

"Karl really didn't try to save me?" Clean-David looked distraught, like he'd been dumped.

"Nope. And that was just the beginning. Time's running out, and I've seen the future. Skid's on her way here, and I can guarantee she's the reason you got that knife in your leg."

A sudden burst of anger rushed into Clean-David; he sat straight and pulled the pistol in front of him, the sag in his shoulders gone, jaw set. He pulled back the pistol bolt and released it in a metallic snap. The weapon was ready to fire.

"I'm sure she did," he said. "But that wasn't me."

A laugh escaped from Dave. He couldn't hold it in anymore. "You and Karl are walking clichés. What'd you do? Take a Comedic Villain class together?"

Clean David pushed himself to his feet, sending the chair wheeling backward until it clanged against a wall. "I don't like you."

3

The man looked harmless and somewhat dazed; a trickle of blood, already thick and sticky, had run down his nose and stopped at his upper lip. Skid slipped the blade back into its sheath. The lab was full of scientists, and this guy in his J. C. Penney slacks and button-down shirt sure looked like one. *Coming back late from lunch, buddy?* His right cheek, flushed pink, had begun to swell. Science Guy didn't look like the kind of person who got himself into situations to be beaten up much, at least not since high school.

"Are you okay?" she asked, moving past Brick, her voice all preschool teacher. The man stepped back, whether from her movement or Brick starting to get ruffled, she couldn't tell. "What happened?"

That concern sounded fake, she thought. *Yeah, definitely fake.*

The man took a deep breath and winced when he let it out. "I was jumped," he said, his eyes never meeting Skid's. "A couple of guys. One of them was named Dave." He paused and took another painful breath. "Then this cloud thing came out of nowhere, and now I'm here and they're not."

Dave?

289

The man's eyes wandered behind her, not toward Brick, but the building. "Where are we, anyway?"

There was something off about Science Guy. "We're at—"

"Telemetrix Cosmetic Testing Facility," Brick interrupted. He turned back to the door and swiped the other Dave's key card. The light blinked green, and the door slid open again. "We're protesting the use of the Barbary macaque to test tinted moisturizer and pomade hair gel. If you're not ready to smash some cages and release members of the only population of well-groomed wild European monkeys, get lost."

Skid's mouth started to move, but she shut it down. She had no idea where this was going, but Brick was selling it hard.

"I just want to use the phone," the man said.

Air conditioning from the lobby of the building brushed against her back, sending a welcome chill through her shoulders. *We have to ditch this guy,* she thought. *But we can't leave him alone.* To her, Science Guy, or whoever he was, seemed as helpless as he most probably was. "What's your name?"

His feet shifted. He still hadn't looked at them. "Marty, Martin," he stuttered. "Martin McClure. I—I sell insurance."

Skid slapped her hand on his shoulder and shoved him through the open door of Lemaître Labs.

"Then, Martin McClure who sells insurance, let's find you a telephone."

4

Karl walked into the lobby behind the woman he was certain was Skid. She had to be. If she were as dangerous as that idiot Collison and his idiot double said, the knife belt was a dead giveaway. But she hadn't stabbed him, so maybe she wasn't as big and bad as the Collisons let on. She certainly wasn't big, but Karl was smart enough to know size and gender had nothing to do with power. This woman could still be Darth-Thanos-Sauron and he didn't want to stay with these two morons long enough to find out.

Chairs and couches lay scattered in pieces around the large room. Gillian's desk was overturned, the telephone and computer monitor she played solitaire on in pieces, crushed by something big and, given the spread of the debris, angry. Karl hoped it had only been Oscar on a rampage. The former Lemaître Labs engineer who specialized in quantum mechanics was safely locked in the engineering portal to the Bridge, looking more like Grendel than a guy who graduated top of his class at Stanford. He should still be beating on the impenetrable engineering portal to the Bridge five floors beneath him. Karl would find out soon enough.

It could have been Doctor Hahn. After watching the Chet Hahn mantis devour one of the Collisons, Karl didn't want to see either of them again, or anything else bigger than the lumberjack-looking man who followed him into the building. *Telemetrix Cosmetic Testing Facility. Monkeys. Hair gel. Why the bull hockey, Paul Bunyan?*

The front doors slid shut behind them with a whoosh.

"What happened in here?" Karl said from between his two guides, guards, protectors, executioners, whatever they were. He stepped over crushed lobby furniture to Gillian's desk. Her purse lay partially under a splintered section of furniture. His breath caught in his throat—the Lemaître Labs lanyard attached to every key card issued to every employee spilled from the bag's main compartment like purse vomit.

Karl bent over the purse. Part of the key card peeked out. It wouldn't get him into the Bridge—not many people had that kind of clearance—but it would get him onto the elevator, and that was all he needed. He just had to grab it. He stretched his hand out and—

"You find something?" the big man asked.

Dang it. Karl reached over the bag and lifted the telephone receiver from the floor. The curly cord dangled uselessly. *Sell it, Karl. Sell it.* His eyes slid up, finally connecting with Skid's. They were dark, hard. He'd avoided looking into the eyes of either of these people before now because his acting skills had peaked in a dramatic sixth-grade performance based on the middle-grade Revolutionary War novel *My Brother Sam is Dead*. He pointed the receiver at her.

"Did you people do this? How can I call my mother to pick me up now?"

Paul Bunyan shook his head and walked around the room, presumably looking for a path friendlier than the dark hallway that stretched before them, but Karl was too pleased with himself to care. *Mother. That was brilliant.* But the key card. He needed that, or he wasn't going anywhere. These two interlopers weren't as smart as Karl Miller the Dimension King, but they might be smart enough to get to the lab even with the elevator off. He had to do something.

"There's one hallway," Paul Bunyan said, pointing predictably toward it. Then he swept his thick arm around the room. "And a door that looks like it could be to another hallway or a supply closet—"

It's a bathroom, moron.

"—or a bathroom."

The big man pulled what looked like cocktail napkins from his front pocket and shuffled through them.

"Bud Light Dave's map shows a conference room, stairs, and the elevator down the hall."

Karl studied Paul Bunyan's face. *Bud Light Dave? Collison?*

The big man gently pushed the napkins back into his pocket and motioned Skid toward the hallway. "Maybe we should go this way."

Move, Karl. His feet didn't do what his brain told them to do, which was to do anything other than stand there like a twat waffle. A vertical tunnel was hidden in the conference room, a tunnel that wasn't booby-trapped. Karl just needed to get to that room and down to the Bridge before these idiots ruined everything. A cough exploded from him; he hit his chest with a fist.

"You okay?" asked the woman who may be Skid.

"Yes," he said, trying to look anywhere but the hallway. Karl could see the plan unfold in his mind. He'd let these two go into the darkness, claim he was afraid of the dark, then get Gillian's key card. He'd follow, notice the conference room door, and say, *There's probably a phone in there.* Then he'd lock the door behind him and leave them to be eaten by the HR cockroaches. He had to fight back a grin. *Brilliant, Dimension King. Simply brilliant.*

"You sure?"

"I don't want to go in there. I—I can't go in the dark. Can you find a phone for me?"

The Skid woman took a step toward the dark, empty hallway. "Sure. Maybe there's one in here."

These two are so stupid.

5

"That guy is so stupid." Brick leaned against a tinted-glass window that spread down the darkened hallway. "No way he's an insurance salesman. I think he's a scientist who got locked out and Hans Grubered us to get back in."

"Hans Grubered?"

If she didn't know Brick, Skid thought his expression would make her worry for her safety.

"You've never seen *Die Hard*?"

Skid shrugged. Then when he didn't respond, she shrugged 2.0. "No. I haven't seen *Die Hard*. I've been living, Brick. Can you expertly throw a knife? I don't think so. It takes practice, and practice takes time." She sighed. So many things she didn't have control over. "Who's this Hands Bieber?"

"Gruber."

"Whatever."

Brick pulled the explorer's pack from his back and dropped it to the floor, then knelt beside it.

"In *Die Hard*, Bruce Willis battles terrorists holding hostages in a high-rise office building. The main terrorist, Hans Gruber, runs into Willis and pretends to be a hostage himself, using a fake name because he's trying to get his hands on something."

She glanced toward the empty entrance of the hall, then down its dark depths in the direction she knew they had to go.

"So, you're saying this guy we just met, who wouldn't look us in the eye, who stumbled over his own name and didn't scan the front office like someone new to a place, might have lied to us?"

Brick set a tin box on the floor and pulled out what looked like a thin club, one end wrapped in oil-soaked cloth. "Yeah. I guess."

"Of course he lied. Jesus, Brick. The way he said he had to call his mother? I can act better than this guy." She fingered the one throwing knife still in her belt and looked down the hallway. "You want to leave him behind?"

Brick shook his head. "Not really. Keep your friends close and your enemies closer. We should take him with us."

Skid clapped her hands. "That's great. This guy who weirds me out should follow us so we can keep an eye on him until he backstabs us." She crossed her arms and drummed fingers on her biceps. "No. I don't trust people who smell like Cheetos."

Brick's shoulders managed a meager shrug. "Whatever. It's your job to keep an eye out for him." He motioned down the black pit of the hallway. "The elevator's that way."

She took a few steps into the darkness. "Okay, let's go."

"We need light," Brick said, the tin box now open. He held a piece of carbon steel in one hand, a flake of flint in the other.

"What are you—"

Before she could finish, Brick struck flint to steel, flint to steel, flint to steel. Sparks danced onto the oiled cloth and ignited in a blaze of orange.

Brick's smile was Christmas morning.

"We're walking down dark corridors going into the depths of enemy territory, Skid. This is a dungeon. I'm actually in a dungeon."

He stood, throwing the pack over one arm, holding the torch over his head with the other. "I've been waiting for this moment since junior high school."

"But the—"

The flames from the torch sent thick, black smoke to cover the ceiling. Moments later, the flame grew and licked the air just under a sprinkler head.

Something clicked, and the Lemaître Labs sprinkler directly overhead, designed to put out random electrical malfunctions, human error, fires of inter-dimensional nature, and apparently medieval torches, burst, dumping forty gallons of water per minute in a heavy spray. Brick's torch died as quickly as he'd brought it to life.

"Damn it."

Skid punched his shoulder, not that he noticed.

"Do you have a flashlight in that purse?" she shouted over the falling water.

"It's an explorer's pack," he said, staring at the dead torch.

"I. Don't. Care," she shouted, punching his arm with each word. "Do. You. Have. A. Flashlight?"

"Yeah. A Maglite. I just thought—" He held the dead stick in front of his face. "Dungeons and Dragons, you know?"

Sharp white light sprang to life at the end of the hall. Emergency lamps triggered by the sprinkler, which was the only one on. Apparently, Brick's torch was too small to signal a lab-wide emergency. As the heavy indoor waterfall soaked through her shirt and into her socks, Skid was relieved she could at least see somewhat down the darkened end of the hall. She turned back from where they came. Marty Martin McClure, insurance salesman, stood in silhouette at the mouth of the hall.

Is that little bastard laughing at us?

"This isn't going to be a proper dungeon without a torch," Brick moaned.

Skid rolled her eyes like a snotty junior high girl. "Maybe we can have it both ways?"

"Huh?"

"Marty Martin McClure," she said. "I don't want him with us because he might screw us over. You want him with us because we can watch him screw us over. How about we just lock him in an office?"

A grin crossed Brick's hairy face. "I'll go grab him. You open a door."

The big man dropped the dead torch onto the floor with a clack and walked toward Hans Gruber.

6

They were gone, but not *gone* gone. That would have been too easy. Skid and the lumberjack were standing near the door to the conference room when Karl moved away from the hallway threshold and pressed himself against the lobby wall, because that's what people did when they were trying to be sneaky. He paused and listened.

"The elevator's that way," the big man said. The next few sentences were muffled.

"Ha," came out of Karl like a suppressed cough. "Good luck taking *that* route with the power off."

Whatever had torn through the lobby hadn't left much intact—chairs, potted plants, the water cooler, the portrait of the president that hangs in every government building, the bookshelves, all crushed and strewn around the room. Some scat might give a hint of what did this, or hair, if it had been Oscar. But Karl didn't think Oscar had stomped this path of destruction. The sasquatch-looking engineer would have slammed through the door to freedom.

An unsettling thought wormed into Karl's mind. *Unless he was hunting for me.* A chill enveloped him. Oscar was still in the building, in engineering, beating on the unbreakable door, possibly ripping his hands to shreds, just to get at him.

He moved with more urgency.

The key card came out of Gillian's purse intact. Karl had worried about that. Everything else in this room had been destroyed, but the key card looked untouched. He hung it around his neck and turned toward the hallway. From down the hall, the woman shouted.

Roaches already? Not yet! He knew he had to get into the confor once room before the roaches came out. "Can't you HR people do anything right?"

He jogged the twenty feet to the entrance of the hall, panting from the exertion. Karl promised himself he'd start using the lab's gym, installed to keep the brainiacs from having an early heart attack.

He found Skid and the lumberjack standing under a fire-suppression sprinkler they'd set off. Seconds later, the emergency lights at the end of the hallway popped on.

"Can you stop being a nerd for five seconds?" she shouted at the lumberjack before looking up to see Karl. She said something to the lumberjack Karl couldn't hear, but the large man began walking toward him.

Oh no.

A minute later, Brick shoved Karl into the conference room, the clang of an office chair being jammed under the hallway doorknob echoed.

That was too easy.

7

Skid's key card didn't work.

"Swipe it again," Brick said, dripping into the puddle they'd made on the floor, the single sprinkler still spraying water down the hall.

She wiped it over the sensor again; it beeped, but the light didn't switch from red to green.

Brick reached over her and swiped the key card the other David had given him from the blood-stained seat of a stolen pickup. It beeped, but nothing else happened.

"The elevator's turned off." Skid's eyes were nearly black in the spotty shadows cast by the emergency lights.

Brick wiped his hand over a dent in the door. "This is weird."

"Does that matter?" Skid snapped. "We still have to get down to the control room."

"Dave called it the Bridge, and yes, it matters," Brick said. He balled up his hand and put it in the dent that looked like a fist, a fist more than twice as big as Brick's. "Does this look like a punch to you?"

"What?" She slapped the sleek metal door and turned to look at the giant fist mark. "Yeah. That's a punch."

"Dave said we couldn't take the stairs," Brick said. "Should we take the stairs? We might want to take the stairs."

She waved him off.

"It's booby-trapped. Poison, bloody vomit, explosive diarrhea, death, blah, blah, blah." She stuck her fingertips into the center crack of the elevator door. "So," she said, grunting as she pulled at the doors; Brick stuck his fingers inside and helped her force them open. The gap revealed a black pit. "Got any bright ideas? I mean, I guess we could wait here for whatever left that mark, or—"

Brick clicked on the Maglite and held it under his face. "I—"

"Jesus, Brick," she interrupted. "Don't."

She couldn't tell if he frowned under all that beard, but he huffed and walked about twenty feet down the hall to the nearest door marked "Accounting," ran his key card over the sensor and walked inside. Skid didn't understand Brick, but she couldn't say she tried hard either. Business owner, giant, nerd, giant nerd, a man she witnessed slaughter the last inhabitants of a village of Orcs, but most probably the nicest guy she'd ever met.

Something crashed inside the room, maybe a computer colliding with the floor. A long, high scrape screeched through the air and the door opened again. A metal office desk flew into the hallway and rolled to a stop against the wall. Brick stepped out after it, unshouldering his explorer's pack and dropping it to the floor.

"So much for stealth," Skid said, wondering just what the hell that was about. "What's the desk for? Your taxes?"

"Nope, and stealth is irrelevant. Hans Gruber's locked up nice and tight, and whatever thing made that dent should have been on top of us by now." The big man reached into the backpack and pulled out a something dangly that could have been an enormous lasso of licorice. "You know what this is?"

"A really big Twizzler?"

He uncoiled the lasso, ignoring her. "It's fifty feet of hempen rope from my explorer's pack, which, by the way, has come in handy more than once." Brick looped the rope around the center of desk and pulled slack on the loose end. "Do you think I should tie a two-half hitch or a bowline knot?"

Skid shook her head. "What am I? Popeye? I don't know how to tie knots."

"You should learn; they come in handy if you're moving, packing, or breaking into a top-secret government lab." He flipped the rope and pulled it tight, grunting as he lifted the desk gently off the floor to test it. "Bowline it is."

"So, what's the plan?"

He shouldered his pack and carried the desk to the elevator before he set it on its side and pushed it against the open maw of the shaft. What used to be a desk was now basically a piton that anchored the rope solidly against the wall on either side of the opening. He smiled at Skid and tossed the remaining coil of rope into the darkness.

"What's so funny?"

Brick scratched his beard with one thick, dirty hand. "We can't use the stairs. We can't use the elevator. We can't apparate."

Jesus. "Appawhat?"

"And I could never climb the rope in gym class." He held out the Maglite.

She snatched the flashlight from his meat hook. It was heavy in her hands. "That elevator shaft better not be deep." She leaned over the desk, shining the high-powered beam into the pit. Light reached the bottom. It was more than fifty feet down because the rope didn't quite reach the top of the elevator car. Skid pulled back and stepped away from what looked like the lair of something wicked.

"It doesn't reach the bottom, Brick," she said, trying to force strength into her voice. "My dad tried to get me to do the tightrope before he settled for the motorcycle. I don't do heights, which made me kind of a failure at the circus."

"It's just an elevator shaft," he said over her shoulder, leaning forward to look into the depths. Brick took the rope and began pulling it up. "Tell you what, I'll lower you down. I'll just tie the rope around your waist with a highwayman's hitch." He pulled up the last of the line and looped the end around Skid's wrist using some kind of witchcraft. "When you get to the bottom, all you have to do is pull the end —" He tugged the last few inches of the rope that stuck from the knot and it fell free of her arm. "—and drop the last four feet—"

"It's at least ten."

"—six feet to the bottom." He gave her a gentle smile that didn't comfort her. "You have nothing to worry about."

She folded her arms over her chest. "And why can't you do it?"

"Like I said, I can't climb ropes. Besides, if I run into trouble, you wouldn't be able to pull me up."

Trouble? She suddenly had difficulty catching her breath. "What kind of trouble?"

"With what we've been through," he said, sliding the rope around her waist and cinching it tight with the knot, "it could be anything." He tried smiling again. It had the same effect as before—nothing. He reached into his pocket and pulled out the other David's key card to dangle it in front of her. "You'd better take this. We still don't know what dimension we're in."

She took it and hung it over her neck, face down, shoulders slumped. Brick bent a knuckle under her chin and gently lifted her face to his. "You're going to be okay."

Why doesn't that sound true? she thought, staring into his kind, hairy, blood-splattered face. She hated to admit she cared for him. Her stomach felt watery, her knees weak. She wasn't in control again, and she hated it. "We're out of options. I don't really have a choice." She threw a leg over the desk. It hung over about sixty feet of nothing. Her eyes shot to Brick. "You have to promise not to drop me."

He opened his mouth, but she cut him off.

"Promise me now."

He threw the rope behind him and pulled it tight across his back, holding the end near Skid's belly in one huge hand, the part that emerged from behind him in the other. He tugged, and she leaned toward him.

"I promise. I will not drop you."

The Maglite in her hand clicked off, and the shaft fell back into darkness. She didn't want to see anything.

"I can't get any more ready for this." She brought her other leg over to sit on the center desk drawer, trying to breathe slowly to keep her heart rate down. "Watch your back for our friend. I think you're right, Marty Martin McClure is Hans Buber."

Brick didn't correct her. "Everything will be fine," he assured her as she slid off the desk and into the pit. The knot held. "Try to face the wall and use your feet to keep you from smashing your face."

Great.

"What was Hans Gruber trying to get his hands on?" she asked, attempting to get her mind off the dark, sixty-foot drop, and the fact that her clothes were still dripping wet and there was a weird guy in the building hiding something from them. The rope lowered slowly. She reached her feet out and bumped into the wall. "You said in *Die Hard*, Gruber used a fake name because he was trying to get his hands on something. What was it?"

She went farther into the pit, the darkness closing in on her like a blanket. A scary, scary blanket.

His voice echoed down the shaft. "A gun."

That doesn't help.

The rope stopped moving, and her still mostly pink shoes came to rest against the wall of the shaft. She looked up from the black cocoon that engulfed her, the dim gray glow of the open doors above doing absolutely nothing to comfort her. She couldn't see Brick, not even his shadow.

"Brick—" she started to say, but it was cut off by a scream.

About that time, Karl vanished again.

CHAPTER FOURTEEN

SEPTEMBER 7, NOW WITH MORE MARSHMALLOWS

1

THE TRESPASSERS to Karl the Dimension King's domain were still standing by the useless elevator door staring into the black depths of the shaft about the time something stirred in the hallway, an indistinct, undulating shape that seemed to move like a jerky 1970s cartoon.

The shifting in the darkness rose through the floor, growing as it came, then sprang at Karl as if it were alive, a Miller wave. He tried to whip Gillian's key card over his head, but it caught on his right ear, the sudden pull leaning him to one side as the dimensional-temporal storm struck him.

This wave was different. There was no rush that pushed Karl's suddenly non-corporeal body through the solid metal and concrete. He couldn't count the layers of earth he ascended through before the wave left him standing in a field. He wasn't in a field, and this time he didn't pee. One second he stood in the dark hall on the first floor of the lab complex, the next he stood in a shower as the dull thud of music came from somewhere.

A mildew-stained vinyl curtain hung limply from a sagging aluminum rod. It was as sad as a beach towel in North Dakota. Shampoo and conditioner bottles, none full, but none quite empty, lined the shower shelf, separated by small chunks of what had begun their existence as bars of Ivory and Irish Spring soaps. There was one razor in the shower, a pink Bic in a plastic cup with the words *In-B-Tween* faded and chipped.

What now? And why do people play bad music so loudly? He almost thought, *Why don't people listen to Lisa Lisa and Cult Jam anymore?* but suppressed it from the childhood fear that people could read his mind.

Karl reached a hand toward the shower wall stained with soap scum and leaned against it, his stomach clenching and unclenching like ab exercises. There were little more than two hours left before the soldiers came back with those monsters, and Karl needed to be at the lab. He *had* to be at the lab. There was much to do, and Oscar was still loose. Oscar should have been locked in engineering, but then who trashed the lobby? Could HR do that much damage, even without opposable thumbs? He tried to calm himself but didn't know how.

A body shifted slightly outside the shower and Karl flinched, sinking back into the dirty tiled wall as much as it would let him. He peed again, only a droplet, enough that he considered scheduling an appointment with a urologist.

"Bleeecchhharrrrff."

Something wet spattered against something else wet.

"Bleeecchhharrrrff."

Then came the smell. Karl pinched fingers over his nose before he threw up, too. Alcohol, that was for sure, mixed with, what? Taco Bell? He slowly pulled the curtain back.

The drunken puker was a man, or more specifically a boy, who might be mistaken for Shaggy on *Scooby-Doo* if his face wasn't in the toilet.

Shaggy let loose again. "Bleeecchhharrrrff."

Karl stepped out of the shower, tiptoeing around the boy's feet. The kid, a college student probably, either didn't know he was there or didn't care.

"Bleeecchhharrrrff."

The gag reflex, present in almost all mammals but rats and horses, kicked in and Karl coughed. He never could stomach someone else vomiting. He lunged for the door, but for an instant his eyes grazed the mirror mounted on the rusty tin medicine cabinet over the sink, the letters TKE and AΣA stuck to the glass.

I'm in a college house. And it was familiar. Those letters—he knew them. Once upon a time, he saw them almost daily on shirts of people he knew. Karl opened the door and stepped into a short hallway with darkened openings to bedrooms. What had been a dull thud in the bathroom was now full-on blaring 1980s German techno mixed with laughter. There was a party in this house. Karl took a step into the hallway. Peeling flowered wallpaper was decorated with wrinkled posters of Real McCoy, La Bouche, and Mouse on Mars. Marty and Suzie loved that music.

"You'll never have this day again," Marty had told him more than thirty years ago.

"No way," he whispered. "This can't be happening."

"Hey, dude," a shaky voice said from behind him. "Shut the door."

Karl walked down the hall, leaving the bathroom wide open.

2

Oh, shit. Ohshitoshitoshitoshitoshit. Without warning, the rope swung outward and to the left, slamming Skid into the metal wall of the elevator shaft. The wind shot out of her. She clung to the rope, now impossibly thin to her, and fought to pull air back into her lungs.

Oxygen dragged through her trachea, the air burning as it went in and out. From above, Brick screamed again, followed by the sound of metal striking something hard.

Skid pulled her body into a ball as the rope swung outward again; in what direction, she couldn't tell.

"Brraaaaaa," came from overhead, but not a scream this time, a bellow. Like in the orc world. Brick wasn't alone.

The rope twisted her in circles, and Skid wondered if she might shit herself. Her feet instinctively thrust themselves out and her shoes struck the side of the elevator shaft. Skid winced at the pain, but the spin slowed as she dragged the shoes along a flat metal surface once, twice, three times. She stopped, her breath not coming any easier.

Brick growled. Berserker Brick was back. His sword clanged off armor again and something hissed.

"Watch out for my fingers, man," another voice yelled before an airy scream echoed down the shaft, then the world fell silent.

Cord's back.

3

When Karl reached the stairs, he knew where he was—Marty and Suzie's graduation party.

This was thirty years ago.

He stood with a hand on the rickety second floor newel post to keep himself upright. It was 1984, and he was back at college. Chuck and Tommy hovered by the keg, probably talking about Advanced Dungeons and Dragons as Marion fixed herself a drink at the makeshift bar on the dining room table. Three people he didn't know sat with sixth-year senior Matt the Rat at the opposite end of the table, playing Quarters. Bobbylicious stood behind the turntable flipping through Marty and Suzie's record collection, his long blond mullet hung behind him like a cape for his head. Karl even remembered the song Bobbylicious spun, "Don't You Forget About Me" by

Simple Minds. Not German techno, but at least European. It was playing when—

Karl turned toward the door, and there he was, Young Karl holding a half-filled cup of warm, flat Diet Coke listening to Marty bitch about grad school and computer entrepreneurs. Suzie pushed Marty, and he walked toward the keg, flipping off Karl's twenty-one-year-old, not-yet-Ph.D. self.

This is why I'm here, he realized. *I have to warn myself about Colleen. Young Karl set down his cup and walked out the door. I have to stop him.*

"Whoa, dude. What happened to your face?" Chuck said as Karl reached the ground floor and turned to follow himself out the door. "Marty. Hey Marty. Old guy alert."

Marty turned, then Suzie, then every face in the room. Karl's step slowed as he took in the house. He remembered this place with the crappy furniture, the crappy sound, the crappy smell. It was awful. All of it.

"Oh my god," Suzie shouted. "You look like—"

"Karl Miller," he said. "That's because I am."

Marty stepped in front of Karl, moving with him as he tried a sidestep. "Dude. Karl just left, but you're, you're—"

"Injured? My face? Yes, I know."

Marty shook his head. "No, old. I mean, you're still dressed the same, and your hair's the same, but—" His drunken eyes finally focused and grew wide. "—you're just old. Who are you, man? This is either going to be really funny or I'm going to hit you."

"Are you Karl's dad, or something," Suzie asked, pushing her way in front of her boyfriend to get a better look.

Karl softened for a second. He'd always liked Suzie. She was nice and smart and funny and too good for Marty. Way too good.

"No, I'm not Karl's dad. I am Karl Miller." He paused and looked around. Everyone's attention was on him. Bobbylicious potted down the music. Karl raised his hands like somebody had a gun on him, although he just wanted to strengthen the attention he already had. "I'm Karl Miller from the future."

One of the guys playing Quarters laughed.

"Whatever. That's not possible," Marty said. "Seriously, who the fuck are you? And it better be good. I'm just drunk enough to call the cops to my own party."

A painful smile danced around Karl's mouth. "Do you remember when you told me, 'You'll never have this day again'?"

Marty took a drink of his fresh beer before answering. "Yeah, I just said that." Confusion leaked over his face.

Karl's arms folded across his chest. "How would I know that?"

"Just, I dunno, whatever."

"I know a lot of things, Marty," Karl said, delight now washing over him. This was going to be fun. Just like everyone else he'd met in life, Karl didn't like his undergrad friends much either. Marty had been his best friend since the first day of freshman year, but in the grand scheme of things, what did that really mean?

"I know you cheated on your college entrance exam," he said. Marty's mouth dropped, but Karl held a hand up in front of his old friend to keep anything from coming out of it. "I'm the only one who knows that, buddy boy. I also know you're afraid of deep water, you caught your folks in your bedroom smoking the pot they found under your mattress when you were a junior in high school, and you had— or maybe still have—a secret crush on your first cousin Karen. You know, the one with the enormous tits."

Karl finished and the room fell silent. Bobbylicious leaned over the turntable glaring with fisheyes at Karl as the album underneath him played through.

"But," Bobbylicious said, his voice too small for his body. "If you're from the future, dude, do you know what happens to us?"

His eyes went to the door. Young Karl was out there, walking home, but Karl knew where home was. His smile came back.

"Sure," he said, raising his voice so everyone could hear. "Chuck, you're going to have a drug problem when you're thirty. Heroine, I think."

The red Solo cup fell from Chuck's hand and hit the floor with a flat clank; cheap foamy beer pooled around his feet. "What?"

Karl turned, pointing at people. "Marion is going to be a third-grade teacher. Tommy will spend a semester abroad and disappear in Romania. You three, I don't know. Matthew the Ratthew Simington is going to sell advertising for a failing small-town newspaper—" His finger lingered on Bobbylicious who looked genuinely frightened.

"What? What man? What about me?"

"You're actually going to be pretty successful. You'll own four or five McDonald's franchises in Kansas City and marry an NFL cheerleader."

Bobbylicious exhaled, sat behind the turntable and didn't move.

"Me, I'm going to run a lab for the United States government and will discover a way to traverse time and space, obviously."

He tried to step around Marty, who moved in front of him again.

"What about me, buddy? What happens to me?" Marty's drunken happy face had hardened into drunken angry face.

Karl sighed. This game wasn't fun anymore. He knew he had to leave before another wave hit and took him away from his younger self. He turned to Suzie.

"I'm sorry, Suzie, but after three years of marriage, this jerk cheats on you with your sister Janet."

Marty's fist came out of nowhere and connected with Karl's jaw. Suzie screamed as Karl stumbled backward into the front door, but there'd been no real power behind the punch. Karl flipped Marty the bird and went outside, the shouts from inside louder than the music had been.

4

Brick's hands moved slowly, easing the rope in a controlled descent, his broad back taking most of Skid's weight as she dropped farther into the darkness. The explorer's pack had been a good find in his Other-Dimension parents' house. Brick had started to put one together in high school and gotten as far as the bedroll, rations, and mess kit—all from the Army/Navy store a few blocks away from his house—before he and Mitch Davees watched *It* late one Saturday and voted unanimously to put their adventures in the sewers on permanent hold. He didn't know if Other-Dimension Brick had gone through with it either. His doppelganger had bought the fifty feet of hempen rope off eBay; the receipt was still in the pack.

Brick peered into the darkness but couldn't see anything other than the top two feet of rope that disappeared into the void. Skid must have turned off the flashlight. He almost called down to her but held back his voice. D&D 101: when exploring a dungeon in known hostile territory, don't call attention to yourself. Sound could attract orcs, ettins, gelatinous cubes, or giant insects.

He shivered. If he could handle orcs, radioactive dinosaurs and zombies, he knew he could handle an ettin and maybe a gelatinous cube, but bugs were gross.

A click, a single click, echoed down the hall. Brick stopped lowering Skid toward the elevator car at the bottom of the shaft and listened. The sound could be anything. Even Hans Gruber. No. He'd locked the suspicious guy safely away. Brick's gaze stretched down the hallway as far as it could through the dim light and harsh shadows cast by the sparse emergency lights. Nothing.

"You're hearing things, Brick," he said to himself and slid Skid a few feet lower. Then the click came again, louder, closer.

"No," a voice behind him said. "I heard it, too."

A scream nearly split Brick's lips, but he swallowed it when he saw Cord. The healthy Cord from dimensions unknown.

"How long have you been here?"

Cord cocked his head and squinted at Brick in an un-Cordlike way. "How long? I've been with you guys the whole time. I suggested Skid go down." He relaxed some and crossed his arms. "I never could climb that rope in gym class."

Another click, then a chitter.

Brick's fists clamped into vices, and Skid stopped again. Something was out there, and it wasn't Hans or apparently Cord. The thing made that noise again, something like a recording on fast-forward. *This is not cool.* The sound came from in front of him, past the nearest emergency light, invisible in the darkness. A knot like he'd swallowed a golf ball grew in his throat, and every horror movie he'd ever seen crept closer to him in the darkness. His muscles tensed.

"Hello," tried to work its way past the golf ball and came out in a squeak.

"What is it?" Cord asked.

A blob moved in the shadows, thick and low to the ground. More clicking, followed by a scuttling as the thing emerged from the darkness like the hallway had given birth. A cockroach the size of a storage trunk stepped into the dim outer haze of the emergency lighting. Brick screamed as the creature shuffled closer, its exoskeleton occasionally clanking against the floor.

A bug. A big. A bug. A big bug. Shit, shit, shit. It broke into a scampering run, and he screamed again.

Skid. Oh, my god, Skid. She hung at least halfway down the elevator shaft and Brick knew if he let go, the fall would kill her—or, worse, would leave her too badly injured too evade the cockroach that climbed down to eat her alive. He twisted his left wrist twice, wrapping the rope around his muscular forearm, and held it tightly. He took the rope with his right hand and wound it around Cord's waist.

"Hey, wait." Cord pulled at the rope but couldn't move it.

"If I fall, don't let Skid drop," he said, tugging as he held all Skid's weight in one arm. He couldn't drop her.

The big orc sword hissed as he pulled it from the explorer's pack, the monster almost atop him, its hissing and chittering flooding his senses. Cord whimpered beside him.

"Come get some," he Bruce-Campbelled and brought the sword down. It clanged off the roach's hard thorax.

The gigantic insect hissed and backpedaled out of Brick's reach, rubbing its head with its two hairy front legs.

"Don't like that, huh?" Brick tried to keep his legs solid beneath him. A warmth rushed through his chest, and he momentarily forgot Skid below him, hanging thirty feet above a painful end.

The monster hissed and charged.

"Brraaaaaa," burst from Brick's throat, and he met the roach with an overhead swipe of the sword; it glanced off the beast's back, not leaving a scratch.

"Chchchchchch," it hissed and lurched backward, its horrid black eyes glaring.

"Come on," Brick roared.

As it charged again, he swung the sword toward its head.

"Watch out for my fingers, man," Cord shouted as the sword whizzed by him.

The roach caught the blade in its mandibles, the ring echoed in the empty hall. The beast tugged at the sword, trying to rip it from Brick's grip.

"Not today, you Kafka-looking son-of-a-bitch," he growled and threw his weight forward. The sword slid into the ugly creature's throat. A hiss ripped through the air followed by a hot white liquid splattering Brick's arm and chest. He twisted the blade, and the cockroach dropped to the floor dead.

Brick tried to slow his breathing, the weight on his left arm forgotten. Adrenaline coursed through his veins.

"That was messed up, Cord," he said.

"Yeah, sure. Can you untie me now?"

"In a second." Brick stuck the nicked orc scimitar in Cord's hands, the blade dripping with what cockroaches had for blood.

"Brick?" Skid's soft voice came from the empty hole in the wall.

He grabbed the rope with his right hand, relieving the pressure on his left. He leaned over the dark hole. "Are you okay?"

The shaft was silent for almost a second too long. "Yeah. Enough. What happened?"

He turned back toward the far end of the hallway. Other shapes shifted in the shadows but didn't come closer. "They have a huge cockroach problem here."

In his mind, he could see the familiar look that was probably on her face. Mock surprise mixed with a dash of *you're an idiot*, topped with a little *why do I even try?*

"Is that a misplaced modifier?" she called upward.

"No," he said. "The roaches are enormous." The shadow-shifting grew more urgent; one would attack soon, maybe all of them. "I have to lower you down now, Skid. There are more up here. I'm going to need both hands."

"Like I have a choice," came from the darkness.

A pang, an emotional sucker punch, caught Brick. He realized he might not see Skid after this.

"Come on," he said. "We gotta make this quick." And he started lowering her again.

6

Young Karl had almost made it to his apartment building by the time Karl the Dimension King caught up with him. Karl didn't want to go inside and relive the crappy apartment. Whatever Karl was going to say to himself, it could be done on the street.

"Hey," he shouted, his jaw starting to ache from Marty's punch. "Karl Miller, wait up."

Young Karl stopped at the last streetlight before the apartment door, a yellow glow surrounding him. If he were surprised to see himself, he didn't show it.

"What do you want?" he asked.

Karl the Dimension King stepped into the yellow light and looked at his younger self. Same shirt, same slacks, same shoes, same hair. *I haven't changed a bit.*

"Do you know who I am?" he asked between wheezes.

His younger self nodded. "Yeah. You're me," he said like he ran into himself from the future all the time. "I've always suspected this might happen. I suppose you have some message for me, or something."

Karl the Dimension King rested his hands on his hips as he tried to slow his breathing; he'd moved faster than he usually moved, and he wasn't Young Karl anymore. He was Cheetos Karl. He held up a finger while he caught his breath. *Was I always this cocky?* "I'm here to warn you about—"

The next Miller Wave slammed into him from behind. A second later he stood in a black, empty hallway; Young Karl stayed in the past.

"Dang it."

7

The rope dropped quickly.

"I'm almost to the end," Brick yelled from above. He sounded so far away.

The feeling in the pit of Skid's stomach was tightened. It was fear, and fear was stupid. She tried to swallow it away.

"Okay," she managed, although her voice wavered. For some reason, she hoped Brick hadn't heard the tremor in her voice. She liked being strong Skid, reliable Skid. When the tears came, she liked to keep them to herself.

The light clicked on under her thumb, glass pointed too close to her face. Skid almost dropped the flashlight in the darkness. *Get your shit together,* she scolded, and pointed the light downward. She'd gone farther than she thought. The top of the elevator car was only about ten feet below her.

Brick lowered her another few feet and the rope stopped.

"I'm here," she said, but the words stuck hard. She coughed and tried again. "I'm here."

Silence greeted her and the fear began to turn into panic. *Come on, Brick. Come on. I can't do this without you. I—*

"Good," came from above. "All you have to do is pull on the end of the rope, and the hitch will come free. It'll be fast, so be ready."

Ready? "Ready for what? I think gravity has it from here."

"The landing," Brick said. "Tuck and roll."

The top of the car lay below, a block of metal lined with support beams and a pulley for the thick metal cable that moved it.

"I'm not a gymnast."

Silence again.

"What's going on up there?"

"The roaches are gathering, and Cord has my scimitar. I don't think he knows what end to use." Brick's voice was low and flat. "You have to go now."

Skid pointed the Maglite onto the car below her. The spot directly beneath her was clear but lined by support beams.

"You can do this," she told herself, and pulled the rope. She dropped into nothingness.

8

When Karl reappeared, that big idiot still stood in the hallway, looming over the body of an HR employee. *I hope that wasn't Janet.* Janet Parman always made chewy snickerdoodle cookies for Christmas. Karl squinted down the dimly lighted hall, which didn't help him see better. *What is that man holding? A sword? Where did he get a sword? This isn't Florida.*

But the lumberjack's sword wasn't his concern. The roaches from HR would take care of him. Karl's concern was himself about thirty years ago. "When you're the project manager at a big government lab, don't hire an asshole named David Collison, no matter who his relatives are," he'd wanted to tell Young Karl before the wave snapped him back to the present.

Karl slowly, carefully pulled out the chair wedged under the doorknob to the conference room, slipped Gillian's key card from around his neck and swiped it over the security sensor. When the light turned green, he pushed the door open and went inside.

This was it. The time for the dimension-traveling soldiers to return ticked closer, and he would be there to see them home, them and their pet monster warriors. He thought he'd get a promotion at the least. Karl once thought a cabinet position was out of his reach, but not now. He'd conquered space and time for his country. He didn't think he was just eligible for a cabinet position; he deserved one.

The hatch, in the short hall that led to the bathroom, came off easily. It took Karl a few minutes to find it, as seamlessly as it fit into the wall, but with a push of his fingertips in the center of the panel, part of the wall moved outward on pneumatic hinges. His fingers fit into the holds and the panel lifted off, revealing a heavy metal door with a touch pad underneath. It took a code to open this door, a code only Karl knew because this secret tunnel led to the BAB-C. He had designed this feature himself, in case an emergency shut down the lab. Karl poked the keypad and the mechanism clicked, sliding open to reveal a downward tunnel with a ladder that seemed to have no end.

As he swung his leg over the ledge and felt for a ladder rung with his shoe, he hoped the lights at the bottom still worked.

9

Bees buzzed in Oscar's head. Not bumblebees, not honeybees, not carpenter bees, but Africanized killer bees. Somewhere buried deep in what was left of Dr. Oscar Montouez, his theoretical physicist's brain calmly assured him there were no bees in there. But the anger that surged and bounced around his thick, hairy skull was just as real as bees.

His beady red eyes glared through the murky glass of a thick, dented metal door. Dave, his friend, stood in the room beyond, and Oscar wondered why he didn't let him inside. Maybe his friend was confused because there were two of him.

This was all Miller's fault. Oscar had come in late for work. He was hungover after drinking beer alone at a local bar. His usual friend had stormed away from work angry. *At Miller. He was mad at Miller.* Then the world went wonky, and he'd forgotten the name of his job. He'd forgotten a lot more since then. Ten minutes at work, and a surging purple cloud burst through the floor and swallowed him. When it spat him back out, Oscar wasn't Oscar anymore. He was something else. Bigger and stronger, certainly, but he could no longer remember what all the machines were for.

Dana saw Oscar first, but it was Marcus who screamed and flung himself through the door from the engineering department and out into the hallway, looking back at the pleading face of Dana as he left her behind. Oscar remembered the terror in her eyes. *Don't hurt me,* she'd said. *Please, don't hurt me.* Oscar didn't. He'd never hurt Dana. He stood still, breathing great breaths through a chest the size of a beer keg, and watched as Dana slowly backed toward the door and followed Marcus into the hallway before turning and running as fast as she could in heels.

His first instinct was to chase her, to catch her and rip her throat out with—*my teeth? No. NO. What are you? An animal?* The urge gnawed at him like a sudden, intolerable hunger, the need to chase what ran, but he caught himself before he'd taken a step. *I am a man.* He would not chase Dana. The one person he would sink his teeth into was the one who had caused all this.

"Mirroo."

10

When Brick turned back to Cord, the man's knee was a mess, and Carla stood next to him looking pissed off. Maybe she was out of cigarettes.

More shapes moved in the darkness. Brick stood solid as a wall, slowly lowering Skid into the elevator shaft, ears alert, eyes trying to penetrate the blackness of the hallway. The white beam of the emergency lights helped, but didn't quite create the same dungeon ambience of his torch. Stupid fire-suppression system. A black lump on the ceiling maneuvered onto a wall and slowly made its way down to the floor.

"Keep your eyes on those things, will you?" Brick nodded at Cord, who had slipped out of the rope and now gripped the sword with both hands.

"Are those cockroaches?" Carla asked.

"Yeah," Brick said, keeping the rope moving steadily.

"Reminds me of home."

He slid more rope down the shaft. It grew taut around him. Skid had reached the end.

"Good luck," he started to shout into the black hole, but the rope suddenly became slack. Skid had gone. Brick couldn't help her anymore.

One of the roaches scrambled from the darkness and rushed Brick. He let the rope fall flat, a smile pulling across his face as he took the orc sword from Cord.

"Oh, yeah," he said, his voice soft, in control. "Come to papa."

The cockroach hissed as it sprang. Brick sidestepped its attack and slammed the gruesome sword between the monster's head and thorax. The head snapped off with a squish, spraying his arms with white goo. The still-scuttling body slammed into the wall. A scream bit through the darkness, probably Cord.

Brick laughed. "I'm getting good at this." He waved at figures crawling over each other in the darkness. "Come on. I don't have all day."

None moved closer. The hot, berserk rage he'd felt in Oreland bubbled inside him. Never in his two decades of playing Dungeons and Dragons had he set foot in a real dungeon. His smile threatened to hurt his face.

"Today," he said toward the darkness, "is a good day for you to die."

Brick stepped over the rope and rushed into the black hole of the deep hallway.

"Uh, Brick," Cord said, too softly for the big man to hear over the blood thundering in his ears.

"Come at me," he screamed and rushed toward the shuffling bodies, his vision red. "Raaaarrrrrr."

An oily, musty smell invaded Brick's nostrils as he jumped amongst the things, swinging the sword. It clanged off a shell on a downward sweep, his rear leg mule-kicked another in the face. It shrieked and fell backward, but Brick swept the sword up and brought it down, point first, into a joint of the first roach's natural armor. He grunted and pried; a hairy leg popped and slid across the floor.

The roach squealed and fell to its side. A second later, the sword point smashed through its armor, piercing its brain. It fell dead. The other monsters backed down the hall, cowering in the darkness, chittering at the giant hairy beast covered in their blood. It had a stinger.

Brick started to charge them again, but another shadow appeared in the darkness. Taller, bigger than the HR department.

Brick took a step back, almost slipping in cockroach goo.

The thing stepped closer to him. It was something out of a horror movie.

"What are you?" he whispered.

"Cree? Krrkrrrkrrrkrrrk, cree?" the thing responded.

Oh, hell no. Brick backed up, his pace never faltering, the orc sword tight in his grip.

"Cree? Krrkrrrkrrrkrrrk, cree?" it repeated, the sound like metal grinding together.

Carla's voice came from somewhere behind him. "Great. Now it's exactly like home."

Brick backed into the light, the berserker rage draining from his system. The not-a-roach followed him into the flood lights. Brick's legs, suddenly weak, threatened to drop him onto the floor. "There's a praying mantis in a lab coat up here, Skid," he called down the open elevator. "This is not cool."

No response from the shaft.

"Cree?" the mantis asked, rubbing its pivoting green eyes with its forearms.

Brick screamed and ran.

11

Fear squirmed in her gut, an annoying tickle she'd learned to strangle and bury with the memory of walking through a bad part of town in her prom dress carrying a gas can. Sixteen-year-old Skid had taken that fear and swallowed it before wrecking the knee of a toothless guy in an Anthrax shirt. "You can do this, Skid," she whispered into the elevator shaft. "You can do this."

The fall lasted for less time than it seemed, which was for-fuck-ing-ever. The knot took two tugs to loosen, then Skid dropped eight feet and landed on the roof of the car. "Tuck and roll," Brick had said. There was no time or space for that. She hit the metal roof with all the grace of a sack of onions. Her left ankle buckled beneath her and pain, motorcycle wreck pain, shot up her leg. She collapsed onto the unforgiving metal.

"Aaaaaahhhhh," she screamed when her ankle bent. The Maglite clanked across the roof of the car before it came to rest with the high-power beam pointing into her face.

Skid lay on her stomach, her head turned toward the light. *I broke it. I broke my ankle. How the hell am I supposed to save the universe with a broken ankle?*

She tried to roll over, but a sharp burst of pain kept her down. Her eyes slammed shut. *Damn it.*

Breathe, said a voice that sounded too much like her father's when she lay broken and bleeding from her motorcycle accident. *Breathe, baby.*

Her eyelids pinched tight. *One, two, three, four, five—*

A far-off clang echoed off the shaft walls from above and made her lose count. Her teeth gritted as she sucked in air. Brick was up there fighting giant cockroaches.

Six, seven, eight, nine, ten.

Skid let the air out slowly and focused on breathing, controlled breathing—in deeply through the nose and out slowly through the mouth. The pain subsided into more of a hot throbbing ache. She opened her eyes and rolled onto her back using her left side as a pivot, keeping her ankle as still as possible. The pain stabbed at her, but there was less of it. Hello Kitty pointed in the direction she was supposed to.

There was no snap, she told herself. *If it was broken, you'd have heard it.*

Brick bellowed from high above, the sound of his sword crashing over and over into what her mind pictured were giant, sentient anime bugs smoking cigars. He laughed and an almost inhuman scream split the darkness.

"I'm glad you're having fun," she said, her voice barely audible, even to herself. "I couldn't even stick the landing." The roof hatch lay less than a foot away. "But I can do this."

She grabbed the hatch and pulled herself to it. Elevators in highly populated buildings had doors in the ceiling that opened so emergency personnel could get passengers out in case of a fire. Hollywood used the trope to get anyone out of a stuck car, but it would never work in real life because the hatch was usually—

Locked. The thing is locked? Skid started to pound on the latch but held back her hand. She'd already made enough noise. Attracting more attention would be stupid.

Unintentional handholds dotted the top of the car. Her hand grasped a crossbeam and she pulled herself nearly on top of the hatch before taking the flashlight and training it onto the lock. The device was simple, just there to keep morons inside the car from trying to be movie heroes. She wiped a sleeve across her face to keep the sweat out of her eyes.

"Ouch," she grunted; she'd shifted her body and her ankle turned. It had already begun to swell. The cuff of her pants felt tight.

Brick screamed far above her. "There's a praying mantis in a lab coat up here, Skid. This is not cool."

No. It's not. Her hand found her belt and clasped a knife hilt, her last one. She whipped it forward, slamming the steel point into the lock and twisting with stuck-jar lid strength. Something snapped, and lock bits scattered onto the metal roof.

"I'm saving your ass this time, Brick." She shuffled off the hatch and pulled it open. It moved easily on well-greased, never-used hinges. Easy white light poured from the hole. She leaned over. The elevator car was empty, its door open.

This was it. Dave's bridge was on this floor. She slipped the blade back into her belt.

"Let's go save the world," she said, then shook her head. "World, worlds, whatever."

Skid grabbed the edge of the opening and slowly lowered herself into the car, her well-toned muscles hardly feeling the weight. She hung by her fingers for five seconds, maybe ten, trying to judge the distance of the fall and how she should land, wishing she'd paid more attention to the Roe Bros. acrobats who did perfect spin jumps off moving horses. *Good luck, Brick,* she thought the second before Brick screamed from above and she let go.

12

Lights, like the energy-saving lights in the frozen food aisle, switched on every ten feet as Karl descended. He promised himself he'd start going to the lab gym when all this was over. First losing his breath chasing Young Karl, now huffing while climbing down a ladder? Pfft. *Come on, Karl. Healthy body, healthy mind.* But he would have given all the money in his wallet right then for a can of Coke.

The bottom finally came. He leaned with his hands on his knees panting until his breath returned. The door that would lead him out of the tunnel was inches from his face. This door took a code to open as well. His soldiers would be back soon. Karl stood tall and punched the code into the keypad. The door beeped and slid open.

13

This time Skid tucked. As her right leg touched the tight carpet she collapsed into a ball and rolled over her shoulder, out of the elevator and into a short, dim hallway lined by a bank of windows. Her left leg hit the wall. She bit her lip to hold back a scream.

She lay still, watching for movement, listening to see if anyone or anything had noticed her entrance. Nothing. The only sound in the hall was her short, sharp breath. She rolled onto her stomach and pushed herself to her knees, the injured ankle throbbing like a drumbeat.

"This—finally—is going to be easy," she said, panting.

Her fingers latched onto the sill of a long window over her head.

Arm muscles contracted and pulled her body off the floor, sweat running into her face.

You can do this. Her elbows hit the sill, and she pulled up onto her good foot. The left hung limply as she looked through the glass.

"Oh, god." Skid's heart pounded. Dave. He sat in a chair in this well-lighted room filled with computer monitors and enough buttons and gauges to make the Bridge of the *Enterprise* feel inadequate. She forgot about the sweat beading on her forehead. Why hadn't Dave shut down the machine?

If Dave saw her, he didn't show it. He kept looking to his right, then down at the floor. He said something toward a corner Skid couldn't see. Someone was in there with him.

She hopped on her right foot to the door, holding onto the window ledge for support. Inside the Bridge, Dave leaned back in his chair, fingers behind his head.

The card reader beeped and changed from red to green at her first sweep, but whether from Dave's key card or the other David's, she couldn't remember. The locking mechanism clicked, and she pulled open the door.

"Hey, Skid," Dave said, propping his legs on a table, grinning like nothing was wrong.

"Is this her?" another voice asked.

She turned and almost dropped her weight onto her left foot. The other voice was also Dave's.

14

"You're Skid, aren't you?" The standing David Collison crossed his arms and leaned his back against the metal wall. The air in the room seemed heavy, the kind of heavy that comes right after a fight, or right before one.

"Maybe," she said, pressing her hand in the doorframe to keep upright. "Who are you?"

"I thought that was obvious." The man's eyes tried to bore into her. "I'm David Collison, Ph.D., just like your boyfriend."

"He's not my—" Skid began to say, but let it go.

Chair Dave slowly stood, one knee popping at the movement. Skid and Clean-David both turned toward him.

"I thought you knew Skid," he said to Clean-David, his forehead creased in confusion. "You warned Karl about her."

Clean-David looked at the floor and nudged something with his toe. "Yeah, about that. I ran into myself during a dimensional shift," he said. "We had a couple beers and dodgy butter chicken at a place called Moe, Larry, and Curry. He told me a woman named Skid was going to kill everybody here."

Dave threw his hands into the air.

"Am I a douche in every dimension but this one?" he asked.

Skid shrugged. "Now that you mention it—"

He couldn't stop his grin from making him look like a goofy kid. "I'm happy to see you."

The pain, the forgotten fear, the fact that two of the same man stood in this room dragged at her mind but didn't overwhelm it. She had a job to do. Skid motioned toward the control panel. "Are you ready?"

Clean-David bent and picked something off the floor, never taking his attention from her. When he stood, she saw the pistol.

"Well," she said, her voice without inflection. "That complicates things."

The man she was sure was the real Dave took a step toward her. "He won't shoot either of us," he said. "He's me, and I wouldn't hurt anybody."

Clean-David raised the gun.

"I'm not you," the man said and waved for Dave to sit down, then turned to face Skid. "Why don't you come in, Skid, if that is your real name." He shook his head. "No, of course it's not. What is it, anyway?"

She grinned. "Blow me."

"Wow." He waved the pistol at Dave again. "You have yourself a keeper." He trained the pistol at Skid. "Please, come in."

"I'm good here. I—"

The bullet buzzed by her head like an angry insect from Mount Olympus and ricocheted down the hallway. The gunshot echoed in the room like the last breath of the shot. Clean-David's smile pulled across his face as if he had hooks on both sides of his mouth.

"I spent a lot of my youth on a farm, Miss Skid," he said. "I know how to shoot. If I'd meant to hit you, I would have."

Before she could move, gears cranked from inside the walls, and the heavy sliding double doors in the back of the lab groaned and split, the smug figure of Martin McClure who sells insurance coming into view on the other side. Behind him stretched a vast chamber of machinery. A giant metal tube jutted into tunnels in opposite, roughly hewn walls. A platform supporting a metal ring webbed with wires rose from the middle of the floor. Inside the ring raged a purple storm.

"Welcome back, Karl," Dave said, his butt firmly back in the office chair. "We missed you."

"Karl?" Suddenly the appearance of Martin McClure who sells insurance made so much more sense.

"That's Karl Miller Ph.Dickhole."

"He Hans Grubered us," Skid said. "Up top."

"He what?" Clean-David asked.

Skid flipped him off. "He pretended to be someone else. What? They don't have *Die Hard* in whatever dimension you're from?"

Dave barked a laugh. "I knew there was a reason I sat by you that night."

"I wish you'd stop saying that."

Karl stepped into the room and a flurry of motion sprang into the window of the engineering door. Skid gasped and shifted her weight as the creature on the other side soundlessly beat on the unbreakable door. Her left foot hit the floor and she let out a howl of pain, falling into the room. The hallway door slid shut behind her.

Karl walked into the Bridge and stood next to Clean-David. "So you're the Skid I've heard so much about." Lightning crackled around the undulating mass of violet inside the ring in the cavern-like room behind him. It might have looked impressive, if she hadn't stopped caring. "I thought as much when I met you and the lumberjack upstairs. Welcome."

This Karl, who had orchestrated a massive universal fuckupery, had walked into the room like Steve Jobs introducing the goddamned iPad. Skid's brain fingered her ace; she knew something he didn't.

Concern traveled across real Dave's face. "Where are Cord and Brick?"

Skid waved him off. "Cord and his 1957 girlfriend are here and there. Brick's upstairs fighting giant insects."

"That's the HR department," Clean-David said. "And the monster on the other side of the door here is Oscar."

Skid was only half-listening. Her eyes were trained on Karl Miller. "What time are your soldiers supposed to be here, Hans?"

Karl looked at his watch. Whatever smile had been there fell off in chunks. "Five minutes ago," he said flatly. "They were supposed to be here five minutes ago."

She pulled herself across the floor, dragging her injured leg behind. Her hand slapped the top of a control panel, and she climbed to her knees. The other followed, and she pulled herself onto her good foot. A red button under a glass case sat four feet to her left; the sasquatch looming by the engineering door was closer. The beast called Oscar didn't look evil, just angry. She slid closer to the red button, Oscar's face now over her shoulder.

"That's because they're not coming," she said.

"What do you mean?" Karl asked, confusion in his voice.

She hopped the last two feet and stopped. The red button under glass, the one that could stop this madness, was within reach.

"I mean I saw them." Her fingers inched toward the button. "In Orcland, or wherever we were. They're dead, Hans. Killed by orc soldiers."

Pink flushed his face, quickly turning to red. Karl the Dimension King's fists clenched; he looked like he might pop.

"You're lying. Those were United States soldiers in Humvees."

The fingers of Skid's left hand toyed with the glass case that protected the button. She flipped it open. The slot for a key, the one her Dave had drawn on a napkin at Dan's Daylight Donuts was empty. She pushed the button, but nothing happened.

"You're looking for this." Karl's voice harsh, verging on panic. A flat, rectangular key on a short chain hung from his right index finger. "Now, tell me what you know."

Her hand dropped from the button and slowly lowered the glass shield. "I saw them," she said. "There were three Humvees, all damaged by what looked like catapults or something. There were no soldiers alive, at least none that we could see."

Karl had stopped breathing and looked like he might collapse. "That's impossible," trickled from his mouth. Then anger flared again, and he pointed a finger at Skid. "Shoot her," he barked.

"What?" Clean-David turned toward Karl. "Why? She can't do anything."

He reached for the pistol, but Clean-David didn't give it to him.

"Hey, Skid," her Dave said, ignoring Karl. "Do you remember the night we met?"

Her brain churned, last Friday flooded it like a bad dream.

"We talked about Erwin Schrödinger," he continued, not giving her a chance to answer.

"You know, the guy with the cat."

"Give me the damn gun," Karl shouted, but he seemed far away.

Erwin Schrödinger? Schrödinger's cat. "Yeah, I remember. You were debating on if you should prevent the zombie catpocalypse."

A smile radiated from his eyes. "I must have made some kind of impression on you."

She grinned. "That's why I punched you."

"This is all very lovely," Karl said, but they took no notice.

"What did you decide was the point about Schrödinger no one understands?"

She picked through the memories of that night. The beer, the knife, Dave disappearing in a whiff of ozone, and Schrödinger. *That's it.*

"He was a horrible pet owner."

She turned her head and looked at the beast named Oscar, his rage a heat she could almost feel. There was a button marked 'Door Release' mounted in the wall to the right of the metal portal, within her reach. She lunged for it, and the world suddenly stopped.

Karl's voice died at the sound of a magnetic lock opening. Clean-David stood silently, the shock on his face frozen in a mask. Dave held his breath. Then the door flew open, banging the wall opposite Skid hard, knocking it off one hinge.

Oscar was loose.

"Mirrooo," the hairy giant roared, the room filled with the deep, guttural sound.

"No," Karl mouthed, turning toward the room where he'd emerged.

Oscar was faster. The Bigfoot-looking physicist burst through the doorway, launched himself over the control station and landed feet from Karl with a scream. Saliva sprayed the scientist's face.

"Mirrooo," he bellowed again and grasped Karl in one gigantic fist. "Mirrooo diya. Mirrooo."

The arm swung like an outfielder tossing out a runner from the warning track; Karl flew from his hand into the cavern, hitting the floor and rolling toward the seething purple storm.

"Mirrooo." Oscar wheeled after Karl, his arms and legs flying in all directions as he ran. "Diya, diya, diya." The beast scooped up the scientist and dove into the ring, disappearing into the churning storm.

The three stood in stunned silence, the zap of lightning from the cavern the only sound.

"I guess I'm in charge here now," both Daves said.

Clean-David pointed the gun at him. "I guess I'm in charge here now," he repeated. "Besides." He pulled a key from his pocket. "Karl wasn't the only one with a key to the BAB-C, but you're not getting this one either."

"Shit," Dave hissed, but the word died when he realized Skid was laughing.

She stood on her one good leg. An identical key hung from her fist.

"How?" Clean-David asked.

"You dropped it," she said. "Or, you will drop the one you're holding in the bathroom hallway of a shitty dance club in about—" She paused for a moment, counting back the days. "—a week ago."

"That's *my* key?" Clean-David raised an arm toward her, the gun working its way upward to her chest.

Skid didn't know she was going to do what she did. It just happened, quickly and smoothly, a motion she'd practiced thousands of times. Her right hand sank to her belt and came up with the last throwing knife. It stayed in her hand for less than a second before it spun through the air and sunk hilt-deep into Clean-David's right thigh, the pop as it sunk in like she'd opened a cantaloupe. The pistol dropped from his hand and skipped across the floor. He screamed. Not as good as Oscar's scream, but not bad.

The Miller ring in the cavern burped and a slight wave bubbled out, swallowing Clean-David before it faded into nothing.

15

The silence in the room was middle school dance awkward. Dave and Skid stood alone on opposite sides of the Bridge, staring at each other.

"Why did he go but we didn't?" Skid asked, breaking the silence.

Dave shook his head. "I don't know. I told you, quantum mechanics might as well be magic. It doesn't behave rationally."

"Yeah." Skid hopped back to the control panel. "I think I get that."

"What's the weirdest thing that happened to you? You know, after I left," he asked. His leg muscles tightened to raise him from the chair, but for some reason they wouldn't move.

"Godzilla Junior, zombie circus master, alien people-eating mushrooms. You know, the usual." She shrugged. "You?"

"I watched a giant praying mantis in a lab coat eat myself from another dimension while I sat in a comfy chair with a sack of peanuts."

"That's not weird."

"The mantis's name was Chet."

She nodded. "Okay, yeah, that's weird."

"I smell bad," Dave said.

"Me, too."

That did it. The shock evaporated and his legs moved, pulling him across the floor in seconds. Dave stopped inches from Skid, afraid to reach out because she might not really be there. Stranger things had happened recently.

"I haven't brushed my teeth in a week," he said.

She closed the inches between them in a slight hop, her face suddenly hot, her stomach less full of butterflies and more full of Coke and Pop Rocks. She laced her fingers behind his neck. "Me neither."

He suddenly looked like a kid who'd thought up a great joke. "Has anyone ever told you how beautiful you are?"

"And kept their teeth?" she said. "None that I remember."

Dave bent forward, his lips parted, but Skid backed away; her mouth dropped open, her eyes grew wide. Her mouth moved, but no words came out; it swung like a gate.

"Skid?" Dave whispered and slowly turned to face the cavern. He didn't like it. Not a damn bit.

The raging purple storm had expanded from the dimension ring, taking up most of the cavern. A foot, like that of an enormous bear, had appeared from the ring and thudded onto the stone floor, its leg covered in scales. Lightning crackled and shot from the circle, flittering along the ceiling. The head of a great, horned lizard slowly emerged from the storm. Another followed, and another. Water sloshed from the ring and splattered onto the floor.

"What is it?" Skid's words were soft, her voice tight.

Dave put an arm around her waist and pulled her tightly to him as another horned head on a long, scaly neck emerged from the storm. It was bigger than the others. Its eyes bore into them. Dave's insides felt like ice.

"I don't know." But something deep inside him did. He concentrated on the seven V-shaped, heads on undulating necks, its scales shone like silver. It had ten horns, and on each one hung a crown. "Oh, shit."

Skid pulled away from him and grabbed the control panel. "Come on. We have to stop this."

Yes, he knew what this was.

"John told us about this."

"John," she said from behind him, flipping the glass shield off the button. "Who the hell's John?"

"John the Apostle. And 'hell's' right." Dave began reciting. "It rose up out of the sea, having seven heads and ten horns, and upon his horns ten crowns, and upon his heads the name of blasphemy."

She slid the key into its slot. "That does not sound good."

"No. It doesn't. That's from Revelation Chapter 13. I think that might be the Devil, Sk—"

"Skid." The voice, deep and booming, echoed through the cavern, stretching into the Bridge and turning her good knee to water. She gripped the control panel hard.

The Devil? It said my name. In the alien mushroom world, Brick had named the dimensions they'd shifted through. Dinosaurs and Nazis, orcs and butterflies. He left out biblical prophecy.

Her hand shot out and turned Dave around, pulling him close and crushing his face to hers. Their lips met. Dave's eyes still closed when she pulled away. The monster over his left shoulder filled her attention. Its shoulders stretched the metal ring to the point of bursting. Lightning spat around it. She patted Dave's face.

"Wake up."

He leaned forward for another kiss and pushed him away.

Dave's eyelids lifted, and the face of a guy at least a six-pack in greeted her. "Huh?"

"I hope you don't look that stupid after sex," she said, turning the key to the 'activate' position. "Are you ready?"

He rested his hand on the red kill button. "Yeah. Did you really just say sex?"

"She did," came the voice from the cavern.

She put her smaller hand over Dave's. The demon behind her said her name again. She swallowed hard.

"Maybe," she said, then pushed as the Miller wave broke free of the ring and swarmed into the room. The kill switch dropped, and the purple cloud swept over them—then every molecule in the known universes shifted at once.

THE STUFF AT THE END

JUNE 27

1

DICE CLATTERED across the thick wooden tabletop. One struck the dull surface of a vintage aluminum napkin holder and flirted with the table's edge before it dropped onto the floor. The remaining three landed on five, three and two. Brick leaned over and plucked the rogue six-sided die off the polished hardwood floor of Manic Muffins and sat back up in his chair.

"Sorry, Tanner," he said, "but you'll have to roll this one again. Floor rolls don't count."

"But it was a six," the boy protested, his face dangerously close to a pout. "Come on, Brick. Let me."

Brick's forehead creased as he leaned over the table, glaring at him, the expression on his face as intimidating as a corgi's. "Floor rolls don't count."

Tanner's mom sat at the next table nibbling a bran muffin and drinking a milky coffee. She brushed her index finger across the screen of an iPad like she'd spilled something on it and ignored them.

"But—"

Brick reached a huge hairy hand a few inches over Tanner's small one and dropped the six-sided die into it.

"Roll," he said. "Everything is random." But Brick knew that wasn't true, not really. Not meeting friends, not zipping through time, not zapping through dimensions, not Skid, not thinking a man who once owned a haunted house would drop from the air with his waitress girlfriend from other-dimension 1957 and land on his couch. It wasn't random that another haunted house would immediately come up for sale in Villisca, Iowa, and Cord would pounce on it. No. Nothing was random. Not even dice rolls. Brick knew Tanner would roll another six.

Tanner dropped the die on the table. It danced for two, three, four clacks, then came to rest on six.

"Ha," he shouted, grinning in defiance. His grin quickly fell into confusion. "Now what?"

Brick smiled. "Now," he said, pointing at the dice. "You add the three highest numbers and write it down."

The boy's mental calculations required fingers and a pencil, but he eventually jotted fourteen onto a sheet of paper marked "character sheet" filled with boxes and grids.

"And this can go for my—" He struck each box with the pencil eraser. "Strength, dex, dex, dexterity, const-it-u-tion, intelligence, wisdom and what's the last one?"

"Charisma."

Tanner looked up at Brick, his face pinched, a mop of blond hair an untrainable mess. "What's charisma?"

The bell over the door rang and Brick pushed his bulk out of the chair. "It's something you have in buckets, kid. Now, roll the dice, all four of them on the table, and keep the highest three each time. None will go higher than eighteen, at least not yet. Those abilities will be what you use to create your character, a fighter, a ranger—"

"A paladin, a wizard," Tanner recited. "Yeah, I know. I can do this. It's easy math, not like fractions."

Brick mussed the boy's hair, like anyone would notice, and glanced up at the new customer. It was Katie; he hadn't seen Katie forever. "Nobody likes fractions."

2

Brick poured her usual coffee before she asked for it. Large and black, no sugar and nothing milky. He set the recyclable cup on the counter and smiled as she approached. Katie hadn't visited Manic Muffins in months, and Brick had been worried. She wasn't getting any younger, after all. She walked to the glass case in her usual black jogging clothes and reached behind her head to tighten her ponytail, also black, but with thick veins of white.

"Where have you been?" he asked. "I was beginning to think you dumped me for Dan's Daylight Donuts."

"With his coffee? Blech," she said, sticking out her tongue. "Not a chance."

She squatted in front of the display counter like few sixty-some-things probably could and eyed the muffins. The middle row held a tray with a few rectangular red ones; crumbs dotted the spaces where others had been. "Is that what I think it is?"

"The Brick? Yeah." He slid open the back of the display case, pulled out the tray and sat it on top of the counter. "Your pick. It's on the house."

Katie scanned the five left on the tray and pointed to one in the back; the red icing seemed thicker. "Damn straight it's on the house. They were my idea."

Silicone-tipped tongs pinched the red velvet cake muffin and Brick fitted it into a brown bag with a paper napkin before folding the top closed. She took it and gave him a five-dollar bill.

"For the coffee," she said. "Keep the rest."

For as long as Katie had come into Manic Muffins, she'd tipped big and acted like she knew him, and Brick didn't know anything about her. What she did for a living, what her last name was, if she was married. He twisted the thin gold band on his own ring finger, looking for the non-existent one on hers.

He picked up the coffee pot again and filled his own cup.

The aluminum door that separated the kitchen from the front room swung open and Beverly stepped out with another tray of red velvet cake muffins, the bottom of the tray resting on her stomach bump. She set the tray on the counter and grinned.

"Oh, hey, Skid," she said. "Long time no see."

Brick froze.

"Yeah." Katie flashed a grin that looked too much like Skid's not to be. "Dave here yet?"

The coffee pot fell from Brick's hand and shattered on the floor.

ACKNOWLEDGMENTS

I wrote *You Had to Build a Time Machine* in three months. That's average for a first draft. For those who haven't yet written your book (as a writer I think everyone wants to write a book), there are a few misconceptions about writing I'd like to clear up. One, writing is basically word-based accountancy with more suspicious web searches. It's quiet, solitary and self-rewarding, which is fine for the author because we're usually socially-crippled introverts. Two, writing is the easy part. Seriously. When I'm in book-mode, I can pound out about 2,000 words I mostly like every day. That may not sound like much, but in three months it adds up. Given my off days when I produce less, travel days when I refuse to utilize my laptop's text-to-speech function while driving, and Family Fridays when pizza and movies take precedent, that adds up to more than 100,000 words. Just enough for a nice sized novel.

That brings us to three: the next nine months make up the hard part. Putting the manuscript in a drawer for a month or more before reading it. Editing it once, twice, three times, maybe more. Waiting for your beta readers (people whose opinion you trust and who won't blow smoke up your butt) to return your manuscript with suggestions. Going through those suggestions, keeping the good ones and discarding the rest (it's your baby, after all). And it's still a piece of putty to the publisher. Your manuscript will be stretched, smushed and molded into something finer than what you sent them.

Tired yet? Boy, I am.

I'd like to thank the people who helped me through this exhausting process. My family, who graciously accepts my role as Daddy Writer Nerd, my beta readers Kelsey Noble, Jacob Hulsey, Gary Darling, and my lovely wife Kim, and the great folks at CamCat Books, Sue Arroyo, Dayna Anderson, Helga Schier, and Cassandra Farrin.

I'd also like to thank podcaster and paranormal scoundrel Tim Binnall who wanted a mention in each one of my novels so he'd be part of the "Offuttverse." Here you go, Tim. In this novel, you're a street.

And lastly, I'd like to thank you, kind reader, without whom I'd have no reason to put this story into print. I hope you enjoyed the novel.

Jason Offutt
Maryville, Missouri
December 2019

ABOUT THE AUTHOR

Jason Offutt writes books. This is infinitely better than what his father trained him to do, which was to drink beer and shout at the television. He is best known for science fiction, such as his end-of-the-world zombie novel *Bad Day for the Apocalypse* (a curious work that doesn't include zombies), his paranormal non-fiction like *Chasing American Monsters* (that does), and his book of humor *How to Kill Monsters Using Common Household Objects* (that not only includes zombies but teaches readers how to remove an infestation of them from their home). He teaches university journalism, cooks for his family, and wastes much of his writing time trying to keep the cat off his lap. You can find more about Jason at his website, www.jasonoffutt.com. There are no pictures of his cat Gary, and it serves him right.

twitter.com/TheJasonOffutt

instagram.com/thejasonoffutt

CamCat Books

Visit Us Online for More Books to Live In:
camcatbooks.com

Follow Us:

CamCatBooks   @CamCatBooks   @CamCatBooks

CPSIA information can be obtained
at www.ICGtesting.com
Printed in the USA
LVHW081541300720
661975LV00014B/227/J